EVIL THING

A VILLAINS GRAPHIC NOVEL

EVIL THING

THING

A VILLAINS GRAPHIC NOVEL

BY
SERENA VALENTINO

ILLUSTRATED BY
ARIELLE JOVELLANOS

COLOR BY
JANET SUNG

LETTERING BY
CHRIS DICKEY

DISNEY HYPERION

LOS ANGELES • NEW YORK

First Edition, September 2021
10 9 8 7 6 5 4 3 2 1
FAC-038091-21204

Printed in the United States of America

This book is set in CC Monologous, CC EvilDoings, CCCheeseAndCrackers/Comicraft
Designed by Phil Buchanan

Library of Congress Cataloging-in-Publication Data:
Names: Valentino, Serena, author. • Jovellanos, Arielle, illustrator. •
   Valentino, Serena. Evil thing.
Title: Evil thing : the graphic novel / Serena Valentino ; illustrated by
   Arielle Jovellanos.
Description: First edition. • Los Angeles : Disney-Hyperion, 2021. •
   Series: Villains graphic novels ; vol 1 • Audience: Ages 13–18 •
   Audience: Grades 10–12 • Summary: "This graphic novel adaptation of
   Serena Valentino's Villains series follows the rise and fall of the
   deranged and glamorous fan favorite, Cruella De Vil. If it doesn't scare
   you, no evil thing will." —Provided by publisher.
Identifiers: LCCN 2020052123 • ISBN 9781368068161 (hardcover) •
   ISBN 9781368076104 (paperback) • ISBN 9781368076111 (ebook)
Subjects: LCSH: Graphic novels. • CYAC: Graphic novels. • De Vil, Cruella
   (Fictitious character)—Fiction. • Villains—Fiction. • Mothers and
   daughters—Fiction. • Puppies—Fiction. • Disney characters—Fiction.
Classification: LCC PZ7.7.V22 Ev 2021 • DDC 741.5/973—dc23
LC record available at https://lccn.loc.gov/2020052123

Reinforced binding
Visit www.DisneyBooks.com

Dedicated, with love, to my awesome dog, Gozer.
And with special thanks to Arielle Jovellanos, Janet Sung,
Jocelyn Davies, and Rachel Stark

— Serena Valentino

To my Mom and Dad, who bought me the *One Hundred and One Dalmatians*
VHS, bedsheets, and beach towels when I was a wee child

—Arielle Jovellanos

To my chosen family and my friend Arielle, whom I cherish

—Janet Sung

CHAPTER ONE
CRUELLA DE VIL

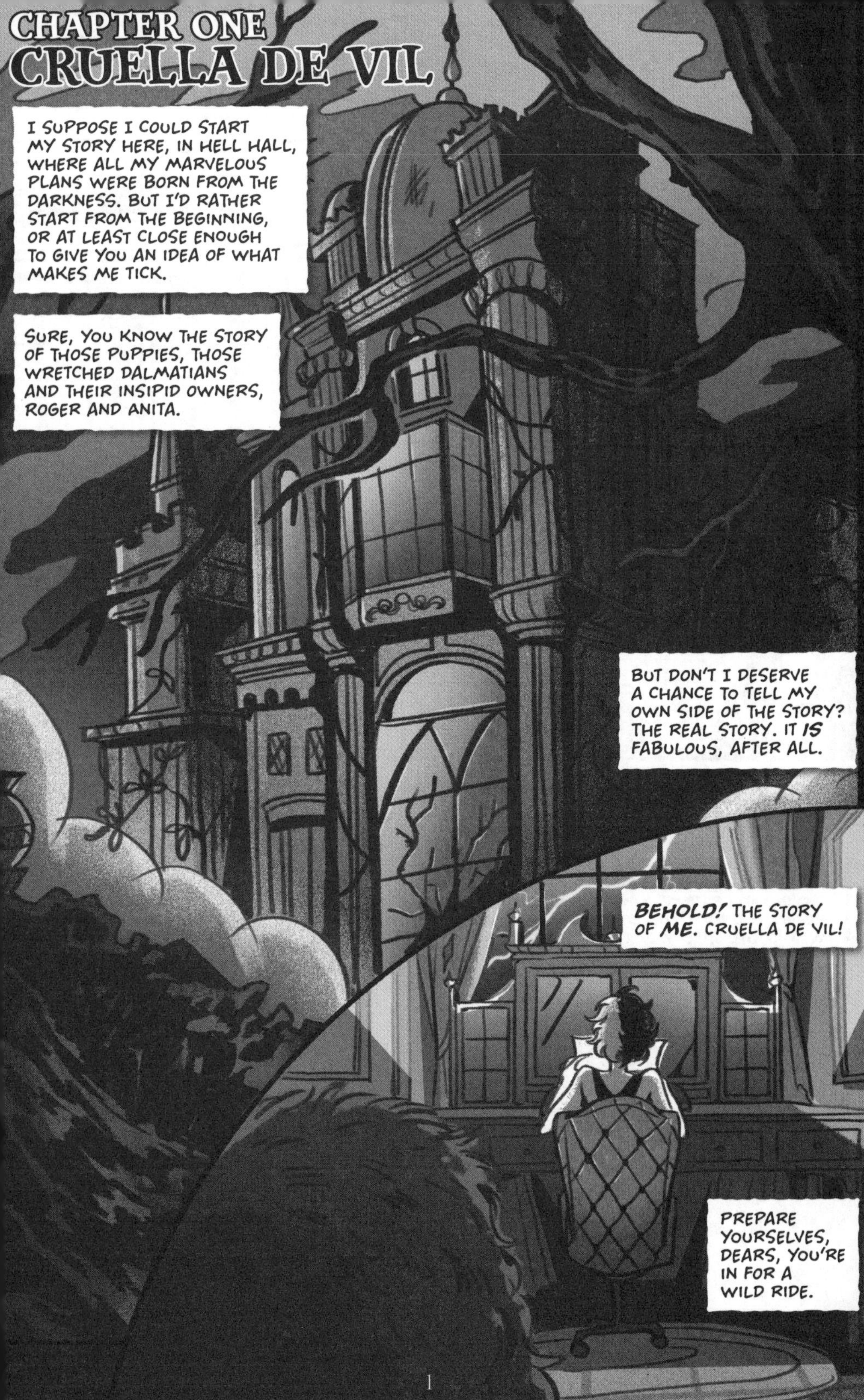
I SUPPOSE I COULD START MY STORY HERE, IN HELL HALL, WHERE ALL MY MARVELOUS PLANS WERE BORN FROM THE DARKNESS. BUT I'D RATHER START FROM THE BEGINNING, OR AT LEAST CLOSE ENOUGH TO GIVE YOU AN IDEA OF WHAT MAKES ME TICK.
SURE, YOU KNOW THE STORY OF THOSE PUPPIES, THOSE WRETCHED DALMATIANS AND THEIR INSIPID OWNERS, ROGER AND ANITA.
BUT DON'T I DESERVE A CHANCE TO TELL MY OWN SIDE OF THE STORY? THE REAL STORY. IT *IS* FABULOUS, AFTER ALL.
BEHOLD! THE STORY OF *ME*. CRUELLA DE VIL!
PREPARE YOURSELVES, DEARS, YOU'RE IN FOR A WILD RIDE.

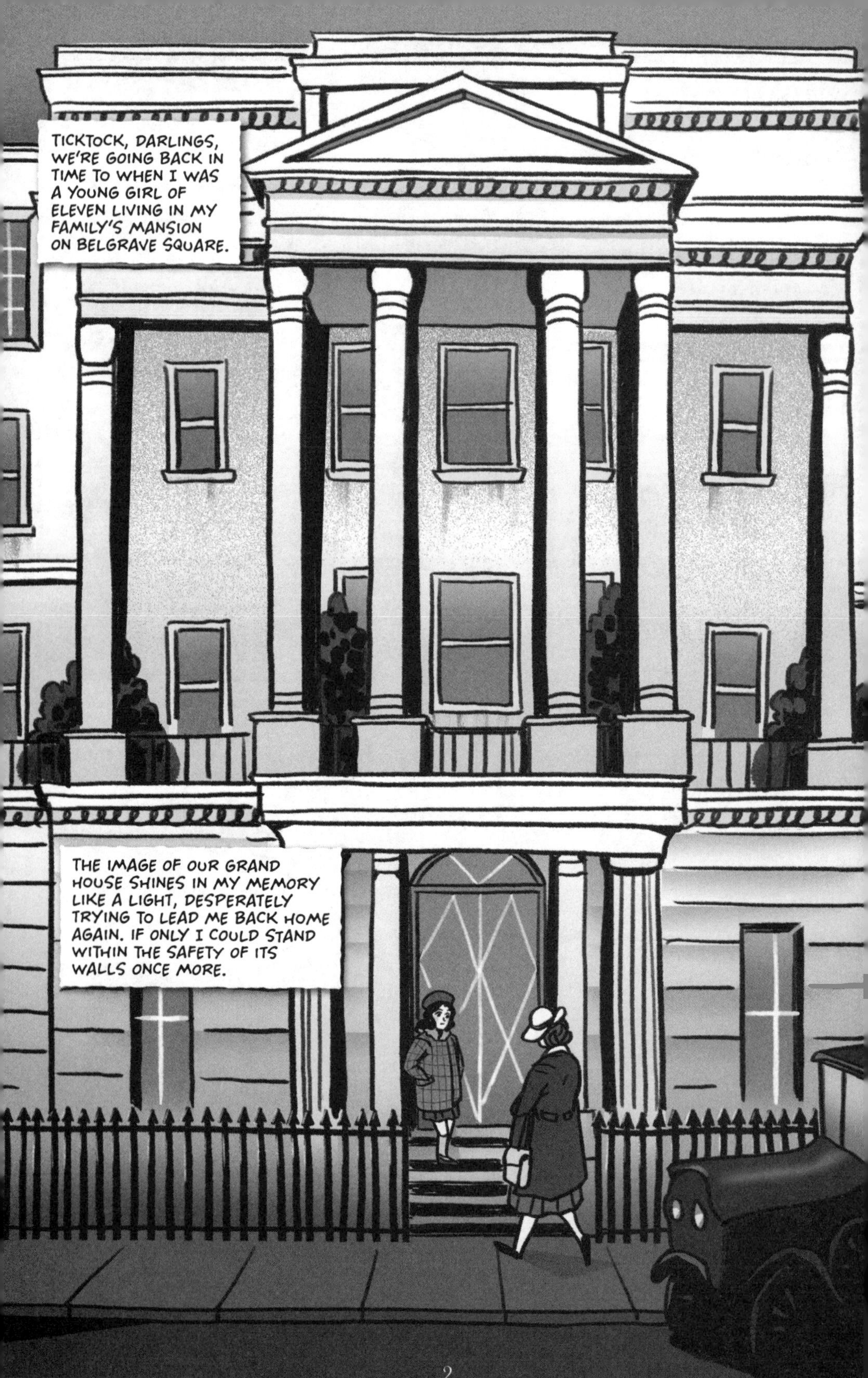
TICKTOCK, DARLINGS, WE'RE GOING BACK IN TIME TO WHEN I WAS A YOUNG GIRL OF ELEVEN LIVING IN MY FAMILY'S MANSION ON BELGRAVE SQUARE.
THE IMAGE OF OUR GRAND HOUSE SHINES IN MY MEMORY LIKE A LIGHT, DESPERATELY TRYING TO LEAD ME BACK HOME AGAIN. IF ONLY I COULD STAND WITHIN THE SAFETY OF ITS WALLS ONCE MORE.

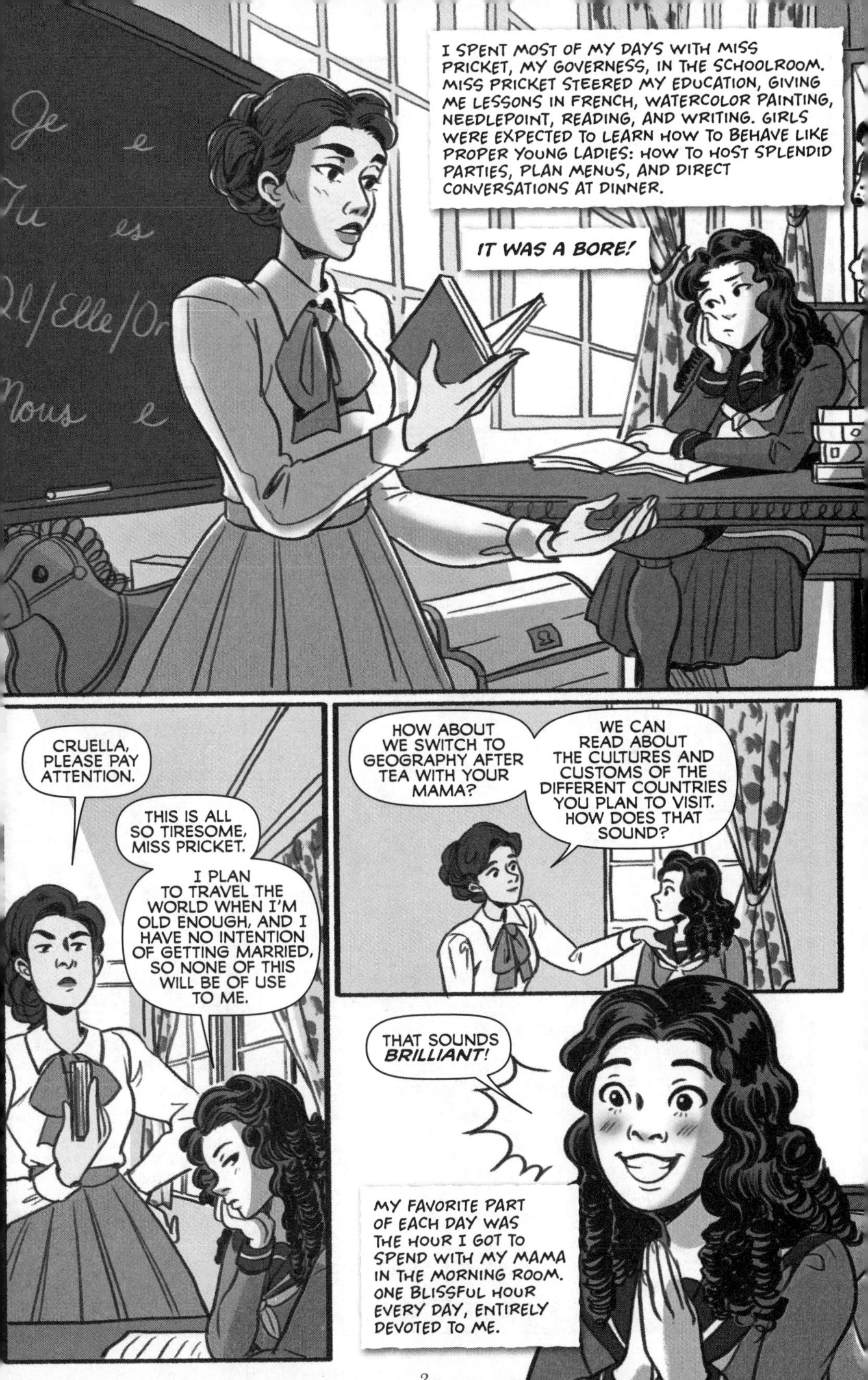
I SPENT MOST OF MY DAYS WITH MISS PRICKET, MY GOVERNESS, IN THE SCHOOLROOM. MISS PRICKET STEERED MY EDUCATION, GIVING ME LESSONS IN FRENCH, WATERCOLOR PAINTING, NEEDLEPOINT, READING, AND WRITING. GIRLS WERE EXPECTED TO LEARN HOW TO BEHAVE LIKE PROPER YOUNG LADIES: HOW TO HOST SPLENDID PARTIES, PLAN MENUS, AND DIRECT CONVERSATIONS AT DINNER.
IT WAS A BORE!
Je e
Tu es
Il/Elle/On
Nous
CRUELLA, PLEASE PAY ATTENTION.
THIS IS ALL SO TIRESOME, MISS PRICKET.
I PLAN TO TRAVEL THE WORLD WHEN I'M OLD ENOUGH, AND I HAVE NO INTENTION OF GETTING MARRIED, SO NONE OF THIS WILL BE OF USE TO ME.
HOW ABOUT WE SWITCH TO GEOGRAPHY AFTER TEA WITH YOUR MAMA?
WE CAN READ ABOUT THE CULTURES AND CUSTOMS OF THE DIFFERENT COUNTRIES YOU PLAN TO VISIT. HOW DOES THAT SOUND?
THAT SOUNDS BRILLIANT!
MY FAVORITE PART OF EACH DAY WAS THE HOUR I GOT TO SPEND WITH MY MAMA IN THE MORNING ROOM. ONE BLISSFUL HOUR EVERY DAY, ENTIRELY DEVOTED TO ME.

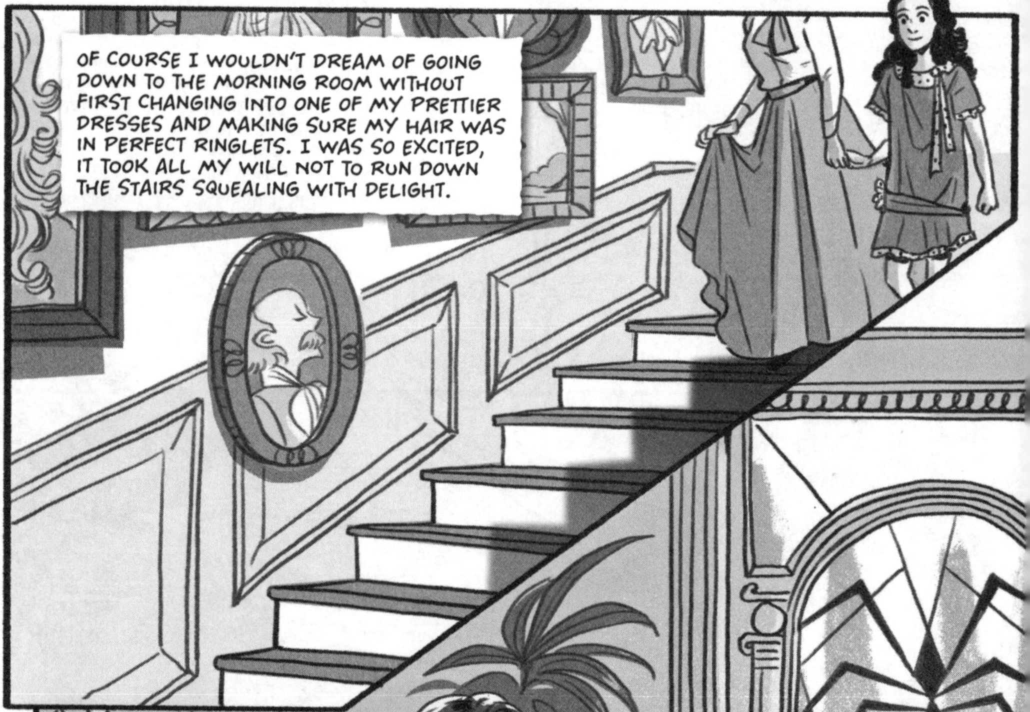
OF COURSE I WOULDN'T DREAM OF GOING DOWN TO THE MORNING ROOM WITHOUT FIRST CHANGING INTO ONE OF MY PRETTIER DRESSES AND MAKING SURE MY HAIR WAS IN PERFECT RINGLETS. I WAS SO EXCITED, IT TOOK ALL MY WILL NOT TO RUN DOWN THE STAIRS SQUEALING WITH DELIGHT.

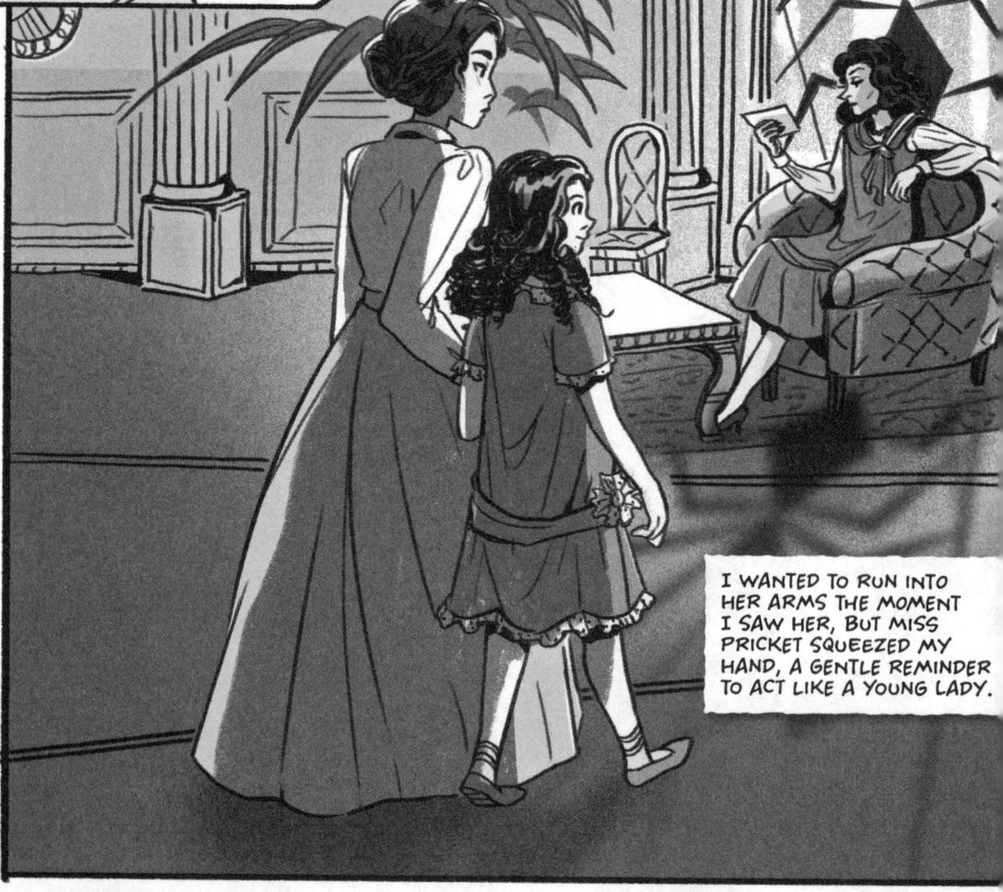
I WANTED TO RUN INTO HER ARMS THE MOMENT I SAW HER, BUT MISS PRICKET SQUEEZED MY HAND, A GENTLE REMINDER TO ACT LIKE A YOUNG LADY.

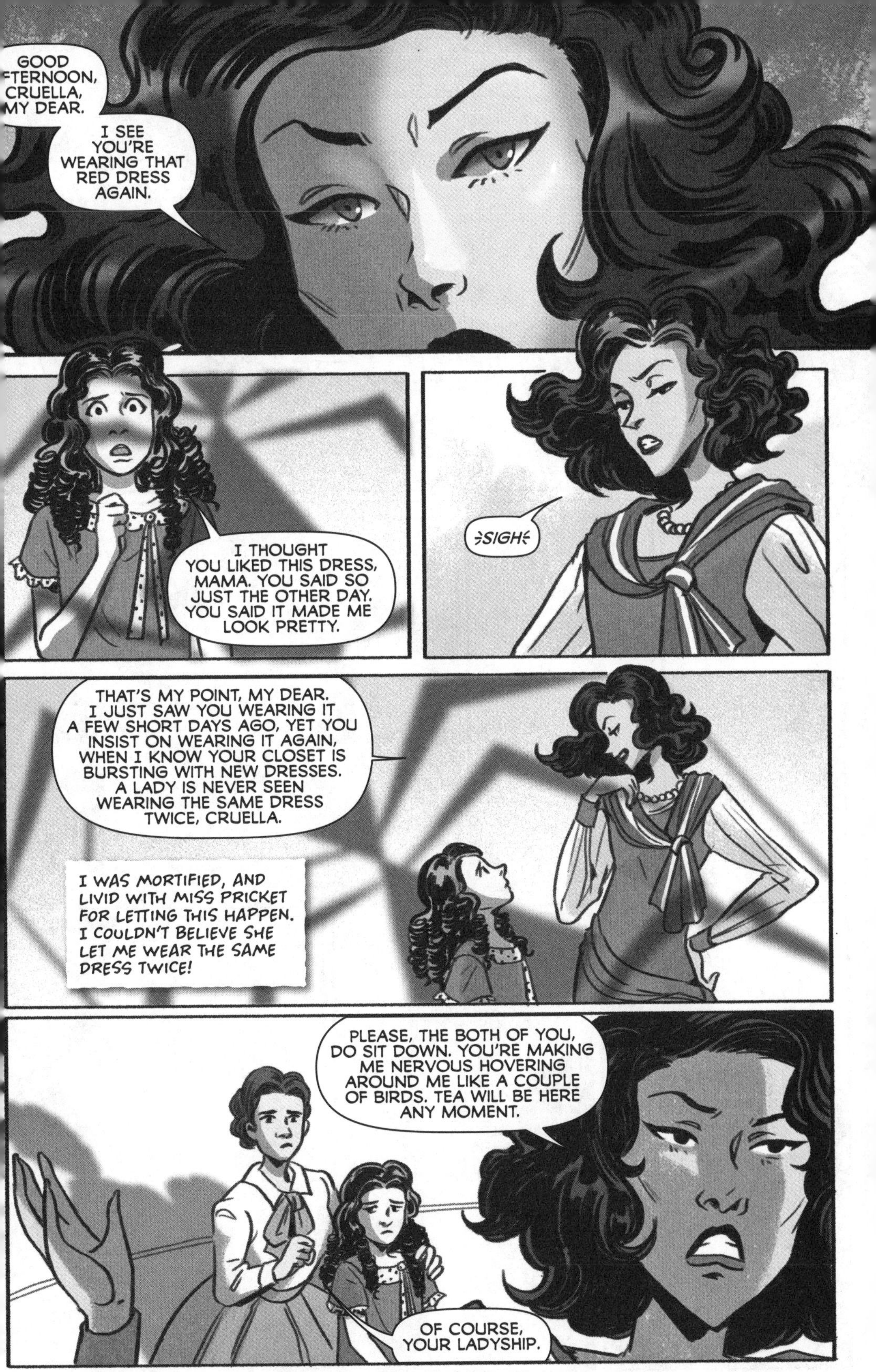
GOOD
FTERNOON,
CRUELLA,
MY DEAR.
I SEE YOU'RE WEARING THAT RED DRESS AGAIN.
I THOUGHT YOU LIKED THIS DRESS, MAMA. YOU SAID SO JUST THE OTHER DAY. YOU SAID IT MADE ME LOOK PRETTY.
SIGH
THAT'S MY POINT, MY DEAR. I JUST SAW YOU WEARING IT A FEW SHORT DAYS AGO, YET YOU INSIST ON WEARING IT AGAIN, WHEN I KNOW YOUR CLOSET IS BURSTING WITH NEW DRESSES. A LADY IS NEVER SEEN WEARING THE SAME DRESS TWICE, CRUELLA.
I WAS MORTIFIED, AND LIVID WITH MISS PRICKET FOR LETTING THIS HAPPEN. I COULDN'T BELIEVE SHE LET ME WEAR THE SAME DRESS TWICE!
PLEASE, THE BOTH OF YOU, DO SIT DOWN. YOU'RE MAKING ME NERVOUS HOVERING AROUND ME LIKE A COUPLE OF BIRDS. TEA WILL BE HERE ANY MOMENT.
OF COURSE, YOUR LADYSHIP.

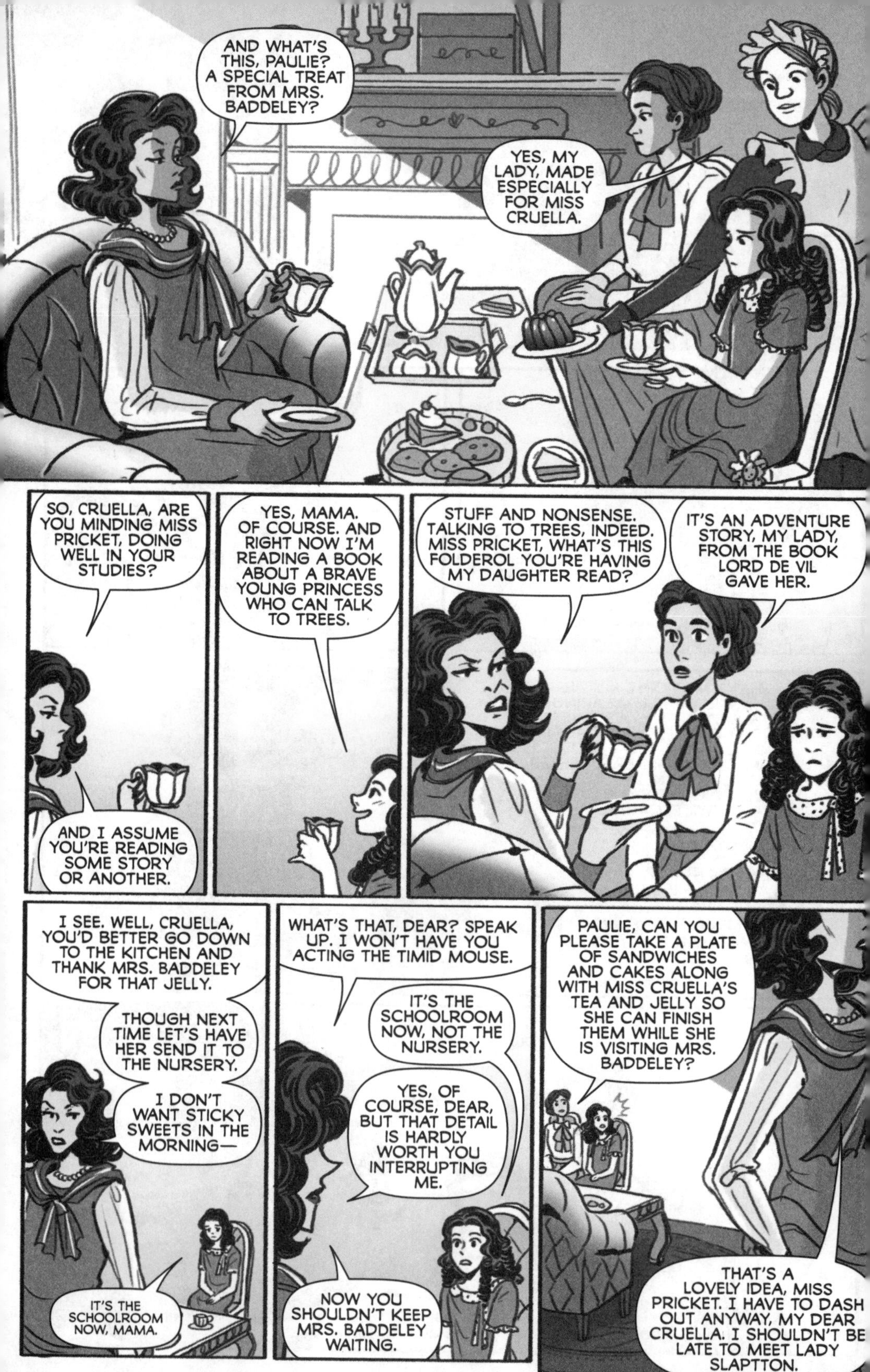

AND WHAT'S THIS, PAULIE? A SPECIAL TREAT FROM MRS. BADDELEY?
YES, MY LADY, MADE ESPECIALLY FOR MISS CRUELLA.
SO, CRUELLA, ARE YOU MINDING MISS PRICKET, DOING WELL IN YOUR STUDIES?
AND I ASSUME YOU'RE READING SOME STORY OR ANOTHER.
YES, MAMA. OF COURSE. AND RIGHT NOW I'M READING A BOOK ABOUT A BRAVE YOUNG PRINCESS WHO CAN TALK TO TREES.
STUFF AND NONSENSE. TALKING TO TREES, INDEED. MISS PRICKET, WHAT'S THIS FOLDEROL YOU'RE HAVING MY DAUGHTER READ?
IT'S AN ADVENTURE STORY, MY LADY, FROM THE BOOK LORD DE VIL GAVE HER.
I SEE. WELL, CRUELLA, YOU'D BETTER GO DOWN TO THE KITCHEN AND THANK MRS. BADDELEY FOR THAT JELLY.
THOUGH NEXT TIME LET'S HAVE HER SEND IT TO THE NURSERY.
I DON'T WANT STICKY SWEETS IN THE MORNING—
IT'S THE SCHOOLROOM NOW, MAMA.
WHAT'S THAT, DEAR? SPEAK UP. I WON'T HAVE YOU ACTING THE TIMID MOUSE.
IT'S THE SCHOOLROOM NOW, NOT THE NURSERY.
YES, OF COURSE, DEAR, BUT THAT DETAIL IS HARDLY WORTH YOU INTERRUPTING ME.
NOW YOU SHOULDN'T KEEP MRS. BADDELEY WAITING.
PAULIE, CAN YOU PLEASE TAKE A PLATE OF SANDWICHES AND CAKES ALONG WITH MISS CRUELLA'S TEA AND JELLY SO SHE CAN FINISH THEM WHILE SHE IS VISITING MRS. BADDELEY?
THAT'S A LOVELY IDEA, MISS PRICKET. I HAVE TO DASH OUT ANYWAY, MY DEAR CRUELLA. I SHOULDN'T BE LATE TO MEET LADY SLAPTTON.

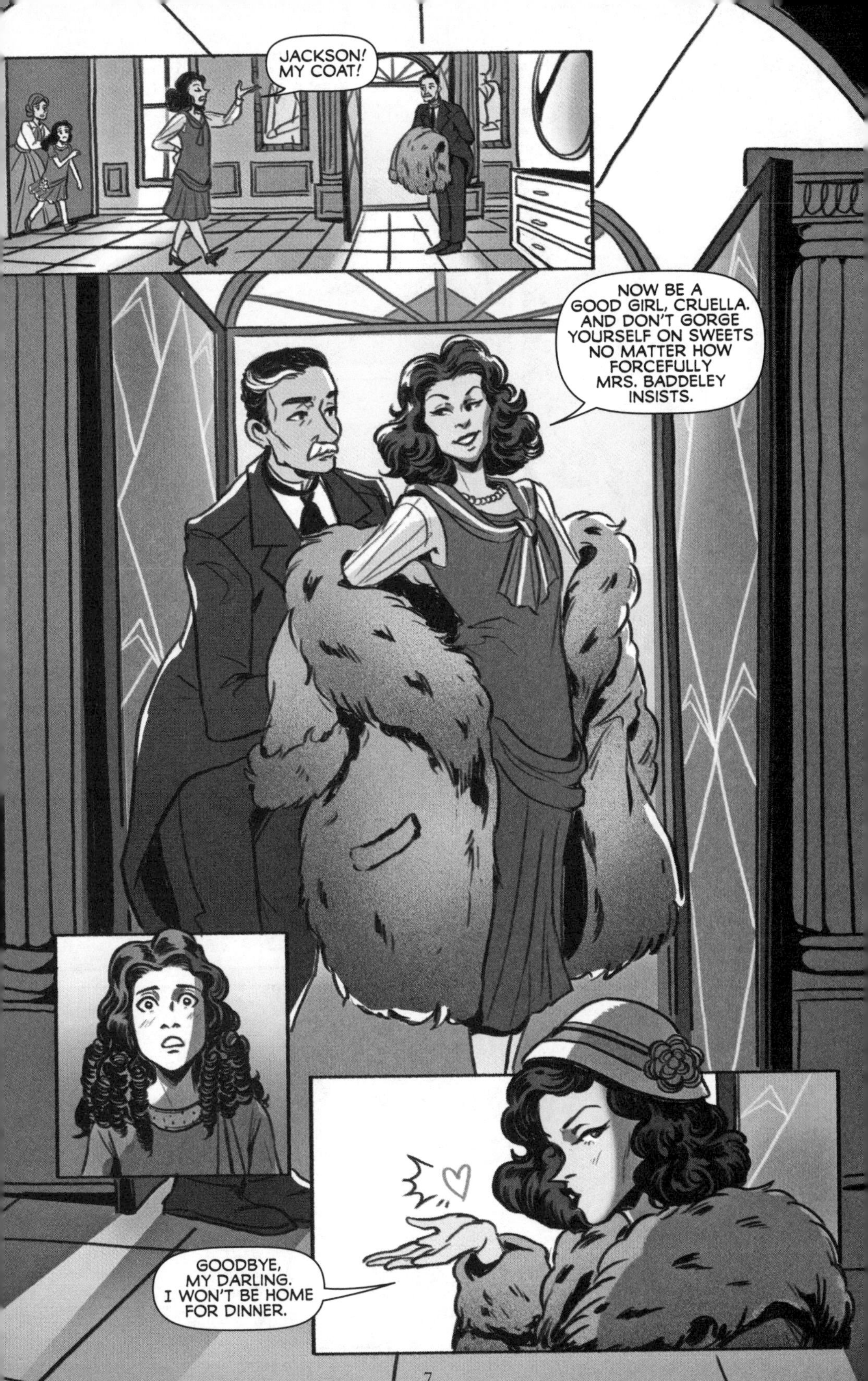
JACKSON! MY COAT!
NOW BE A GOOD GIRL, CRUELLA. AND DON'T GORGE YOURSELF ON SWEETS NO MATTER HOW FORCEFULLY MRS. BADDELEY INSISTS.
GOODBYE, MY DARLING. I WON'T BE HOME FOR DINNER.

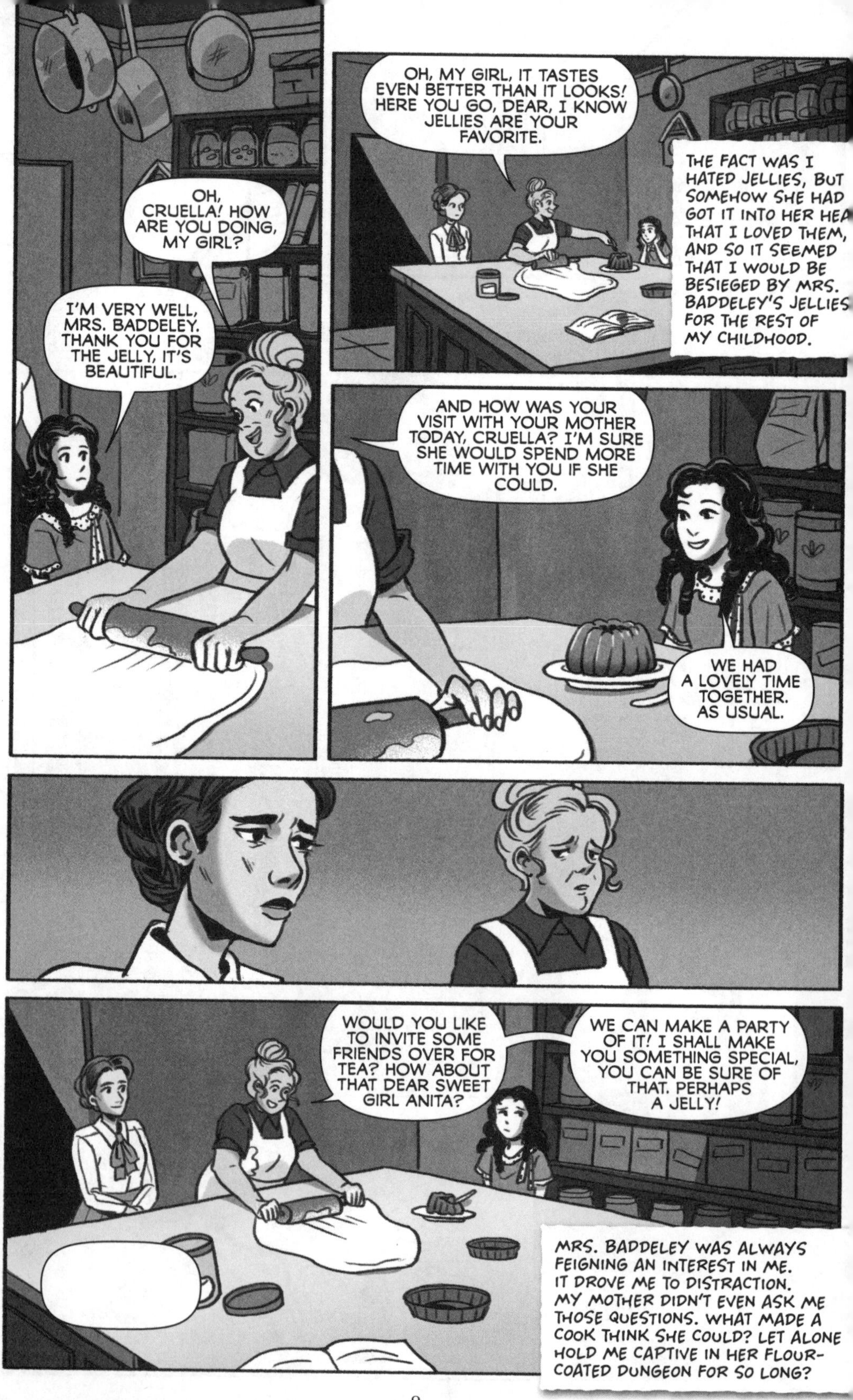
OH, CRUELLA! HOW ARE YOU DOING, MY GIRL?
I'M VERY WELL, MRS. BADDELEY. THANK YOU FOR THE JELLY, IT'S BEAUTIFUL.
OH, MY GIRL, IT TASTES EVEN BETTER THAN IT LOOKS! HERE YOU GO, DEAR, I KNOW JELLIES ARE YOUR FAVORITE.
THE FACT WAS I HATED JELLIES, BUT SOMEHOW SHE HAD GOT IT INTO HER HEA THAT I LOVED THEM, AND SO IT SEEMED THAT I WOULD BE BESIEGED BY MRS. BADDELEY'S JELLIES FOR THE REST OF MY CHILDHOOD.
AND HOW WAS YOUR VISIT WITH YOUR MOTHER TODAY, CRUELLA? I'M SURE SHE WOULD SPEND MORE TIME WITH YOU IF SHE COULD.
WE HAD A LOVELY TIME TOGETHER. AS USUAL.
WOULD YOU LIKE TO INVITE SOME FRIENDS OVER FOR TEA? HOW ABOUT THAT DEAR SWEET GIRL ANITA?
WE CAN MAKE A PARTY OF IT! I SHALL MAKE YOU SOMETHING SPECIAL, YOU CAN BE SURE OF THAT. PERHAPS A JELLY!
MRS. BADDELEY WAS ALWAYS FEIGNING AN INTEREST IN ME. IT DROVE ME TO DISTRACTION. MY MOTHER DIDN'T EVEN ASK ME THOSE QUESTIONS. WHAT MADE A COOK THINK SHE COULD? LET ALONE HOLD ME CAPTIVE IN HER FLOUR-COATED DUNGEON FOR SO LONG?

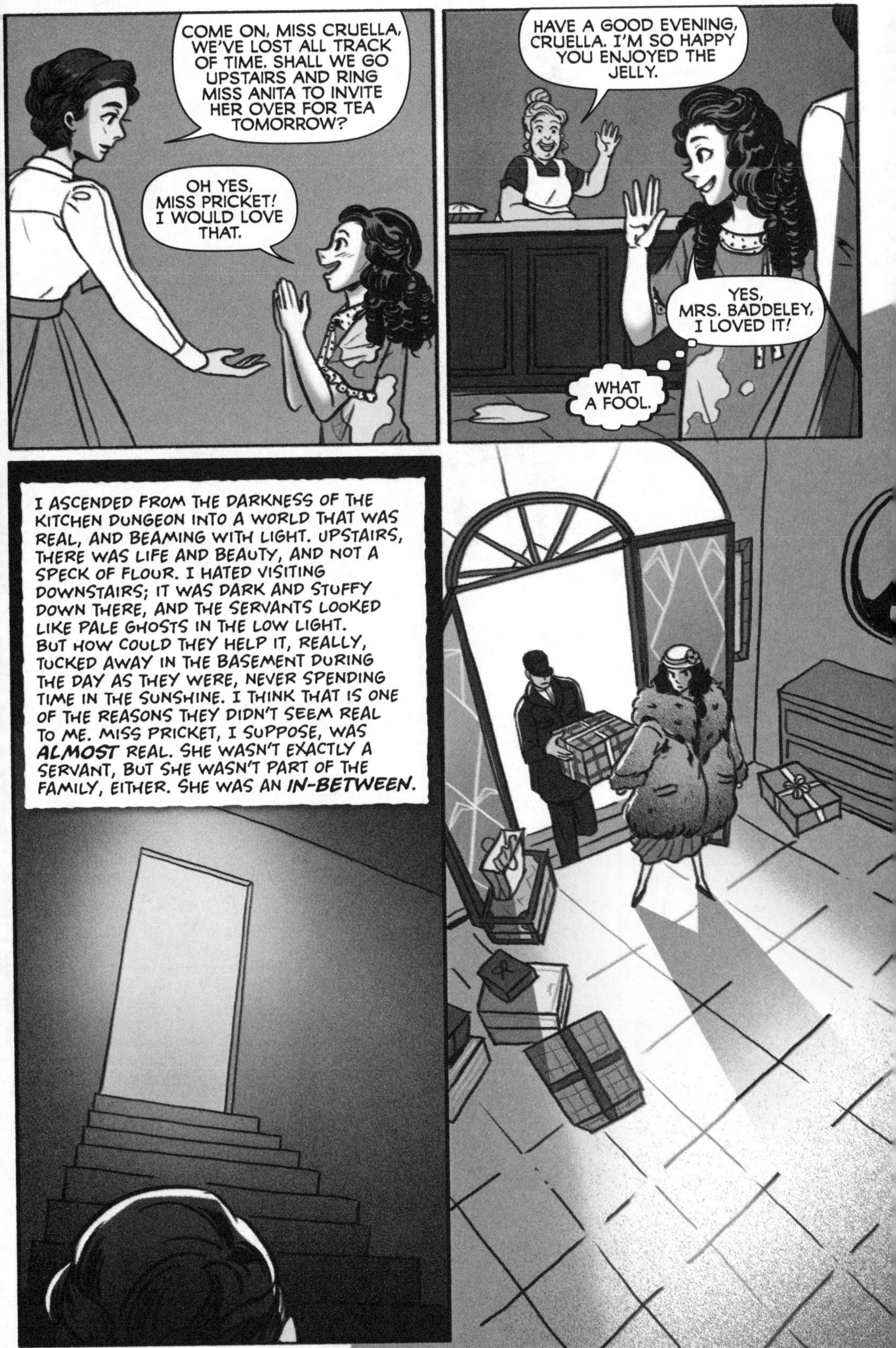
COME ON, MISS CRUELLA, WE'VE LOST ALL TRACK OF TIME. SHALL WE GO UPSTAIRS AND RING MISS ANITA TO INVITE HER OVER FOR TEA TOMORROW?
OH YES, MISS PRICKET! I WOULD LOVE THAT.
HAVE A GOOD EVENING, CRUELLA. I'M SO HAPPY YOU ENJOYED THE JELLY.
YES, MRS. BADDELEY, I LOVED IT!
WHAT A FOOL.
I ASCENDED FROM THE DARKNESS OF THE KITCHEN DUNGEON INTO A WORLD THAT WAS REAL, AND BEAMING WITH LIGHT. UPSTAIRS, THERE WAS LIFE AND BEAUTY, AND NOT A SPECK OF FLOUR. I HATED VISITING DOWNSTAIRS; IT WAS DARK AND STUFFY DOWN THERE, AND THE SERVANTS LOOKED LIKE PALE GHOSTS IN THE LOW LIGHT. BUT HOW COULD THEY HELP IT, REALLY, TUCKED AWAY IN THE BASEMENT DURING THE DAY AS THEY WERE, NEVER SPENDING TIME IN THE SUNSHINE. I THINK THAT IS ONE OF THE REASONS THEY DIDN'T SEEM REAL TO ME. MISS PRICKET, I SUPPOSE, WAS ALMOST REAL. SHE WASN'T EXACTLY A SERVANT, BUT SHE WASN'T PART OF THE FAMILY, EITHER. SHE WAS AN IN-BETWEEN.

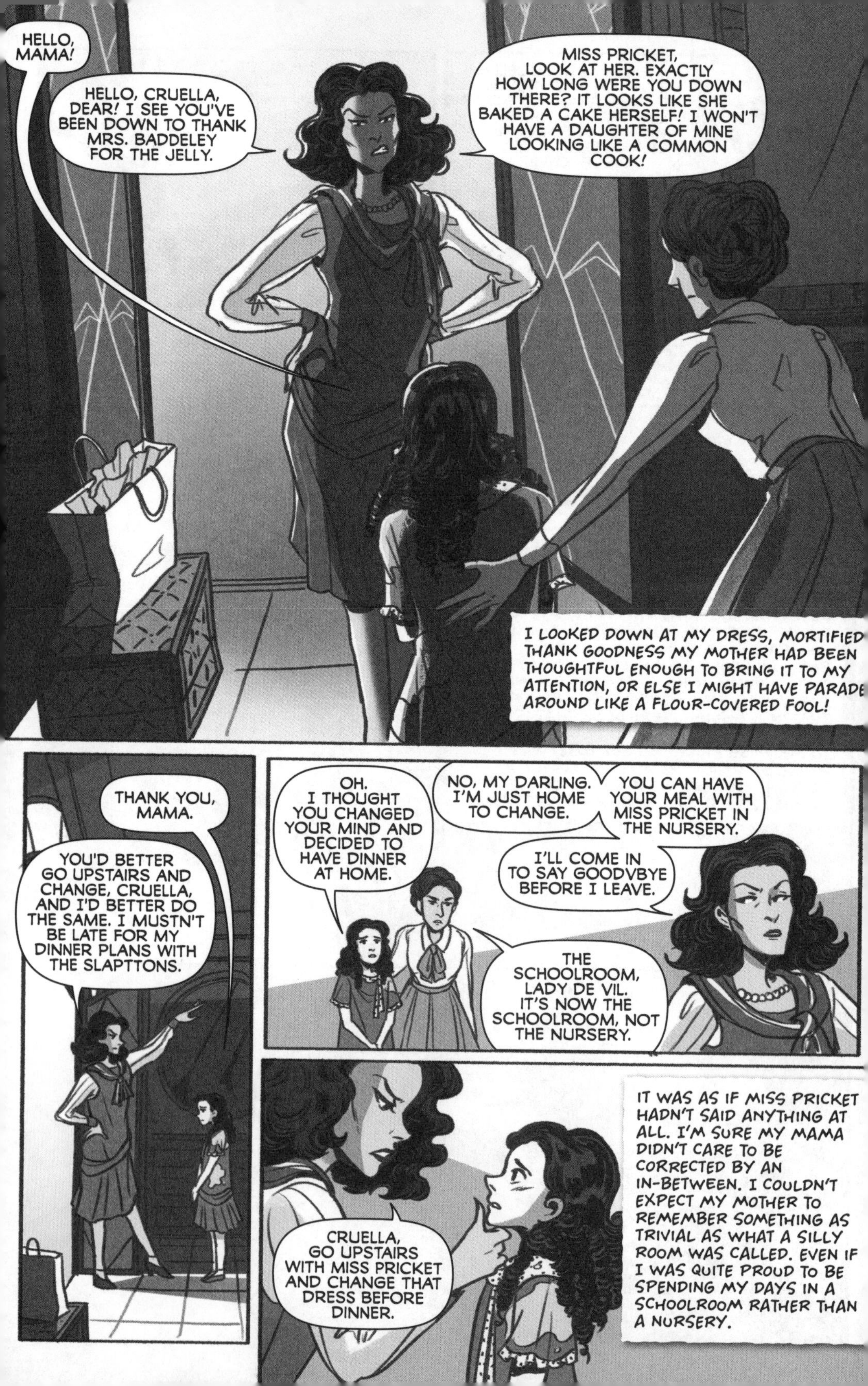
HELLO, MAMA!
HELLO, CRUELLA, DEAR! I SEE YOU'VE BEEN DOWN TO THANK MRS. BADDELEY FOR THE JELLY.
MISS PRICKET, LOOK AT HER. EXACTLY HOW LONG WERE YOU DOWN THERE? IT LOOKS LIKE SHE BAKED A CAKE HERSELF! I WON'T HAVE A DAUGHTER OF MINE LOOKING LIKE A COMMON COOK!
I LOOKED DOWN AT MY DRESS, MORTIFIED. THANK GOODNESS MY MOTHER HAD BEEN THOUGHTFUL ENOUGH TO BRING IT TO MY ATTENTION, OR ELSE I MIGHT HAVE PARADE AROUND LIKE A FLOUR-COVERED FOOL!
THANK YOU, MAMA.
YOU'D BETTER GO UPSTAIRS AND CHANGE, CRUELLA, AND I'D BETTER DO THE SAME. I MUSTN'T BE LATE FOR MY DINNER PLANS WITH THE SLAPTTONS.
OH. I THOUGHT YOU CHANGED YOUR MIND AND DECIDED TO HAVE DINNER AT HOME.
NO, MY DARLING. I'M JUST HOME TO CHANGE.
YOU CAN HAVE YOUR MEAL WITH MISS PRICKET IN THE NURSERY.
I'LL COME IN TO SAY GOODVBYE BEFORE I LEAVE.
THE SCHOOLROOM, LADY DE VIL. IT'S NOW THE SCHOOLROOM, NOT THE NURSERY.
CRUELLA, GO UPSTAIRS WITH MISS PRICKET AND CHANGE THAT DRESS BEFORE DINNER.
IT WAS AS IF MISS PRICKET HADN'T SAID ANYTHING AT ALL. I'M SURE MY MAMA DIDN'T CARE TO BE CORRECTED BY AN IN-BETWEEN. I COULDN'T EXPECT MY MOTHER TO REMEMBER SOMETHING AS TRIVIAL AS WHAT A SILLY ROOM WAS CALLED. EVEN IF I WAS QUITE PROUD TO BE SPENDING MY DAYS IN A SCHOOLROOM RATHER THAN A NURSERY.

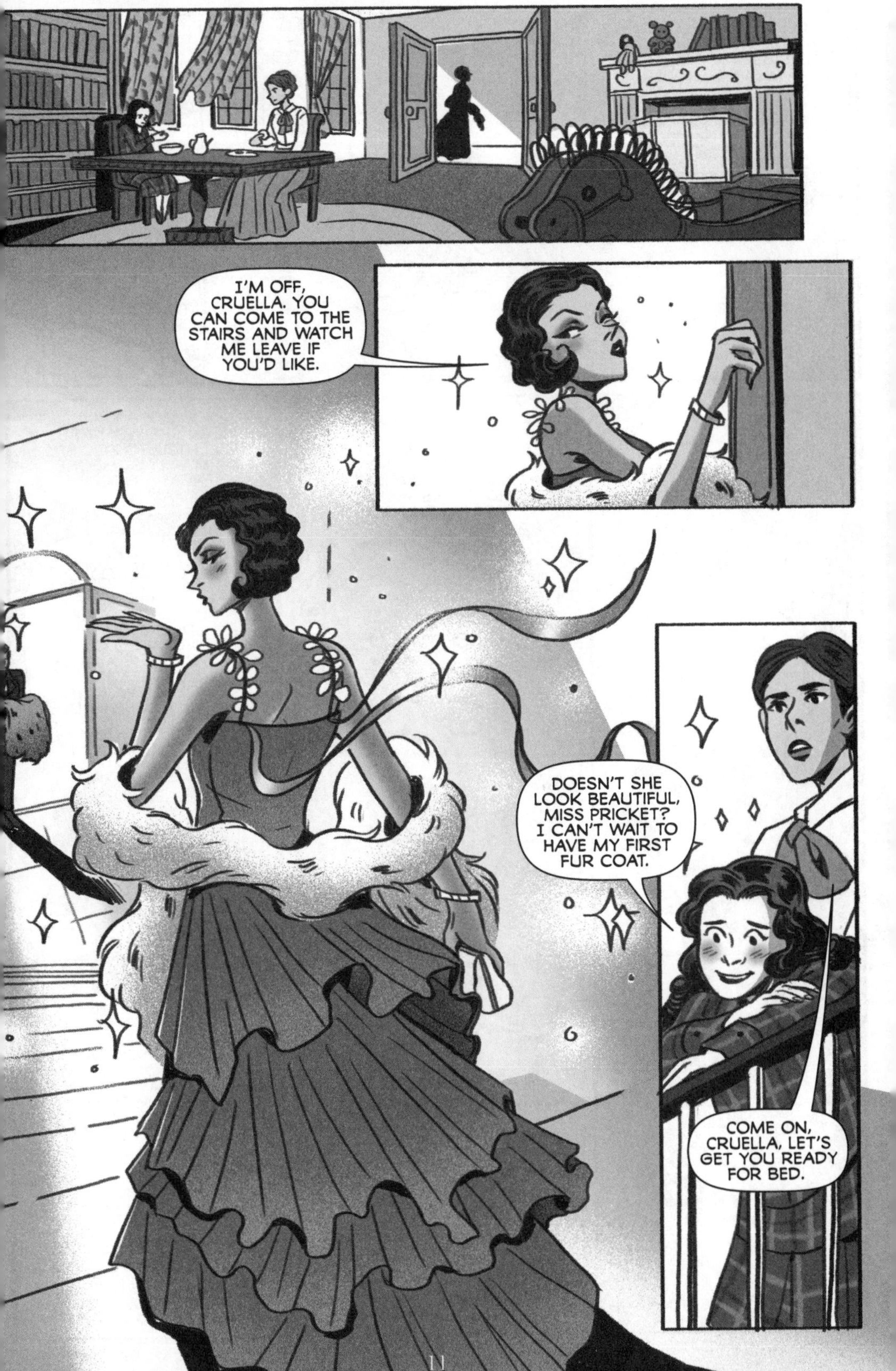
I'M OFF, CRUELLA. YOU CAN COME TO THE STAIRS AND WATCH ME LEAVE IF YOU'D LIKE.
DOESN'T SHE LOOK BEAUTIFUL, MISS PRICKET? I CAN'T WAIT TO HAVE MY FIRST FUR COAT.
COME ON, CRUELLA, LET'S GET YOU READY FOR BED.

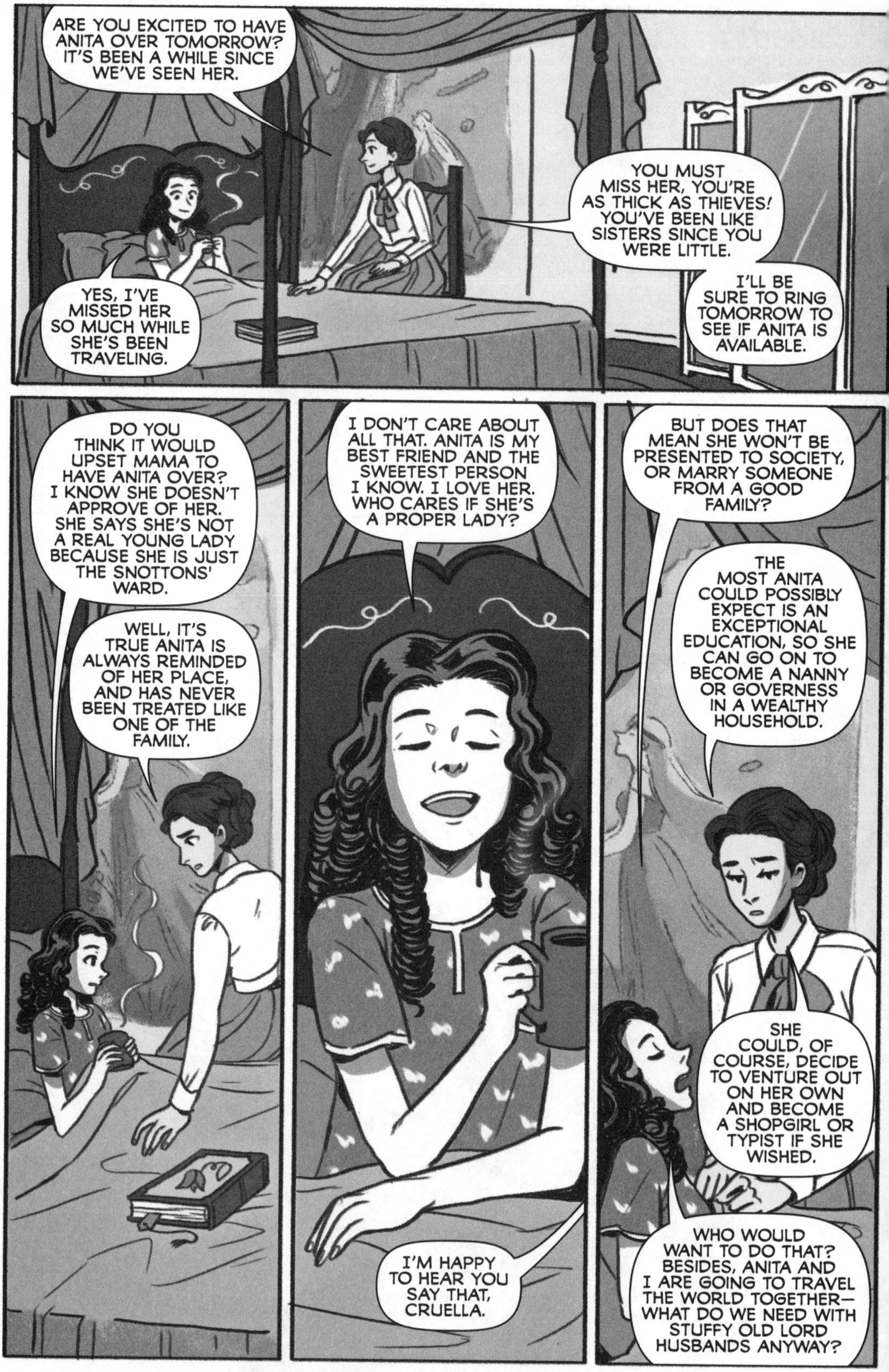

ARE YOU EXCITED TO HAVE ANITA OVER TOMORROW? IT'S BEEN A WHILE SINCE WE'VE SEEN HER.
YES, I'VE MISSED HER SO MUCH WHILE SHE'S BEEN TRAVELING.
YOU MUST MISS HER, YOU'RE AS THICK AS THIEVES! YOU'VE BEEN LIKE SISTERS SINCE YOU WERE LITTLE.
I'LL BE SURE TO RING TOMORROW TO SEE IF ANITA IS AVAILABLE.
DO YOU THINK IT WOULD UPSET MAMA TO HAVE ANITA OVER? I KNOW SHE DOESN'T APPROVE OF HER. SHE SAYS SHE'S NOT A REAL YOUNG LADY BECAUSE SHE IS JUST THE SNOTTONS' WARD.
WELL, IT'S TRUE ANITA IS ALWAYS REMINDED OF HER PLACE, AND HAS NEVER BEEN TREATED LIKE ONE OF THE FAMILY.
I DON'T CARE ABOUT ALL THAT. ANITA IS MY BEST FRIEND AND THE SWEETEST PERSON I KNOW. I LOVE HER. WHO CARES IF SHE'S A PROPER LADY?
I'M HAPPY TO HEAR YOU SAY THAT, CRUELLA.
BUT DOES THAT MEAN SHE WON'T BE PRESENTED TO SOCIETY, OR MARRY SOMEONE FROM A GOOD FAMILY?
THE MOST ANITA COULD POSSIBLY EXPECT IS AN EXCEPTIONAL EDUCATION, SO SHE CAN GO ON TO BECOME A NANNY OR GOVERNESS IN A WEALTHY HOUSEHOLD.
SHE COULD, OF COURSE, DECIDE TO VENTURE OUT ON HER OWN AND BECOME A SHOPGIRL OR TYPIST IF SHE WISHED.
WHO WOULD WANT TO DO THAT? BESIDES, ANITA AND I ARE GOING TO TRAVEL THE WORLD TOGETHER—WHAT DO WE NEED WITH STUFFY OLD LORD HUSBANDS ANYWAY?

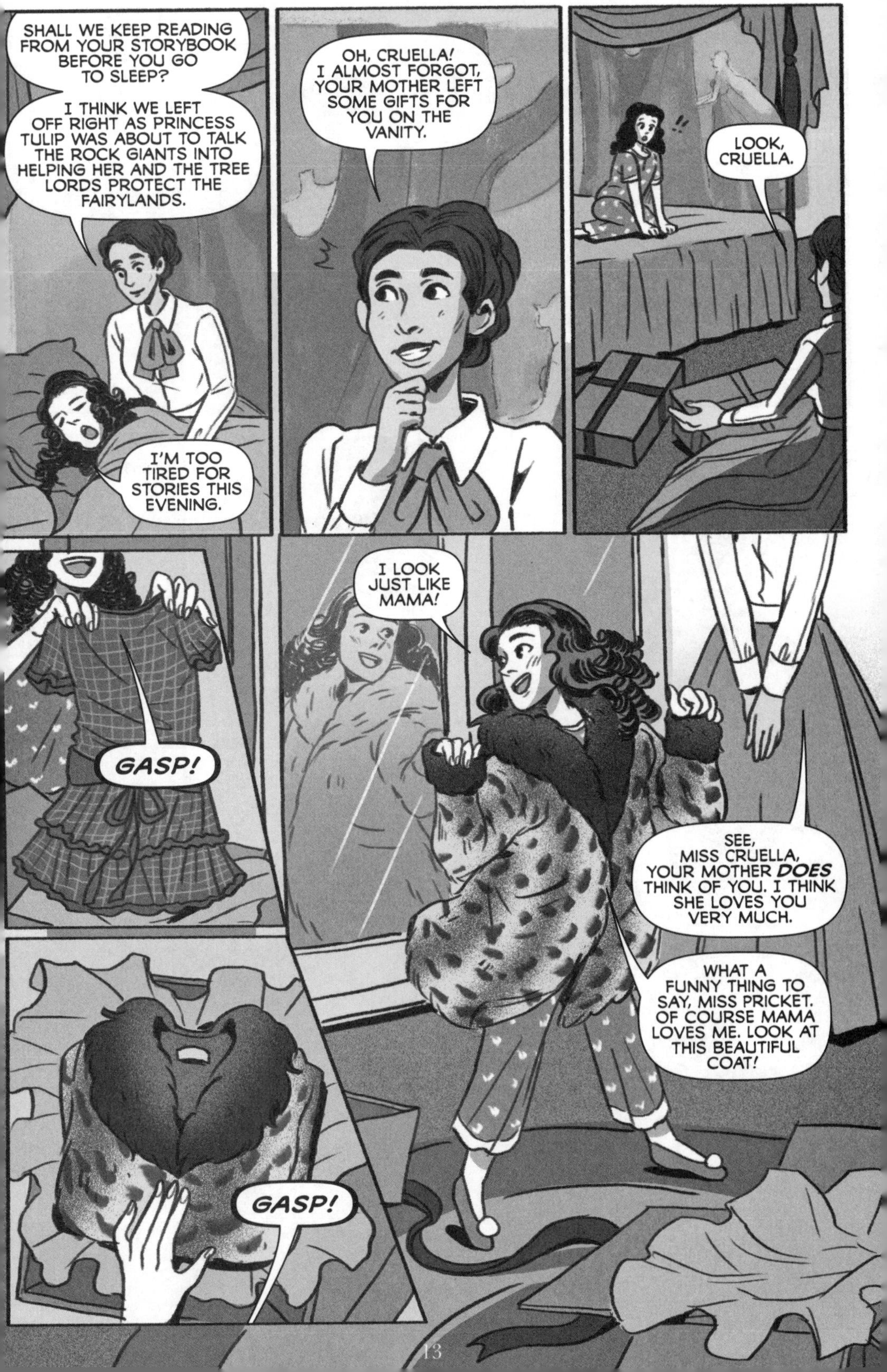

SHALL WE KEEP READING FROM YOUR STORYBOOK BEFORE YOU GO TO SLEEP?
I THINK WE LEFT OFF RIGHT AS PRINCESS TULIP WAS ABOUT TO TALK THE ROCK GIANTS INTO HELPING HER AND THE TREE LORDS PROTECT THE FAIRYLANDS.
I'M TOO TIRED FOR STORIES THIS EVENING.
OH, CRUELLA! I ALMOST FORGOT, YOUR MOTHER LEFT SOME GIFTS FOR YOU ON THE VANITY.
!!
LOOK, CRUELLA.
GASP!
GASP!
I LOOK JUST LIKE MAMA!
SEE, MISS CRUELLA, YOUR MOTHER ***DOES*** THINK OF YOU. I THINK SHE LOVES YOU VERY MUCH.
WHAT A FUNNY THING TO SAY, MISS PRICKET. OF COURSE MAMA LOVES ME. LOOK AT THIS BEAUTIFUL COAT!

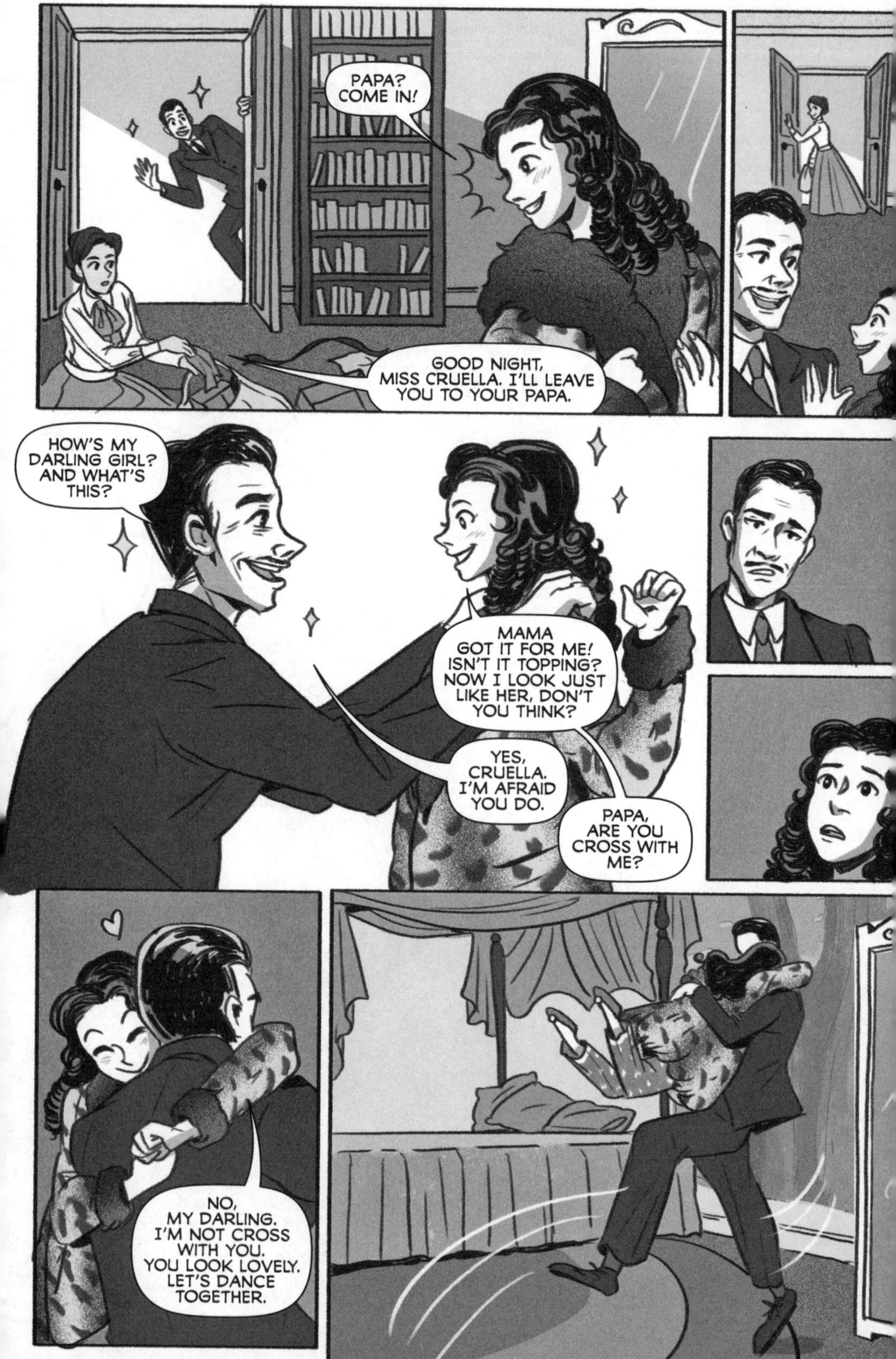
PAPA? COME IN!
GOOD NIGHT, MISS CRUELLA. I'LL LEAVE YOU TO YOUR PAPA.
HOW'S MY DARLING GIRL? AND WHAT'S THIS?
MAMA GOT IT FOR ME! ISN'T IT TOPPING? NOW I LOOK JUST LIKE HER, DON'T YOU THINK?
YES, CRUELLA. I'M AFRAID YOU DO.
PAPA, ARE YOU CROSS WITH ME?
NO, MY DARLING. I'M NOT CROSS WITH YOU. YOU LOOK LOVELY. LET'S DANCE TOGETHER.

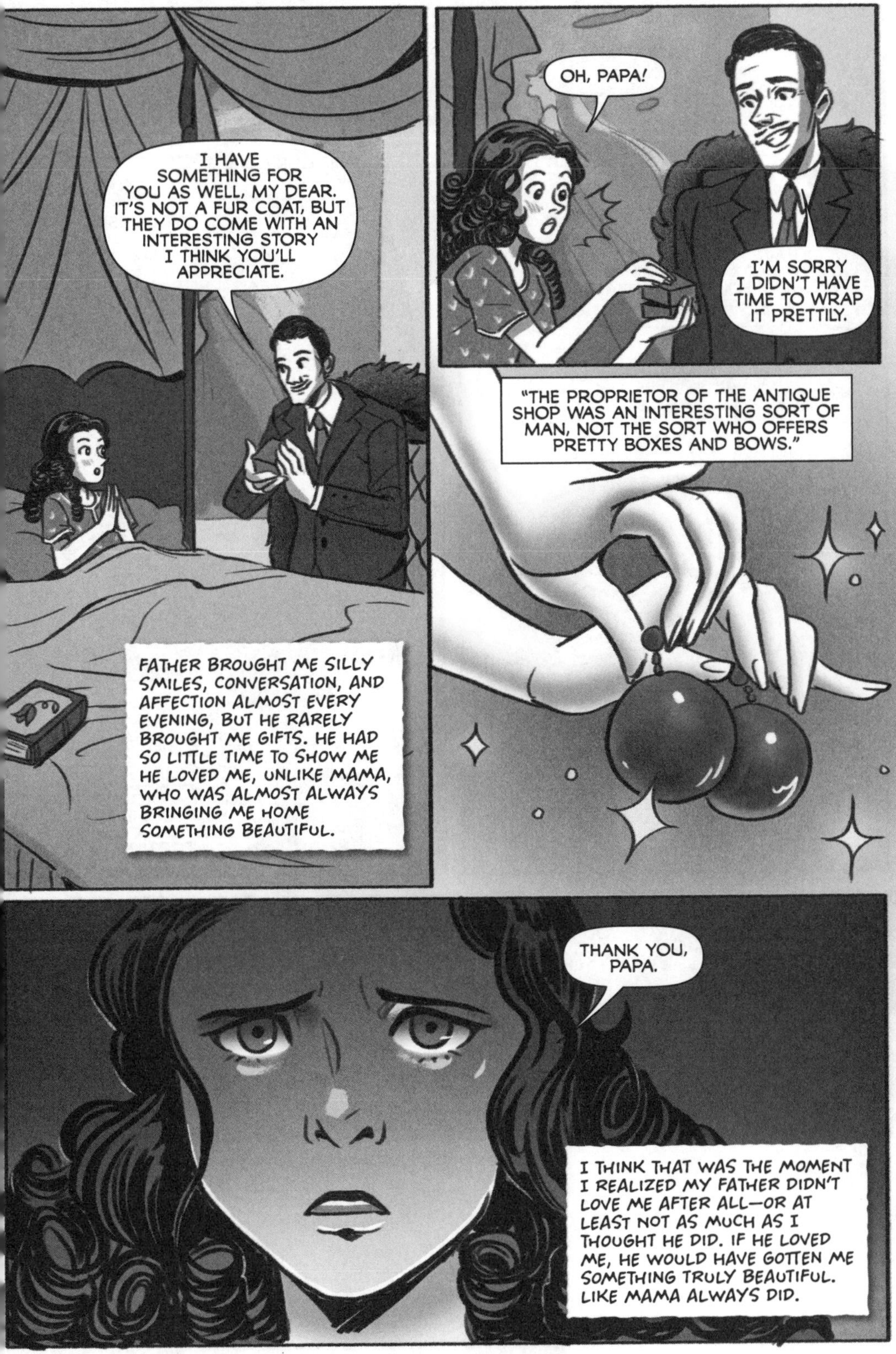
I HAVE SOMETHING FOR YOU AS WELL, MY DEAR. IT'S NOT A FUR COAT, BUT THEY DO COME WITH AN INTERESTING STORY I THINK YOU'LL APPRECIATE.
FATHER BROUGHT ME SILLY SMILES, CONVERSATION, AND AFFECTION ALMOST EVERY EVENING, BUT HE RARELY BROUGHT ME GIFTS. HE HAD SO LITTLE TIME TO SHOW ME HE LOVED ME, UNLIKE MAMA, WHO WAS ALMOST ALWAYS BRINGING ME HOME SOMETHING BEAUTIFUL.
OH, PAPA!
I'M SORRY I DIDN'T HAVE TIME TO WRAP IT PRETTILY.
"THE PROPRIETOR OF THE ANTIQUE SHOP WAS AN INTERESTING SORT OF MAN, NOT THE SORT WHO OFFERS PRETTY BOXES AND BOWS."
THANK YOU, PAPA.
I THINK THAT WAS THE MOMENT I REALIZED MY FATHER DIDN'T LOVE ME AFTER ALL—OR AT LEAST NOT AS MUCH AS I THOUGHT HE DID. IF HE LOVED ME, HE WOULD HAVE GOTTEN ME SOMETHING TRULY BEAUTIFUL. LIKE MAMA ALWAYS DID.

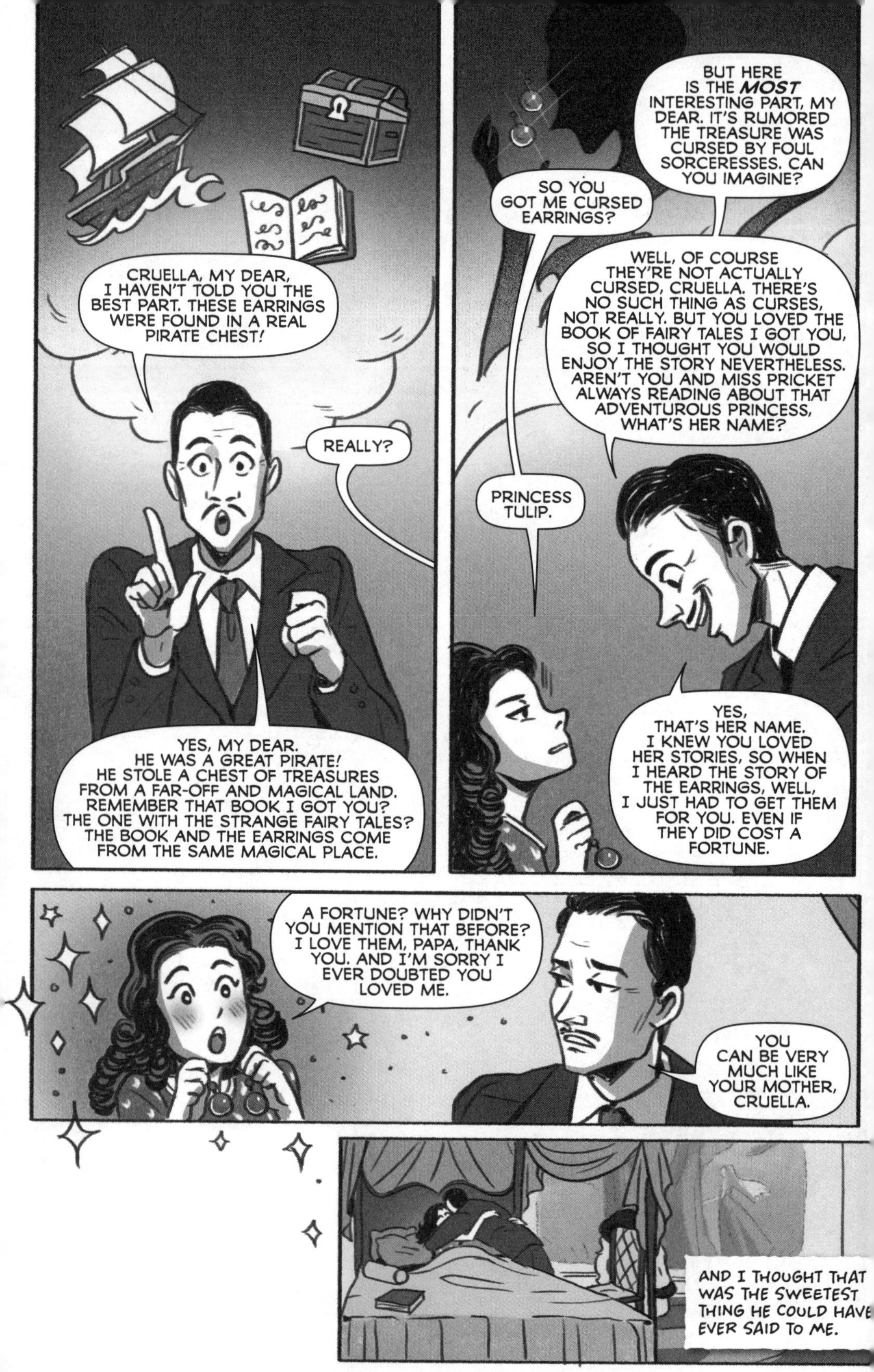
CRUELLA, MY DEAR, I HAVEN'T TOLD YOU THE BEST PART. THESE EARRINGS WERE FOUND IN A REAL PIRATE CHEST!
REALLY?
YES, MY DEAR. HE WAS A GREAT PIRATE! HE STOLE A CHEST OF TREASURES FROM A FAR-OFF AND MAGICAL LAND. REMEMBER THAT BOOK I GOT YOU? THE ONE WITH THE STRANGE FAIRY TALES? THE BOOK AND THE EARRINGS COME FROM THE SAME MAGICAL PLACE.
BUT HERE IS THE *MOST* INTERESTING PART, MY DEAR. IT'S RUMORED THE TREASURE WAS CURSED BY FOUL SORCERESSES. CAN YOU IMAGINE?
SO YOU GOT ME CURSED EARRINGS?
WELL, OF COURSE THEY'RE NOT ACTUALLY CURSED, CRUELLA. THERE'S NO SUCH THING AS CURSES, NOT REALLY. BUT YOU LOVED THE BOOK OF FAIRY TALES I GOT YOU, SO I THOUGHT YOU WOULD ENJOY THE STORY NEVERTHELESS. AREN'T YOU AND MISS PRICKET ALWAYS READING ABOUT THAT ADVENTUROUS PRINCESS, WHAT'S HER NAME?
PRINCESS TULIP.
YES, THAT'S HER NAME. I KNEW YOU LOVED HER STORIES, SO WHEN I HEARD THE STORY OF THE EARRINGS, WELL, I JUST HAD TO GET THEM FOR YOU. EVEN IF THEY DID COST A FORTUNE.
A FORTUNE? WHY DIDN'T YOU MENTION THAT BEFORE? I LOVE THEM, PAPA, THANK YOU. AND I'M SORRY I EVER DOUBTED YOU LOVED ME.
YOU CAN BE VERY MUCH LIKE YOUR MOTHER, CRUELLA.
AND I THOUGHT THAT WAS THE SWEETEST THING HE COULD HAVE EVER SAID TO ME.

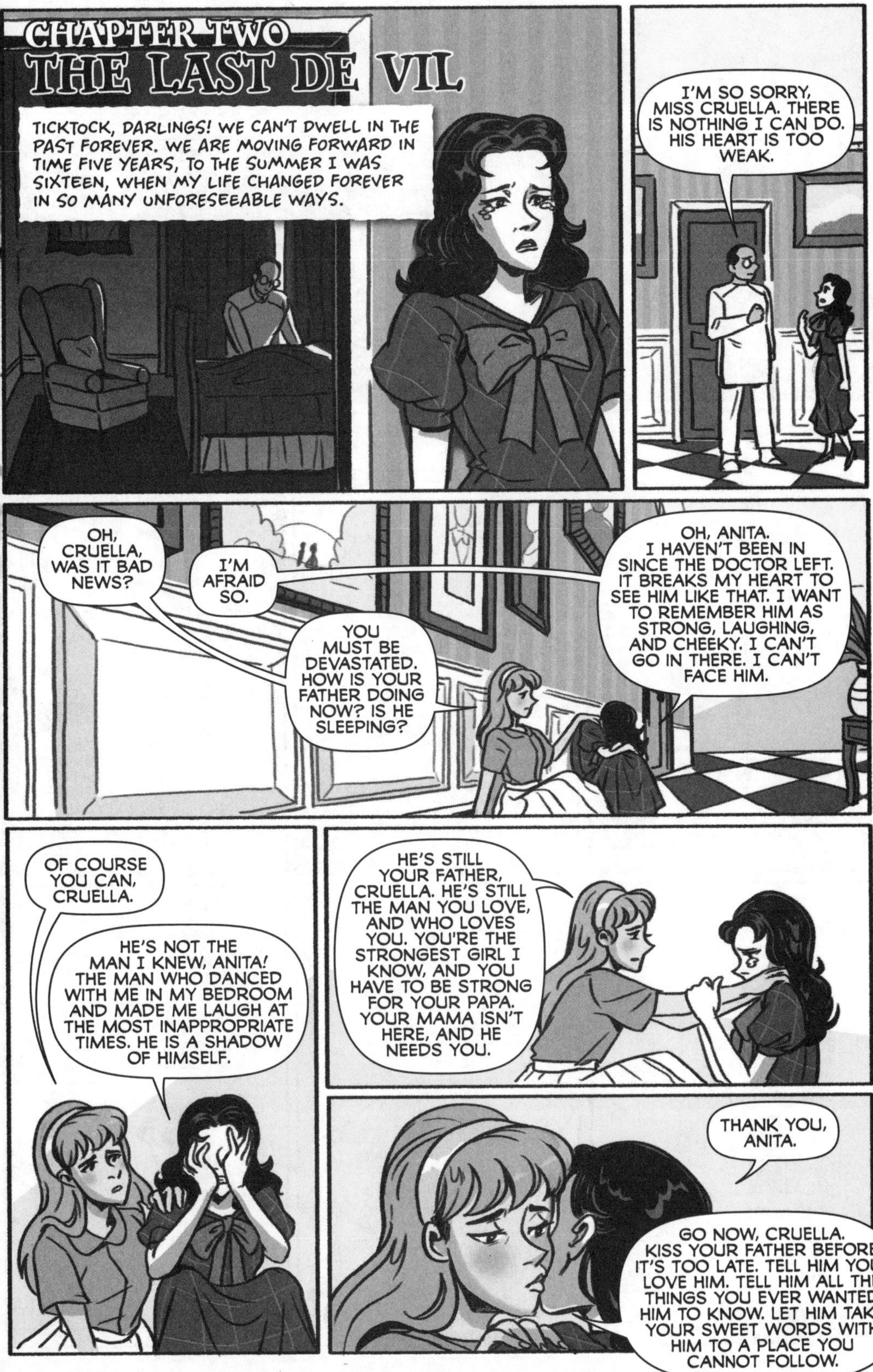
CHAPTER TWO
THE LAST DE VIL
TICKTOCK, DARLINGS! WE CAN'T DWELL IN THE PAST FOREVER. WE ARE MOVING FORWARD IN TIME FIVE YEARS, TO THE SUMMER I WAS SIXTEEN, WHEN MY LIFE CHANGED FOREVER IN SO MANY UNFORESEEABLE WAYS.
I'M SO SORRY, MISS CRUELLA. THERE IS NOTHING I CAN DO. HIS HEART IS TOO WEAK.
OH, CRUELLA, WAS IT BAD NEWS?
I'M AFRAID SO.
YOU MUST BE DEVASTATED. HOW IS YOUR FATHER DOING NOW? IS HE SLEEPING?
OH, ANITA. I HAVEN'T BEEN IN SINCE THE DOCTOR LEFT. IT BREAKS MY HEART TO SEE HIM LIKE THAT. I WANT TO REMEMBER HIM AS STRONG, LAUGHING, AND CHEEKY. I CAN'T GO IN THERE. I CAN'T FACE HIM.
OF COURSE YOU CAN, CRUELLA.
HE'S NOT THE MAN I KNEW, ANITA! THE MAN WHO DANCED WITH ME IN MY BEDROOM AND MADE ME LAUGH AT THE MOST INAPPROPRIATE TIMES. HE IS A SHADOW OF HIMSELF.
HE'S STILL YOUR FATHER, CRUELLA. HE'S STILL THE MAN YOU LOVE, AND WHO LOVES YOU. YOU'RE THE STRONGEST GIRL I KNOW, AND YOU HAVE TO BE STRONG FOR YOUR PAPA. YOUR MAMA ISN'T HERE, AND HE NEEDS YOU.
THANK YOU, ANITA.
GO NOW, CRUELLA. KISS YOUR FATHER BEFORE IT'S TOO LATE. TELL HIM YOU LOVE HIM. TELL HIM ALL THE THINGS YOU EVER WANTED HIM TO KNOW. LET HIM TAKE YOUR SWEET WORDS WITH HIM TO A PLACE YOU CANNOT FOLLOW.

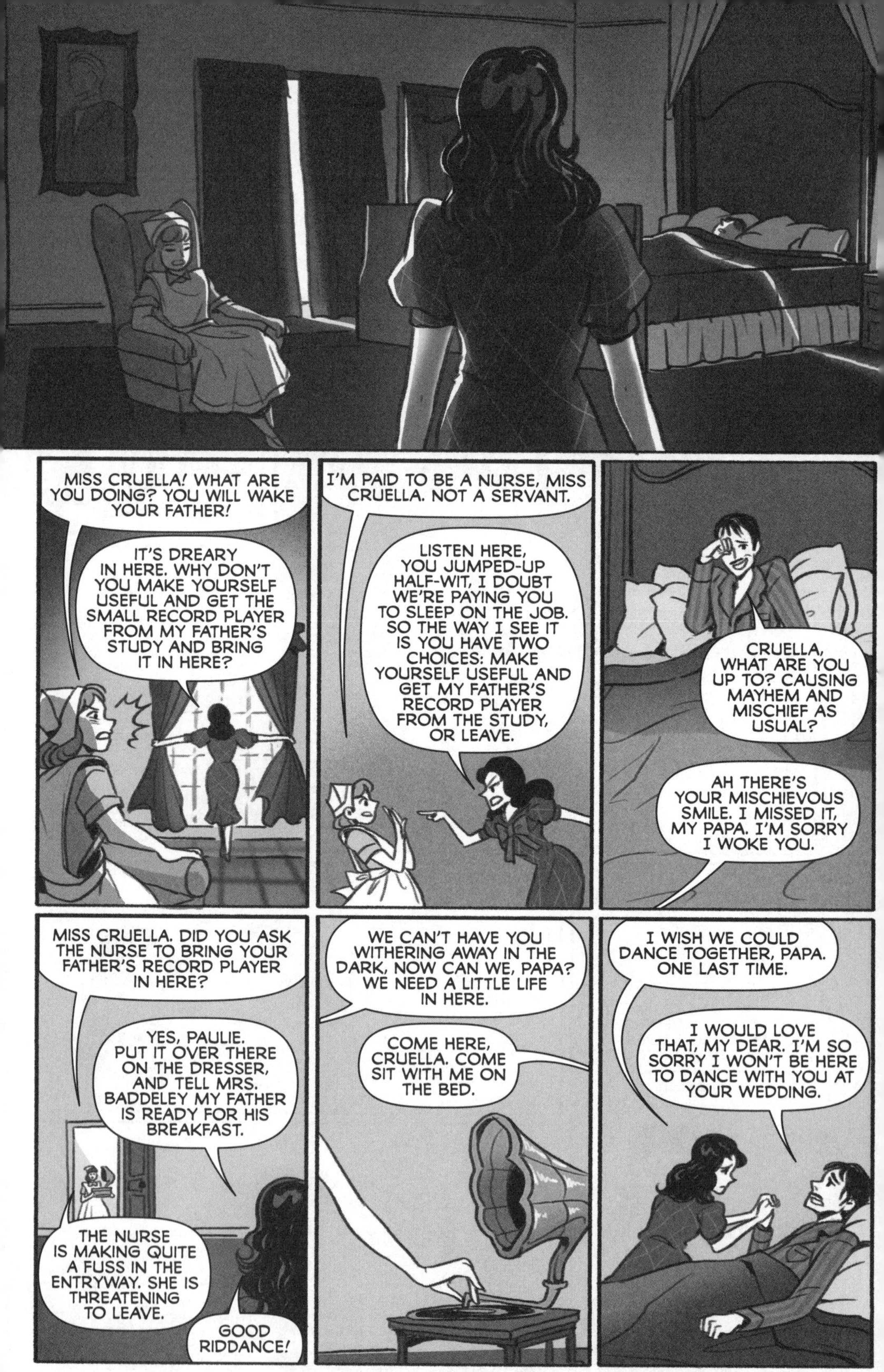
MISS CRUELLA! WHAT ARE YOU DOING? YOU WILL WAKE YOUR FATHER!
IT'S DREARY IN HERE. WHY DON'T YOU MAKE YOURSELF USEFUL AND GET THE SMALL RECORD PLAYER FROM MY FATHER'S STUDY AND BRING IT IN HERE?
I'M PAID TO BE A NURSE, MISS CRUELLA. NOT A SERVANT.
LISTEN HERE, YOU JUMPED-UP HALF-WIT, I DOUBT WE'RE PAYING YOU TO SLEEP ON THE JOB. SO THE WAY I SEE IT IS YOU HAVE TWO CHOICES: MAKE YOURSELF USEFUL AND GET MY FATHER'S RECORD PLAYER FROM THE STUDY, OR LEAVE.
CRUELLA, WHAT ARE YOU UP TO? CAUSING MAYHEM AND MISCHIEF AS USUAL?
AH THERE'S YOUR MISCHIEVOUS SMILE. I MISSED IT, MY PAPA. I'M SORRY I WOKE YOU.
MISS CRUELLA. DID YOU ASK THE NURSE TO BRING YOUR FATHER'S RECORD PLAYER IN HERE?
YES, PAULIE. PUT IT OVER THERE ON THE DRESSER, AND TELL MRS. BADDELEY MY FATHER IS READY FOR HIS BREAKFAST.
THE NURSE IS MAKING QUITE A FUSS IN THE ENTRYWAY. SHE IS THREATENING TO LEAVE.
GOOD RIDDANCE!
WE CAN'T HAVE YOU WITHERING AWAY IN THE DARK, NOW CAN WE, PAPA? WE NEED A LITTLE LIFE IN HERE.
COME HERE, CRUELLA. COME SIT WITH ME ON THE BED.
I WISH WE COULD DANCE TOGETHER, PAPA. ONE LAST TIME.
I WOULD LOVE THAT, MY DEAR. I'M SO SORRY I WON'T BE HERE TO DANCE WITH YOU AT YOUR WEDDING.

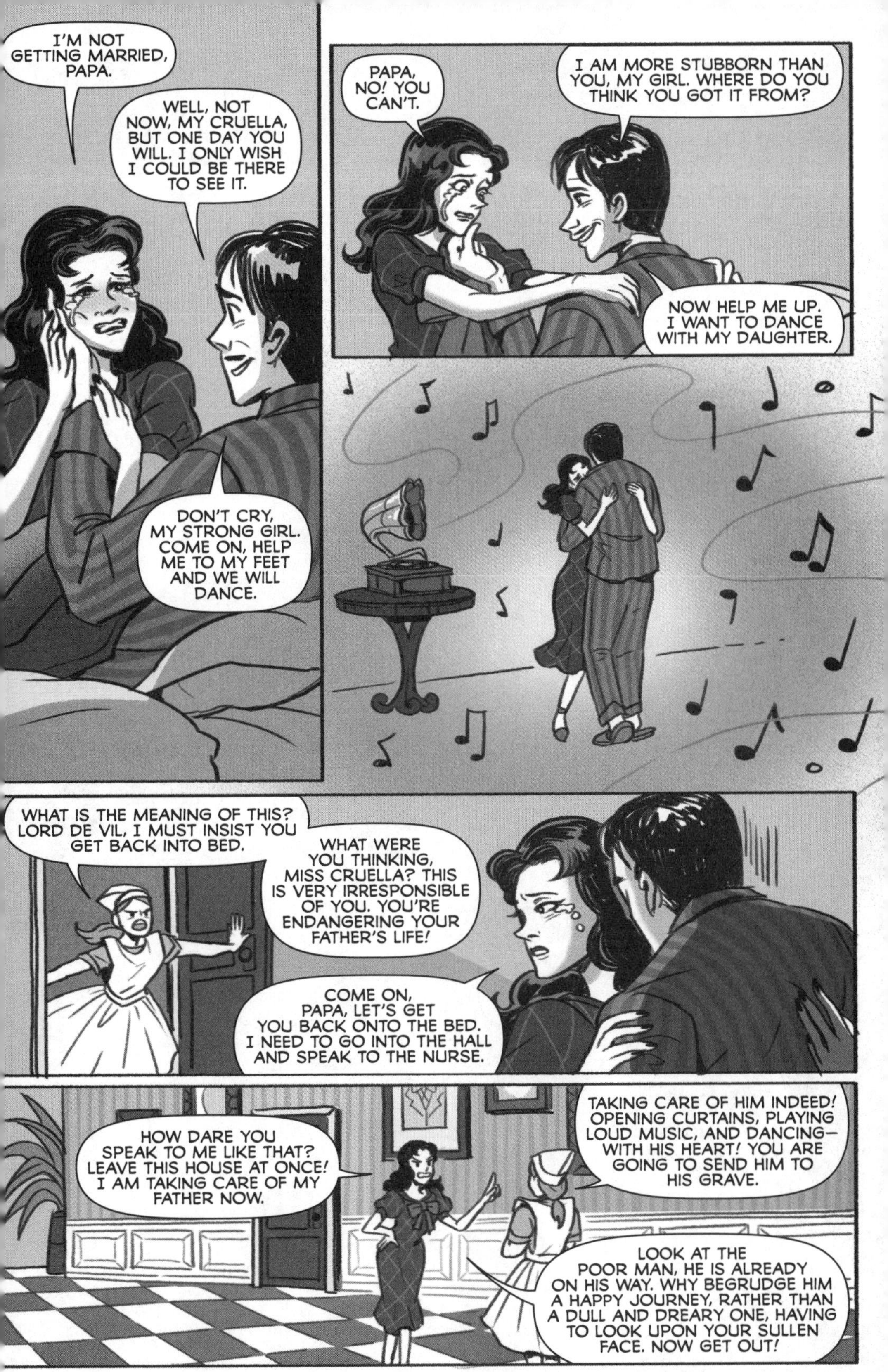
I'M NOT GETTING MARRIED, PAPA.
WELL, NOT NOW, MY CRUELLA, BUT ONE DAY YOU WILL. I ONLY WISH I COULD BE THERE TO SEE IT.
DON'T CRY, MY STRONG GIRL. COME ON, HELP ME TO MY FEET AND WE WILL DANCE.
PAPA, NO! YOU CAN'T.
I AM MORE STUBBORN THAN YOU, MY GIRL. WHERE DO YOU THINK YOU GOT IT FROM?
NOW HELP ME UP. I WANT TO DANCE WITH MY DAUGHTER.
WHAT IS THE MEANING OF THIS? LORD DE VIL, I MUST INSIST YOU GET BACK INTO BED.
WHAT WERE YOU THINKING, MISS CRUELLA? THIS IS VERY IRRESPONSIBLE OF YOU. YOU'RE ENDANGERING YOUR FATHER'S LIFE!
COME ON, PAPA, LET'S GET YOU BACK ONTO THE BED. I NEED TO GO INTO THE HALL AND SPEAK TO THE NURSE.
HOW DARE YOU SPEAK TO ME LIKE THAT? LEAVE THIS HOUSE AT ONCE! I AM TAKING CARE OF MY FATHER NOW.
TAKING CARE OF HIM INDEED! OPENING CURTAINS, PLAYING LOUD MUSIC, AND DANCING—WITH HIS HEART! YOU ARE GOING TO SEND HIM TO HIS GRAVE.
LOOK AT THE POOR MAN, HE IS ALREADY ON HIS WAY. WHY BEGRUDGE HIM A HAPPY JOURNEY, RATHER THAN A DULL AND DREARY ONE, HAVING TO LOOK UPON YOUR SULLEN FACE. NOW GET OUT!

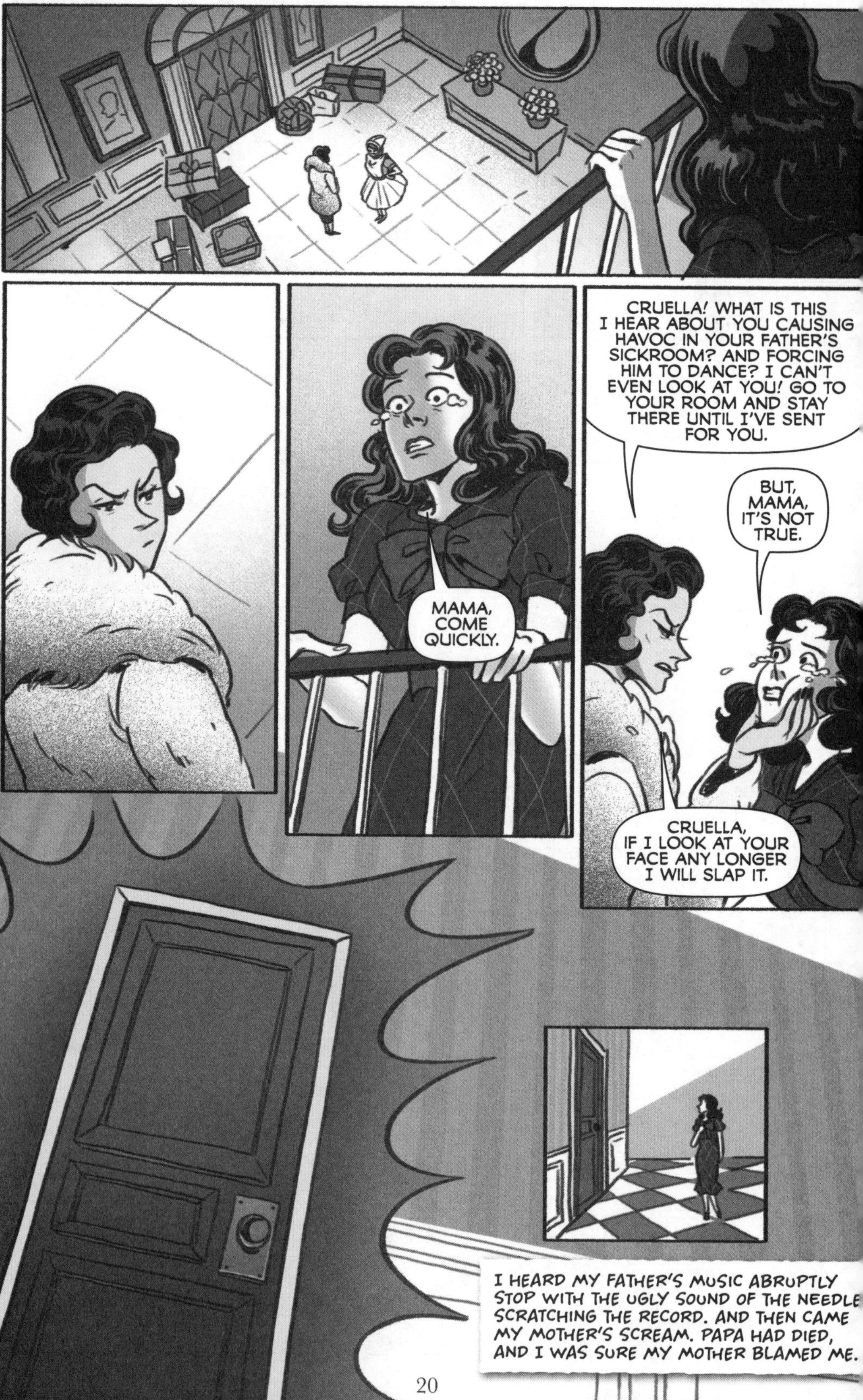

MAMA, COME QUICKLY.
CRUELLA! WHAT IS THIS I HEAR ABOUT YOU CAUSING HAVOC IN YOUR FATHER'S SICKROOM? AND FORCING HIM TO DANCE? I CAN'T EVEN LOOK AT YOU! GO TO YOUR ROOM AND STAY THERE UNTIL I'VE SENT FOR YOU.
BUT, MAMA, IT'S NOT TRUE.
CRUELLA, IF I LOOK AT YOUR FACE ANY LONGER I WILL SLAP IT.
I HEARD MY FATHER'S MUSIC ABRUPTLY STOP WITH THE UGLY SOUND OF THE NEEDLE SCRATCHING THE RECORD. AND THEN CAME MY MOTHER'S SCREAM. PAPA HAD DIED, AND I WAS SURE MY MOTHER BLAMED ME.

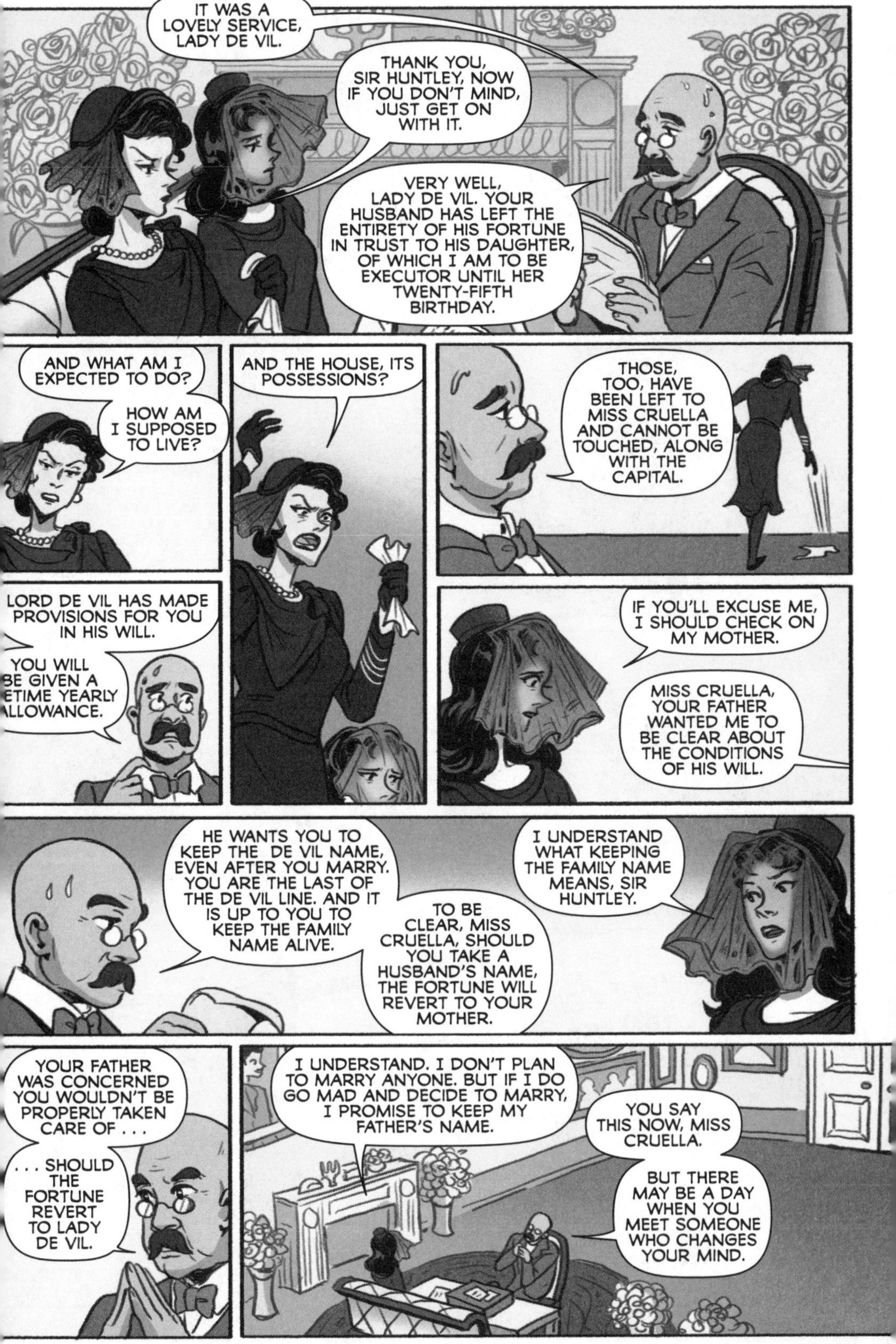
IT WAS A LOVELY SERVICE, LADY DE VIL.
THANK YOU, SIR HUNTLEY, NOW IF YOU DON'T MIND, JUST GET ON WITH IT.
VERY WELL, LADY DE VIL. YOUR HUSBAND HAS LEFT THE ENTIRETY OF HIS FORTUNE IN TRUST TO HIS DAUGHTER, OF WHICH I AM TO BE EXECUTOR UNTIL HER TWENTY-FIFTH BIRTHDAY.
AND WHAT AM I EXPECTED TO DO?
HOW AM I SUPPOSED TO LIVE?
LORD DE VIL HAS MADE PROVISIONS FOR YOU IN HIS WILL.
YOU WILL BE GIVEN A ETIME YEARLY LLOWANCE.
AND THE HOUSE, ITS POSSESSIONS?
THOSE, TOO, HAVE BEEN LEFT TO MISS CRUELLA AND CANNOT BE TOUCHED, ALONG WITH THE CAPITAL.
IF YOU'LL EXCUSE ME, I SHOULD CHECK ON MY MOTHER.
MISS CRUELLA, YOUR FATHER WANTED ME TO BE CLEAR ABOUT THE CONDITIONS OF HIS WILL.
HE WANTS YOU TO KEEP THE DE VIL NAME, EVEN AFTER YOU MARRY. YOU ARE THE LAST OF THE DE VIL LINE. AND IT IS UP TO YOU TO KEEP THE FAMILY NAME ALIVE.
TO BE CLEAR, MISS CRUELLA, SHOULD YOU TAKE A HUSBAND'S NAME, THE FORTUNE WILL REVERT TO YOUR MOTHER.
I UNDERSTAND WHAT KEEPING THE FAMILY NAME MEANS, SIR HUNTLEY.
YOUR FATHER WAS CONCERNED YOU WOULDN'T BE PROPERLY TAKEN CARE OF . . .
. . . SHOULD THE FORTUNE REVERT TO LADY DE VIL.
I UNDERSTAND. I DON'T PLAN TO MARRY ANYONE. BUT IF I DO GO MAD AND DECIDE TO MARRY, I PROMISE TO KEEP MY FATHER'S NAME.
YOU SAY THIS NOW, MISS CRUELLA.
BUT THERE MAY BE A DAY WHEN YOU MEET SOMEONE WHO CHANGES YOUR MIND.

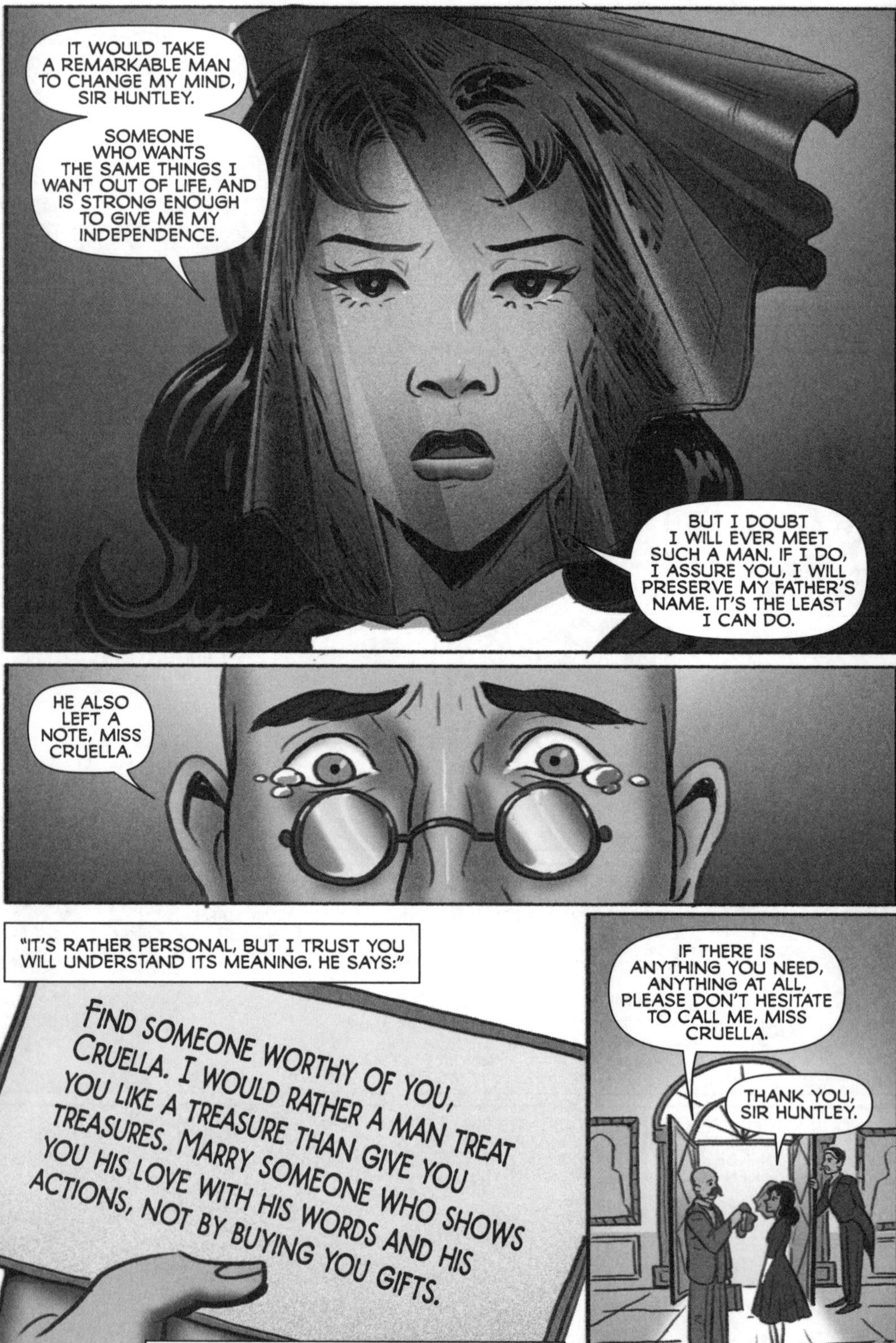
IT WOULD TAKE A REMARKABLE MAN TO CHANGE MY MIND, SIR HUNTLEY.
SOMEONE WHO WANTS THE SAME THINGS I WANT OUT OF LIFE, AND IS STRONG ENOUGH TO GIVE ME MY INDEPENDENCE.
BUT I DOUBT I WILL EVER MEET SUCH A MAN. IF I DO, I ASSURE YOU, I WILL PRESERVE MY FATHER'S NAME. IT'S THE LEAST I CAN DO.
HE ALSO LEFT A NOTE, MISS CRUELLA.
"IT'S RATHER PERSONAL, BUT I TRUST YOU WILL UNDERSTAND ITS MEANING. HE SAYS:"
FIND SOMEONE WORTHY OF YOU, CRUELLA. I WOULD RATHER A MAN TREAT YOU LIKE A TREASURE THAN GIVE YOU TREASURES. MARRY SOMEONE WHO SHOWS YOU HIS LOVE WITH HIS WORDS AND HIS ACTIONS, NOT BY BUYING YOU GIFTS.
"THANK YOU, SIR HUNTLEY, I BELIEVE I UNDERSTAND. NOW IF YOU'LL EXCUSE ME, I NEED TO CHECK ON MY MOTHER."
IF THERE IS ANYTHING YOU NEED, ANYTHING AT ALL, PLEASE DON'T HESITATE TO CALL ME, MISS CRUELLA.
THANK YOU, SIR HUNTLEY.

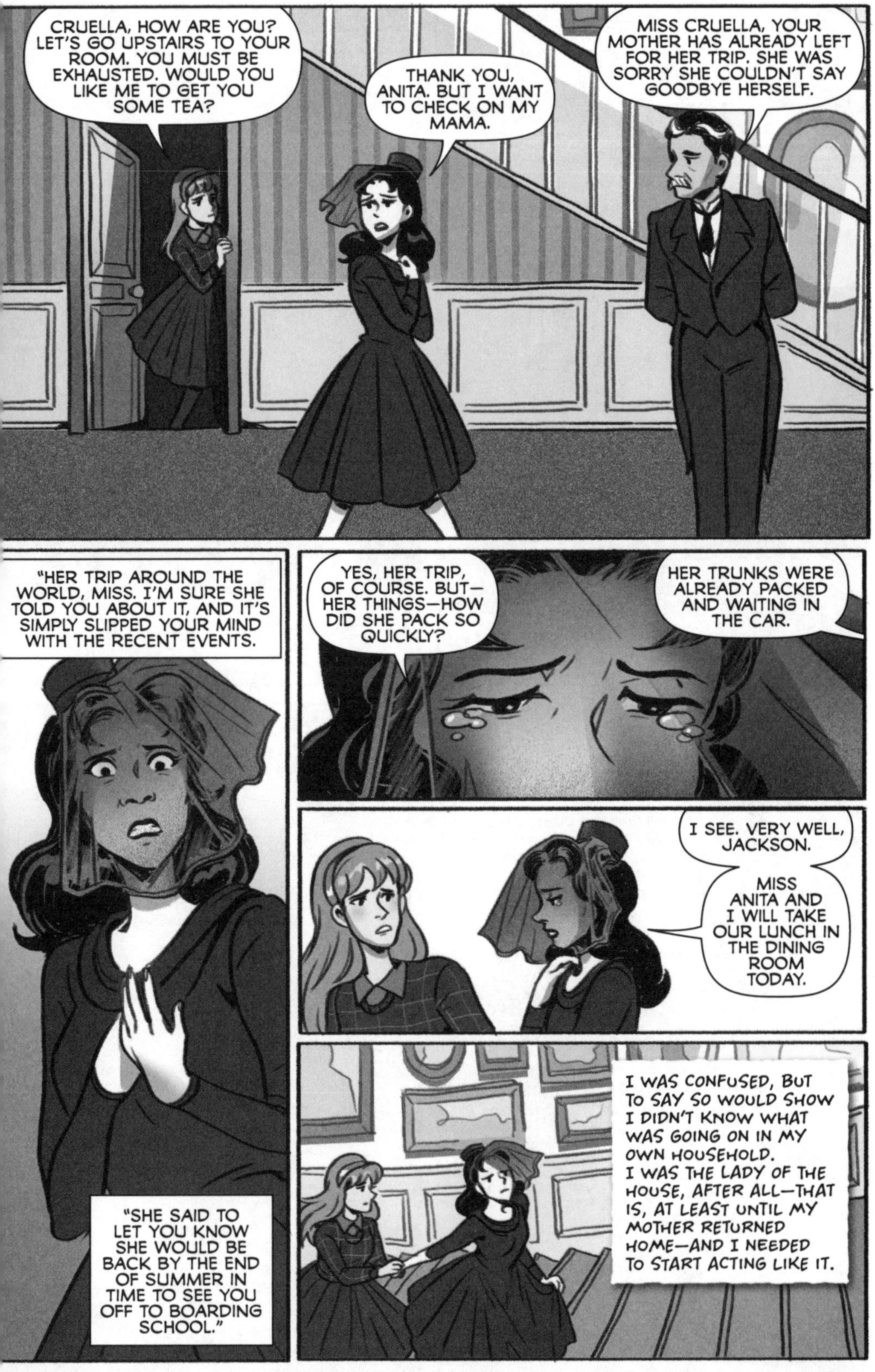
CRUELLA, HOW ARE YOU? LET'S GO UPSTAIRS TO YOUR ROOM. YOU MUST BE EXHAUSTED. WOULD YOU LIKE ME TO GET YOU SOME TEA?
THANK YOU, ANITA. BUT I WANT TO CHECK ON MY MAMA.
MISS CRUELLA, YOUR MOTHER HAS ALREADY LEFT FOR HER TRIP. SHE WAS SORRY SHE COULDN'T SAY GOODBYE HERSELF.
"HER TRIP AROUND THE WORLD, MISS. I'M SURE SHE TOLD YOU ABOUT IT, AND IT'S SIMPLY SLIPPED YOUR MIND WITH THE RECENT EVENTS.
"SHE SAID TO LET YOU KNOW SHE WOULD BE BACK BY THE END OF SUMMER IN TIME TO SEE YOU OFF TO BOARDING SCHOOL."
YES, HER TRIP, OF COURSE. BUT— HER THINGS—HOW DID SHE PACK SO QUICKLY?
HER TRUNKS WERE ALREADY PACKED AND WAITING IN THE CAR.
I SEE. VERY WELL, JACKSON.
MISS ANITA AND I WILL TAKE OUR LUNCH IN THE DINING ROOM TODAY.
I WAS CONFUSED, BUT TO SAY SO WOULD SHOW I DIDN'T KNOW WHAT WAS GOING ON IN MY OWN HOUSEHOLD. I WAS THE LADY OF THE HOUSE, AFTER ALL—THAT IS, AT LEAST UNTIL MY MOTHER RETURNED HOME—AND I NEEDED TO START ACTING LIKE IT.

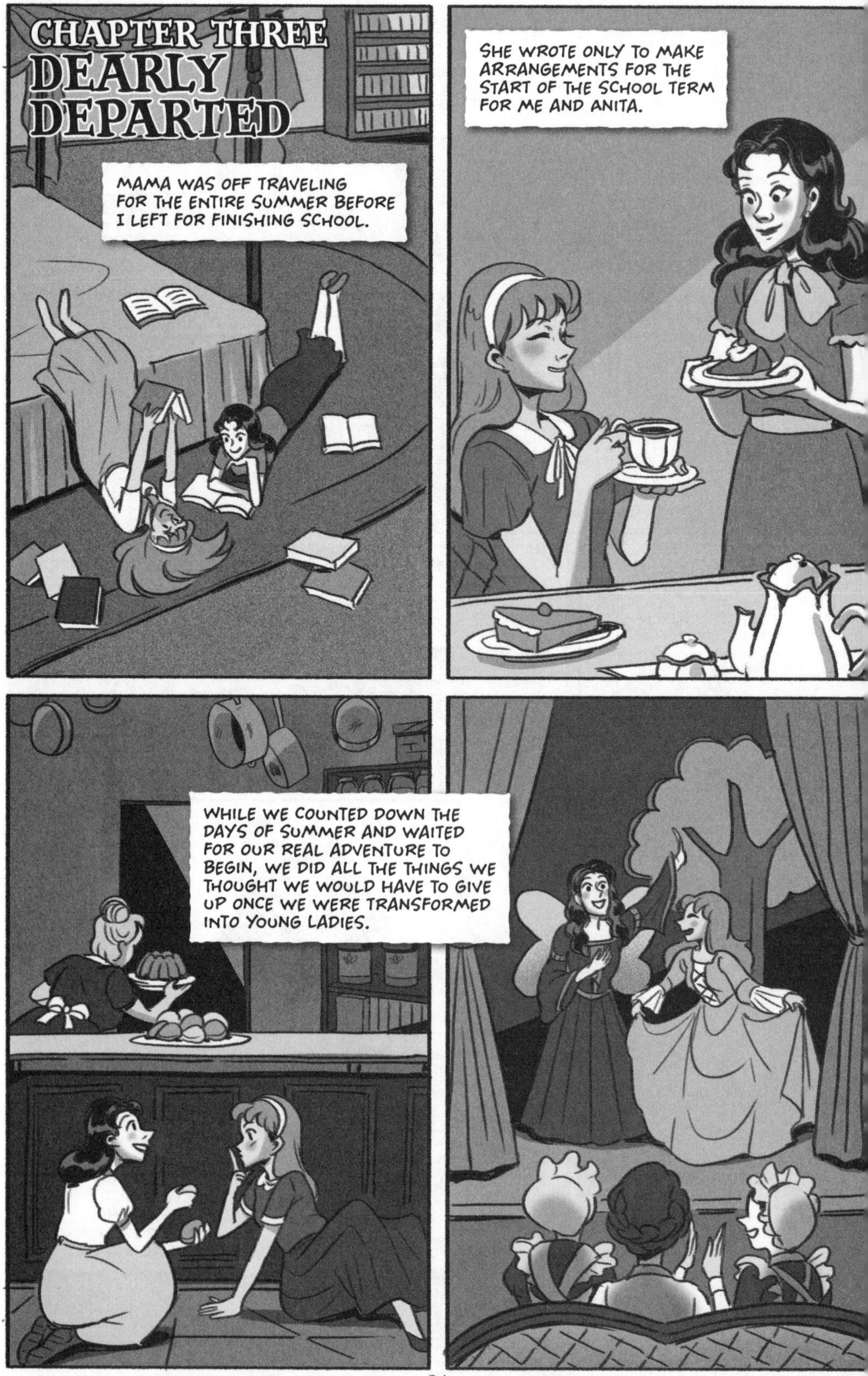
CHAPTER THREE
DEARLY DEPARTED
MAMA WAS OFF TRAVELING FOR THE ENTIRE SUMMER BEFORE I LEFT FOR FINISHING SCHOOL.
SHE WROTE ONLY TO MAKE ARRANGEMENTS FOR THE START OF THE SCHOOL TERM FOR ME AND ANITA.
WHILE WE COUNTED DOWN THE DAYS OF SUMMER AND WAITED FOR OUR REAL ADVENTURE TO BEGIN, WE DID ALL THE THINGS WE THOUGHT WE WOULD HAVE TO GIVE UP ONCE WE WERE TRANSFORMED INTO YOUNG LADIES.

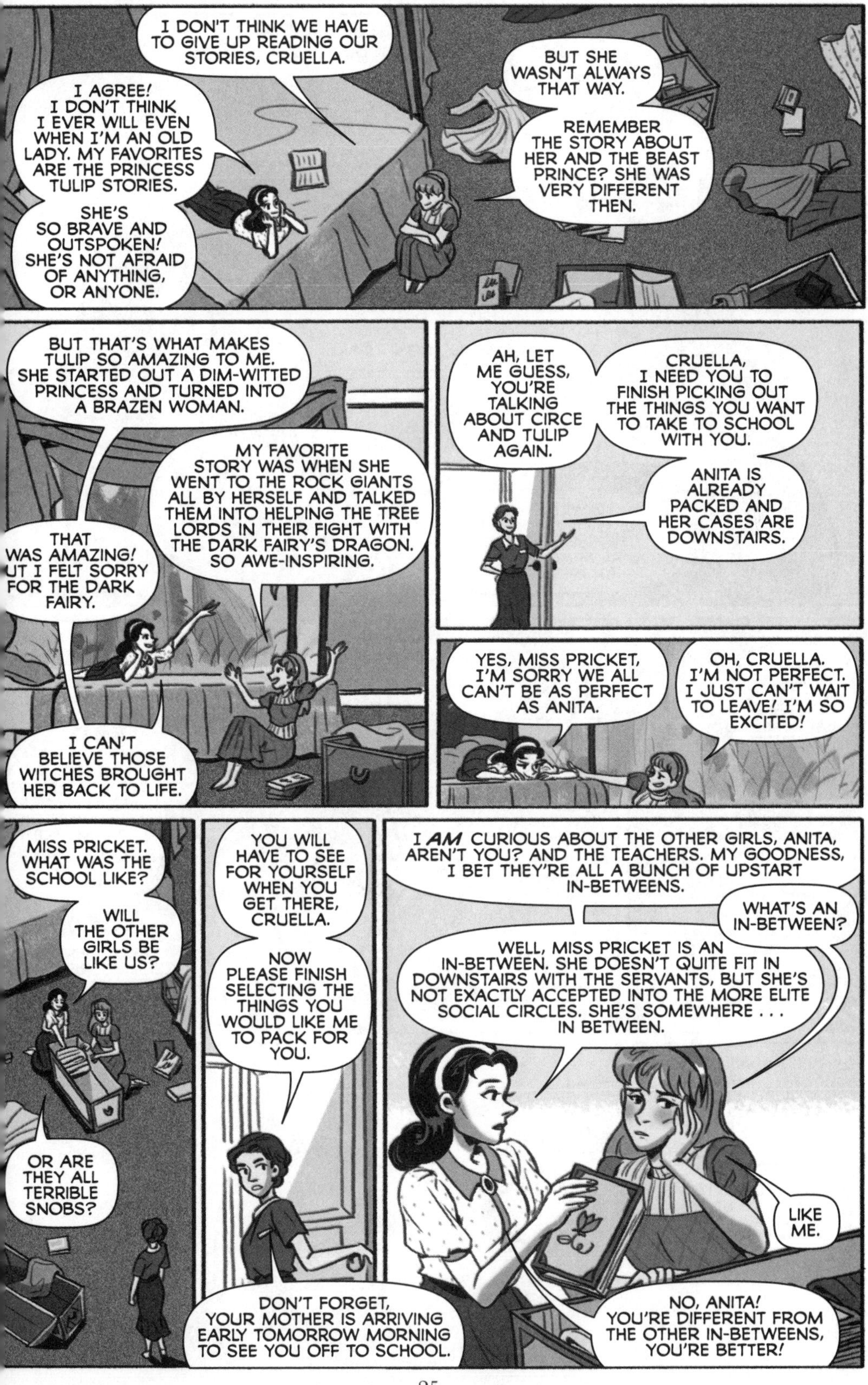
I DON'T THINK WE HAVE TO GIVE UP READING OUR STORIES, CRUELLA.
I AGREE! I DON'T THINK I EVER WILL EVEN WHEN I'M AN OLD LADY. MY FAVORITES ARE THE PRINCESS TULIP STORIES.
SHE'S SO BRAVE AND OUTSPOKEN! SHE'S NOT AFRAID OF ANYTHING, OR ANYONE.
BUT SHE WASN'T ALWAYS THAT WAY.
REMEMBER THE STORY ABOUT HER AND THE BEAST PRINCE? SHE WAS VERY DIFFERENT THEN.
BUT THAT'S WHAT MAKES TULIP SO AMAZING TO ME. SHE STARTED OUT A DIM-WITTED PRINCESS AND TURNED INTO A BRAZEN WOMAN.
MY FAVORITE STORY WAS WHEN SHE WENT TO THE ROCK GIANTS ALL BY HERSELF AND TALKED THEM INTO HELPING THE TREE LORDS IN THEIR FIGHT WITH THE DARK FAIRY'S DRAGON. SO AWE-INSPIRING.
THAT WAS AMAZING! UT I FELT SORRY FOR THE DARK FAIRY.
I CAN'T BELIEVE THOSE WITCHES BROUGHT HER BACK TO LIFE.
AH, LET ME GUESS, YOU'RE TALKING ABOUT CIRCE AND TULIP AGAIN.
CRUELLA, I NEED YOU TO FINISH PICKING OUT THE THINGS YOU WANT TO TAKE TO SCHOOL WITH YOU.
ANITA IS ALREADY PACKED AND HER CASES ARE DOWNSTAIRS.
YES, MISS PRICKET, I'M SORRY WE ALL CAN'T BE AS PERFECT AS ANITA.
OH, CRUELLA. I'M NOT PERFECT. I JUST CAN'T WAIT TO LEAVE! I'M SO EXCITED!
MISS PRICKET. WHAT WAS THE SCHOOL LIKE?
WILL THE OTHER GIRLS BE LIKE US?
OR ARE THEY ALL TERRIBLE SNOBS?
YOU WILL HAVE TO SEE FOR YOURSELF WHEN YOU GET THERE, CRUELLA.
NOW PLEASE FINISH SELECTING THE THINGS YOU WOULD LIKE ME TO PACK FOR YOU.
DON'T FORGET, YOUR MOTHER IS ARRIVING EARLY TOMORROW MORNING TO SEE YOU OFF TO SCHOOL.
I *AM* CURIOUS ABOUT THE OTHER GIRLS, ANITA, AREN'T YOU? AND THE TEACHERS. MY GOODNESS, I BET THEY'RE ALL A BUNCH OF UPSTART IN-BETWEENS.
WHAT'S AN IN-BETWEEN?
WELL, MISS PRICKET IS AN IN-BETWEEN. SHE DOESN'T QUITE FIT IN DOWNSTAIRS WITH THE SERVANTS, BUT SHE'S NOT EXACTLY ACCEPTED INTO THE MORE ELITE SOCIAL CIRCLES. SHE'S SOMEWHERE . . . IN BETWEEN.
LIKE ME.
NO, ANITA! YOU'RE DIFFERENT FROM THE OTHER IN-BETWEENS, YOU'RE BETTER!

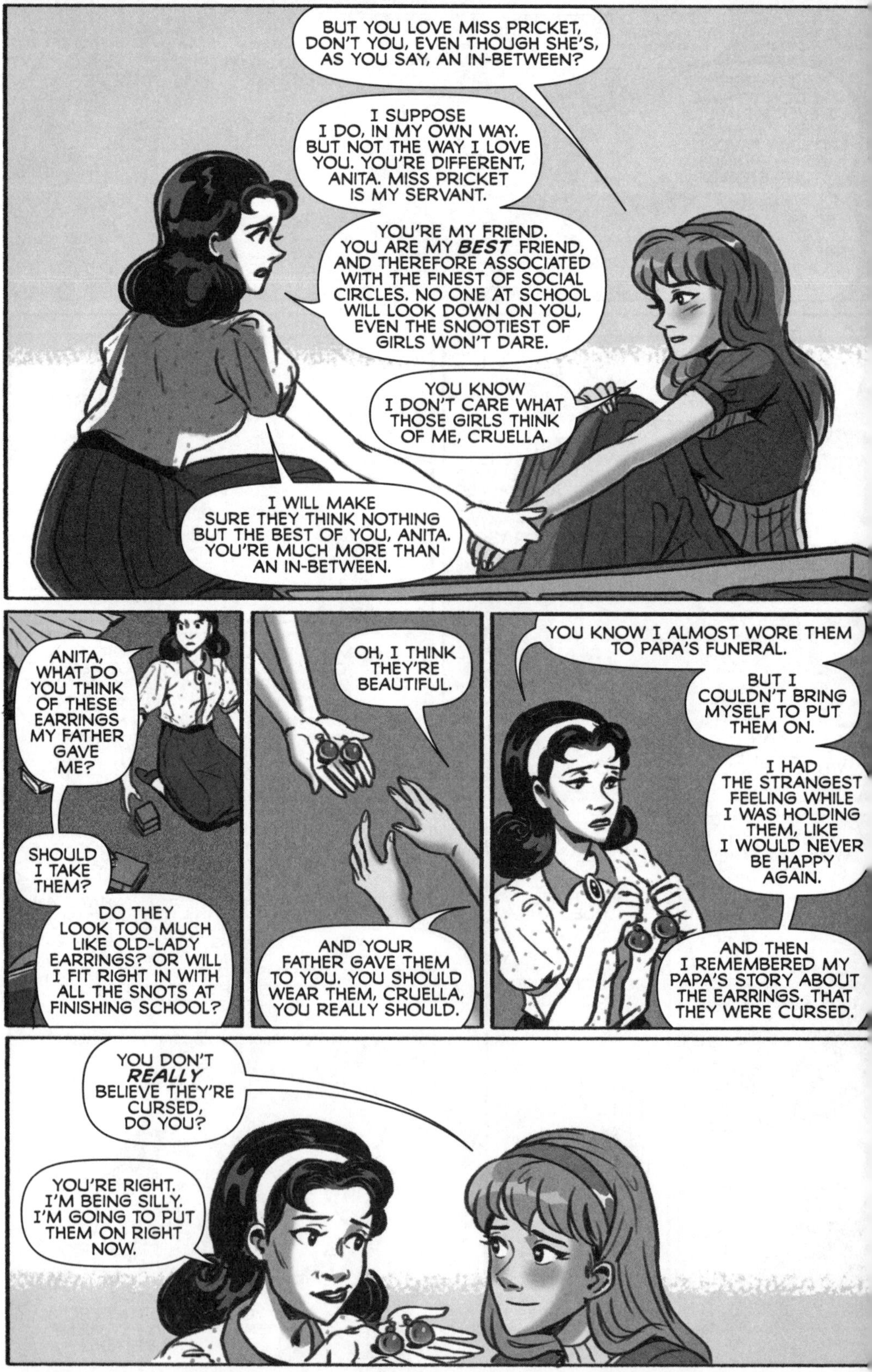

BUT YOU LOVE MISS PRICKET, DON'T YOU, EVEN THOUGH SHE'S, AS YOU SAY, AN IN-BETWEEN?
I SUPPOSE I DO, IN MY OWN WAY. BUT NOT THE WAY I LOVE YOU. YOU'RE DIFFERENT, ANITA. MISS PRICKET IS MY SERVANT.
YOU'RE MY FRIEND. YOU ARE MY ***BEST*** FRIEND, AND THEREFORE ASSOCIATED WITH THE FINEST OF SOCIAL CIRCLES. NO ONE AT SCHOOL WILL LOOK DOWN ON YOU, EVEN THE SNOOTIEST OF GIRLS WON'T DARE.
YOU KNOW I DON'T CARE WHAT THOSE GIRLS THINK OF ME, CRUELLA.
I WILL MAKE SURE THEY THINK NOTHING BUT THE BEST OF YOU, ANITA. YOU'RE MUCH MORE THAN AN IN-BETWEEN.
ANITA, WHAT DO YOU THINK OF THESE EARRINGS MY FATHER GAVE ME?
SHOULD I TAKE THEM?
DO THEY LOOK TOO MUCH LIKE OLD-LADY EARRINGS? OR WILL I FIT RIGHT IN WITH ALL THE SNOTS AT FINISHING SCHOOL?
OH, I THINK THEY'RE BEAUTIFUL.
AND YOUR FATHER GAVE THEM TO YOU. YOU SHOULD WEAR THEM, CRUELLA, YOU REALLY SHOULD.
YOU KNOW I ALMOST WORE THEM TO PAPA'S FUNERAL.
BUT I COULDN'T BRING MYSELF TO PUT THEM ON.
I HAD THE STRANGEST FEELING WHILE I WAS HOLDING THEM, LIKE I WOULD NEVER BE HAPPY AGAIN.
AND THEN I REMEMBERED MY PAPA'S STORY ABOUT THE EARRINGS. THAT THEY WERE CURSED.
YOU DON'T ***REALLY*** BELIEVE THEY'RE CURSED, DO YOU?
YOU'RE RIGHT. I'M BEING SILLY. I'M GOING TO PUT THEM ON RIGHT NOW.

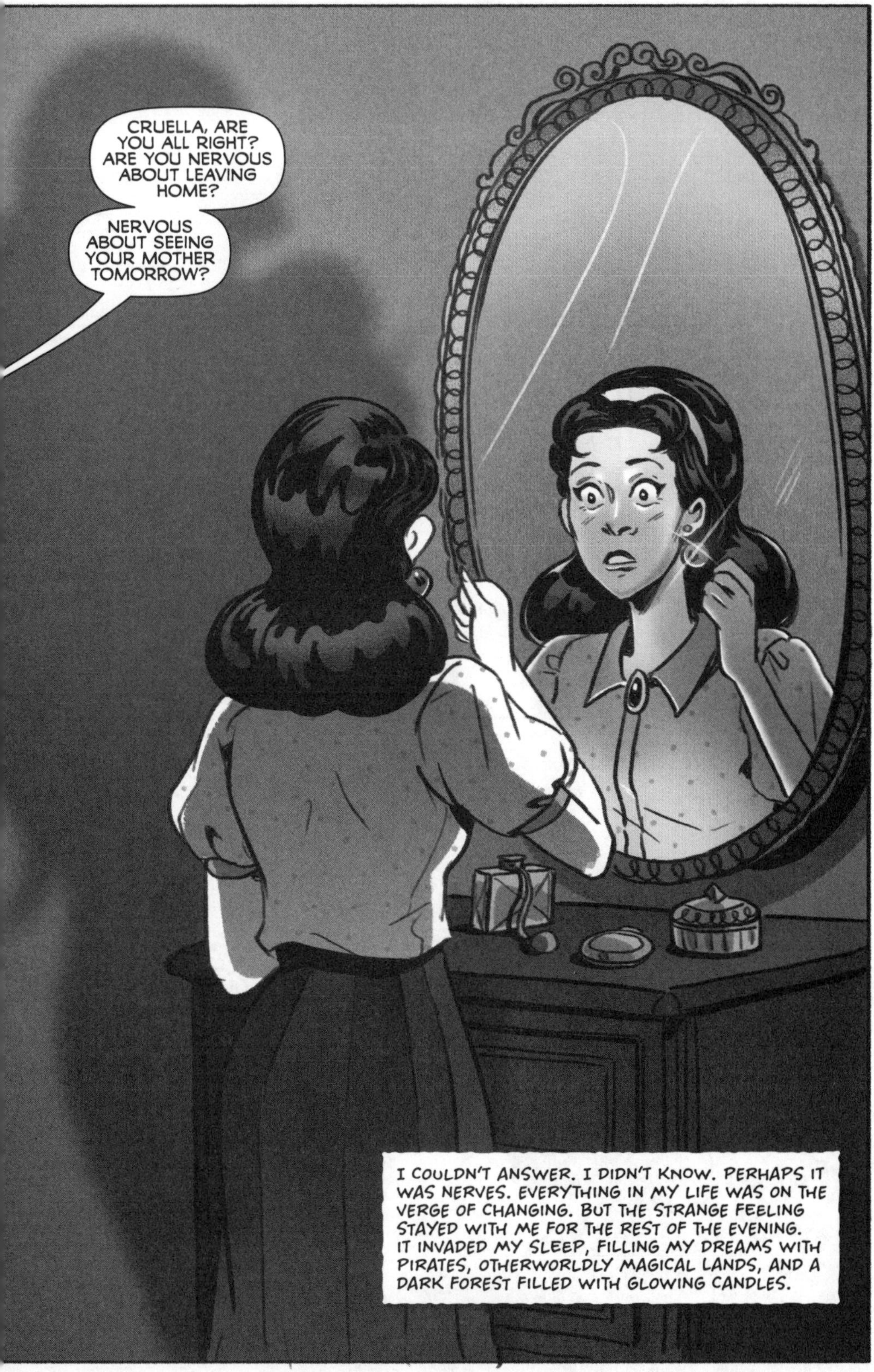
CRUELLA, ARE YOU ALL RIGHT? ARE YOU NERVOUS ABOUT LEAVING HOME?
NERVOUS ABOUT SEEING YOUR MOTHER TOMORROW?
I COULDN'T ANSWER. I DIDN'T KNOW. PERHAPS IT WAS NERVES. EVERYTHING IN MY LIFE WAS ON THE VERGE OF CHANGING. BUT THE STRANGE FEELING STAYED WITH ME FOR THE REST OF THE EVENING. IT INVADED MY SLEEP, FILLING MY DREAMS WITH PIRATES, OTHERWORLDLY MAGICAL LANDS, AND A DARK FOREST FILLED WITH GLOWING CANDLES.

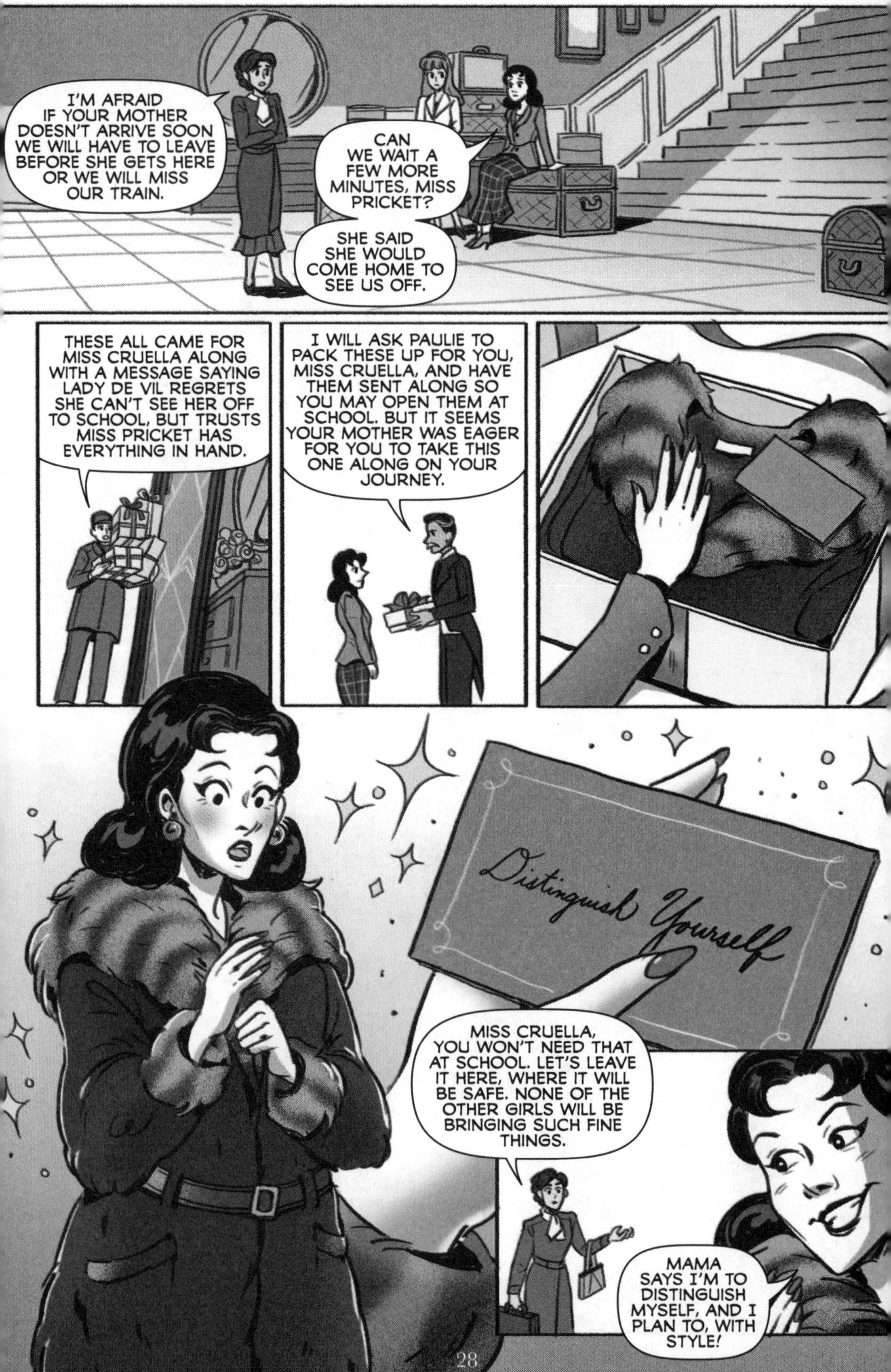
I'M AFRAID IF YOUR MOTHER DOESN'T ARRIVE SOON WE WILL HAVE TO LEAVE BEFORE SHE GETS HERE OR WE WILL MISS OUR TRAIN.
CAN WE WAIT A FEW MORE MINUTES, MISS PRICKET?
SHE SAID SHE WOULD COME HOME TO SEE US OFF.
THESE ALL CAME FOR MISS CRUELLA ALONG WITH A MESSAGE SAYING LADY DE VIL REGRETS SHE CAN'T SEE HER OFF TO SCHOOL, BUT TRUSTS MISS PRICKET HAS EVERYTHING IN HAND.
I WILL ASK PAULIE TO PACK THESE UP FOR YOU, MISS CRUELLA, AND HAVE THEM SENT ALONG SO YOU MAY OPEN THEM AT SCHOOL. BUT IT SEEMS YOUR MOTHER WAS EAGER FOR YOU TO TAKE THIS ONE ALONG ON YOUR JOURNEY.
Distinguish Yourself
MISS CRUELLA, YOU WON'T NEED THAT AT SCHOOL. LET'S LEAVE IT HERE, WHERE IT WILL BE SAFE. NONE OF THE OTHER GIRLS WILL BE BRINGING SUCH FINE THINGS.
MAMA SAYS I'M TO DISTINGUISH MYSELF, AND I PLAN TO, WITH STYLE!

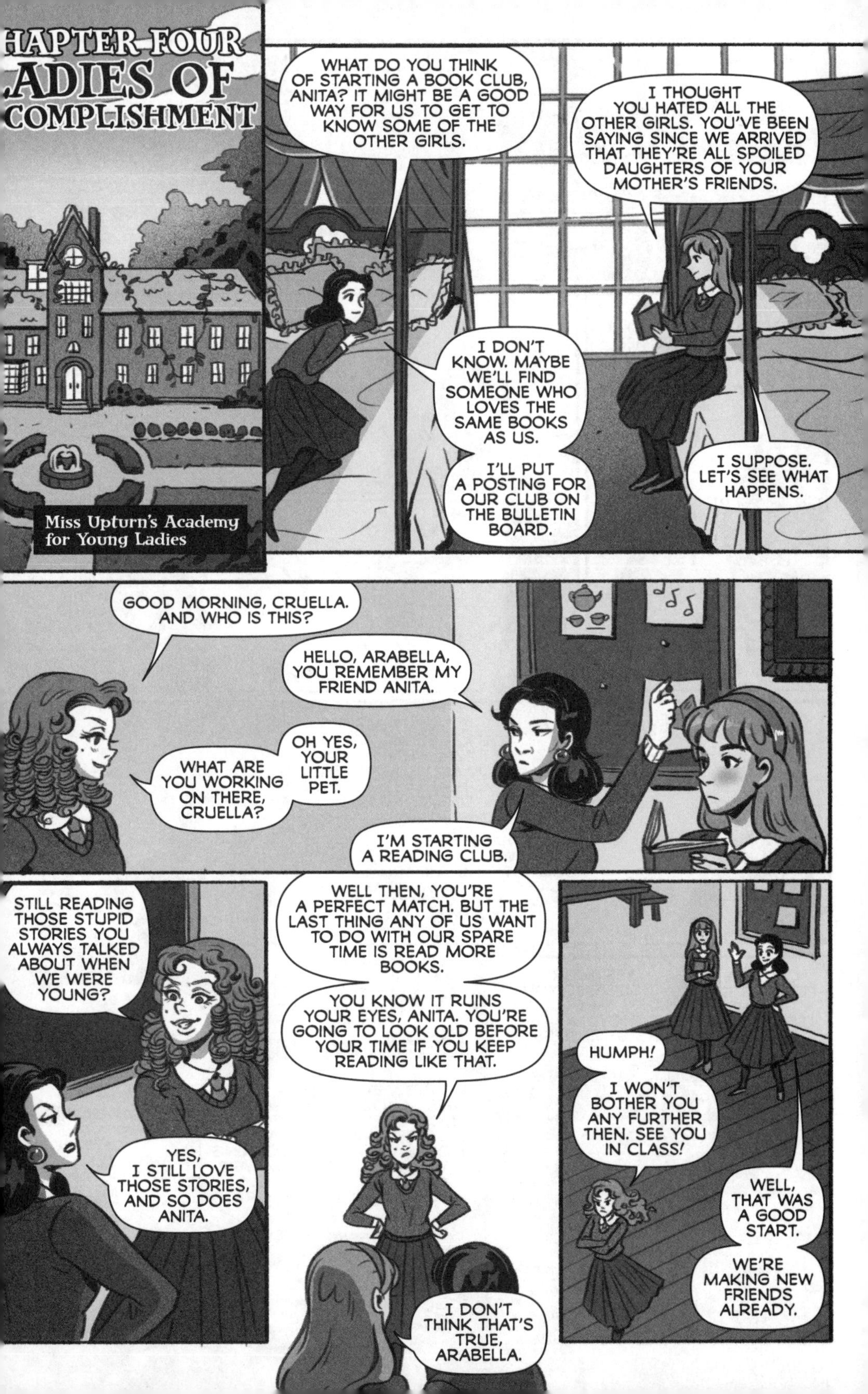
HAPTER FOUR
ADIES OF
COMPLISHMENT
Miss Upturn's Academy for Young Ladies
WHAT DO YOU THINK OF STARTING A BOOK CLUB, ANITA? IT MIGHT BE A GOOD WAY FOR US TO GET TO KNOW SOME OF THE OTHER GIRLS.
I THOUGHT YOU HATED ALL THE OTHER GIRLS. YOU'VE BEEN SAYING SINCE WE ARRIVED THAT THEY'RE ALL SPOILED DAUGHTERS OF YOUR MOTHER'S FRIENDS.
I DON'T KNOW. MAYBE WE'LL FIND SOMEONE WHO LOVES THE SAME BOOKS AS US.
I'LL PUT A POSTING FOR OUR CLUB ON THE BULLETIN BOARD.
I SUPPOSE. LET'S SEE WHAT HAPPENS.
GOOD MORNING, CRUELLA. AND WHO IS THIS?
HELLO, ARABELLA, YOU REMEMBER MY FRIEND ANITA.
OH YES, YOUR LITTLE PET.
WHAT ARE YOU WORKING ON THERE, CRUELLA?
I'M STARTING A READING CLUB.
STILL READING THOSE STUPID STORIES YOU ALWAYS TALKED ABOUT WHEN WE WERE YOUNG?
YES, I STILL LOVE THOSE STORIES, AND SO DOES ANITA.
WELL THEN, YOU'RE A PERFECT MATCH. BUT THE LAST THING ANY OF US WANT TO DO WITH OUR SPARE TIME IS READ MORE BOOKS.
YOU KNOW IT RUINS YOUR EYES, ANITA. YOU'RE GOING TO LOOK OLD BEFORE YOUR TIME IF YOU KEEP READING LIKE THAT.
I DON'T THINK THAT'S TRUE, ARABELLA.
HUMPH!
I WON'T BOTHER YOU ANY FURTHER THEN. SEE YOU IN CLASS!
WELL, THAT WAS A GOOD START.
WE'RE MAKING NEW FRIENDS ALREADY.

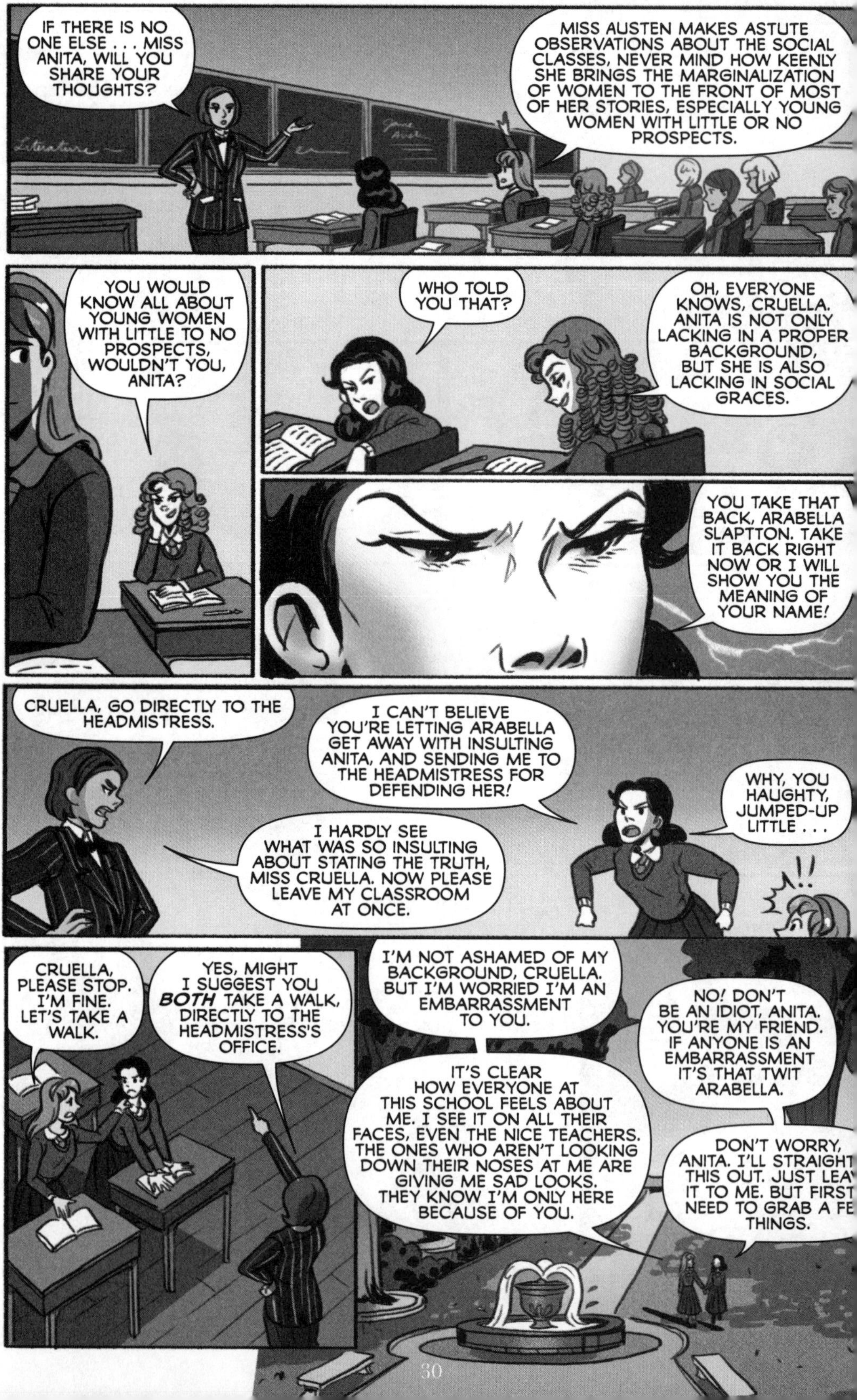
IF THERE IS NO ONE ELSE . . . MISS ANITA, WILL YOU SHARE YOUR THOUGHTS?
MISS AUSTEN MAKES ASTUTE OBSERVATIONS ABOUT THE SOCIAL CLASSES, NEVER MIND HOW KEENLY SHE BRINGS THE MARGINALIZATION OF WOMEN TO THE FRONT OF MOST OF HER STORIES, ESPECIALLY YOUNG WOMEN WITH LITTLE OR NO PROSPECTS.
YOU WOULD KNOW ALL ABOUT YOUNG WOMEN WITH LITTLE TO NO PROSPECTS, WOULDN'T YOU, ANITA?
WHO TOLD YOU THAT?
OH, EVERYONE KNOWS, CRUELLA. ANITA IS NOT ONLY LACKING IN A PROPER BACKGROUND, BUT SHE IS ALSO LACKING IN SOCIAL GRACES.
YOU TAKE THAT BACK, ARABELLA SLAPTTON. TAKE IT BACK RIGHT NOW OR I WILL SHOW YOU THE MEANING OF YOUR NAME!
CRUELLA, GO DIRECTLY TO THE HEADMISTRESS.
I CAN'T BELIEVE YOU'RE LETTING ARABELLA GET AWAY WITH INSULTING ANITA, AND SENDING ME TO THE HEADMISTRESS FOR DEFENDING HER!
I HARDLY SEE WHAT WAS SO INSULTING ABOUT STATING THE TRUTH, MISS CRUELLA. NOW PLEASE LEAVE MY CLASSROOM AT ONCE.
WHY, YOU HAUGHTY, JUMPED-UP LITTLE . . .
!!
CRUELLA, PLEASE STOP. I'M FINE. LET'S TAKE A WALK.
YES, MIGHT I SUGGEST YOU BOTH TAKE A WALK, DIRECTLY TO THE HEADMISTRESS'S OFFICE.
I'M NOT ASHAMED OF MY BACKGROUND, CRUELLA. BUT I'M WORRIED I'M AN EMBARRASSMENT TO YOU.
NO! DON'T BE AN IDIOT, ANITA. YOU'RE MY FRIEND. IF ANYONE IS AN EMBARRASSMENT IT'S THAT TWIT ARABELLA.
IT'S CLEAR HOW EVERYONE AT THIS SCHOOL FEELS ABOUT ME. I SEE IT ON ALL THEIR FACES, EVEN THE NICE TEACHERS. THE ONES WHO AREN'T LOOKING DOWN THEIR NOSES AT ME ARE GIVING ME SAD LOOKS. THEY KNOW I'M ONLY HERE BECAUSE OF YOU.
DON'T WORRY, ANITA. I'LL STRAIGHT THIS OUT. JUST LEA IT TO ME. BUT FIRST NEED TO GRAB A FE THINGS.

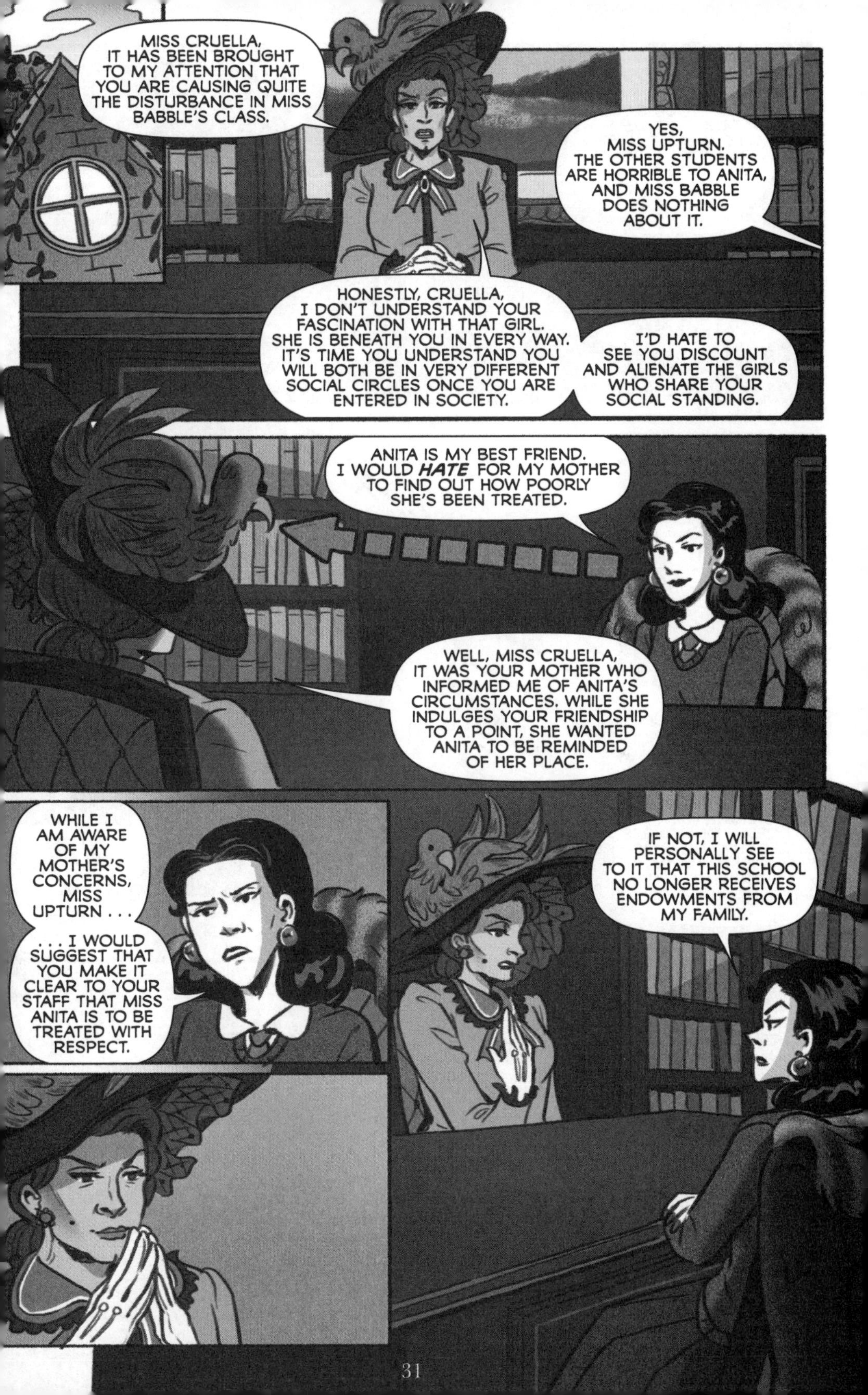
MISS CRUELLA, IT HAS BEEN BROUGHT TO MY ATTENTION THAT YOU ARE CAUSING QUITE THE DISTURBANCE IN MISS BABBLE'S CLASS.
YES, MISS UPTURN. THE OTHER STUDENTS ARE HORRIBLE TO ANITA, AND MISS BABBLE DOES NOTHING ABOUT IT.
HONESTLY, CRUELLA, I DON'T UNDERSTAND YOUR FASCINATION WITH THAT GIRL. SHE IS BENEATH YOU IN EVERY WAY. IT'S TIME YOU UNDERSTAND YOU WILL BOTH BE IN VERY DIFFERENT SOCIAL CIRCLES ONCE YOU ARE ENTERED IN SOCIETY.
I'D HATE TO SEE YOU DISCOUNT AND ALIENATE THE GIRLS WHO SHARE YOUR SOCIAL STANDING.
ANITA IS MY BEST FRIEND. I WOULD ***HATE*** FOR MY MOTHER TO FIND OUT HOW POORLY SHE'S BEEN TREATED.
WELL, MISS CRUELLA, IT WAS YOUR MOTHER WHO INFORMED ME OF ANITA'S CIRCUMSTANCES. WHILE SHE INDULGES YOUR FRIENDSHIP TO A POINT, SHE WANTED ANITA TO BE REMINDED OF HER PLACE.
WHILE I AM AWARE OF MY MOTHER'S CONCERNS, MISS UPTURN . . .
. . . I WOULD SUGGEST THAT YOU MAKE IT CLEAR TO YOUR STAFF THAT MISS ANITA IS TO BE TREATED WITH RESPECT.
IF NOT, I WILL PERSONALLY SEE TO IT THAT THIS SCHOOL NO LONGER RECEIVES ENDOWMENTS FROM MY FAMILY.

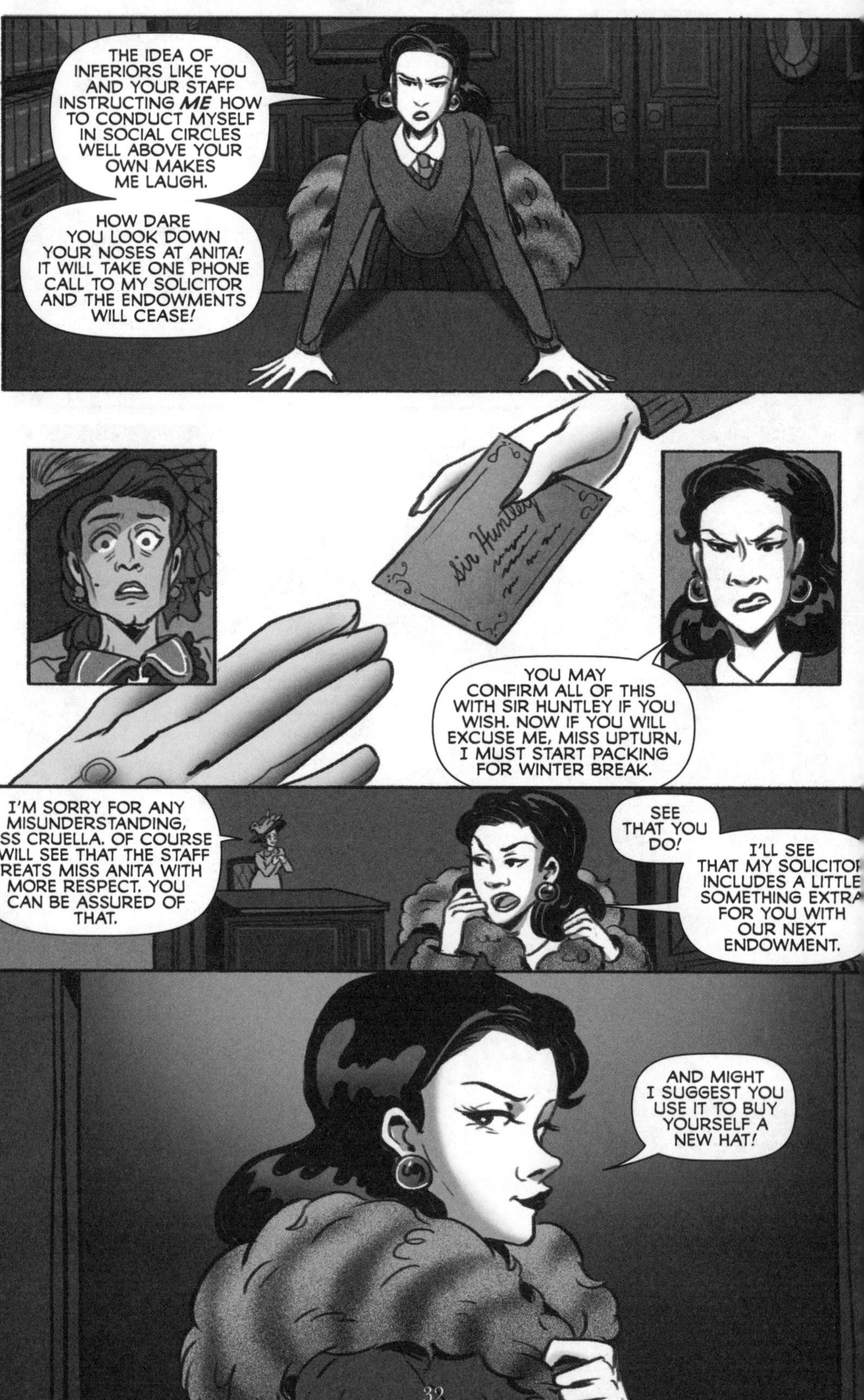
THE IDEA OF INFERIORS LIKE YOU AND YOUR STAFF INSTRUCTING *ME* HOW TO CONDUCT MYSELF IN SOCIAL CIRCLES WELL ABOVE YOUR OWN MAKES ME LAUGH.
HOW DARE YOU LOOK DOWN YOUR NOSES AT ANITA! IT WILL TAKE ONE PHONE CALL TO MY SOLICITOR AND THE ENDOWMENTS WILL CEASE!
Sir Huntley
YOU MAY CONFIRM ALL OF THIS WITH SIR HUNTLEY IF YOU WISH. NOW IF YOU WILL EXCUSE ME, MISS UPTURN, I MUST START PACKING FOR WINTER BREAK.
I'M SORRY FOR ANY MISUNDERSTANDING, MISS CRUELLA. OF COURSE I WILL SEE THAT THE STAFF TREATS MISS ANITA WITH MORE RESPECT. YOU CAN BE ASSURED OF THAT.
SEE THAT YOU DO!
I'LL SEE THAT MY SOLICITO INCLUDES A LITTL SOMETHING EXTR FOR YOU WITH OUR NEXT ENDOWMENT.
AND MIGHT I SUGGEST YOU USE IT TO BUY YOURSELF A NEW HAT!

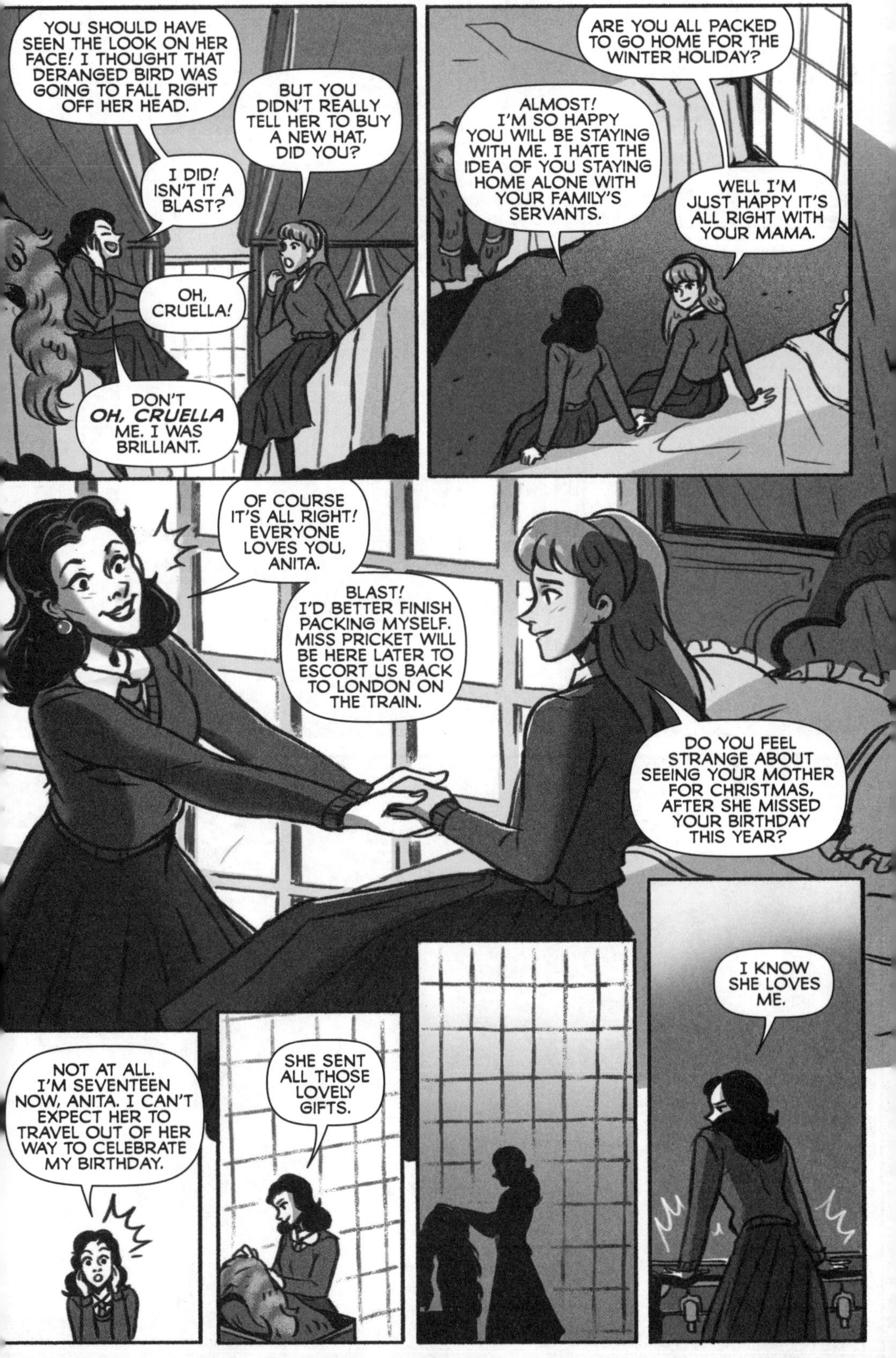
YOU SHOULD HAVE SEEN THE LOOK ON HER FACE! I THOUGHT THAT DERANGED BIRD WAS GOING TO FALL RIGHT OFF HER HEAD.
BUT YOU DIDN'T REALLY TELL HER TO BUY A NEW HAT, DID YOU?
I DID! ISN'T IT A BLAST?
OH, CRUELLA!
DON'T *OH, CRUELLA* ME. I WAS BRILLIANT.
ARE YOU ALL PACKED TO GO HOME FOR THE WINTER HOLIDAY?
ALMOST! I'M SO HAPPY YOU WILL BE STAYING WITH ME. I HATE THE IDEA OF YOU STAYING HOME ALONE WITH YOUR FAMILY'S SERVANTS.
WELL I'M JUST HAPPY IT'S ALL RIGHT WITH YOUR MAMA.
OF COURSE IT'S ALL RIGHT! EVERYONE LOVES YOU, ANITA.
BLAST! I'D BETTER FINISH PACKING MYSELF. MISS PRICKET WILL BE HERE LATER TO ESCORT US BACK TO LONDON ON THE TRAIN.
DO YOU FEEL STRANGE ABOUT SEEING YOUR MOTHER FOR CHRISTMAS, AFTER SHE MISSED YOUR BIRTHDAY THIS YEAR?
NOT AT ALL. I'M SEVENTEEN NOW, ANITA. I CAN'T EXPECT HER TO TRAVEL OUT OF HER WAY TO CELEBRATE MY BIRTHDAY.
SHE SENT ALL THOSE LOVELY GIFTS.
I KNOW SHE LOVES ME.

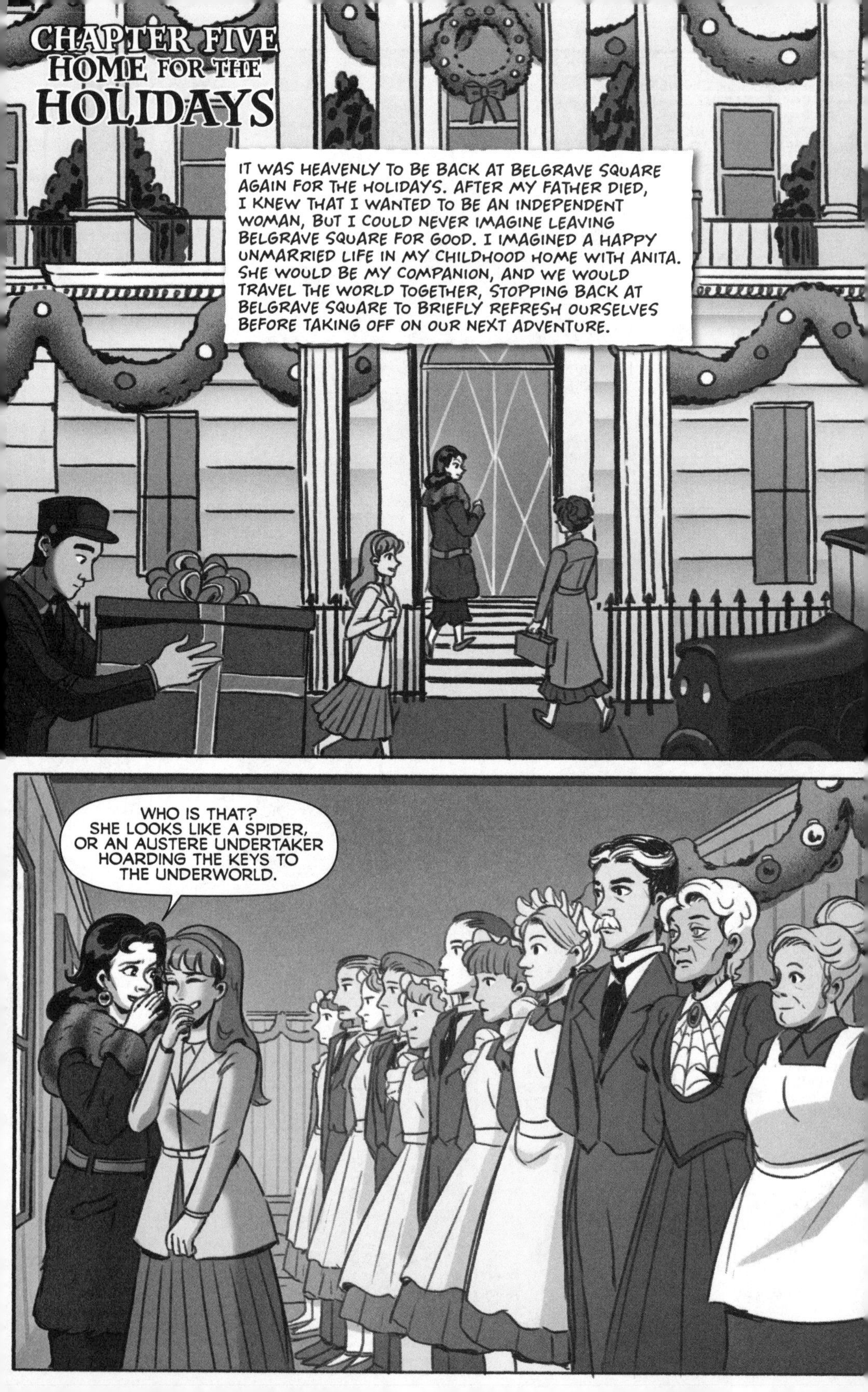
CHAPTER FIVE
HOME FOR THE HOLIDAYS
IT WAS HEAVENLY TO BE BACK AT BELGRAVE SQUARE AGAIN FOR THE HOLIDAYS. AFTER MY FATHER DIED, I KNEW THAT I WANTED TO BE AN INDEPENDENT WOMAN, BUT I COULD NEVER IMAGINE LEAVING BELGRAVE SQUARE FOR GOOD. I IMAGINED A HAPPY UNMARRIED LIFE IN MY CHILDHOOD HOME WITH ANITA. SHE WOULD BE MY COMPANION, AND WE WOULD TRAVEL THE WORLD TOGETHER, STOPPING BACK AT BELGRAVE SQUARE TO BRIEFLY REFRESH OURSELVES BEFORE TAKING OFF ON OUR NEXT ADVENTURE.
WHO IS THAT? SHE LOOKS LIKE A SPIDER, OR AN AUSTERE UNDERTAKER HOARDING THE KEYS TO THE UNDERWORLD.

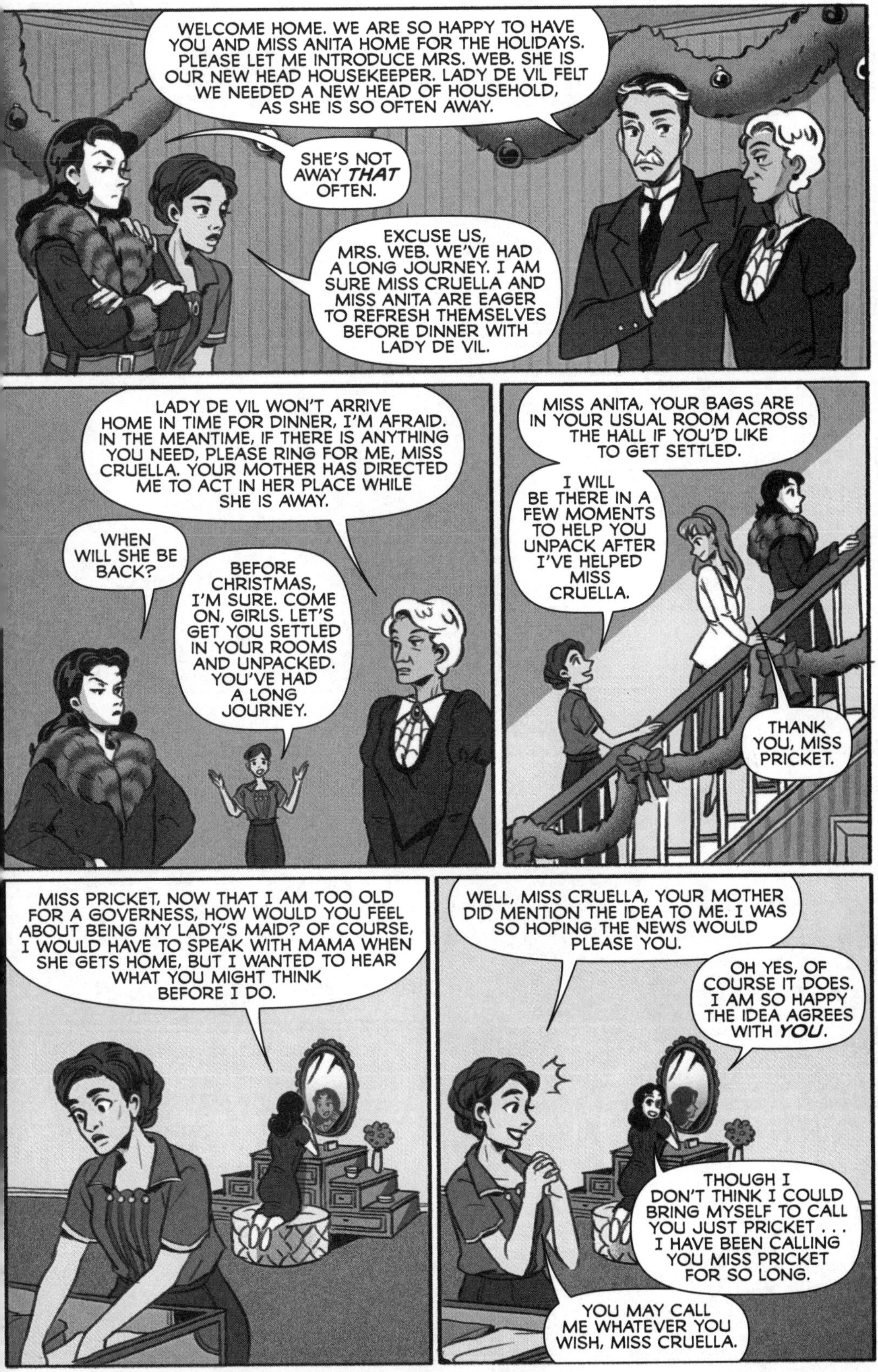
WELCOME HOME. WE ARE SO HAPPY TO HAVE YOU AND MISS ANITA HOME FOR THE HOLIDAYS. PLEASE LET ME INTRODUCE MRS. WEB. SHE IS OUR NEW HEAD HOUSEKEEPER. LADY DE VIL FELT WE NEEDED A NEW HEAD OF HOUSEHOLD, AS SHE IS SO OFTEN AWAY.
SHE'S NOT AWAY *THAT* OFTEN.
EXCUSE US, MRS. WEB. WE'VE HAD A LONG JOURNEY. I AM SURE MISS CRUELLA AND MISS ANITA ARE EAGER TO REFRESH THEMSELVES BEFORE DINNER WITH LADY DE VIL.
LADY DE VIL WON'T ARRIVE HOME IN TIME FOR DINNER, I'M AFRAID. IN THE MEANTIME, IF THERE IS ANYTHING YOU NEED, PLEASE RING FOR ME, MISS CRUELLA. YOUR MOTHER HAS DIRECTED ME TO ACT IN HER PLACE WHILE SHE IS AWAY.
WHEN WILL SHE BE BACK?
BEFORE CHRISTMAS, I'M SURE. COME ON, GIRLS. LET'S GET YOU SETTLED IN YOUR ROOMS AND UNPACKED. YOU'VE HAD A LONG JOURNEY.
MISS ANITA, YOUR BAGS ARE IN YOUR USUAL ROOM ACROSS THE HALL IF YOU'D LIKE TO GET SETTLED.
I WILL BE THERE IN A FEW MOMENTS TO HELP YOU UNPACK AFTER I'VE HELPED MISS CRUELLA.
THANK YOU, MISS PRICKET.
MISS PRICKET, NOW THAT I AM TOO OLD FOR A GOVERNESS, HOW WOULD YOU FEEL ABOUT BEING MY LADY'S MAID? OF COURSE, I WOULD HAVE TO SPEAK WITH MAMA WHEN SHE GETS HOME, BUT I WANTED TO HEAR WHAT YOU MIGHT THINK BEFORE I DO.
WELL, MISS CRUELLA, YOUR MOTHER DID MENTION THE IDEA TO ME. I WAS SO HOPING THE NEWS WOULD PLEASE YOU.
OH YES, OF COURSE IT DOES. I AM SO HAPPY THE IDEA AGREES WITH *YOU*.
THOUGH I DON'T THINK I COULD BRING MYSELF TO CALL YOU JUST PRICKET . . . I HAVE BEEN CALLING YOU MISS PRICKET FOR SO LONG.
YOU MAY CALL ME WHATEVER YOU WISH, MISS CRUELLA.

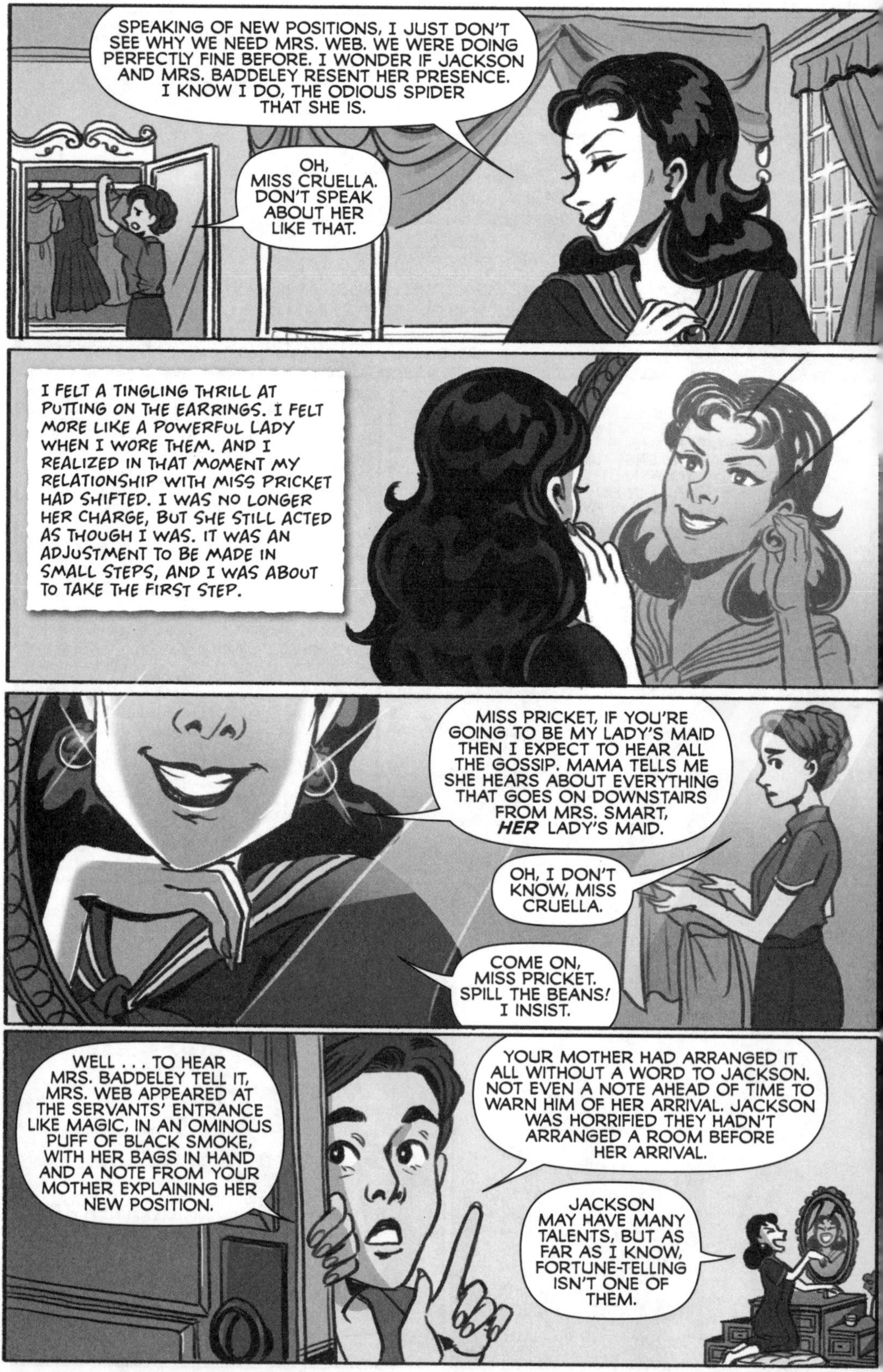
SPEAKING OF NEW POSITIONS, I JUST DON'T SEE WHY WE NEED MRS. WEB. WE WERE DOING PERFECTLY FINE BEFORE. I WONDER IF JACKSON AND MRS. BADDELEY RESENT HER PRESENCE. I KNOW I DO, THE ODIOUS SPIDER THAT SHE IS.
OH, MISS CRUELLA. DON'T SPEAK ABOUT HER LIKE THAT.
I FELT A TINGLING THRILL AT PUTTING ON THE EARRINGS. I FELT MORE LIKE A POWERFUL LADY WHEN I WORE THEM. AND I REALIZED IN THAT MOMENT MY RELATIONSHIP WITH MISS PRICKET HAD SHIFTED. I WAS NO LONGER HER CHARGE, BUT SHE STILL ACTED AS THOUGH I WAS. IT WAS AN ADJUSTMENT TO BE MADE IN SMALL STEPS, AND I WAS ABOUT TO TAKE THE FIRST STEP.
MISS PRICKET, IF YOU'RE GOING TO BE MY LADY'S MAID THEN I EXPECT TO HEAR ALL THE GOSSIP. MAMA TELLS ME SHE HEARS ABOUT EVERYTHING THAT GOES ON DOWNSTAIRS FROM MRS. SMART, ***HER*** LADY'S MAID.
OH, I DON'T KNOW, MISS CRUELLA.
COME ON, MISS PRICKET. SPILL THE BEANS! I INSIST.
WELL . . . TO HEAR MRS. BADDELEY TELL IT, MRS. WEB APPEARED AT THE SERVANTS' ENTRANCE LIKE MAGIC, IN AN OMINOUS PUFF OF BLACK SMOKE, WITH HER BAGS IN HAND AND A NOTE FROM YOUR MOTHER EXPLAINING HER NEW POSITION.
YOUR MOTHER HAD ARRANGED IT ALL WITHOUT A WORD TO JACKSON. NOT EVEN A NOTE AHEAD OF TIME TO WARN HIM OF HER ARRIVAL. JACKSON WAS HORRIFIED THEY HADN'T ARRANGED A ROOM BEFORE HER ARRIVAL.
JACKSON MAY HAVE MANY TALENTS, BUT AS FAR AS I KNOW, FORTUNE-TELLING ISN'T ONE OF THEM.

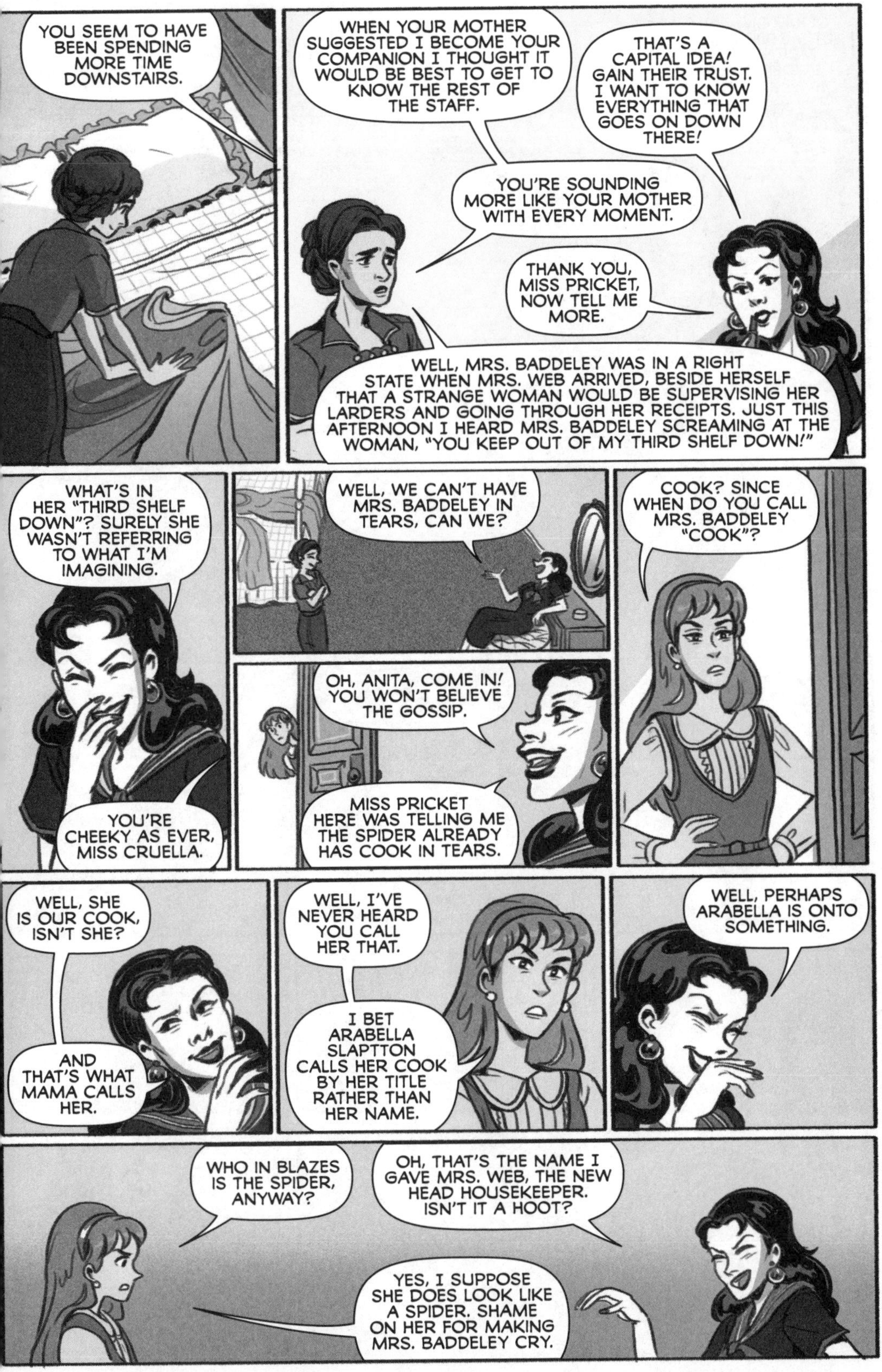
YOU SEEM TO HAVE BEEN SPENDING MORE TIME DOWNSTAIRS.
WHEN YOUR MOTHER SUGGESTED I BECOME YOUR COMPANION I THOUGHT IT WOULD BE BEST TO GET TO KNOW THE REST OF THE STAFF.
THAT'S A CAPITAL IDEA! GAIN THEIR TRUST. I WANT TO KNOW EVERYTHING THAT GOES ON DOWN THERE!
YOU'RE SOUNDING MORE LIKE YOUR MOTHER WITH EVERY MOMENT.
THANK YOU, MISS PRICKET, NOW TELL ME MORE.
WELL, MRS. BADDELEY WAS IN A RIGHT STATE WHEN MRS. WEB ARRIVED, BESIDE HERSELF THAT A STRANGE WOMAN WOULD BE SUPERVISING HER LARDERS AND GOING THROUGH HER RECEIPTS. JUST THIS AFTERNOON I HEARD MRS. BADDELEY SCREAMING AT THE WOMAN, "YOU KEEP OUT OF MY THIRD SHELF DOWN!"
WHAT'S IN HER "THIRD SHELF DOWN"? SURELY SHE WASN'T REFERRING TO WHAT I'M IMAGINING.
YOU'RE CHEEKY AS EVER, MISS CRUELLA.
WELL, WE CAN'T HAVE MRS. BADDELEY IN TEARS, CAN WE?
OH, ANITA, COME IN! YOU WON'T BELIEVE THE GOSSIP.
MISS PRICKET HERE WAS TELLING ME THE SPIDER ALREADY HAS COOK IN TEARS.
COOK? SINCE WHEN DO YOU CALL MRS. BADDELEY "COOK"?
WELL, SHE IS OUR COOK, ISN'T SHE?
AND THAT'S WHAT MAMA CALLS HER.
WELL, I'VE NEVER HEARD YOU CALL HER THAT.
I BET ARABELLA SLAPTTON CALLS HER COOK BY HER TITLE RATHER THAN HER NAME.
WELL, PERHAPS ARABELLA IS ONTO SOMETHING.
WHO IN BLAZES IS THE SPIDER, ANYWAY?
OH, THAT'S THE NAME I GAVE MRS. WEB, THE NEW HEAD HOUSEKEEPER. ISN'T IT A HOOT?
YES, I SUPPOSE SHE DOES LOOK LIKE A SPIDER. SHAME ON HER FOR MAKING MRS. BADDELEY CRY.

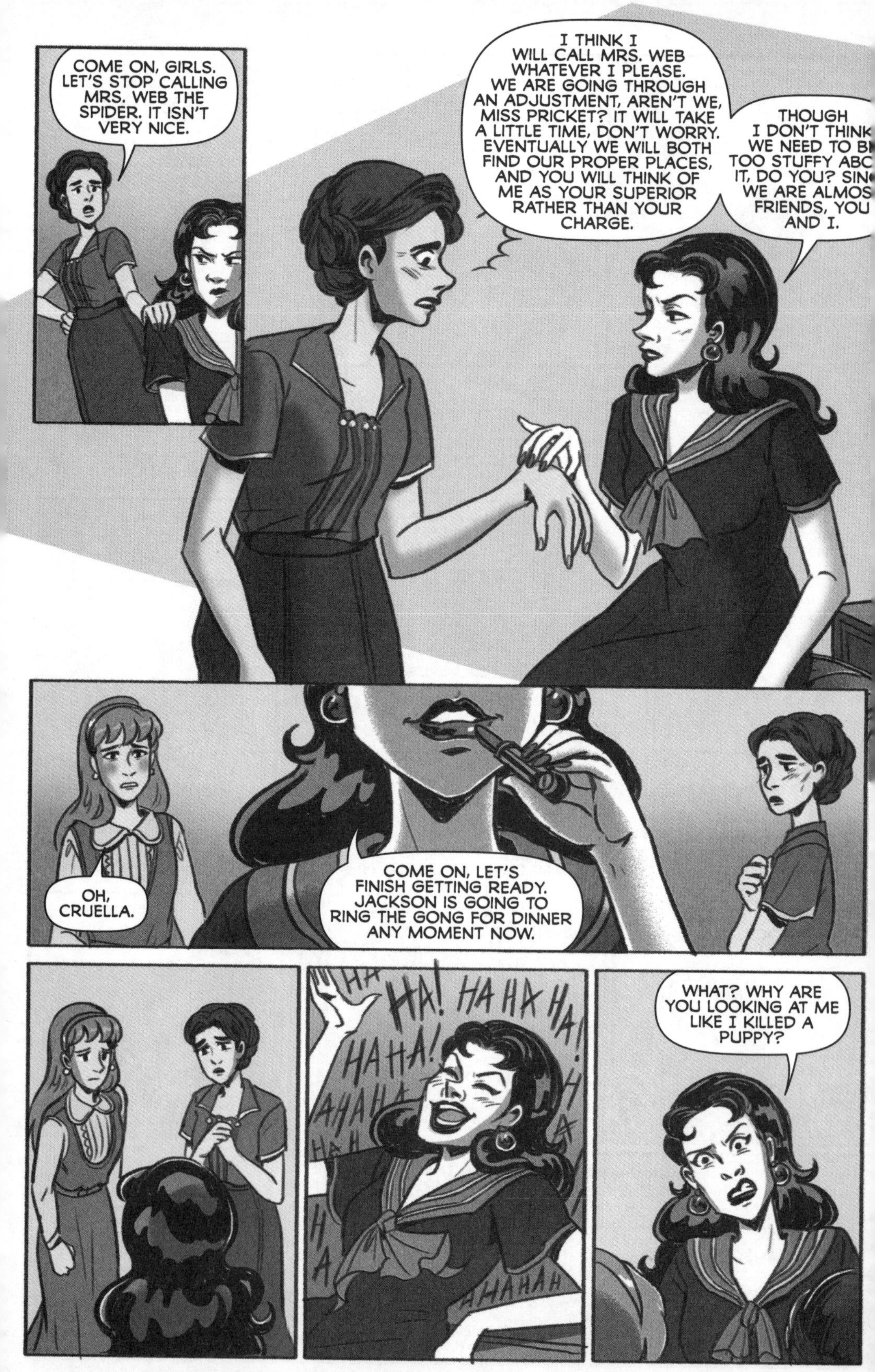
COME ON, GIRLS. LET'S STOP CALLING MRS. WEB THE SPIDER. IT ISN'T VERY NICE.
I THINK I WILL CALL MRS. WEB WHATEVER I PLEASE. WE ARE GOING THROUGH AN ADJUSTMENT, AREN'T WE, MISS PRICKET? IT WILL TAKE A LITTLE TIME, DON'T WORRY. EVENTUALLY WE WILL BOTH FIND OUR PROPER PLACES, AND YOU WILL THINK OF ME AS YOUR SUPERIOR RATHER THAN YOUR CHARGE.
THOUGH I DON'T THINK WE NEED TO B TOO STUFFY ABC IT, DO YOU? SIN WE ARE ALMOS FRIENDS, YOU AND I.
OH, CRUELLA.
COME ON, LET'S FINISH GETTING READY. JACKSON IS GOING TO RING THE GONG FOR DINNER ANY MOMENT NOW.
HA! HA HA HA! HAHA!
WHAT? WHY ARE YOU LOOKING AT ME LIKE I KILLED A PUPPY?

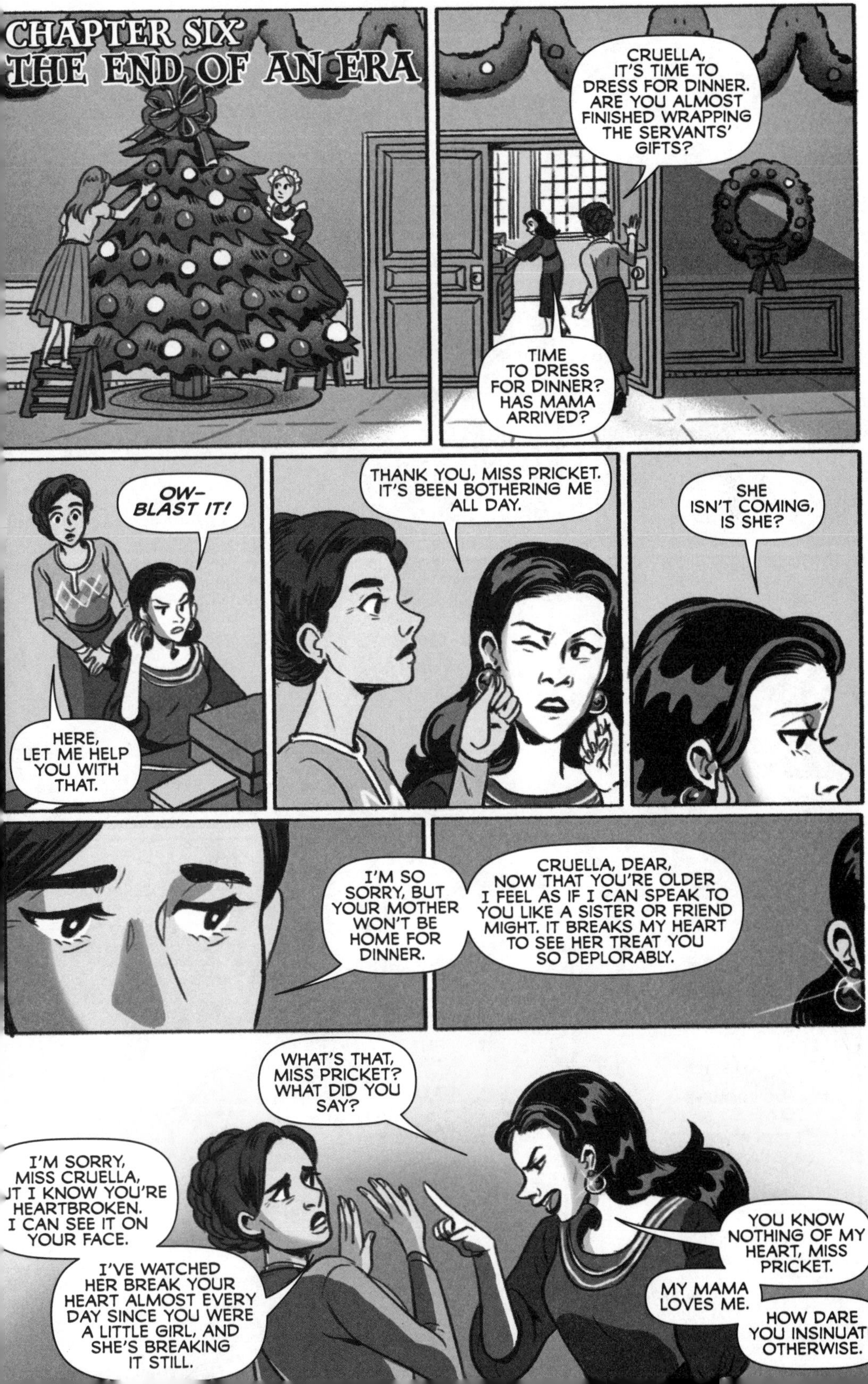
CHAPTER SIX
THE END OF AN ERA
CRUELLA, IT'S TIME TO DRESS FOR DINNER. ARE YOU ALMOST FINISHED WRAPPING THE SERVANTS' GIFTS?
TIME TO DRESS FOR DINNER? HAS MAMA ARRIVED?
OW— BLAST IT!
HERE, LET ME HELP YOU WITH THAT.
THANK YOU, MISS PRICKET. IT'S BEEN BOTHERING ME ALL DAY.
SHE ISN'T COMING, IS SHE?
I'M SO SORRY, BUT YOUR MOTHER WON'T BE HOME FOR DINNER.
CRUELLA, DEAR, NOW THAT YOU'RE OLDER I FEEL AS IF I CAN SPEAK TO YOU LIKE A SISTER OR FRIEND MIGHT. IT BREAKS MY HEART TO SEE HER TREAT YOU SO DEPLORABLY.
WHAT'S THAT, MISS PRICKET? WHAT DID YOU SAY?
I'M SORRY, MISS CRUELLA, UT I KNOW YOU'RE HEARTBROKEN. I CAN SEE IT ON YOUR FACE.
I'VE WATCHED HER BREAK YOUR HEART ALMOST EVERY DAY SINCE YOU WERE A LITTLE GIRL, AND SHE'S BREAKING IT STILL.
YOU KNOW NOTHING OF MY HEART, MISS PRICKET.
MY MAMA LOVES ME.
HOW DARE YOU INSINUATE OTHERWISE.

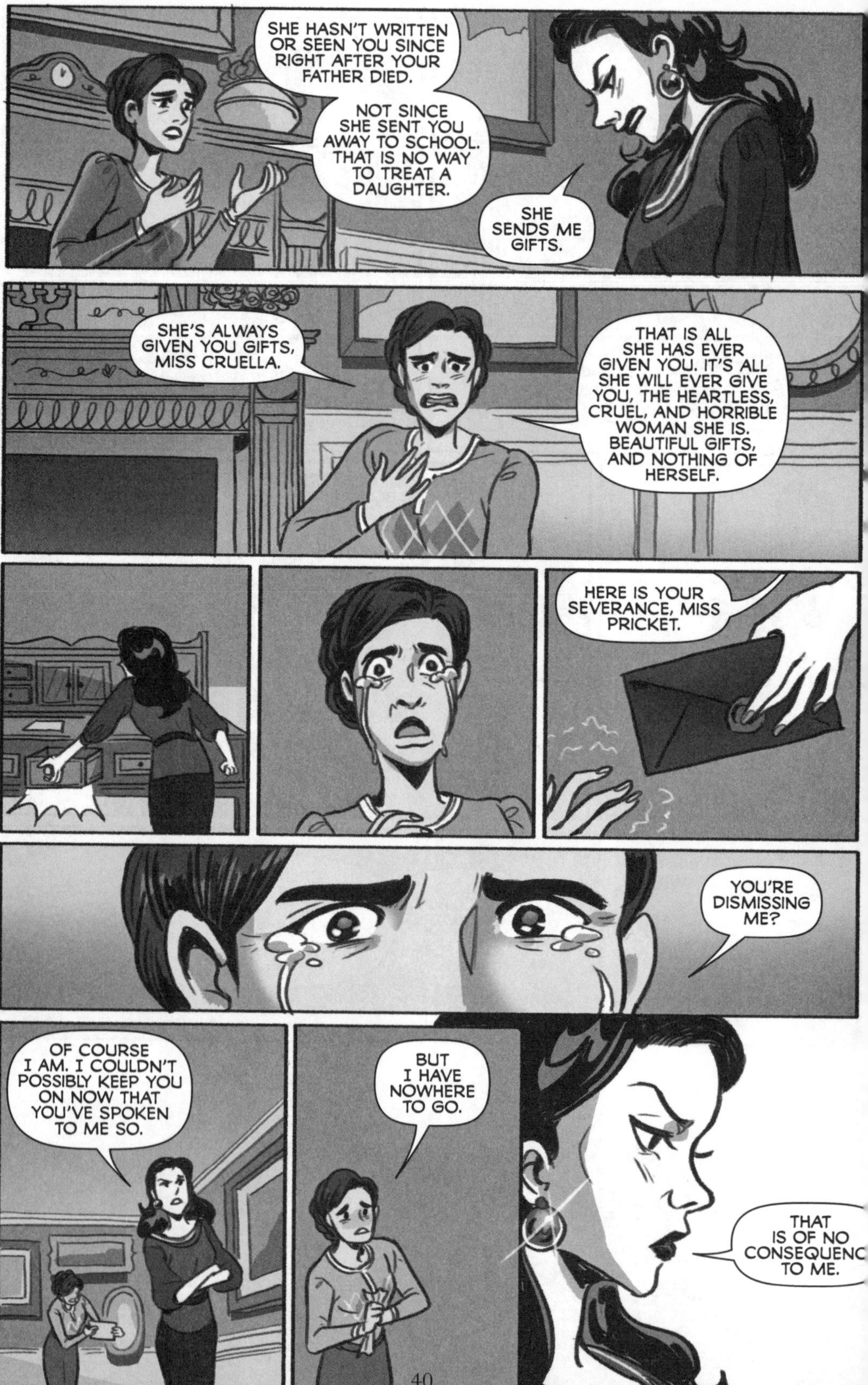
SHE HASN'T WRITTEN OR SEEN YOU SINCE RIGHT AFTER YOUR FATHER DIED.
NOT SINCE SHE SENT YOU AWAY TO SCHOOL. THAT IS NO WAY TO TREAT A DAUGHTER.
SHE SENDS ME GIFTS.
SHE'S ALWAYS GIVEN YOU GIFTS, MISS CRUELLA.
THAT IS ALL SHE HAS EVER GIVEN YOU. IT'S ALL SHE WILL EVER GIVE YOU, THE HEARTLESS, CRUEL, AND HORRIBLE WOMAN SHE IS. BEAUTIFUL GIFTS, AND NOTHING OF HERSELF.
HERE IS YOUR SEVERANCE, MISS PRICKET.
YOU'RE DISMISSING ME?
OF COURSE I AM. I COULDN'T POSSIBLY KEEP YOU ON NOW THAT YOU'VE SPOKEN TO ME SO.
BUT I HAVE NOWHERE TO GO.
THAT IS OF NO CONSEQUENC TO ME.

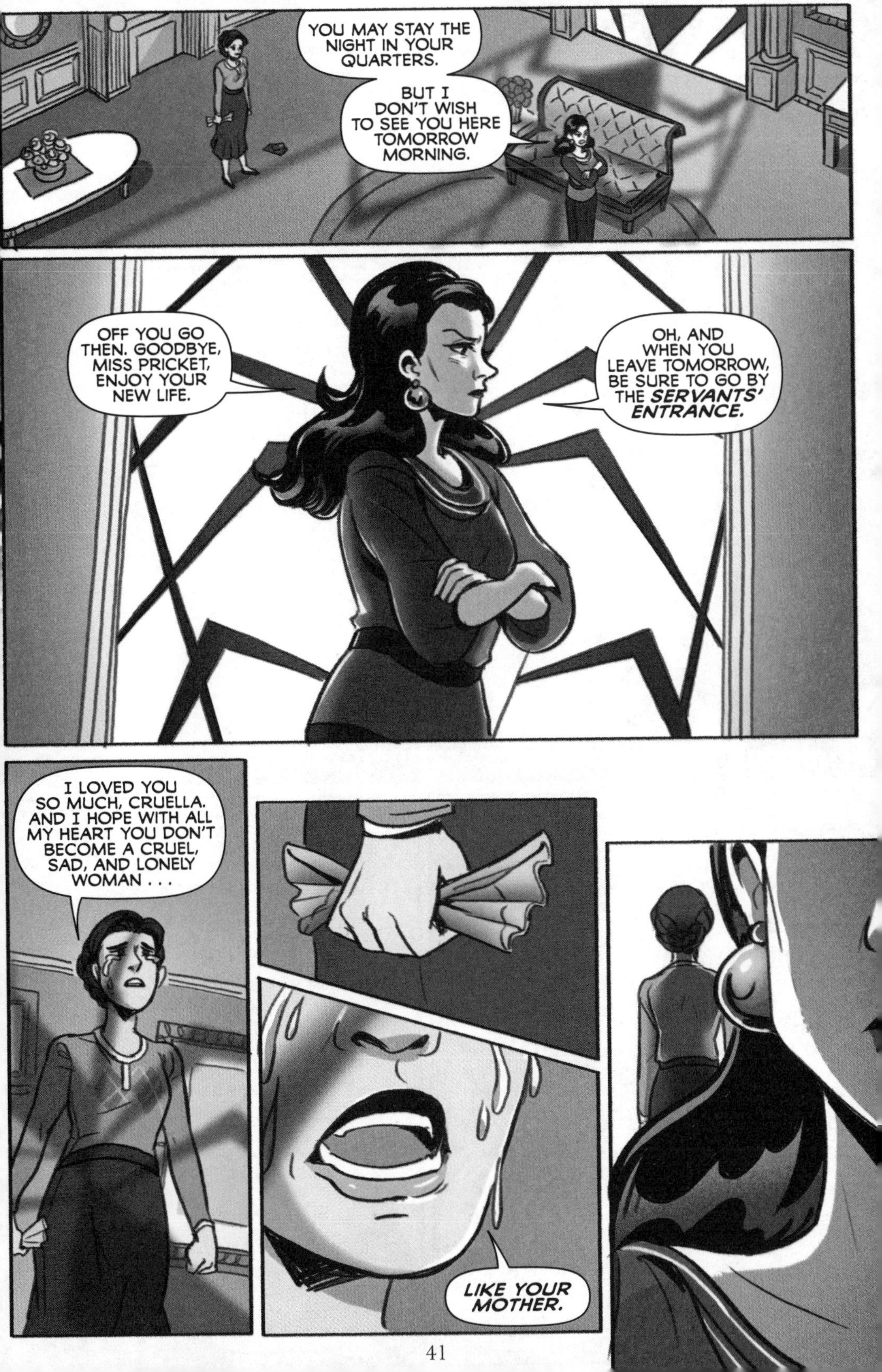
YOU MAY STAY THE NIGHT IN YOUR QUARTERS.
BUT I DON'T WISH TO SEE YOU HERE TOMORROW MORNING.
OFF YOU GO THEN. GOODBYE, MISS PRICKET, ENJOY YOUR NEW LIFE.
OH, AND WHEN YOU LEAVE TOMORROW, BE SURE TO GO BY THE *SERVANTS' ENTRANCE.*
I LOVED YOU SO MUCH, CRUELLA. AND I HOPE WITH ALL MY HEART YOU DON'T BECOME A CRUEL, SAD, AND LONELY WOMAN . . .
LIKE YOUR MOTHER.

CHAPTER SEVEN
CHRISTMAS EVE

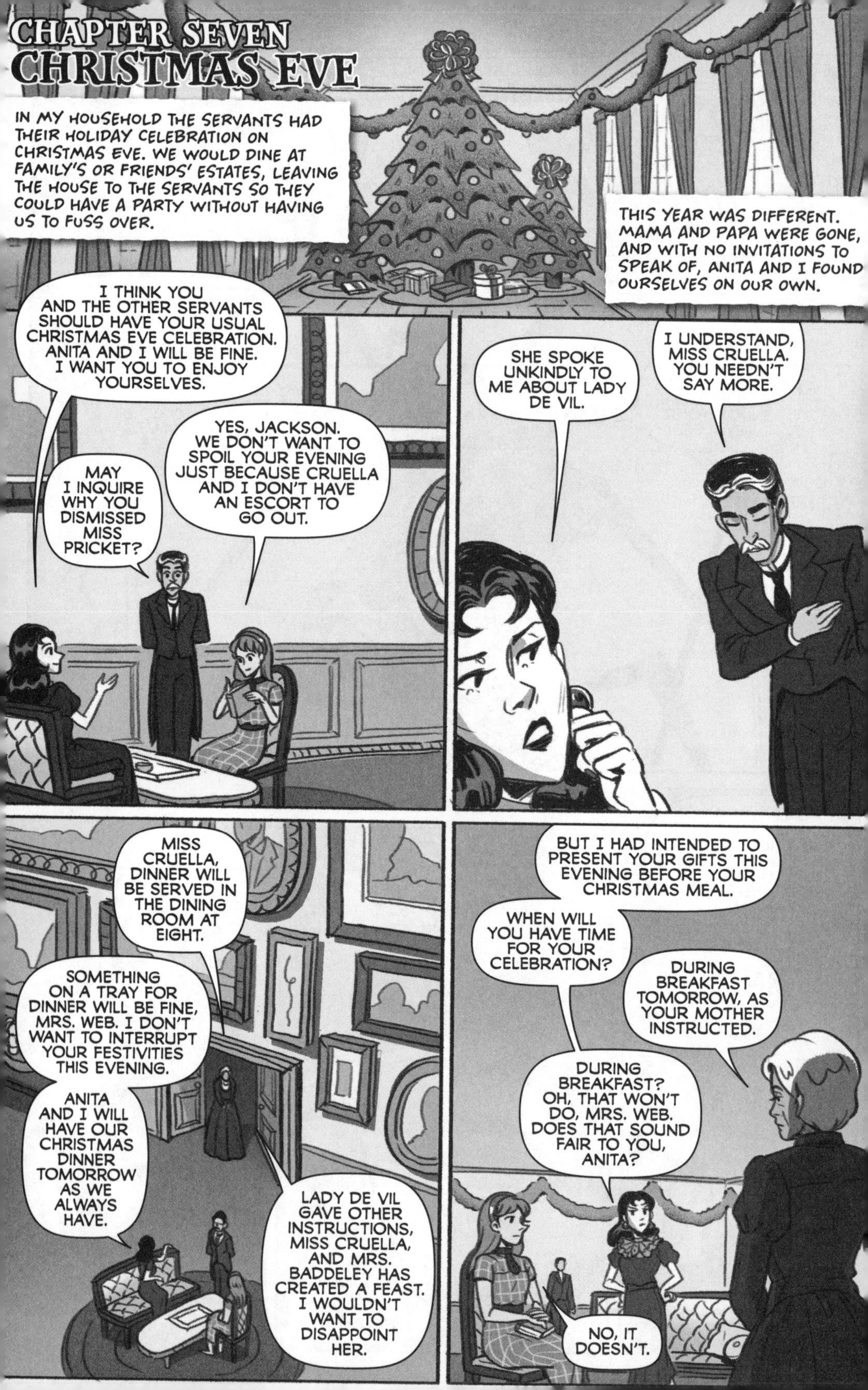
IN MY HOUSEHOLD THE SERVANTS HAD THEIR HOLIDAY CELEBRATION ON CHRISTMAS EVE. WE WOULD DINE AT FAMILY'S OR FRIENDS' ESTATES, LEAVING THE HOUSE TO THE SERVANTS SO THEY COULD HAVE A PARTY WITHOUT HAVING US TO FUSS OVER.
THIS YEAR WAS DIFFERENT. MAMA AND PAPA WERE GONE, AND WITH NO INVITATIONS TO SPEAK OF, ANITA AND I FOUND OURSELVES ON OUR OWN.
I THINK YOU AND THE OTHER SERVANTS SHOULD HAVE YOUR USUAL CHRISTMAS EVE CELEBRATION. ANITA AND I WILL BE FINE. I WANT YOU TO ENJOY YOURSELVES.
YES, JACKSON. WE DON'T WANT TO SPOIL YOUR EVENING JUST BECAUSE CRUELLA AND I DON'T HAVE AN ESCORT TO GO OUT.
MAY I INQUIRE WHY YOU DISMISSED MISS PRICKET?
SHE SPOKE UNKINDLY TO ME ABOUT LADY DE VIL.
I UNDERSTAND, MISS CRUELLA. YOU NEEDN'T SAY MORE.
MISS CRUELLA, DINNER WILL BE SERVED IN THE DINING ROOM AT EIGHT.
SOMETHING ON A TRAY FOR DINNER WILL BE FINE, MRS. WEB. I DON'T WANT TO INTERRUPT YOUR FESTIVITIES THIS EVENING.
ANITA AND I WILL HAVE OUR CHRISTMAS DINNER TOMORROW AS WE ALWAYS HAVE.
LADY DE VIL GAVE OTHER INSTRUCTIONS, MISS CRUELLA, AND MRS. BADDELEY HAS CREATED A FEAST. I WOULDN'T WANT TO DISAPPOINT HER.
BUT I HAD INTENDED TO PRESENT YOUR GIFTS THIS EVENING BEFORE YOUR CHRISTMAS MEAL.
WHEN WILL YOU HAVE TIME FOR YOUR CELEBRATION?
DURING BREAKFAST TOMORROW, AS YOUR MOTHER INSTRUCTED.
DURING BREAKFAST? OH, THAT WON'T DO, MRS. WEB. DOES THAT SOUND FAIR TO YOU, ANITA?
NO, IT DOESN'T.

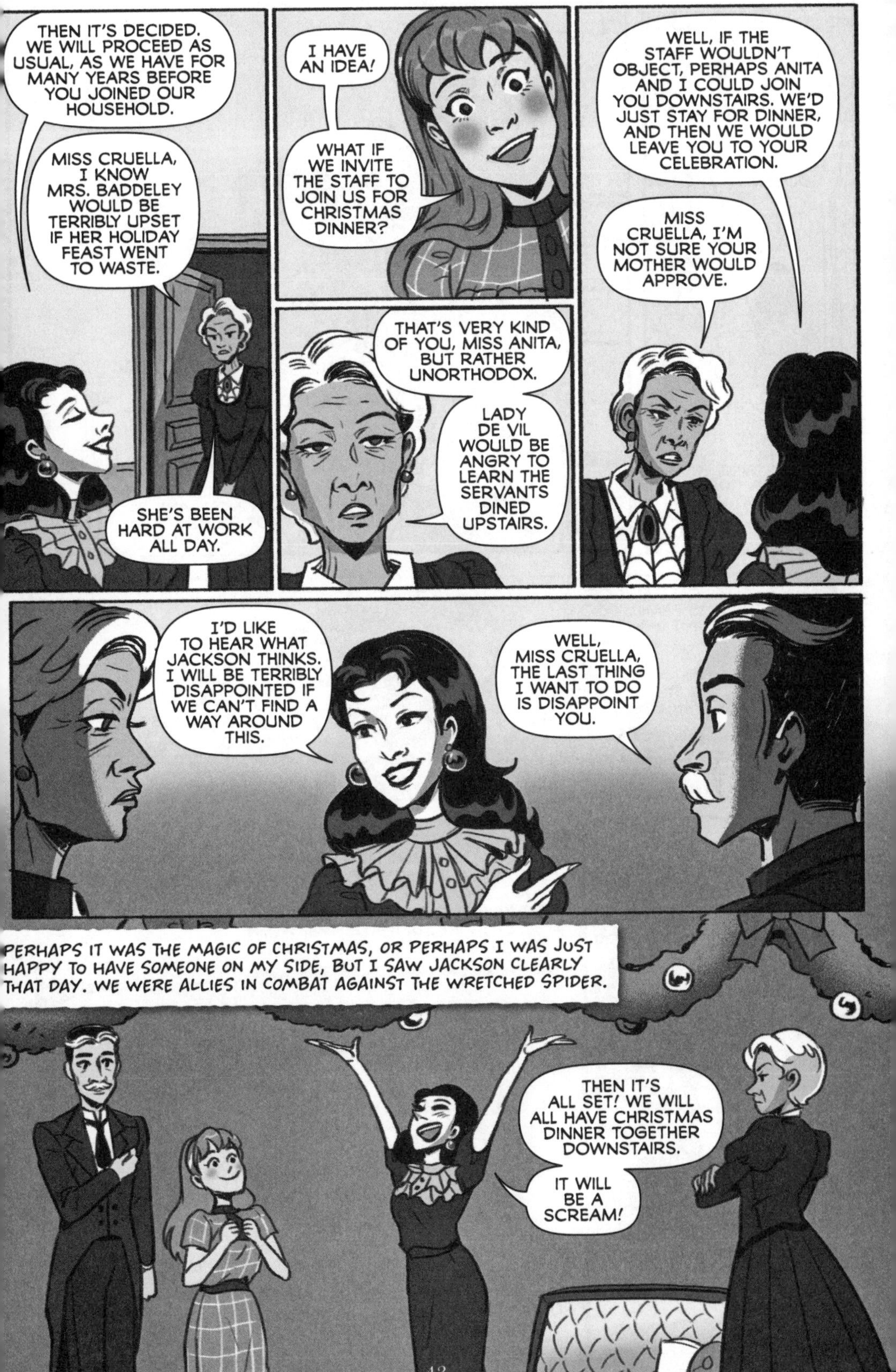
THEN IT'S DECIDED. WE WILL PROCEED AS USUAL, AS WE HAVE FOR MANY YEARS BEFORE YOU JOINED OUR HOUSEHOLD.
MISS CRUELLA, I KNOW MRS. BADDELEY WOULD BE TERRIBLY UPSET IF HER HOLIDAY FEAST WENT TO WASTE.
SHE'S BEEN HARD AT WORK ALL DAY.
I HAVE AN IDEA!
WHAT IF WE INVITE THE STAFF TO JOIN US FOR CHRISTMAS DINNER?
THAT'S VERY KIND OF YOU, MISS ANITA, BUT RATHER UNORTHODOX.
LADY DE VIL WOULD BE ANGRY TO LEARN THE SERVANTS DINED UPSTAIRS.
WELL, IF THE STAFF WOULDN'T OBJECT, PERHAPS ANITA AND I COULD JOIN YOU DOWNSTAIRS. WE'D JUST STAY FOR DINNER, AND THEN WE WOULD LEAVE YOU TO YOUR CELEBRATION.
MISS CRUELLA, I'M NOT SURE YOUR MOTHER WOULD APPROVE.
I'D LIKE TO HEAR WHAT JACKSON THINKS. I WILL BE TERRIBLY DISAPPOINTED IF WE CAN'T FIND A WAY AROUND THIS.
WELL, MISS CRUELLA, THE LAST THING I WANT TO DO IS DISAPPOINT YOU.
PERHAPS IT WAS THE MAGIC OF CHRISTMAS, OR PERHAPS I WAS JUST HAPPY TO HAVE SOMEONE ON MY SIDE, BUT I SAW JACKSON CLEARLY THAT DAY. WE WERE ALLIES IN COMBAT AGAINST THE WRETCHED SPIDER.
THEN IT'S ALL SET! WE WILL ALL HAVE CHRISTMAS DINNER TOGETHER DOWNSTAIRS.
IT WILL BE A SCREAM!

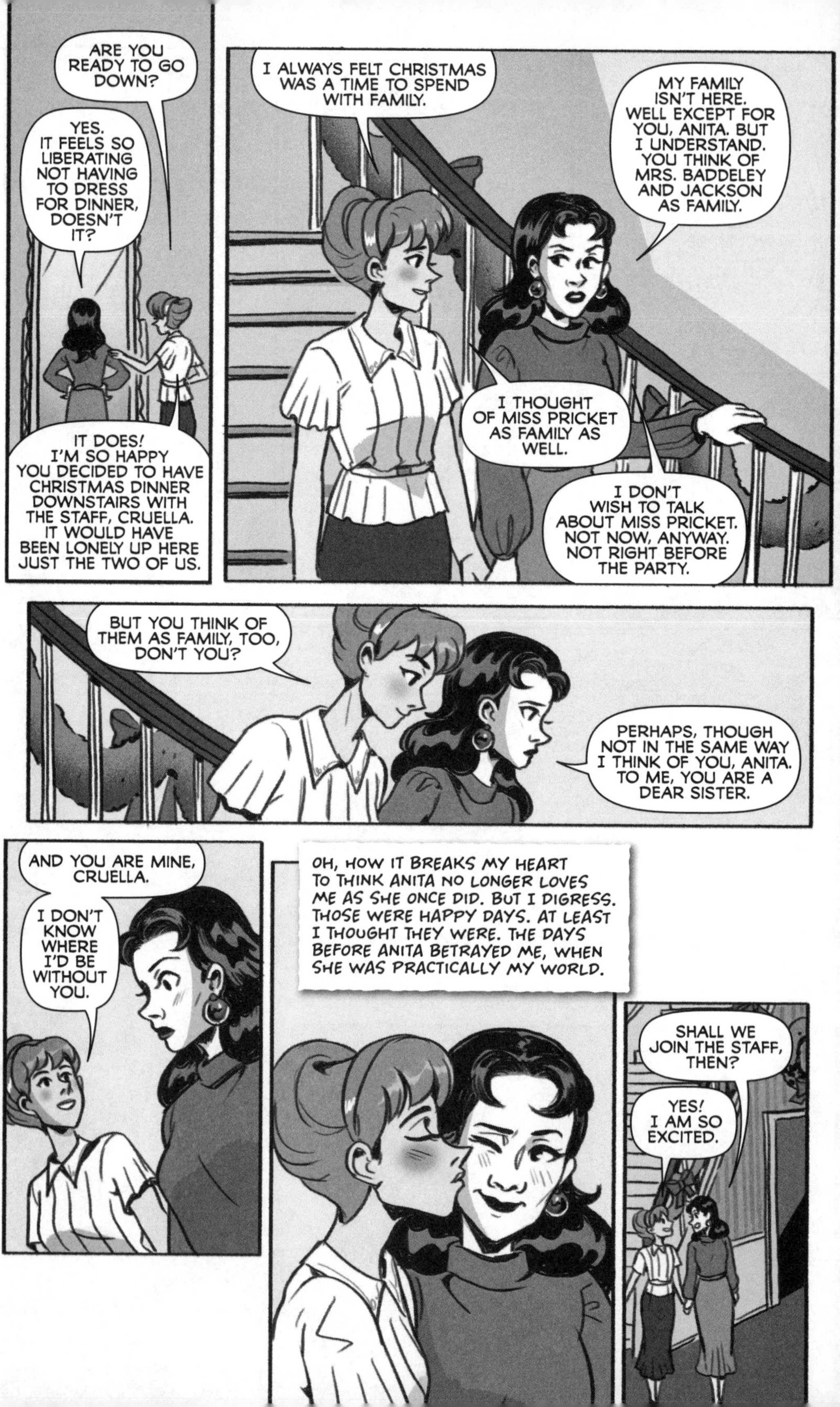
ARE YOU READY TO GO DOWN?
YES. IT FEELS SO LIBERATING NOT HAVING TO DRESS FOR DINNER, DOESN'T IT?
IT DOES! I'M SO HAPPY YOU DECIDED TO HAVE CHRISTMAS DINNER DOWNSTAIRS WITH THE STAFF, CRUELLA. IT WOULD HAVE BEEN LONELY UP HERE JUST THE TWO OF US.
I ALWAYS FELT CHRISTMAS WAS A TIME TO SPEND WITH FAMILY.
MY FAMILY ISN'T HERE. WELL EXCEPT FOR YOU, ANITA. BUT I UNDERSTAND. YOU THINK OF MRS. BADDELEY AND JACKSON AS FAMILY.
I THOUGHT OF MISS PRICKET AS FAMILY AS WELL.
I DON'T WISH TO TALK ABOUT MISS PRICKET. NOT NOW, ANYWAY. NOT RIGHT BEFORE THE PARTY.
BUT YOU THINK OF THEM AS FAMILY, TOO, DON'T YOU?
PERHAPS, THOUGH NOT IN THE SAME WAY I THINK OF YOU, ANITA. TO ME, YOU ARE A DEAR SISTER.
AND YOU ARE MINE, CRUELLA.
I DON'T KNOW WHERE I'D BE WITHOUT YOU.
OH, HOW IT BREAKS MY HEART TO THINK ANITA NO LONGER LOVES ME AS SHE ONCE DID. BUT I DIGRESS. THOSE WERE HAPPY DAYS. AT LEAST I THOUGHT THEY WERE. THE DAYS BEFORE ANITA BETRAYED ME, WHEN SHE WAS PRACTICALLY MY WORLD.
SHALL WE JOIN THE STAFF, THEN?
YES! I AM SO EXCITED.

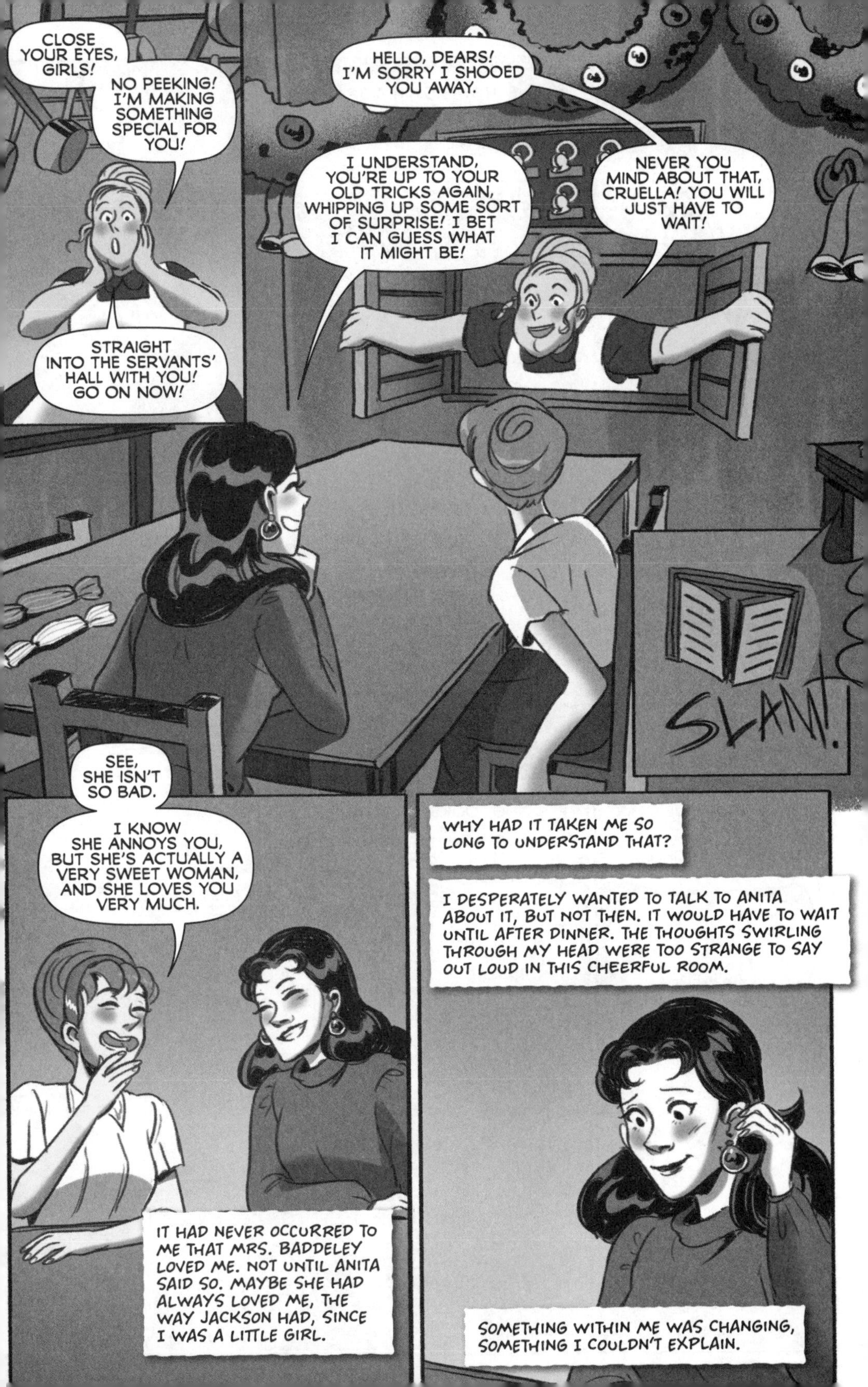

CLOSE YOUR EYES, GIRLS!
NO PEEKING! I'M MAKING SOMETHING SPECIAL FOR YOU!
STRAIGHT INTO THE SERVANTS' HALL WITH YOU! GO ON NOW!
HELLO, DEARS! I'M SORRY I SHOOED YOU AWAY.
I UNDERSTAND, YOU'RE UP TO YOUR OLD TRICKS AGAIN, WHIPPING UP SOME SORT OF SURPRISE! I BET I CAN GUESS WHAT IT MIGHT BE!
NEVER YOU MIND ABOUT THAT, CRUELLA! YOU WILL JUST HAVE TO WAIT!
SLAM!
SEE, SHE ISN'T SO BAD.
I KNOW SHE ANNOYS YOU, BUT SHE'S ACTUALLY A VERY SWEET WOMAN, AND SHE LOVES YOU VERY MUCH.
IT HAD NEVER OCCURRED TO ME THAT MRS. BADDELEY LOVED ME. NOT UNTIL ANITA SAID SO. MAYBE SHE HAD ALWAYS LOVED ME, THE WAY JACKSON HAD, SINCE I WAS A LITTLE GIRL.
WHY HAD IT TAKEN ME SO LONG TO UNDERSTAND THAT?
I DESPERATELY WANTED TO TALK TO ANITA ABOUT IT, BUT NOT THEN. IT WOULD HAVE TO WAIT UNTIL AFTER DINNER. THE THOUGHTS SWIRLING THROUGH MY HEAD WERE TOO STRANGE TO SAY OUT LOUD IN THIS CHEERFUL ROOM.
SOMETHING WITHIN ME WAS CHANGING, SOMETHING I COULDN'T EXPLAIN.

IT WAS SUCH A GRAND EVENING OF EATING, DRINKING, AND LISTENING TO CHRISTMAS MUSIC ON THE WIRELESS.

I WOULD LIKE TO PROPOSE A TOAST! TO MRS. BADDELEY, FOR THIS DELICIOUS MEAL!

TO MRS. BADDELEY!

OH, MRS. BADDELEY, YOU WONDERFUL DEAR WOMAN, YOU REMEMBERED HOW MUCH I LOVE YOUR CHEESE STRAWS!

OH YES, MY DEAR. I HAVE REMEMBERED ALL YOUR FAVORITES. AND MISS CRUELLA'S AS WELL.

I SEE THAT, MRS. BADDELEY. PUDDING LOOKS AMAZING. BUT I WONDER IF WE WILL HAVE ROOM AFTER EATING ALL OF THIS?

OH, YOU HAVEN'T SEEN THE HALF OF IT. YOU HAVEN'T EVEN SEEN MY SURPRISE.

OH BLAST! I WAS SO EXCITED FOR OUR LITTLE PARTY I FORGOT TO PRESENT YOU WITH YOUR GIFTS! LET ME RUN UPSTAIRS AND GET THEM!

NO, MISS CRUELLA. SIT. MRS. BADDELEY HAS BEEN WORKING ON YOUR SURPRISE ALL DAY.

BESIDES, YOU ARE OUR GIFT THIS EVENING. WE'RE SO HAPPY TO HAVE YOU AND MISS ANITA WITH US.

OH, PLEASE STAY.

SEE, THESE PEOPLE LOVE YOU, CRUELLA.

WHO BUT YOU COULD GET JACKSON TO WEAR A PAPER CROWN?

I THINK IT'S TIME PAULIE BRINGS IN MRS. BADDELEY'S CHRISTMAS SURPRISE.

46

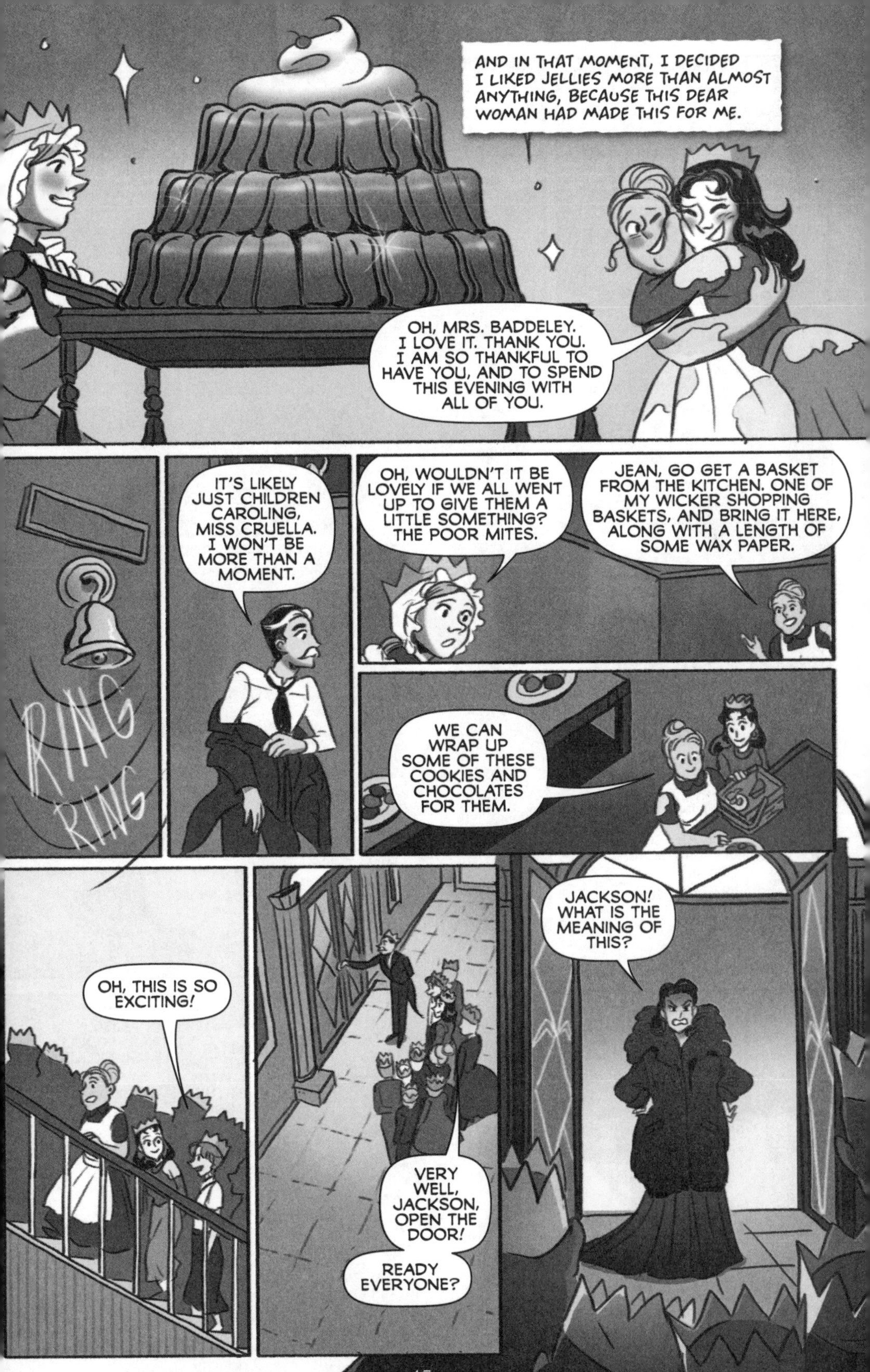
AND IN THAT MOMENT, I DECIDED I LIKED JELLIES MORE THAN ALMOST ANYTHING, BECAUSE THIS DEAR WOMAN HAD MADE THIS FOR ME.
OH, MRS. BADDELEY. I LOVE IT. THANK YOU. I AM SO THANKFUL TO HAVE YOU, AND TO SPEND THIS EVENING WITH ALL OF YOU.
RING RING
IT'S LIKELY JUST CHILDREN CAROLING, MISS CRUELLA. I WON'T BE MORE THAN A MOMENT.
OH, WOULDN'T IT BE LOVELY IF WE ALL WENT UP TO GIVE THEM A LITTLE SOMETHING? THE POOR MITES.
JEAN, GO GET A BASKET FROM THE KITCHEN. ONE OF MY WICKER SHOPPING BASKETS, AND BRING IT HERE, ALONG WITH A LENGTH OF SOME WAX PAPER.
WE CAN WRAP UP SOME OF THESE COOKIES AND CHOCOLATES FOR THEM.
OH, THIS IS SO EXCITING!
READY EVERYONE?
VERY WELL, JACKSON, OPEN THE DOOR!
JACKSON! WHAT IS THE MEANING OF THIS?

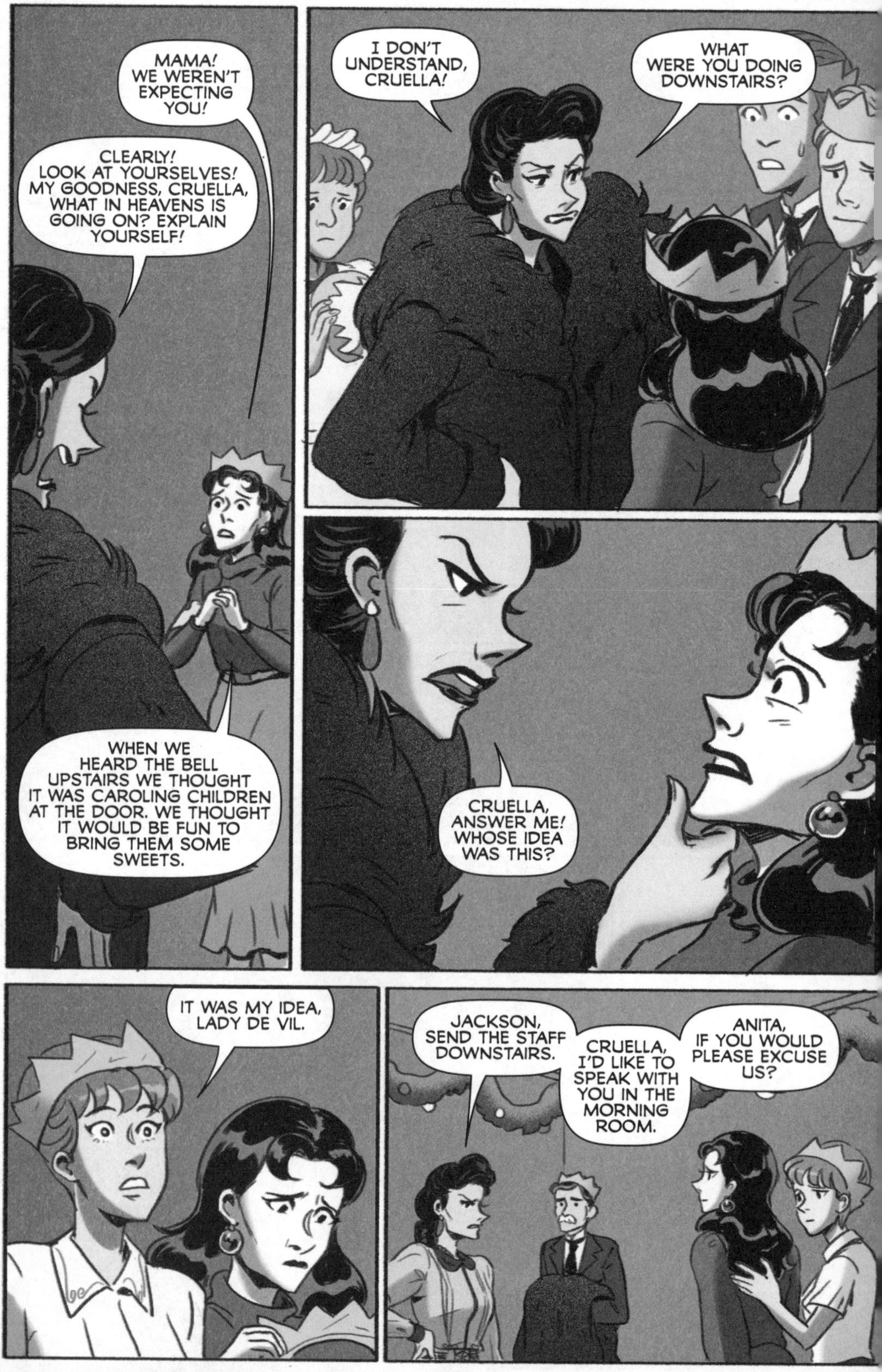
MAMA! WE WEREN'T EXPECTING YOU!
CLEARLY! LOOK AT YOURSELVES! MY GOODNESS, CRUELLA, WHAT IN HEAVENS IS GOING ON? EXPLAIN YOURSELF!
WHEN WE HEARD THE BELL UPSTAIRS WE THOUGHT IT WAS CAROLING CHILDREN AT THE DOOR. WE THOUGHT IT WOULD BE FUN TO BRING THEM SOME SWEETS.
I DON'T UNDERSTAND, CRUELLA!
WHAT WERE YOU DOING DOWNSTAIRS?
CRUELLA, ANSWER ME! WHOSE IDEA WAS THIS?
IT WAS MY IDEA, LADY DE VIL.
JACKSON, SEND THE STAFF DOWNSTAIRS.
CRUELLA, I'D LIKE TO SPEAK WITH YOU IN THE MORNING ROOM.
ANITA, IF YOU WOULD PLEASE EXCUSE US?

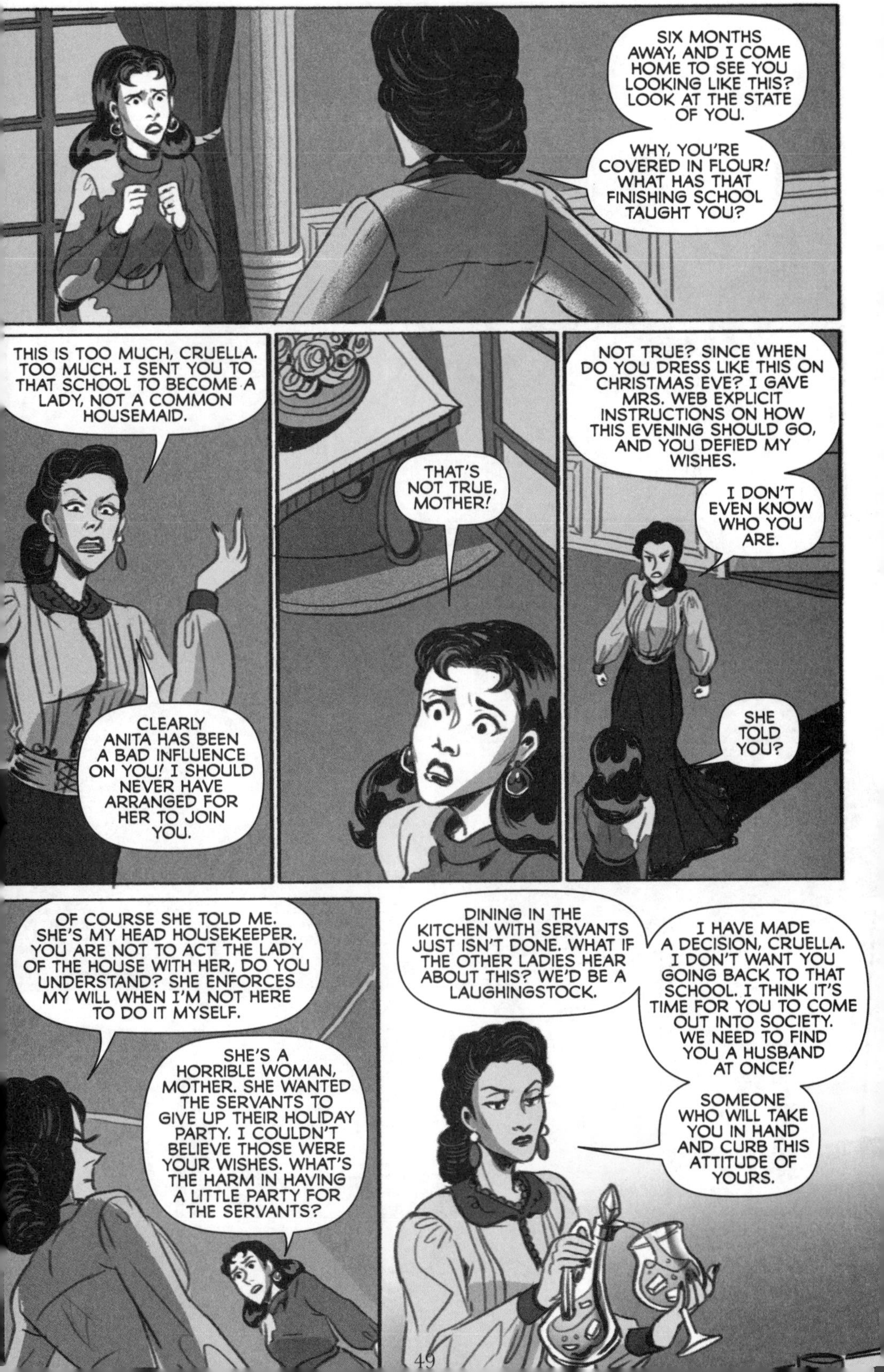
SIX MONTHS AWAY, AND I COME HOME TO SEE YOU LOOKING LIKE THIS? LOOK AT THE STATE OF YOU.
WHY, YOU'RE COVERED IN FLOUR! WHAT HAS THAT FINISHING SCHOOL TAUGHT YOU?
THIS IS TOO MUCH, CRUELLA. TOO MUCH. I SENT YOU TO THAT SCHOOL TO BECOME A LADY, NOT A COMMON HOUSEMAID.
CLEARLY ANITA HAS BEEN A BAD INFLUENCE ON YOU! I SHOULD NEVER HAVE ARRANGED FOR HER TO JOIN YOU.
THAT'S NOT TRUE, MOTHER!
NOT TRUE? SINCE WHEN DO YOU DRESS LIKE THIS ON CHRISTMAS EVE? I GAVE MRS. WEB EXPLICIT INSTRUCTIONS ON HOW THIS EVENING SHOULD GO, AND YOU DEFIED MY WISHES.
I DON'T EVEN KNOW WHO YOU ARE.
SHE TOLD YOU?
OF COURSE SHE TOLD ME. SHE'S MY HEAD HOUSEKEEPER. YOU ARE NOT TO ACT THE LADY OF THE HOUSE WITH HER, DO YOU UNDERSTAND? SHE ENFORCES MY WILL WHEN I'M NOT HERE TO DO IT MYSELF.
SHE'S A HORRIBLE WOMAN, MOTHER. SHE WANTED THE SERVANTS TO GIVE UP THEIR HOLIDAY PARTY. I COULDN'T BELIEVE THOSE WERE YOUR WISHES. WHAT'S THE HARM IN HAVING A LITTLE PARTY FOR THE SERVANTS?
DINING IN THE KITCHEN WITH SERVANTS JUST ISN'T DONE. WHAT IF THE OTHER LADIES HEAR ABOUT THIS? WE'D BE A LAUGHINGSTOCK.
I HAVE MADE A DECISION, CRUELLA. I DON'T WANT YOU GOING BACK TO THAT SCHOOL. I THINK IT'S TIME FOR YOU TO COME OUT INTO SOCIETY. WE NEED TO FIND YOU A HUSBAND AT ONCE!
SOMEONE WHO WILL TAKE YOU IN HAND AND CURB THIS ATTITUDE OF YOURS.

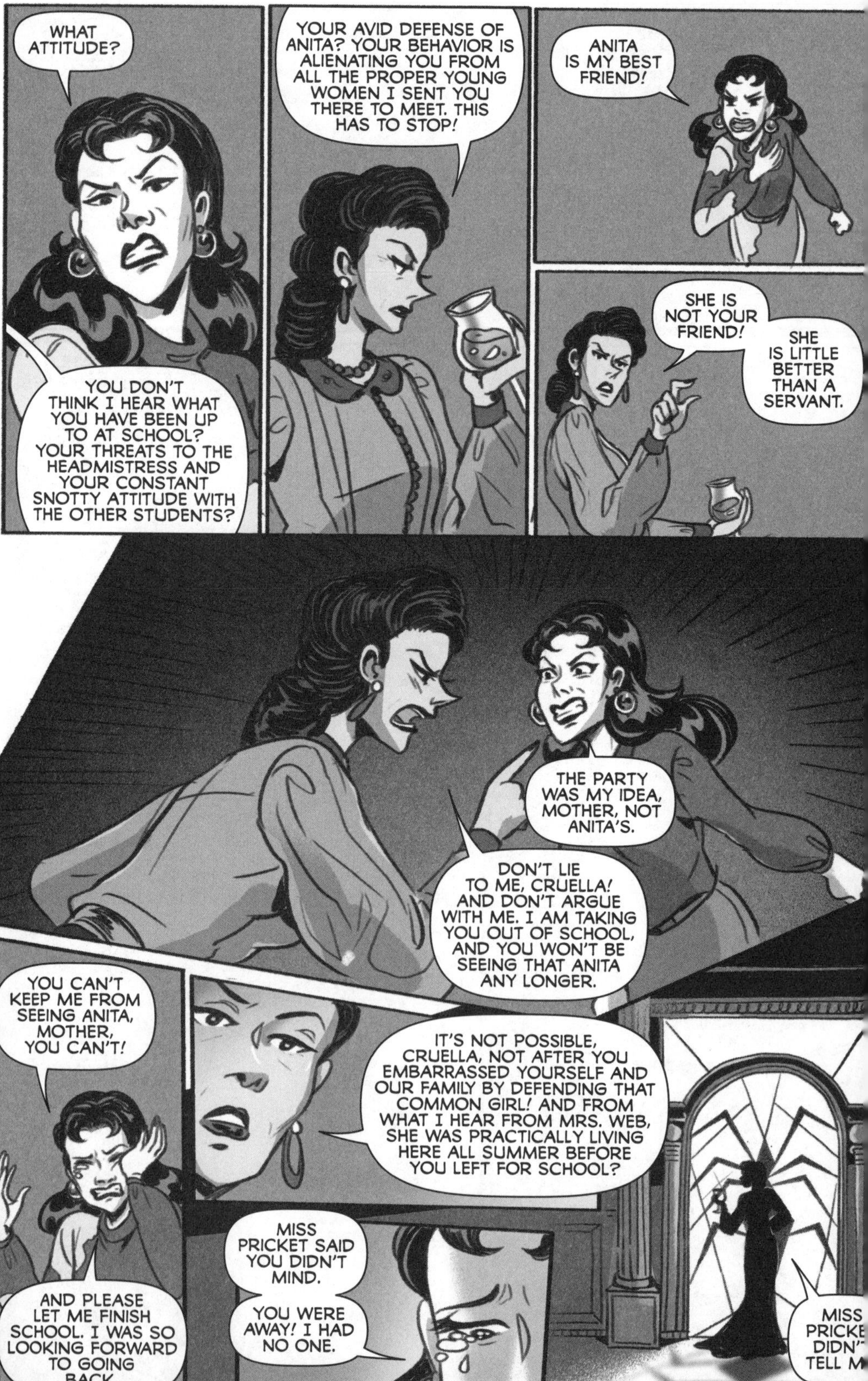
WHAT ATTITUDE?
YOU DON'T THINK I HEAR WHAT YOU HAVE BEEN UP TO AT SCHOOL? YOUR THREATS TO THE HEADMISTRESS AND YOUR CONSTANT SNOTTY ATTITUDE WITH THE OTHER STUDENTS?
YOUR AVID DEFENSE OF ANITA? YOUR BEHAVIOR IS ALIENATING YOU FROM ALL THE PROPER YOUNG WOMEN I SENT YOU THERE TO MEET. THIS HAS TO STOP!
ANITA IS MY BEST FRIEND!
SHE IS NOT YOUR FRIEND!
SHE IS LITTLE BETTER THAN A SERVANT.
THE PARTY WAS MY IDEA, MOTHER, NOT ANITA'S.
DON'T LIE TO ME, CRUELLA! AND DON'T ARGUE WITH ME. I AM TAKING YOU OUT OF SCHOOL, AND YOU WON'T BE SEEING THAT ANITA ANY LONGER.
YOU CAN'T KEEP ME FROM SEEING ANITA, MOTHER, YOU CAN'T!
IT'S NOT POSSIBLE, CRUELLA, NOT AFTER YOU EMBARRASSED YOURSELF AND OUR FAMILY BY DEFENDING THAT COMMON GIRL! AND FROM WHAT I HEAR FROM MRS. WEB, SHE WAS PRACTICALLY LIVING HERE ALL SUMMER BEFORE YOU LEFT FOR SCHOOL?
AND PLEASE LET ME FINISH SCHOOL. I WAS SO LOOKING FORWARD TO GOING BACK.
MISS PRICKET SAID YOU DIDN'T MIND.
YOU WERE AWAY! I HAD NO ONE.
MISS PRICKE DIDN' TELL M

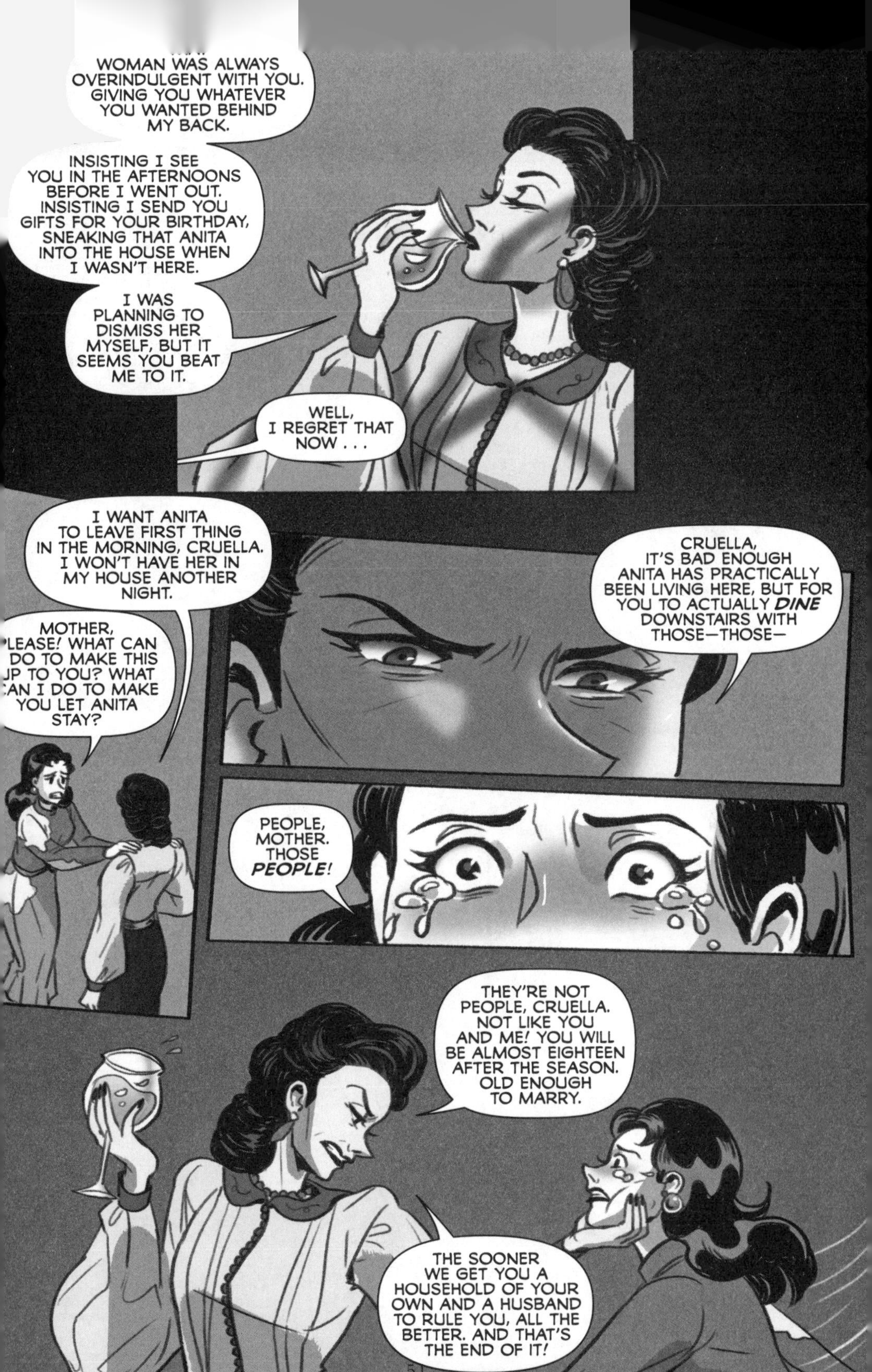
WOMAN WAS ALWAYS OVERINDULGENT WITH YOU. GIVING YOU WHATEVER YOU WANTED BEHIND MY BACK.
INSISTING I SEE YOU IN THE AFTERNOONS BEFORE I WENT OUT. INSISTING I SEND YOU GIFTS FOR YOUR BIRTHDAY, SNEAKING THAT ANITA INTO THE HOUSE WHEN I WASN'T HERE.
I WAS PLANNING TO DISMISS HER MYSELF, BUT IT SEEMS YOU BEAT ME TO IT.
WELL, I REGRET THAT NOW . . .
I WANT ANITA TO LEAVE FIRST THING IN THE MORNING, CRUELLA. I WON'T HAVE HER IN MY HOUSE ANOTHER NIGHT.
MOTHER, LEASE! WHAT CAN DO TO MAKE THIS JP TO YOU? WHAT AN I DO TO MAKE YOU LET ANITA STAY?
CRUELLA, IT'S BAD ENOUGH ANITA HAS PRACTICALLY BEEN LIVING HERE, BUT FOR YOU TO ACTUALLY *DINE* DOWNSTAIRS WITH THOSE—THOSE—
PEOPLE, MOTHER. THOSE *PEOPLE*!
THEY'RE NOT PEOPLE, CRUELLA. NOT LIKE YOU AND ME! YOU WILL BE ALMOST EIGHTEEN AFTER THE SEASON. OLD ENOUGH TO MARRY.
THE SOONER WE GET YOU A HOUSEHOLD OF YOUR OWN AND A HUSBAND TO RULE YOU, ALL THE BETTER. AND THAT'S THE END OF IT!

CHAPTER EIGHT
DISTINGUISH YOURSELF

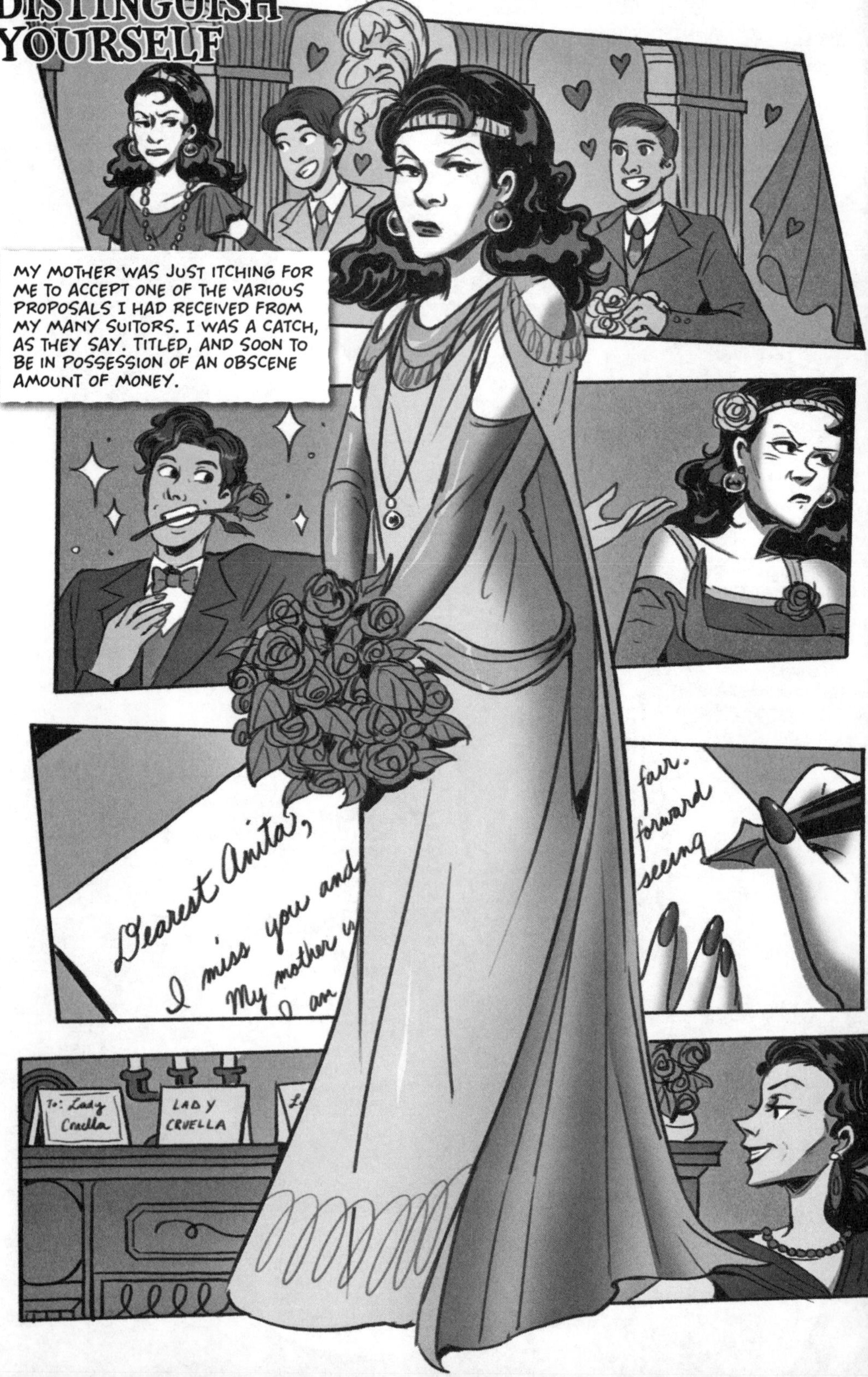
MY MOTHER WAS JUST ITCHING FOR ME TO ACCEPT ONE OF THE VARIOUS PROPOSALS I HAD RECEIVED FROM MY MANY SUITORS. I WAS A CATCH, AS THEY SAY. TITLED, AND SOON TO BE IN POSSESSION OF AN OBSCENE AMOUNT OF MONEY.
Dearest Anita,
I miss you and
My mother
fair.
forward
seeing
To: Lady Cruella
LADY CRUELLA

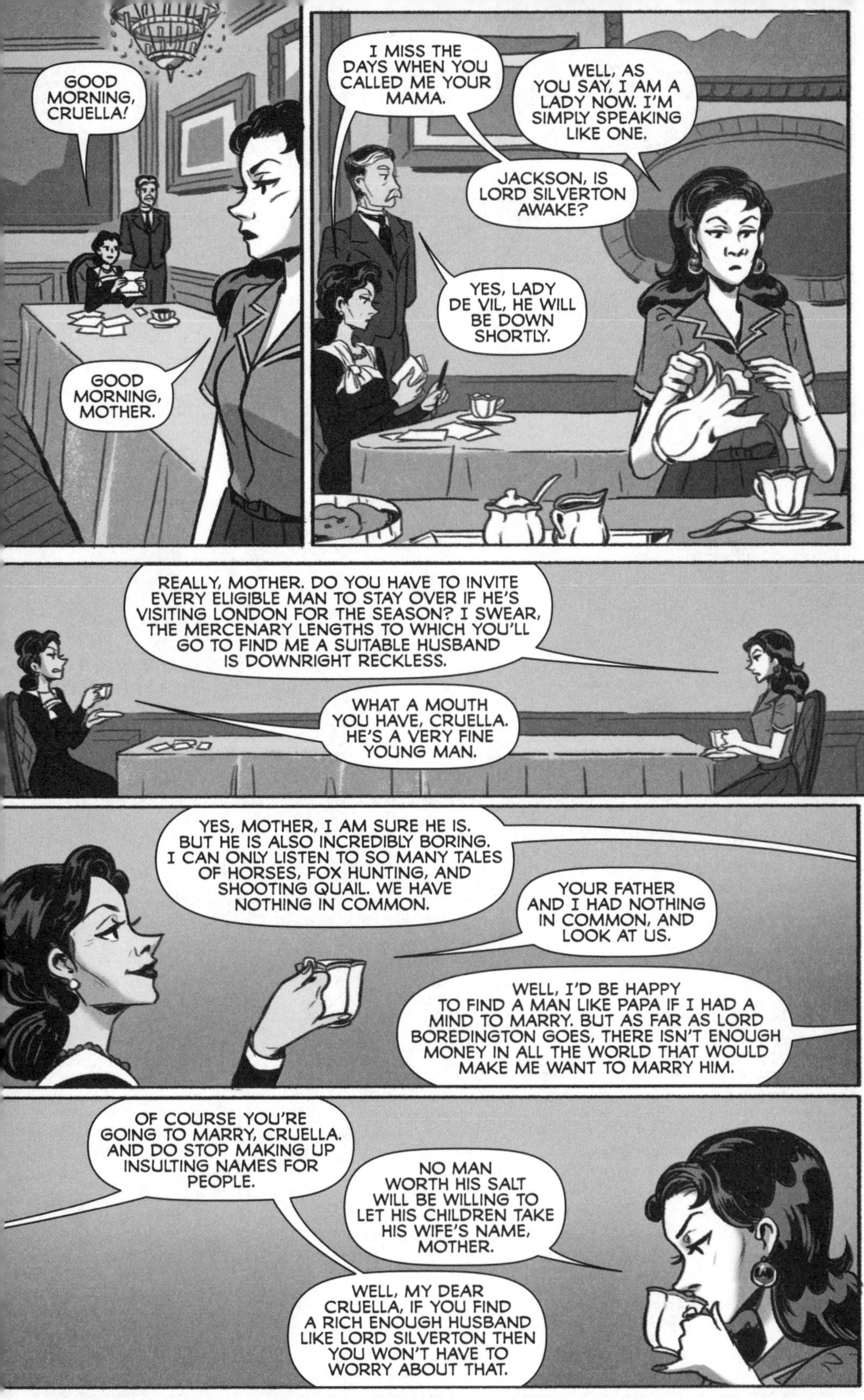

GOOD MORNING, CRUELLA!
GOOD MORNING, MOTHER.
I MISS THE DAYS WHEN YOU CALLED ME YOUR MAMA.
WELL, AS YOU SAY, I AM A LADY NOW. I'M SIMPLY SPEAKING LIKE ONE.
JACKSON, IS LORD SILVERTON AWAKE?
YES, LADY DE VIL, HE WILL BE DOWN SHORTLY.
REALLY, MOTHER. DO YOU HAVE TO INVITE EVERY ELIGIBLE MAN TO STAY OVER IF HE'S VISITING LONDON FOR THE SEASON? I SWEAR, THE MERCENARY LENGTHS TO WHICH YOU'LL GO TO FIND ME A SUITABLE HUSBAND IS DOWNRIGHT RECKLESS.
WHAT A MOUTH YOU HAVE, CRUELLA. HE'S A VERY FINE YOUNG MAN.
YES, MOTHER, I AM SURE HE IS. BUT HE IS ALSO INCREDIBLY BORING. I CAN ONLY LISTEN TO SO MANY TALES OF HORSES, FOX HUNTING, AND SHOOTING QUAIL. WE HAVE NOTHING IN COMMON.
YOUR FATHER AND I HAD NOTHING IN COMMON, AND LOOK AT US.
WELL, I'D BE HAPPY TO FIND A MAN LIKE PAPA IF I HAD A MIND TO MARRY. BUT AS FAR AS LORD BOREDINGTON GOES, THERE ISN'T ENOUGH MONEY IN ALL THE WORLD THAT WOULD MAKE ME WANT TO MARRY HIM.
OF COURSE YOU'RE GOING TO MARRY, CRUELLA. AND DO STOP MAKING UP INSULTING NAMES FOR PEOPLE.
NO MAN WORTH HIS SALT WILL BE WILLING TO LET HIS CHILDREN TAKE HIS WIFE'S NAME, MOTHER.
WELL, MY DEAR CRUELLA, IF YOU FIND A RICH ENOUGH HUSBAND LIKE LORD SILVERTON THEN YOU WON'T HAVE TO WORRY ABOUT THAT.

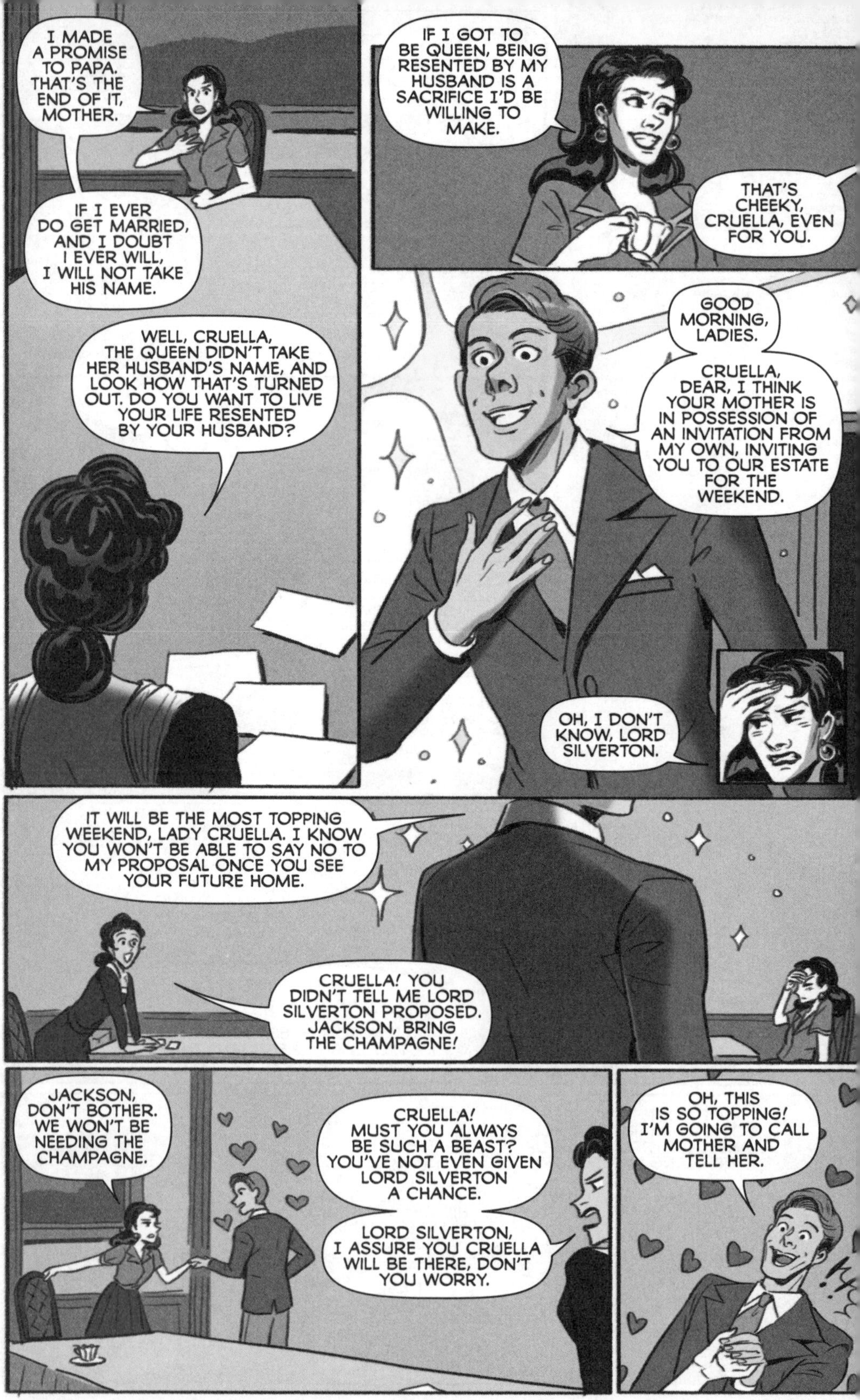
I MADE A PROMISE TO PAPA. THAT'S THE END OF IT, MOTHER.
IF I EVER DO GET MARRIED, AND I DOUBT I EVER WILL, I WILL NOT TAKE HIS NAME.
WELL, CRUELLA, THE QUEEN DIDN'T TAKE HER HUSBAND'S NAME, AND LOOK HOW THAT'S TURNED OUT. DO YOU WANT TO LIVE YOUR LIFE RESENTED BY YOUR HUSBAND?
IF I GOT TO BE QUEEN, BEING RESENTED BY MY HUSBAND IS A SACRIFICE I'D BE WILLING TO MAKE.
THAT'S CHEEKY, CRUELLA, EVEN FOR YOU.
GOOD MORNING, LADIES.
CRUELLA, DEAR, I THINK YOUR MOTHER IS IN POSSESSION OF AN INVITATION FROM MY OWN, INVITING YOU TO OUR ESTATE FOR THE WEEKEND.
OH, I DON'T KNOW, LORD SILVERTON.
IT WILL BE THE MOST TOPPING WEEKEND, LADY CRUELLA. I KNOW YOU WON'T BE ABLE TO SAY NO TO MY PROPOSAL ONCE YOU SEE YOUR FUTURE HOME.
CRUELLA! YOU DIDN'T TELL ME LORD SILVERTON PROPOSED. JACKSON, BRING THE CHAMPAGNE!
JACKSON, DON'T BOTHER. WE WON'T BE NEEDING THE CHAMPAGNE.
CRUELLA! MUST YOU ALWAYS BE SUCH A BEAST? YOU'VE NOT EVEN GIVEN LORD SILVERTON A CHANCE.
LORD SILVERTON, I ASSURE YOU CRUELLA WILL BE THERE, DON'T YOU WORRY.
OH, THIS IS SO TOPPING! I'M GOING TO CALL MOTHER AND TELL HER.

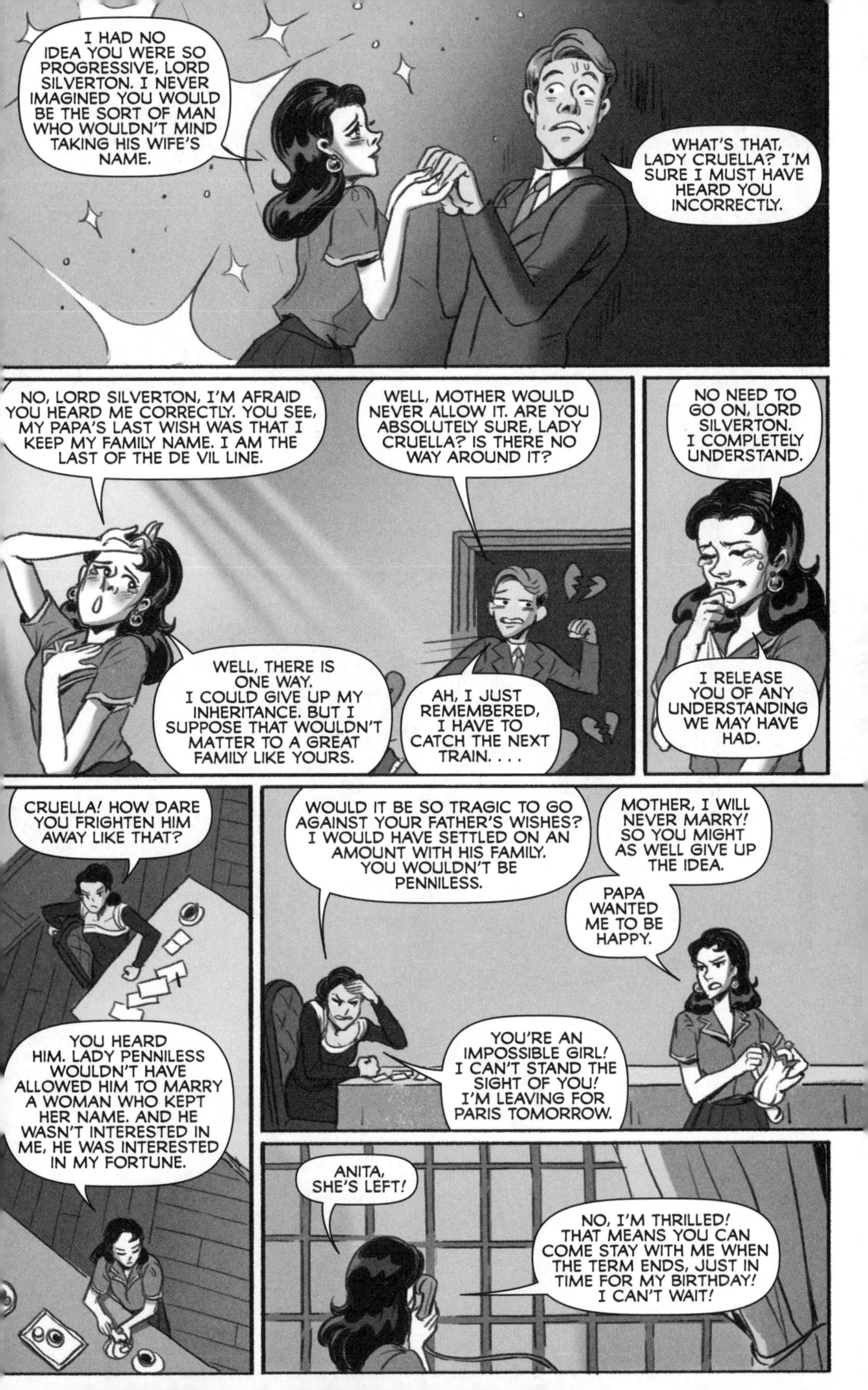
I HAD NO IDEA YOU WERE SO PROGRESSIVE, LORD SILVERTON. I NEVER IMAGINED YOU WOULD BE THE SORT OF MAN WHO WOULDN'T MIND TAKING HIS WIFE'S NAME.
WHAT'S THAT, LADY CRUELLA? I'M SURE I MUST HAVE HEARD YOU INCORRECTLY.
NO, LORD SILVERTON, I'M AFRAID YOU HEARD ME CORRECTLY. YOU SEE, MY PAPA'S LAST WISH WAS THAT I KEEP MY FAMILY NAME. I AM THE LAST OF THE DE VIL LINE.
WELL, MOTHER WOULD NEVER ALLOW IT. ARE YOU ABSOLUTELY SURE, LADY CRUELLA? IS THERE NO WAY AROUND IT?
WELL, THERE IS ONE WAY. I COULD GIVE UP MY INHERITANCE. BUT I SUPPOSE THAT WOULDN'T MATTER TO A GREAT FAMILY LIKE YOURS.
AH, I JUST REMEMBERED, I HAVE TO CATCH THE NEXT TRAIN. . . .
NO NEED TO GO ON, LORD SILVERTON. I COMPLETELY UNDERSTAND.
I RELEASE YOU OF ANY UNDERSTANDING WE MAY HAVE HAD.
CRUELLA! HOW DARE YOU FRIGHTEN HIM AWAY LIKE THAT?
YOU HEARD HIM. LADY PENNILESS WOULDN'T HAVE ALLOWED HIM TO MARRY A WOMAN WHO KEPT HER NAME. AND HE WASN'T INTERESTED IN ME, HE WAS INTERESTED IN MY FORTUNE.
WOULD IT BE SO TRAGIC TO GO AGAINST YOUR FATHER'S WISHES? I WOULD HAVE SETTLED ON AN AMOUNT WITH HIS FAMILY. YOU WOULDN'T BE PENNILESS.
MOTHER, I WILL NEVER MARRY! SO YOU MIGHT AS WELL GIVE UP THE IDEA.
PAPA WANTED ME TO BE HAPPY.
YOU'RE AN IMPOSSIBLE GIRL! I CAN'T STAND THE SIGHT OF YOU! I'M LEAVING FOR PARIS TOMORROW.
ANITA, SHE'S LEFT!
NO, I'M THRILLED! THAT MEANS YOU CAN COME STAY WITH ME WHEN THE TERM ENDS, JUST IN TIME FOR MY BIRTHDAY! I CAN'T WAIT!

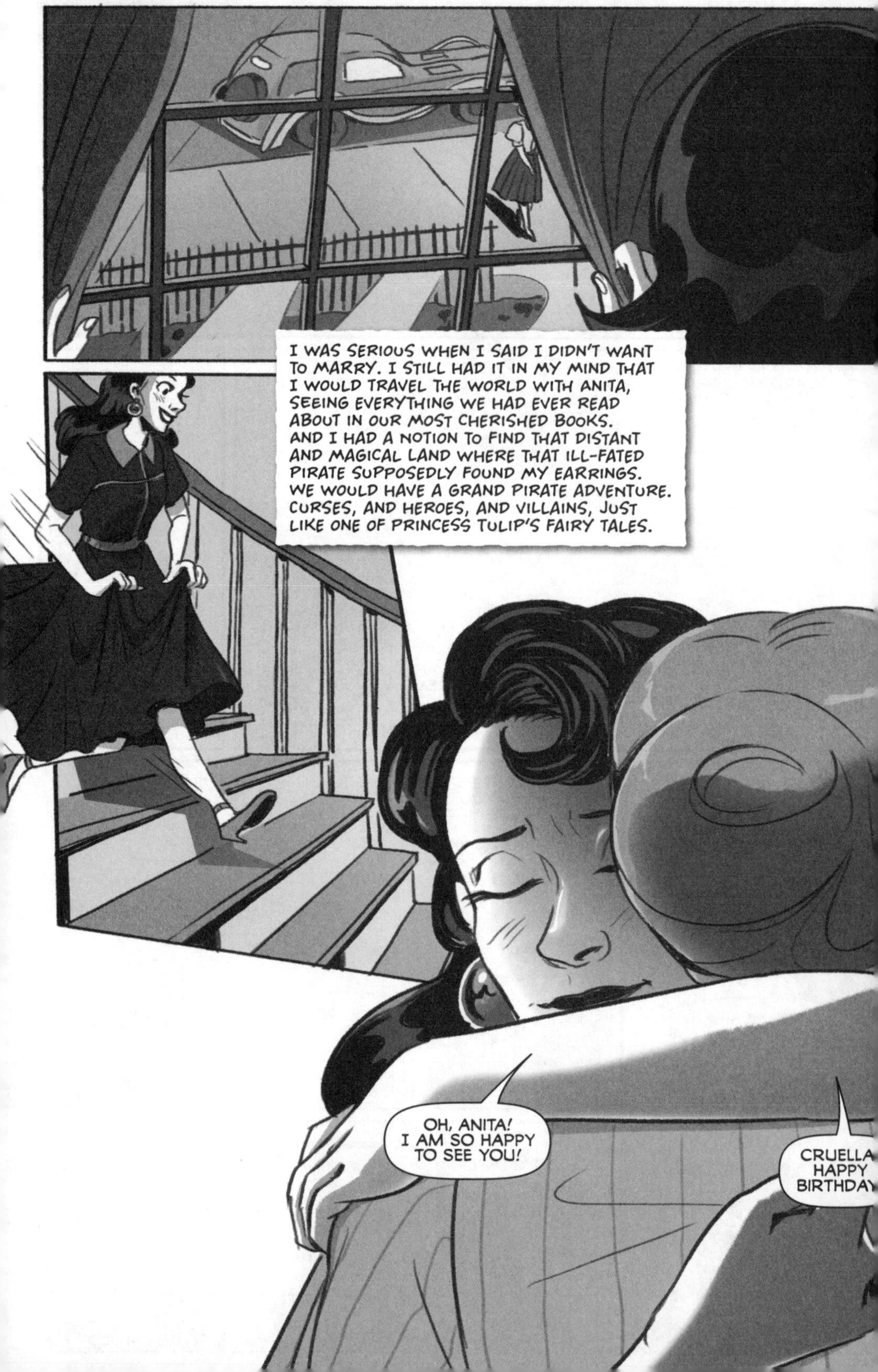
I WAS SERIOUS WHEN I SAID I DIDN'T WANT TO MARRY. I STILL HAD IT IN MY MIND THAT I WOULD TRAVEL THE WORLD WITH ANITA, SEEING EVERYTHING WE HAD EVER READ ABOUT IN OUR MOST CHERISHED BOOKS. AND I HAD A NOTION TO FIND THAT DISTANT AND MAGICAL LAND WHERE THAT ILL-FATED PIRATE SUPPOSEDLY FOUND MY EARRINGS. WE WOULD HAVE A GRAND PIRATE ADVENTURE. CURSES, AND HEROES, AND VILLAINS, JUST LIKE ONE OF PRINCESS TULIP'S FAIRY TALES.
OH, ANITA! I AM SO HAPPY TO SEE YOU!
CRUELLA HAPPY BIRTHDAY

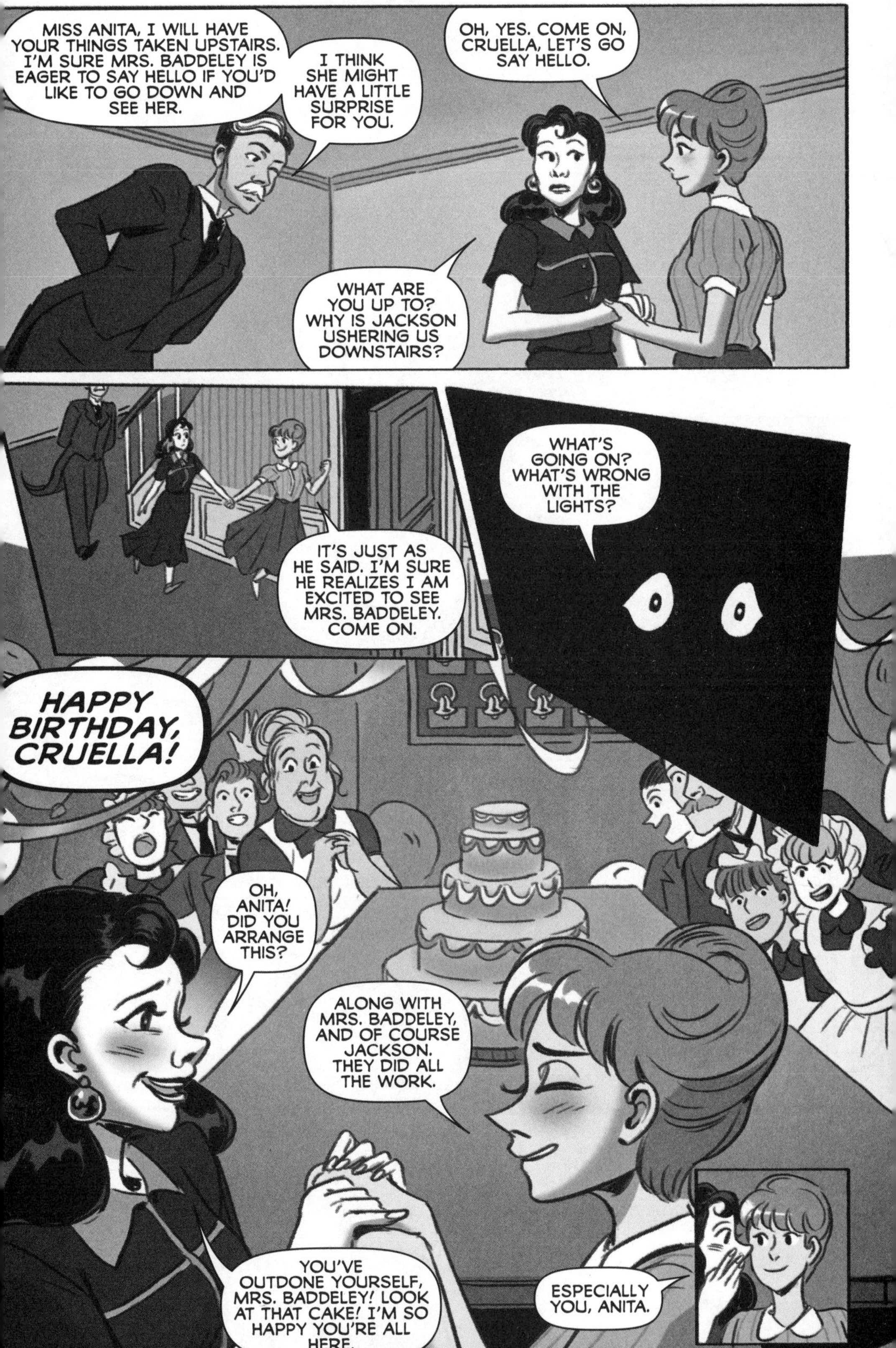
MISS ANITA, I WILL HAVE YOUR THINGS TAKEN UPSTAIRS. I'M SURE MRS. BADDELEY IS EAGER TO SAY HELLO IF YOU'D LIKE TO GO DOWN AND SEE HER.
I THINK SHE MIGHT HAVE A LITTLE SURPRISE FOR YOU.
OH, YES. COME ON, CRUELLA, LET'S GO SAY HELLO.
WHAT ARE YOU UP TO? WHY IS JACKSON USHERING US DOWNSTAIRS?
IT'S JUST AS HE SAID. I'M SURE HE REALIZES I AM EXCITED TO SEE MRS. BADDELEY. COME ON.
WHAT'S GOING ON? WHAT'S WRONG WITH THE LIGHTS?
HAPPY BIRTHDAY, CRUELLA!
OH, ANITA! DID YOU ARRANGE THIS?
ALONG WITH MRS. BADDELEY, AND OF COURSE JACKSON. THEY DID ALL THE WORK.
YOU'VE OUTDONE YOURSELF, MRS. BADDELEY! LOOK AT THAT CAKE! I'M SO HAPPY YOU'RE ALL HERE.
ESPECIALLY YOU, ANITA.

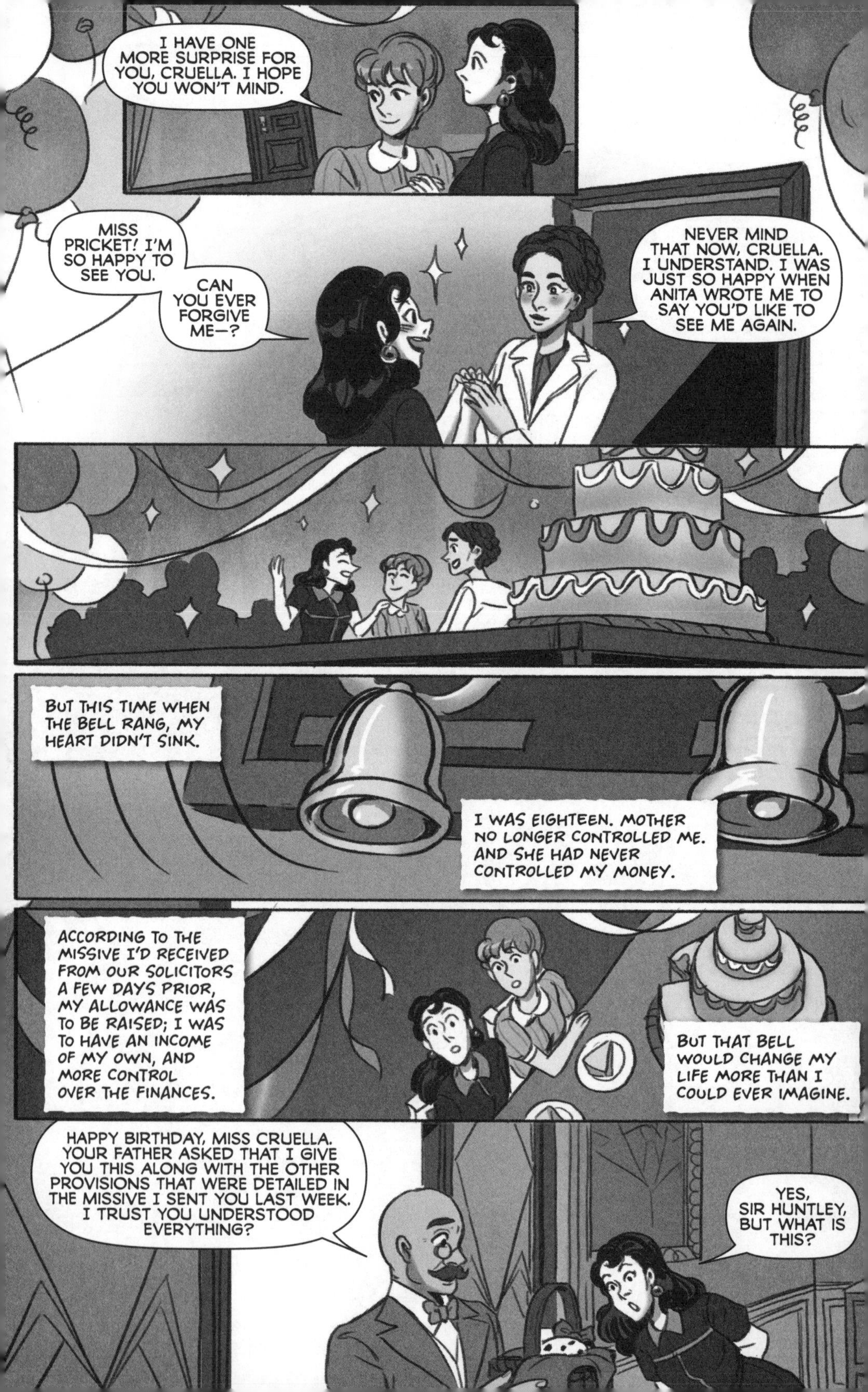
I HAVE ONE MORE SURPRISE FOR YOU, CRUELLA. I HOPE YOU WON'T MIND.
MISS PRICKET! I'M SO HAPPY TO SEE YOU.
CAN YOU EVER FORGIVE ME—?
NEVER MIND THAT NOW, CRUELLA. I UNDERSTAND. I WAS JUST SO HAPPY WHEN ANITA WROTE ME TO SAY YOU'D LIKE TO SEE ME AGAIN.
BUT THIS TIME WHEN THE BELL RANG, MY HEART DIDN'T SINK.
I WAS EIGHTEEN. MOTHER NO LONGER CONTROLLED ME. AND SHE HAD NEVER CONTROLLED MY MONEY.
ACCORDING TO THE MISSIVE I'D RECEIVED FROM OUR SOLICITORS A FEW DAYS PRIOR, MY ALLOWANCE WAS TO BE RAISED; I WAS TO HAVE AN INCOME OF MY OWN, AND MORE CONTROL OVER THE FINANCES.
BUT THAT BELL WOULD CHANGE MY LIFE MORE THAN I COULD EVER IMAGINE.
HAPPY BIRTHDAY, MISS CRUELLA. YOUR FATHER ASKED THAT I GIVE YOU THIS ALONG WITH THE OTHER PROVISIONS THAT WERE DETAILED IN THE MISSIVE I SENT YOU LAST WEEK. I TRUST YOU UNDERSTOOD EVERYTHING?
YES, SIR HUNTLEY, BUT WHAT IS THIS?

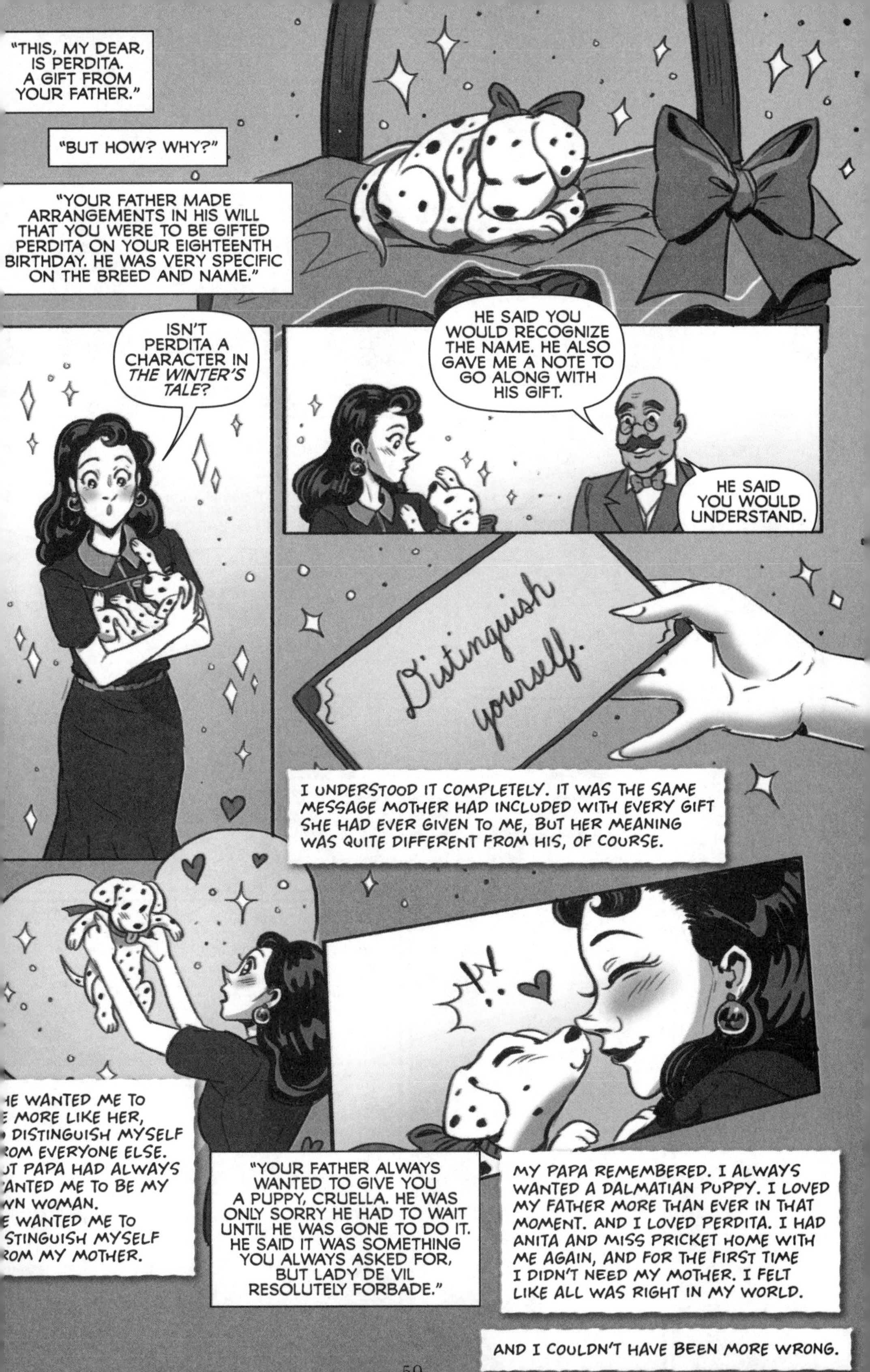

"THIS, MY DEAR, IS PERDITA. A GIFT FROM YOUR FATHER."
"BUT HOW? WHY?"
"YOUR FATHER MADE ARRANGEMENTS IN HIS WILL THAT YOU WERE TO BE GIFTED PERDITA ON YOUR EIGHTEENTH BIRTHDAY. HE WAS VERY SPECIFIC ON THE BREED AND NAME."
ISN'T PERDITA A CHARACTER IN *THE WINTER'S TALE*?
HE SAID YOU WOULD RECOGNIZE THE NAME. HE ALSO GAVE ME A NOTE TO GO ALONG WITH HIS GIFT.
HE SAID YOU WOULD UNDERSTAND.
Distinguish yourself.
I UNDERSTOOD IT COMPLETELY. IT WAS THE SAME MESSAGE MOTHER HAD INCLUDED WITH EVERY GIFT SHE HAD EVER GIVEN TO ME, BUT HER MEANING WAS QUITE DIFFERENT FROM HIS, OF COURSE.
!
IE WANTED ME TO E MORE LIKE HER, DISTINGUISH MYSELF ROM EVERYONE ELSE. JT PAPA HAD ALWAYS ANTED ME TO BE MY WN WOMAN. E WANTED ME TO STINGUISH MYSELF ROM MY MOTHER.
"YOUR FATHER ALWAYS WANTED TO GIVE YOU A PUPPY, CRUELLA. HE WAS ONLY SORRY HE HAD TO WAIT UNTIL HE WAS GONE TO DO IT. HE SAID IT WAS SOMETHING YOU ALWAYS ASKED FOR, BUT LADY DE VIL RESOLUTELY FORBADE."
MY PAPA REMEMBERED. I ALWAYS WANTED A DALMATIAN PUPPY. I LOVED MY FATHER MORE THAN EVER IN THAT MOMENT. AND I LOVED PERDITA. I HAD ANITA AND MISS PRICKET HOME WITH ME AGAIN, AND FOR THE FIRST TIME I DIDN'T NEED MY MOTHER. I FELT LIKE ALL WAS RIGHT IN MY WORLD.
AND I COULDN'T HAVE BEEN MORE WRONG.

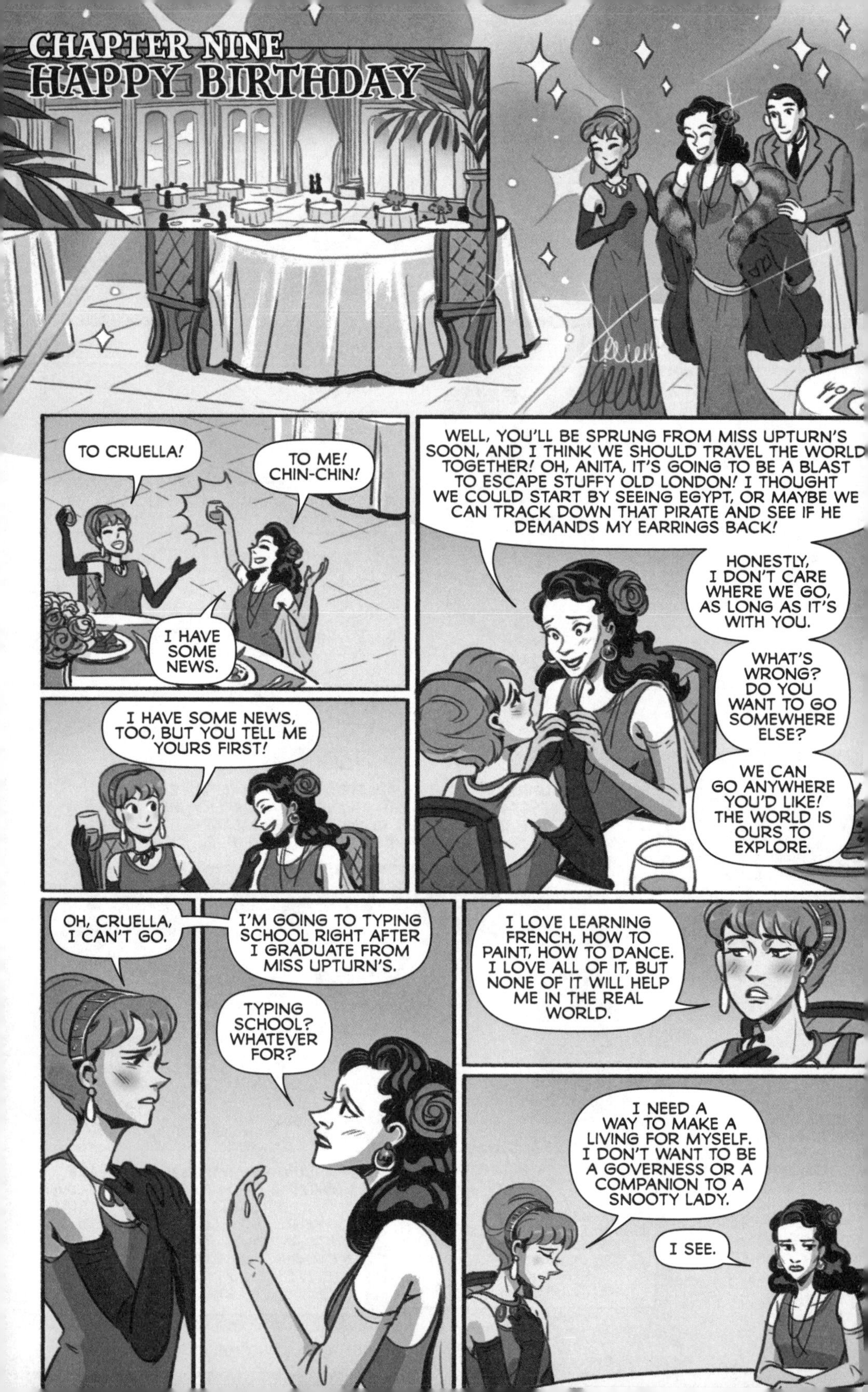
CHAPTER NINE
HAPPY BIRTHDAY
TO CRUELLA!
TO ME! CHIN-CHIN!
I HAVE SOME NEWS.
I HAVE SOME NEWS, TOO, BUT YOU TELL ME YOURS FIRST!
WELL, YOU'LL BE SPRUNG FROM MISS UPTURN'S SOON, AND I THINK WE SHOULD TRAVEL THE WORLD TOGETHER! OH, ANITA, IT'S GOING TO BE A BLAST TO ESCAPE STUFFY OLD LONDON! I THOUGHT WE COULD START BY SEEING EGYPT, OR MAYBE WE CAN TRACK DOWN THAT PIRATE AND SEE IF HE DEMANDS MY EARRINGS BACK!
HONESTLY, I DON'T CARE WHERE WE GO, AS LONG AS IT'S WITH YOU.
WHAT'S WRONG? DO YOU WANT TO GO SOMEWHERE ELSE?
WE CAN GO ANYWHERE YOU'D LIKE! THE WORLD IS OURS TO EXPLORE.
OH, CRUELLA, I CAN'T GO.
I'M GOING TO TYPING SCHOOL RIGHT AFTER I GRADUATE FROM MISS UPTURN'S.
TYPING SCHOOL? WHATEVER FOR?
I LOVE LEARNING FRENCH, HOW TO PAINT, HOW TO DANCE. I LOVE ALL OF IT, BUT NONE OF IT WILL HELP ME IN THE REAL WORLD.
I NEED A WAY TO MAKE A LIVING FOR MYSELF. I DON'T WANT TO BE A GOVERNESS OR A COMPANION TO A SNOOTY LADY.
I SEE.

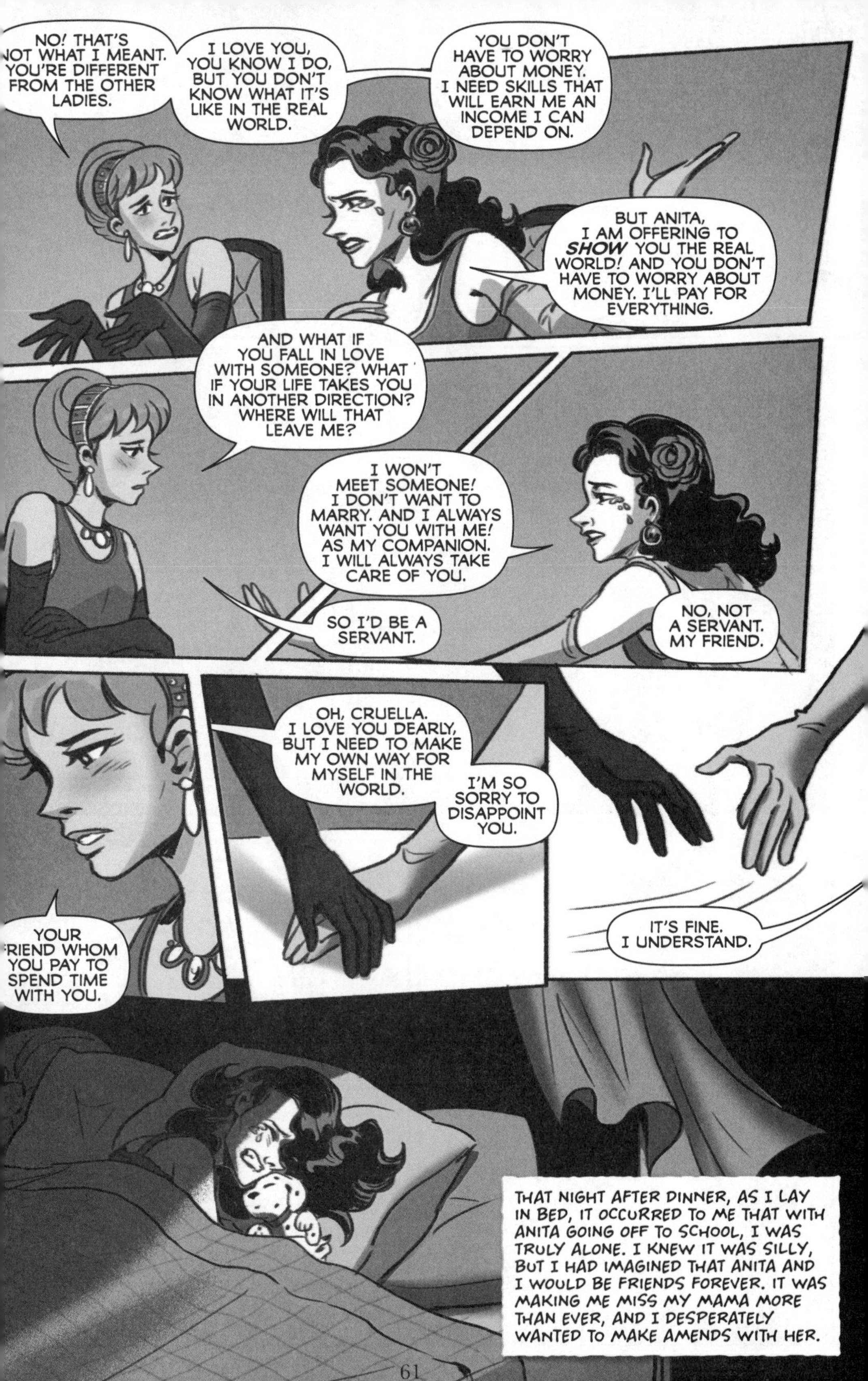

NO! THAT'S NOT WHAT I MEANT. YOU'RE DIFFERENT FROM THE OTHER LADIES.
I LOVE YOU, YOU KNOW I DO, BUT YOU DON'T KNOW WHAT IT'S LIKE IN THE REAL WORLD.
YOU DON'T HAVE TO WORRY ABOUT MONEY. I NEED SKILLS THAT WILL EARN ME AN INCOME I CAN DEPEND ON.
BUT ANITA, I AM OFFERING TO *SHOW* YOU THE REAL WORLD! AND YOU DON'T HAVE TO WORRY ABOUT MONEY. I'LL PAY FOR EVERYTHING.
AND WHAT IF YOU FALL IN LOVE WITH SOMEONE? WHAT IF YOUR LIFE TAKES YOU IN ANOTHER DIRECTION? WHERE WILL THAT LEAVE ME?
I WON'T MEET SOMEONE! I DON'T WANT TO MARRY. AND I ALWAYS WANT YOU WITH ME! AS MY COMPANION. I WILL ALWAYS TAKE CARE OF YOU.
SO I'D BE A SERVANT.
NO, NOT A SERVANT. MY FRIEND.
YOUR FRIEND WHOM YOU PAY TO SPEND TIME WITH YOU.
OH, CRUELLA. I LOVE YOU DEARLY, BUT I NEED TO MAKE MY OWN WAY FOR MYSELF IN THE WORLD.
I'M SO SORRY TO DISAPPOINT YOU.
IT'S FINE. I UNDERSTAND.
THAT NIGHT AFTER DINNER, AS I LAY IN BED, IT OCCURRED TO ME THAT WITH ANITA GOING OFF TO SCHOOL, I WAS TRULY ALONE. I KNEW IT WAS SILLY, BUT I HAD IMAGINED THAT ANITA AND I WOULD BE FRIENDS FOREVER. IT WAS MAKING ME MISS MY MAMA MORE THAN EVER, AND I DESPERATELY WANTED TO MAKE AMENDS WITH HER.

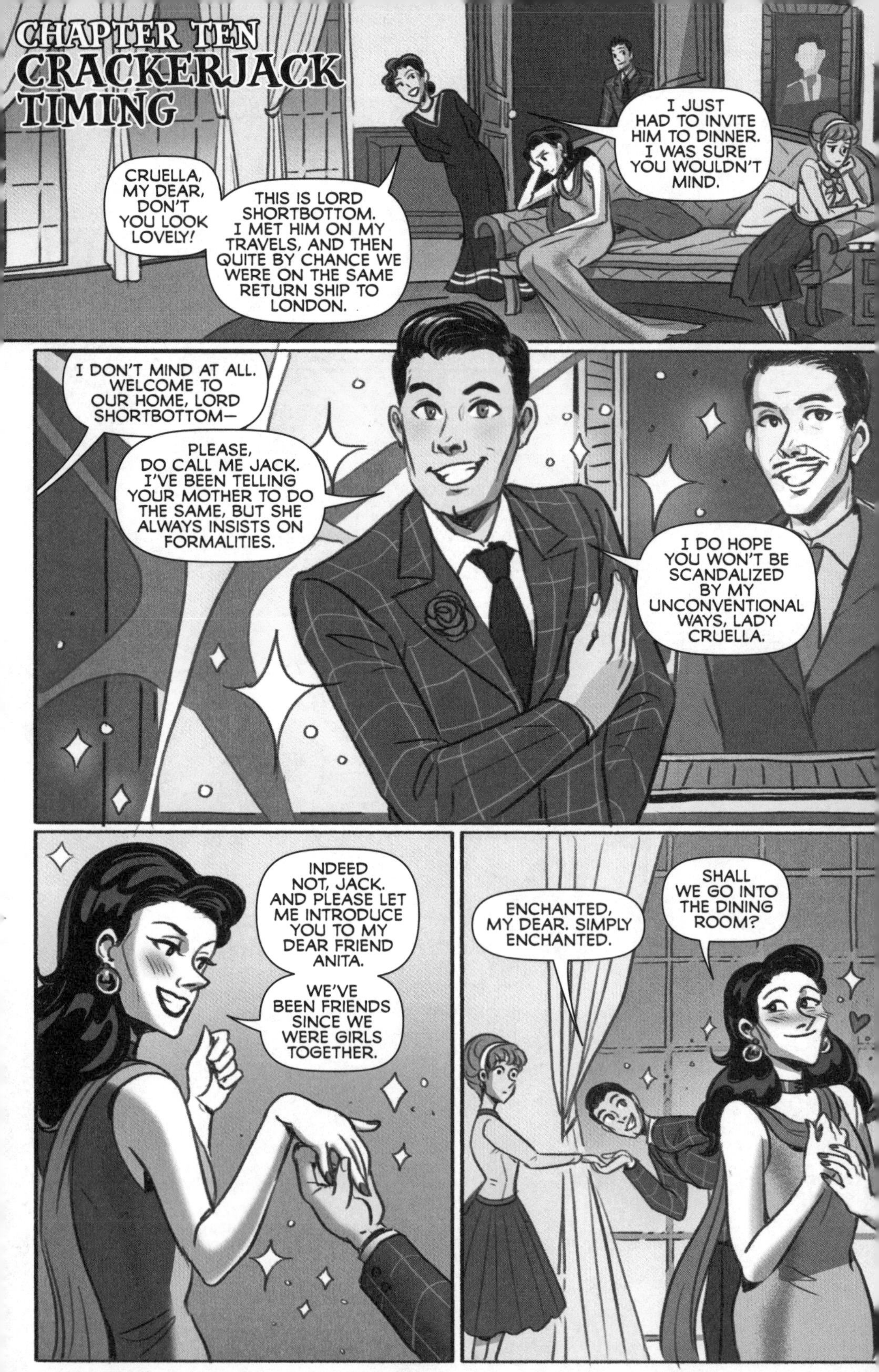
CHAPTER TEN
CRACKERJACK TIMING
CRUELLA, MY DEAR, DON'T YOU LOOK LOVELY!
THIS IS LORD SHORTBOTTOM. I MET HIM ON MY TRAVELS, AND THEN QUITE BY CHANCE WE WERE ON THE SAME RETURN SHIP TO LONDON.
I JUST HAD TO INVITE HIM TO DINNER. I WAS SURE YOU WOULDN'T MIND.
I DON'T MIND AT ALL. WELCOME TO OUR HOME, LORD SHORTBOTTOM—
PLEASE, DO CALL ME JACK. I'VE BEEN TELLING YOUR MOTHER TO DO THE SAME, BUT SHE ALWAYS INSISTS ON FORMALITIES.
I DO HOPE YOU WON'T BE SCANDALIZED BY MY UNCONVENTIONAL WAYS, LADY CRUELLA.
INDEED NOT, JACK. AND PLEASE LET ME INTRODUCE YOU TO MY DEAR FRIEND ANITA.
WE'VE BEEN FRIENDS SINCE WE WERE GIRLS TOGETHER.
ENCHANTED, MY DEAR. SIMPLY ENCHANTED.
SHALL WE GO INTO THE DINING ROOM?

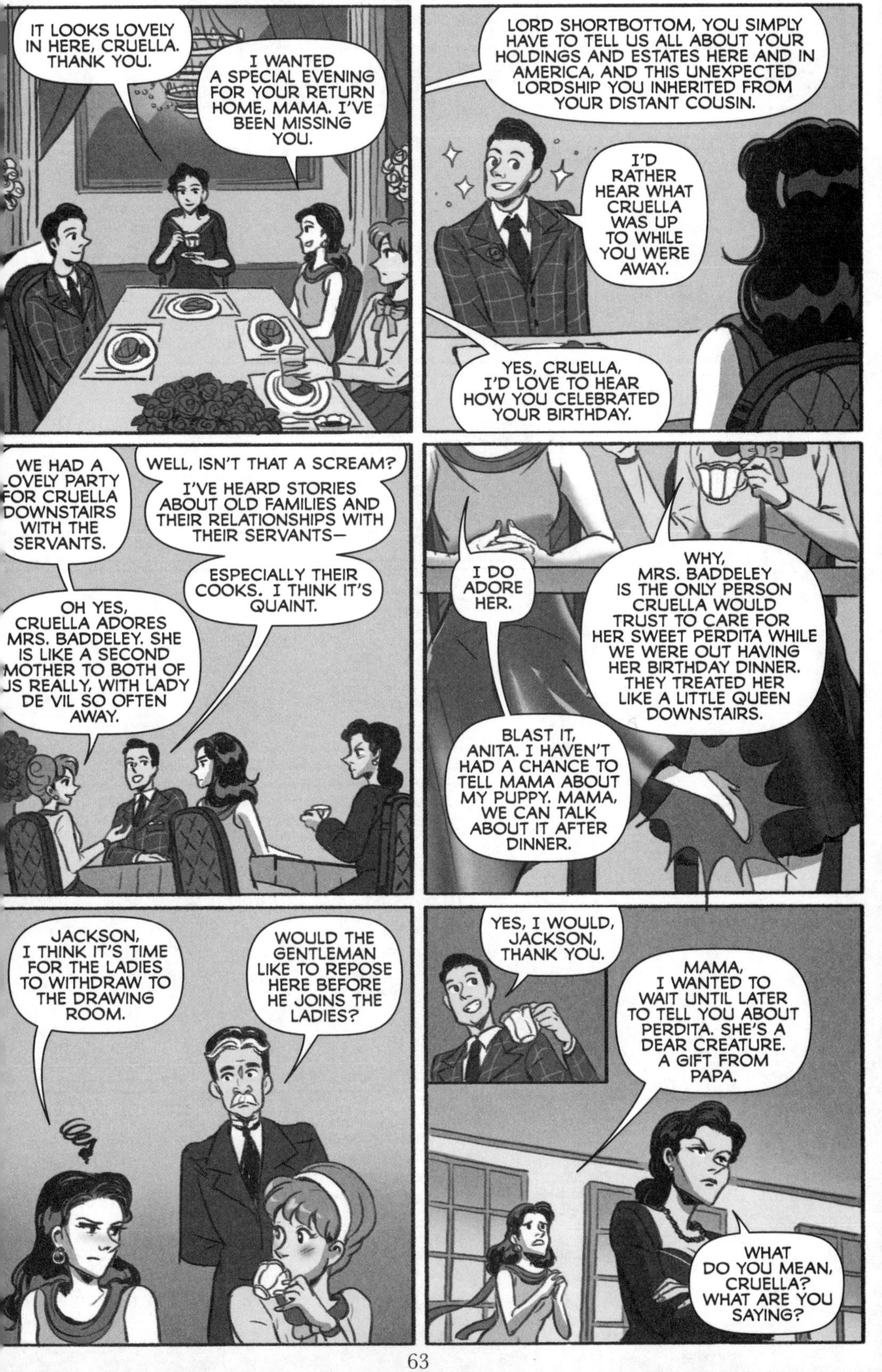
IT LOOKS LOVELY IN HERE, CRUELLA. THANK YOU.
I WANTED A SPECIAL EVENING FOR YOUR RETURN HOME, MAMA. I'VE BEEN MISSING YOU.
LORD SHORTBOTTOM, YOU SIMPLY HAVE TO TELL US ALL ABOUT YOUR HOLDINGS AND ESTATES HERE AND IN AMERICA, AND THIS UNEXPECTED LORDSHIP YOU INHERITED FROM YOUR DISTANT COUSIN.
I'D RATHER HEAR WHAT CRUELLA WAS UP TO WHILE YOU WERE AWAY.
YES, CRUELLA, I'D LOVE TO HEAR HOW YOU CELEBRATED YOUR BIRTHDAY.
WE HAD A LOVELY PARTY FOR CRUELLA DOWNSTAIRS WITH THE SERVANTS.
WELL, ISN'T THAT A SCREAM?
I'VE HEARD STORIES ABOUT OLD FAMILIES AND THEIR RELATIONSHIPS WITH THEIR SERVANTS—
ESPECIALLY THEIR COOKS. I THINK IT'S QUAINT.
OH YES, CRUELLA ADORES MRS. BADDELEY. SHE IS LIKE A SECOND MOTHER TO BOTH OF US REALLY, WITH LADY DE VIL SO OFTEN AWAY.
I DO ADORE HER.
WHY, MRS. BADDELEY IS THE ONLY PERSON CRUELLA WOULD TRUST TO CARE FOR HER SWEET PERDITA WHILE WE WERE OUT HAVING HER BIRTHDAY DINNER. THEY TREATED HER LIKE A LITTLE QUEEN DOWNSTAIRS.
BLAST IT, ANITA. I HAVEN'T HAD A CHANCE TO TELL MAMA ABOUT MY PUPPY. MAMA, WE CAN TALK ABOUT IT AFTER DINNER.
JACKSON, I THINK IT'S TIME FOR THE LADIES TO WITHDRAW TO THE DRAWING ROOM.
WOULD THE GENTLEMAN LIKE TO REPOSE HERE BEFORE HE JOINS THE LADIES?
YES, I WOULD, JACKSON, THANK YOU.
MAMA, I WANTED TO WAIT UNTIL LATER TO TELL YOU ABOUT PERDITA. SHE'S A DEAR CREATURE. A GIFT FROM PAPA.
WHAT DO YOU MEAN, CRUELLA? WHAT ARE YOU SAYING?

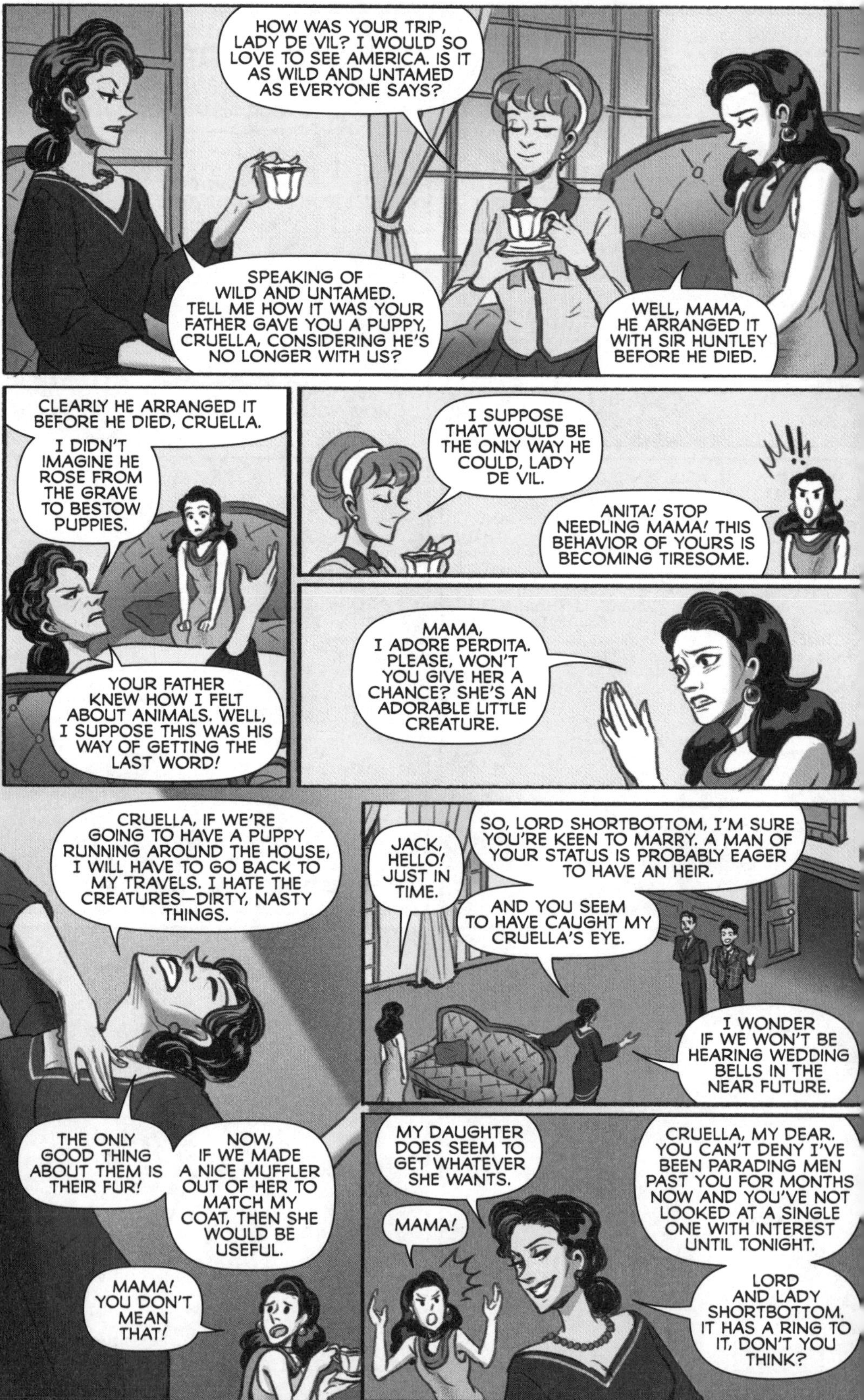
HOW WAS YOUR TRIP, LADY DE VIL? I WOULD SO LOVE TO SEE AMERICA. IS IT AS WILD AND UNTAMED AS EVERYONE SAYS?
SPEAKING OF WILD AND UNTAMED. TELL ME HOW IT WAS YOUR FATHER GAVE YOU A PUPPY, CRUELLA, CONSIDERING HE'S NO LONGER WITH US?
WELL, MAMA, HE ARRANGED IT WITH SIR HUNTLEY BEFORE HE DIED.
CLEARLY HE ARRANGED IT BEFORE HE DIED, CRUELLA.
I DIDN'T IMAGINE HE ROSE FROM THE GRAVE TO BESTOW PUPPIES.
YOUR FATHER KNEW HOW I FELT ABOUT ANIMALS. WELL, I SUPPOSE THIS WAS HIS WAY OF GETTING THE LAST WORD!
I SUPPOSE THAT WOULD BE THE ONLY WAY HE COULD, LADY DE VIL.
ANITA! STOP NEEDLING MAMA! THIS BEHAVIOR OF YOURS IS BECOMING TIRESOME.
MAMA, I ADORE PERDITA. PLEASE, WON'T YOU GIVE HER A CHANCE? SHE'S AN ADORABLE LITTLE CREATURE.
CRUELLA, IF WE'RE GOING TO HAVE A PUPPY RUNNING AROUND THE HOUSE, I WILL HAVE TO GO BACK TO MY TRAVELS. I HATE THE CREATURES—DIRTY, NASTY THINGS.
THE ONLY GOOD THING ABOUT THEM IS THEIR FUR!
NOW, IF WE MADE A NICE MUFFLER OUT OF HER TO MATCH MY COAT, THEN SHE WOULD BE USEFUL.
MAMA! YOU DON'T MEAN THAT!
JACK, HELLO! JUST IN TIME.
SO, LORD SHORTBOTTOM, I'M SURE YOU'RE KEEN TO MARRY. A MAN OF YOUR STATUS IS PROBABLY EAGER TO HAVE AN HEIR.
AND YOU SEEM TO HAVE CAUGHT MY CRUELLA'S EYE.
I WONDER IF WE WON'T BE HEARING WEDDING BELLS IN THE NEAR FUTURE.
MY DAUGHTER DOES SEEM TO GET WHATEVER SHE WANTS.
MAMA!
CRUELLA, MY DEAR. YOU CAN'T DENY I'VE BEEN PARADING MEN PAST YOU FOR MONTHS NOW AND YOU'VE NOT LOOKED AT A SINGLE ONE WITH INTEREST UNTIL TONIGHT.
LORD AND LADY SHORTBOTTOM. IT HAS A RING TO IT, DON'T YOU THINK?

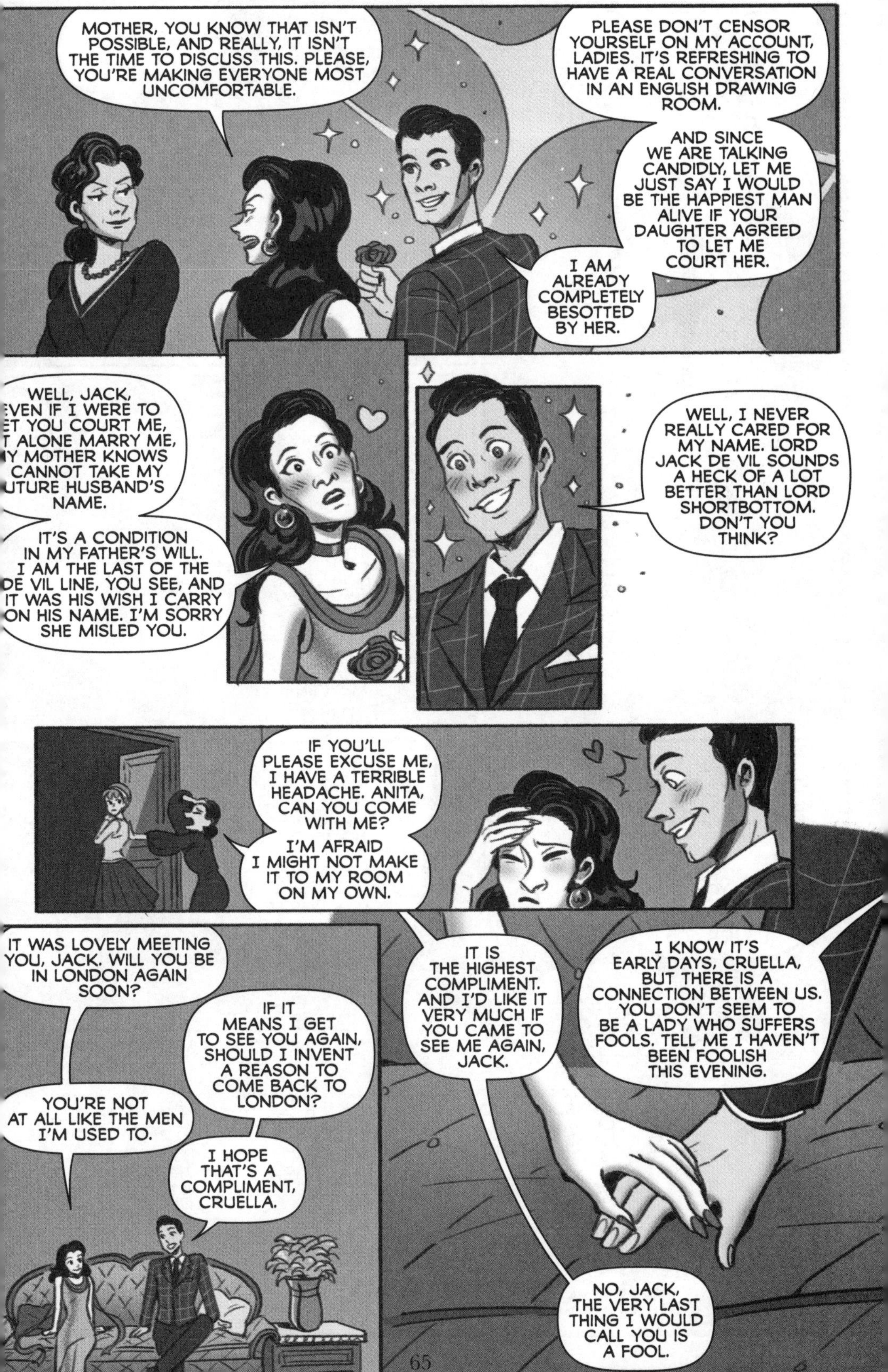
MOTHER, YOU KNOW THAT ISN'T POSSIBLE, AND REALLY, IT ISN'T THE TIME TO DISCUSS THIS. PLEASE, YOU'RE MAKING EVERYONE MOST UNCOMFORTABLE.
PLEASE DON'T CENSOR YOURSELF ON MY ACCOUNT, LADIES. IT'S REFRESHING TO HAVE A REAL CONVERSATION IN AN ENGLISH DRAWING ROOM.
AND SINCE WE ARE TALKING CANDIDLY, LET ME JUST SAY I WOULD BE THE HAPPIEST MAN ALIVE IF YOUR DAUGHTER AGREED TO LET ME COURT HER.
I AM ALREADY COMPLETELY BESOTTED BY HER.
WELL, JACK, EVEN IF I WERE TO ET YOU COURT ME, T ALONE MARRY ME, Y MOTHER KNOWS CANNOT TAKE MY UTURE HUSBAND'S NAME.
IT'S A CONDITION IN MY FATHER'S WILL. I AM THE LAST OF THE DE VIL LINE, YOU SEE, AND IT WAS HIS WISH I CARRY ON HIS NAME. I'M SORRY SHE MISLED YOU.
WELL, I NEVER REALLY CARED FOR MY NAME. LORD JACK DE VIL SOUNDS A HECK OF A LOT BETTER THAN LORD SHORTBOTTOM. DON'T YOU THINK?
IF YOU'LL PLEASE EXCUSE ME, I HAVE A TERRIBLE HEADACHE. ANITA, CAN YOU COME WITH ME?
I'M AFRAID I MIGHT NOT MAKE IT TO MY ROOM ON MY OWN.
IT WAS LOVELY MEETING YOU, JACK. WILL YOU BE IN LONDON AGAIN SOON?
IF IT MEANS I GET TO SEE YOU AGAIN, SHOULD I INVENT A REASON TO COME BACK TO LONDON?
YOU'RE NOT AT ALL LIKE THE MEN I'M USED TO.
I HOPE THAT'S A COMPLIMENT, CRUELLA.
IT IS THE HIGHEST COMPLIMENT. AND I'D LIKE IT VERY MUCH IF YOU CAME TO SEE ME AGAIN, JACK.
I KNOW IT'S EARLY DAYS, CRUELLA, BUT THERE IS A CONNECTION BETWEEN US. YOU DON'T SEEM TO BE A LADY WHO SUFFERS FOOLS. TELL ME I HAVEN'T BEEN FOOLISH THIS EVENING.
NO, JACK, THE VERY LAST THING I WOULD CALL YOU IS A FOOL.

CHAPTER ELEVEN
GOODBYE, PERDITA

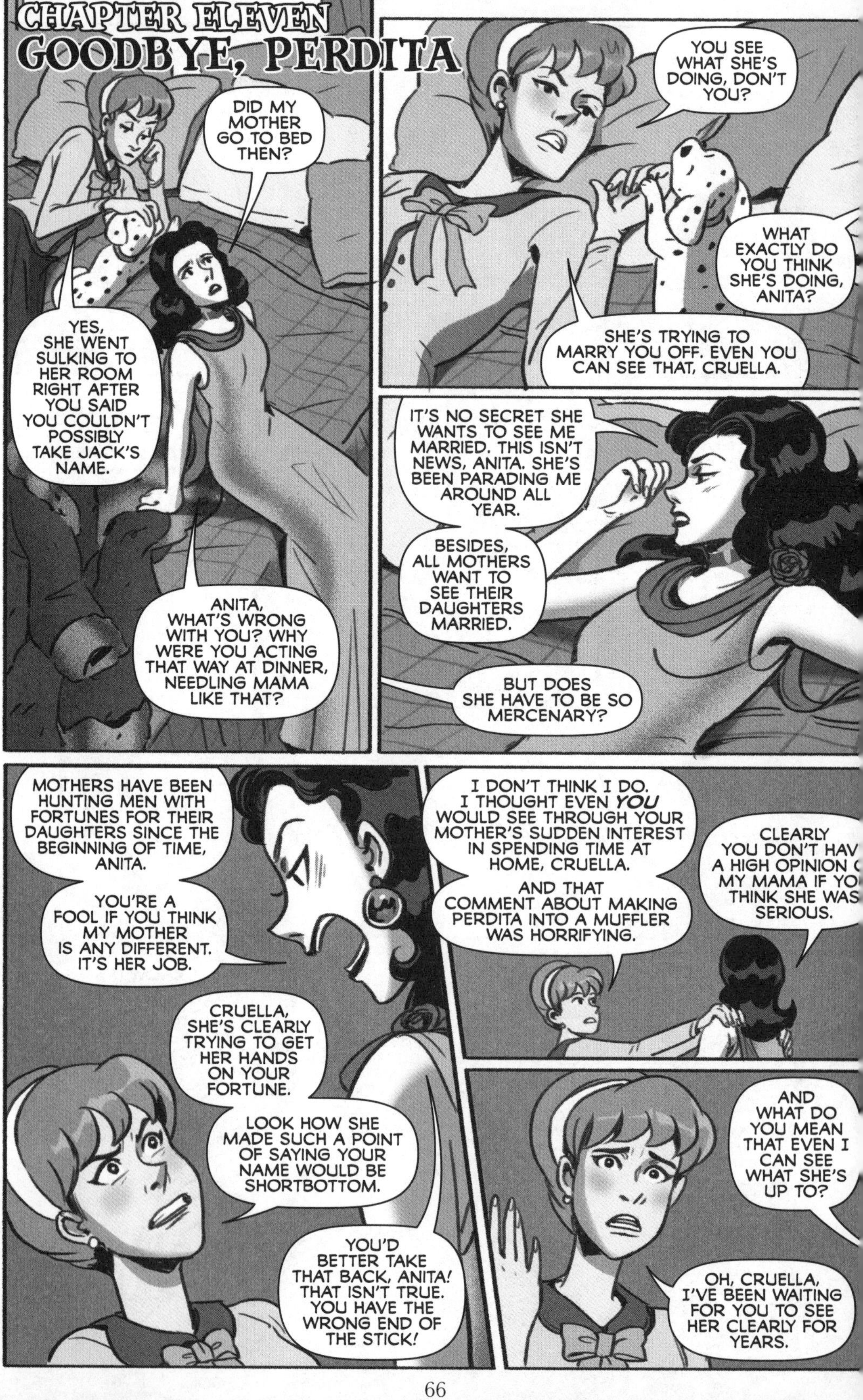
DID MY MOTHER GO TO BED THEN?
YES, SHE WENT SULKING TO HER ROOM RIGHT AFTER YOU SAID YOU COULDN'T POSSIBLY TAKE JACK'S NAME.
ANITA, WHAT'S WRONG WITH YOU? WHY WERE YOU ACTING THAT WAY AT DINNER, NEEDLING MAMA LIKE THAT?
YOU SEE WHAT SHE'S DOING, DON'T YOU?
WHAT EXACTLY DO YOU THINK SHE'S DOING, ANITA?
SHE'S TRYING TO MARRY YOU OFF. EVEN YOU CAN SEE THAT, CRUELLA.
IT'S NO SECRET SHE WANTS TO SEE ME MARRIED. THIS ISN'T NEWS, ANITA. SHE'S BEEN PARADING ME AROUND ALL YEAR.
BESIDES, ALL MOTHERS WANT TO SEE THEIR DAUGHTERS MARRIED.
BUT DOES SHE HAVE TO BE SO MERCENARY?
MOTHERS HAVE BEEN HUNTING MEN WITH FORTUNES FOR THEIR DAUGHTERS SINCE THE BEGINNING OF TIME, ANITA.
YOU'RE A FOOL IF YOU THINK MY MOTHER IS ANY DIFFERENT. IT'S HER JOB.
CRUELLA, SHE'S CLEARLY TRYING TO GET HER HANDS ON YOUR FORTUNE.
LOOK HOW SHE MADE SUCH A POINT OF SAYING YOUR NAME WOULD BE SHORTBOTTOM.
YOU'D BETTER TAKE THAT BACK, ANITA! THAT ISN'T TRUE. YOU HAVE THE WRONG END OF THE STICK!
I DON'T THINK I DO. I THOUGHT EVEN *YOU* WOULD SEE THROUGH YOUR MOTHER'S SUDDEN INTEREST IN SPENDING TIME AT HOME, CRUELLA.
AND THAT COMMENT ABOUT MAKING PERDITA INTO A MUFFLER WAS HORRIFYING.
CLEARLY YOU DON'T HAV A HIGH OPINION MY MAMA IF YO THINK SHE WAS SERIOUS.
AND WHAT DO YOU MEAN THAT EVEN I CAN SEE WHAT SHE'S UP TO?
OH, CRUELLA, I'VE BEEN WAITING FOR YOU TO SEE HER CLEARLY FOR YEARS.

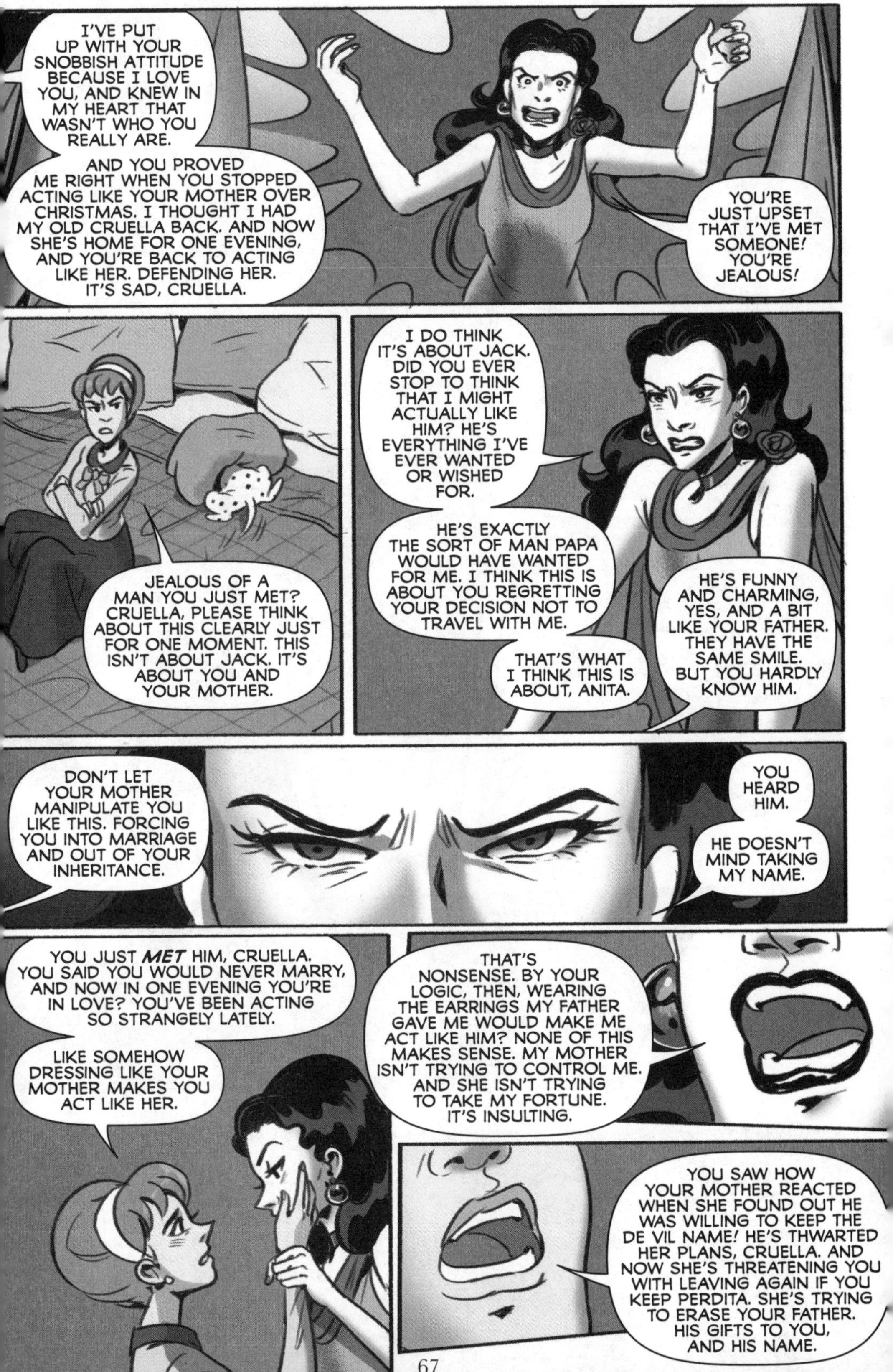
I'VE PUT UP WITH YOUR SNOBBISH ATTITUDE BECAUSE I LOVE YOU, AND KNEW IN MY HEART THAT WASN'T WHO YOU REALLY ARE.
AND YOU PROVED ME RIGHT WHEN YOU STOPPED ACTING LIKE YOUR MOTHER OVER CHRISTMAS. I THOUGHT I HAD MY OLD CRUELLA BACK. AND NOW SHE'S HOME FOR ONE EVENING, AND YOU'RE BACK TO ACTING LIKE HER. DEFENDING HER. IT'S SAD, CRUELLA.
YOU'RE JUST UPSET THAT I'VE MET SOMEONE! YOU'RE JEALOUS!
JEALOUS OF A MAN YOU JUST MET? CRUELLA, PLEASE THINK ABOUT THIS CLEARLY JUST FOR ONE MOMENT. THIS ISN'T ABOUT JACK. IT'S ABOUT YOU AND YOUR MOTHER.
I DO THINK IT'S ABOUT JACK. DID YOU EVER STOP TO THINK THAT I MIGHT ACTUALLY LIKE HIM? HE'S EVERYTHING I'VE EVER WANTED OR WISHED FOR.
HE'S EXACTLY THE SORT OF MAN PAPA WOULD HAVE WANTED FOR ME. I THINK THIS IS ABOUT YOU REGRETTING YOUR DECISION NOT TO TRAVEL WITH ME.
THAT'S WHAT I THINK THIS IS ABOUT, ANITA.
HE'S FUNNY AND CHARMING, YES, AND A BIT LIKE YOUR FATHER. THEY HAVE THE SAME SMILE. BUT YOU HARDLY KNOW HIM.
DON'T LET YOUR MOTHER MANIPULATE YOU LIKE THIS. FORCING YOU INTO MARRIAGE AND OUT OF YOUR INHERITANCE.
YOU HEARD HIM.
HE DOESN'T MIND TAKING MY NAME.
YOU JUST *MET* HIM, CRUELLA. YOU SAID YOU WOULD NEVER MARRY, AND NOW IN ONE EVENING YOU'RE IN LOVE? YOU'VE BEEN ACTING SO STRANGELY LATELY.
LIKE SOMEHOW DRESSING LIKE YOUR MOTHER MAKES YOU ACT LIKE HER.
THAT'S NONSENSE. BY YOUR LOGIC, THEN, WEARING THE EARRINGS MY FATHER GAVE ME WOULD MAKE ME ACT LIKE HIM? NONE OF THIS MAKES SENSE. MY MOTHER ISN'T TRYING TO CONTROL ME. AND SHE ISN'T TRYING TO TAKE MY FORTUNE. IT'S INSULTING.
YOU SAW HOW YOUR MOTHER REACTED WHEN SHE FOUND OUT HE WAS WILLING TO KEEP THE DE VIL NAME! HE'S THWARTED HER PLANS, CRUELLA. AND NOW SHE'S THREATENING YOU WITH LEAVING AGAIN IF YOU KEEP PERDITA. SHE'S TRYING TO ERASE YOUR FATHER. HIS GIFTS TO YOU, AND HIS NAME.

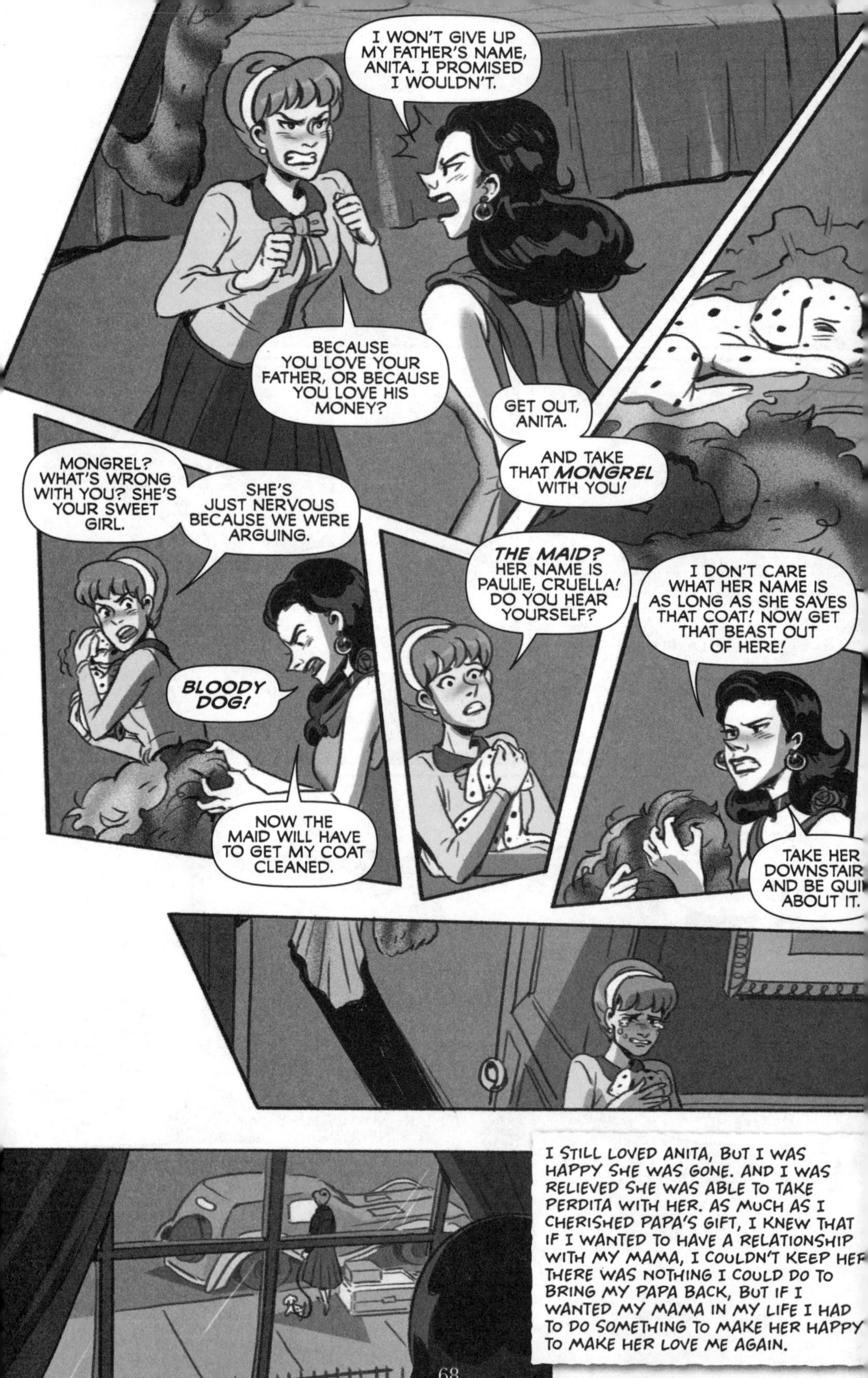
I WON'T GIVE UP MY FATHER'S NAME, ANITA. I PROMISED I WOULDN'T.
BECAUSE YOU LOVE YOUR FATHER, OR BECAUSE YOU LOVE HIS MONEY?
GET OUT, ANITA.
AND TAKE THAT *MONGREL* WITH YOU!
MONGREL? WHAT'S WRONG WITH YOU? SHE'S YOUR SWEET GIRL.
SHE'S JUST NERVOUS BECAUSE WE WERE ARGUING.
BLOODY DOG!
NOW THE MAID WILL HAVE TO GET MY COAT CLEANED.
THE MAID? HER NAME IS PAULIE, CRUELLA! DO YOU HEAR YOURSELF?
I DON'T CARE WHAT HER NAME IS AS LONG AS SHE SAVES THAT COAT! NOW GET THAT BEAST OUT OF HERE!
TAKE HER DOWNSTAIR AND BE QUI ABOUT IT.
I STILL LOVED ANITA, BUT I WAS HAPPY SHE WAS GONE. AND I WAS RELIEVED SHE WAS ABLE TO TAKE PERDITA WITH HER. AS MUCH AS I CHERISHED PAPA'S GIFT, I KNEW THAT IF I WANTED TO HAVE A RELATIONSHIP WITH MY MAMA, I COULDN'T KEEP HER THERE WAS NOTHING I COULD DO TO BRING MY PAPA BACK, BUT IF I WANTED MY MAMA IN MY LIFE I HAD TO DO SOMETHING TO MAKE HER HAPPY TO MAKE HER LOVE ME AGAIN.

HAPTER TWELVE
ICKTOCK

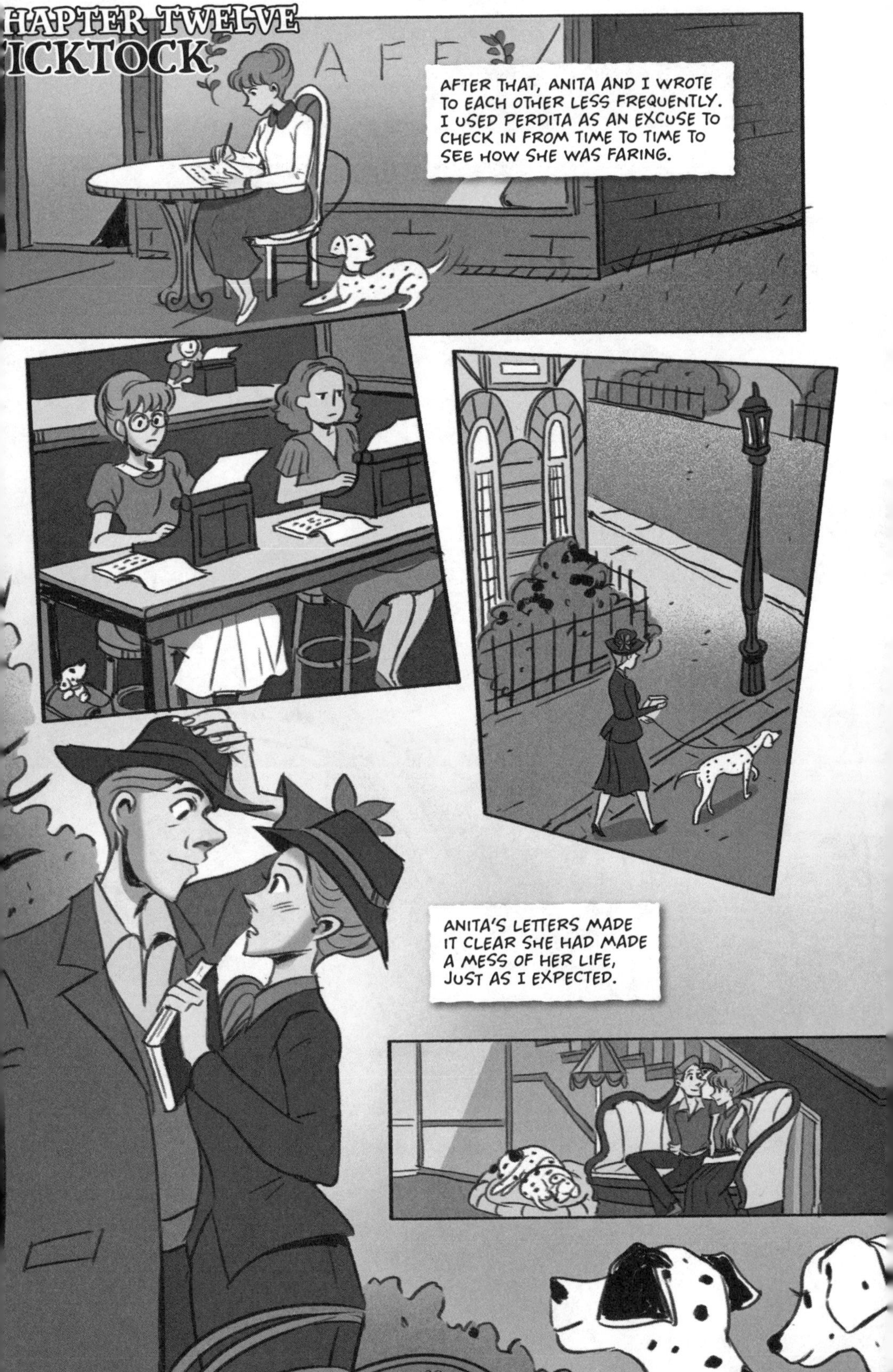
AFTER THAT, ANITA AND I WROTE TO EACH OTHER LESS FREQUENTLY. I USED PERDITA AS AN EXCUSE TO CHECK IN FROM TIME TO TIME TO SEE HOW SHE WAS FARING.
ANITA'S LETTERS MADE IT CLEAR SHE HAD MADE A MESS OF HER LIFE, JUST AS I EXPECTED.

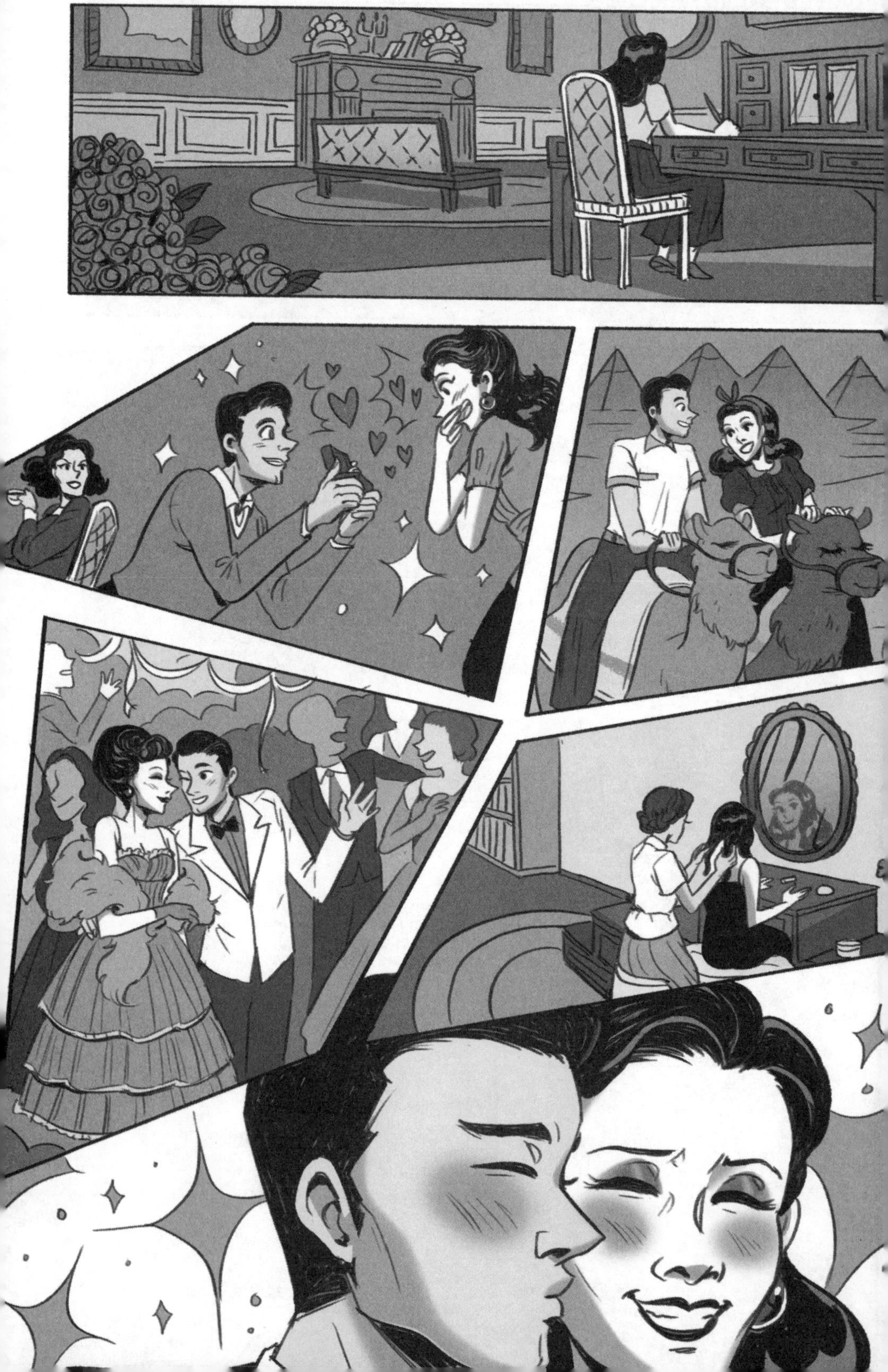

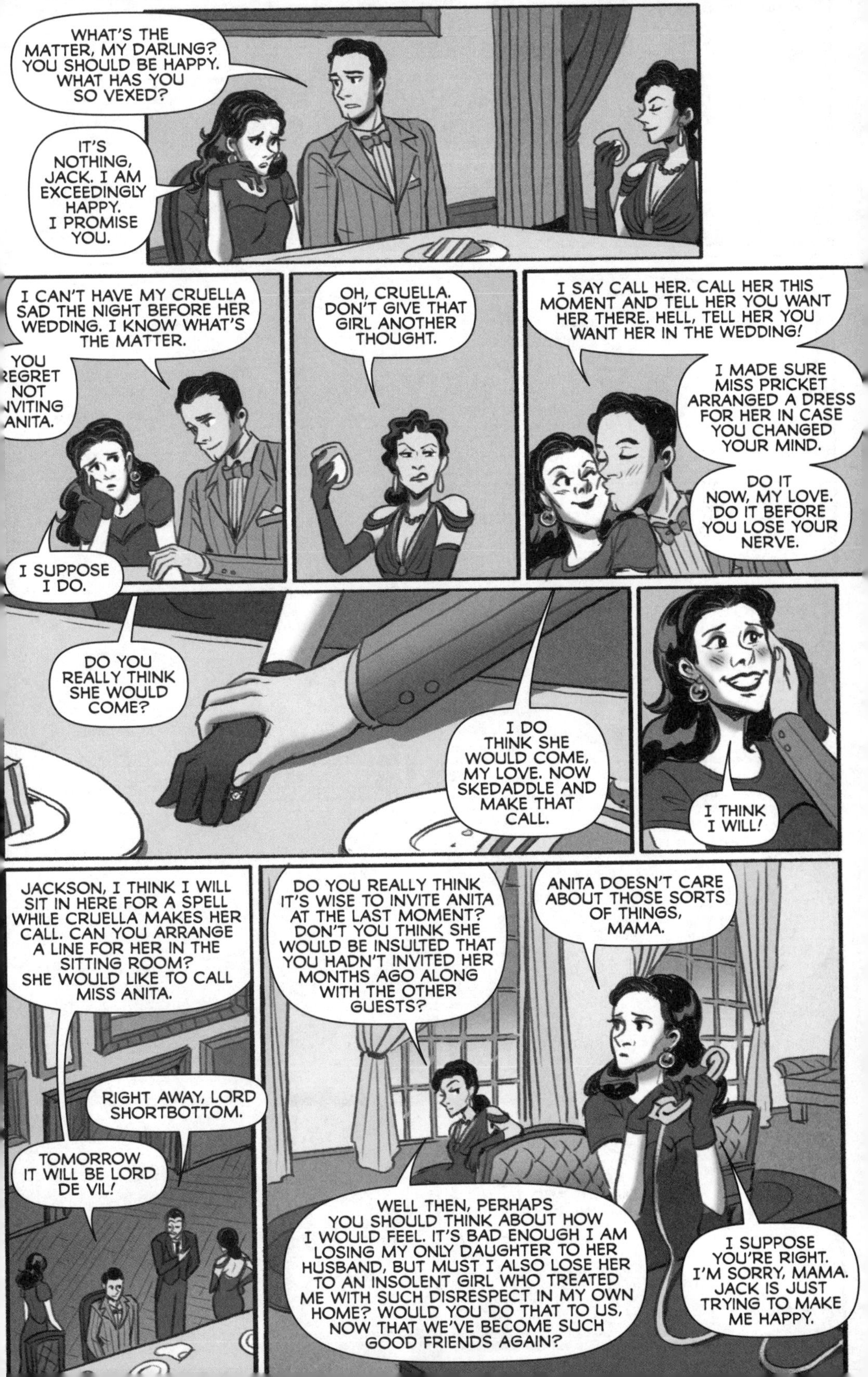
WHAT'S THE MATTER, MY DARLING? YOU SHOULD BE HAPPY. WHAT HAS YOU SO VEXED?
IT'S NOTHING, JACK. I AM EXCEEDINGLY HAPPY. I PROMISE YOU.
I CAN'T HAVE MY CRUELLA SAD THE NIGHT BEFORE HER WEDDING. I KNOW WHAT'S THE MATTER.
YOU REGRET NOT INVITING ANITA.
I SUPPOSE I DO.
OH, CRUELLA. DON'T GIVE THAT GIRL ANOTHER THOUGHT.
I SAY CALL HER. CALL HER THIS MOMENT AND TELL HER YOU WANT HER THERE. HELL, TELL HER YOU WANT HER IN THE WEDDING!
I MADE SURE MISS PRICKET ARRANGED A DRESS FOR HER IN CASE YOU CHANGED YOUR MIND.
DO IT NOW, MY LOVE. DO IT BEFORE YOU LOSE YOUR NERVE.
DO YOU REALLY THINK SHE WOULD COME?
I DO THINK SHE WOULD COME, MY LOVE. NOW SKEDADDLE AND MAKE THAT CALL.
I THINK I WILL!
JACKSON, I THINK I WILL SIT IN HERE FOR A SPELL WHILE CRUELLA MAKES HER CALL. CAN YOU ARRANGE A LINE FOR HER IN THE SITTING ROOM? SHE WOULD LIKE TO CALL MISS ANITA.
RIGHT AWAY, LORD SHORTBOTTOM.
TOMORROW IT WILL BE LORD DE VIL!
DO YOU REALLY THINK IT'S WISE TO INVITE ANITA AT THE LAST MOMENT? DON'T YOU THINK SHE WOULD BE INSULTED THAT YOU HADN'T INVITED HER MONTHS AGO ALONG WITH THE OTHER GUESTS?
ANITA DOESN'T CARE ABOUT THOSE SORTS OF THINGS, MAMA.
WELL THEN, PERHAPS YOU SHOULD THINK ABOUT HOW I WOULD FEEL. IT'S BAD ENOUGH I AM LOSING MY ONLY DAUGHTER TO HER HUSBAND, BUT MUST I ALSO LOSE HER TO AN INSOLENT GIRL WHO TREATED ME WITH SUCH DISRESPECT IN MY OWN HOME? WOULD YOU DO THAT TO US, NOW THAT WE'VE BECOME SUCH GOOD FRIENDS AGAIN?
I SUPPOSE YOU'RE RIGHT. I'M SORRY, MAMA. JACK IS JUST TRYING TO MAKE ME HAPPY.

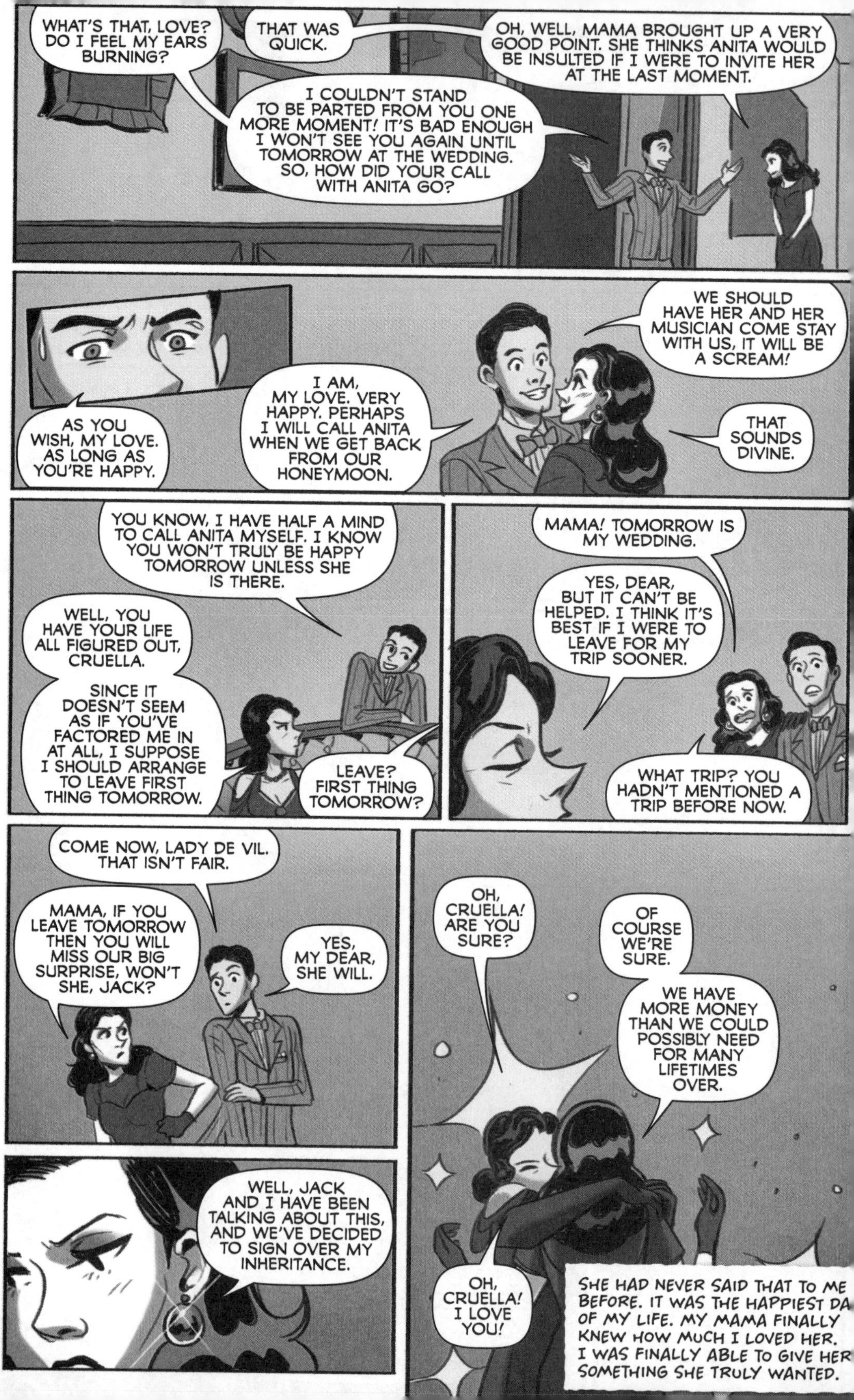
WHAT'S THAT, LOVE? DO I FEEL MY EARS BURNING?
THAT WAS QUICK.
I COULDN'T STAND TO BE PARTED FROM YOU ONE MORE MOMENT! IT'S BAD ENOUGH I WON'T SEE YOU AGAIN UNTIL TOMORROW AT THE WEDDING. SO, HOW DID YOUR CALL WITH ANITA GO?
OH, WELL, MAMA BROUGHT UP A VERY GOOD POINT. SHE THINKS ANITA WOULD BE INSULTED IF I WERE TO INVITE HER AT THE LAST MOMENT.
AS YOU WISH, MY LOVE. AS LONG AS YOU'RE HAPPY.
I AM, MY LOVE. VERY HAPPY. PERHAPS I WILL CALL ANITA WHEN WE GET BACK FROM OUR HONEYMOON.
WE SHOULD HAVE HER AND HER MUSICIAN COME STAY WITH US, IT WILL BE A SCREAM!
THAT SOUNDS DIVINE.
YOU KNOW, I HAVE HALF A MIND TO CALL ANITA MYSELF. I KNOW YOU WON'T TRULY BE HAPPY TOMORROW UNLESS SHE IS THERE.
WELL, YOU HAVE YOUR LIFE ALL FIGURED OUT, CRUELLA.
SINCE IT DOESN'T SEEM AS IF YOU'VE FACTORED ME IN AT ALL, I SUPPOSE I SHOULD ARRANGE TO LEAVE FIRST THING TOMORROW.
LEAVE? FIRST THING TOMORROW?
MAMA! TOMORROW IS MY WEDDING.
YES, DEAR, BUT IT CAN'T BE HELPED. I THINK IT'S BEST IF I WERE TO LEAVE FOR MY TRIP SOONER.
WHAT TRIP? YOU HADN'T MENTIONED A TRIP BEFORE NOW.
COME NOW, LADY DE VIL. THAT ISN'T FAIR.
MAMA, IF YOU LEAVE TOMORROW THEN YOU WILL MISS OUR BIG SURPRISE, WON'T SHE, JACK?
YES, MY DEAR, SHE WILL.
WELL, JACK AND I HAVE BEEN TALKING ABOUT THIS, AND WE'VE DECIDED TO SIGN OVER MY INHERITANCE.
OH, CRUELLA! ARE YOU SURE?
OF COURSE WE'RE SURE.
WE HAVE MORE MONEY THAN WE COULD POSSIBLY NEED FOR MANY LIFETIMES OVER.
OH, CRUELLA! I LOVE YOU!
SHE HAD NEVER SAID THAT TO ME BEFORE. IT WAS THE HAPPIEST DA[Y] OF MY LIFE. MY MAMA FINALLY KNEW HOW MUCH I LOVED HER. I WAS FINALLY ABLE TO GIVE HER SOMETHING SHE TRULY WANTED.

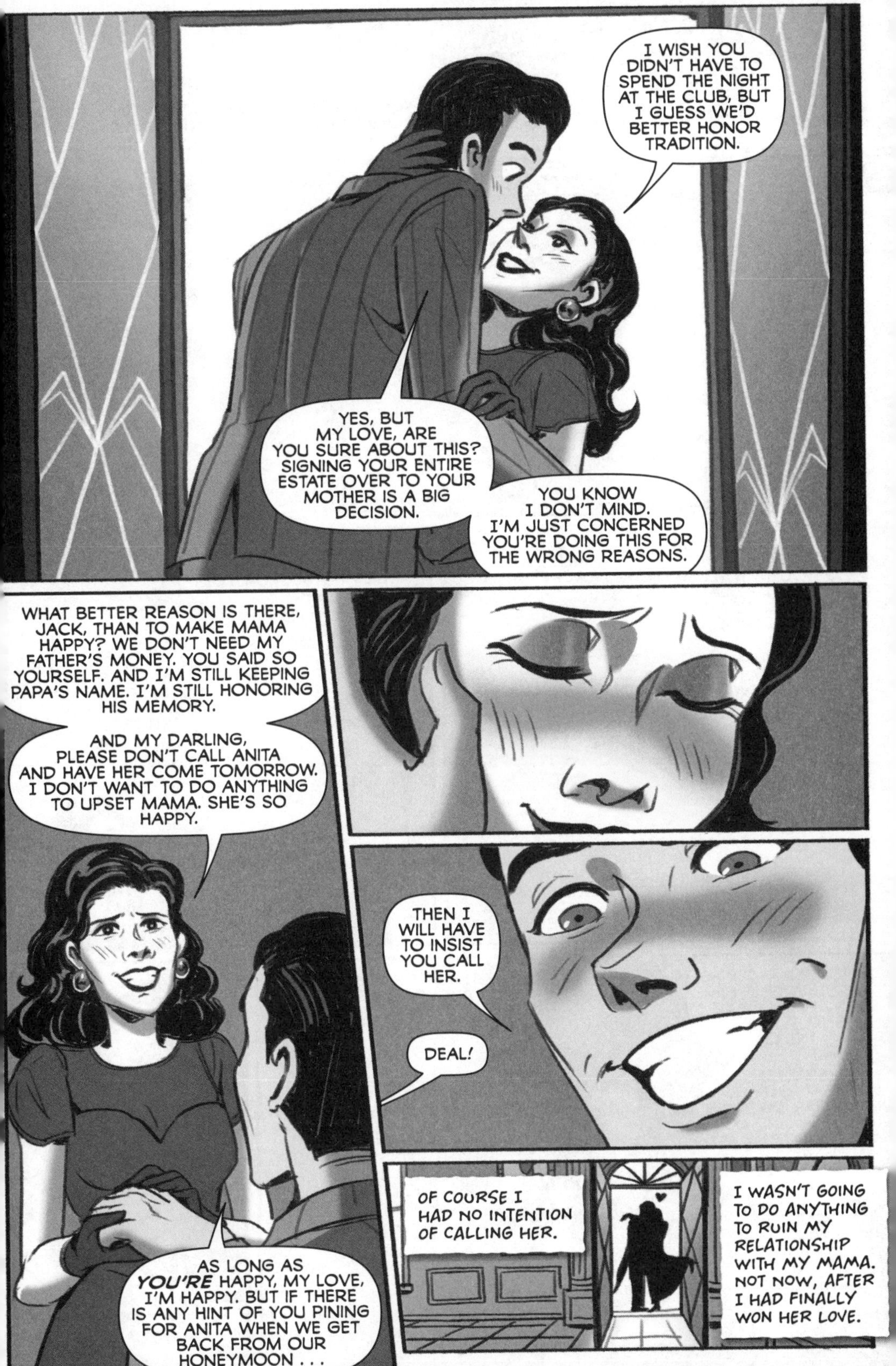
I WISH YOU DIDN'T HAVE TO SPEND THE NIGHT AT THE CLUB, BUT I GUESS WE'D BETTER HONOR TRADITION.
YES, BUT MY LOVE, ARE YOU SURE ABOUT THIS? SIGNING YOUR ENTIRE ESTATE OVER TO YOUR MOTHER IS A BIG DECISION.
YOU KNOW I DON'T MIND. I'M JUST CONCERNED YOU'RE DOING THIS FOR THE WRONG REASONS.
WHAT BETTER REASON IS THERE, JACK, THAN TO MAKE MAMA HAPPY? WE DON'T NEED MY FATHER'S MONEY. YOU SAID SO YOURSELF. AND I'M STILL KEEPING PAPA'S NAME. I'M STILL HONORING HIS MEMORY.
AND MY DARLING, PLEASE DON'T CALL ANITA AND HAVE HER COME TOMORROW. I DON'T WANT TO DO ANYTHING TO UPSET MAMA. SHE'S SO HAPPY.
AS LONG AS *YOU'RE* HAPPY, MY LOVE, I'M HAPPY. BUT IF THERE IS ANY HINT OF YOU PINING FOR ANITA WHEN WE GET BACK FROM OUR HONEYMOON . . .
THEN I WILL HAVE TO INSIST YOU CALL HER.
DEAL!
OF COURSE I HAD NO INTENTION OF CALLING HER.
I WASN'T GOING TO DO ANYTHING TO RUIN MY RELATIONSHIP WITH MY MAMA. NOT NOW, AFTER I HAD FINALLY WON HER LOVE.

CHAPTER THIRTEEN
SIR HUNTLEY'S RESERVATIONS

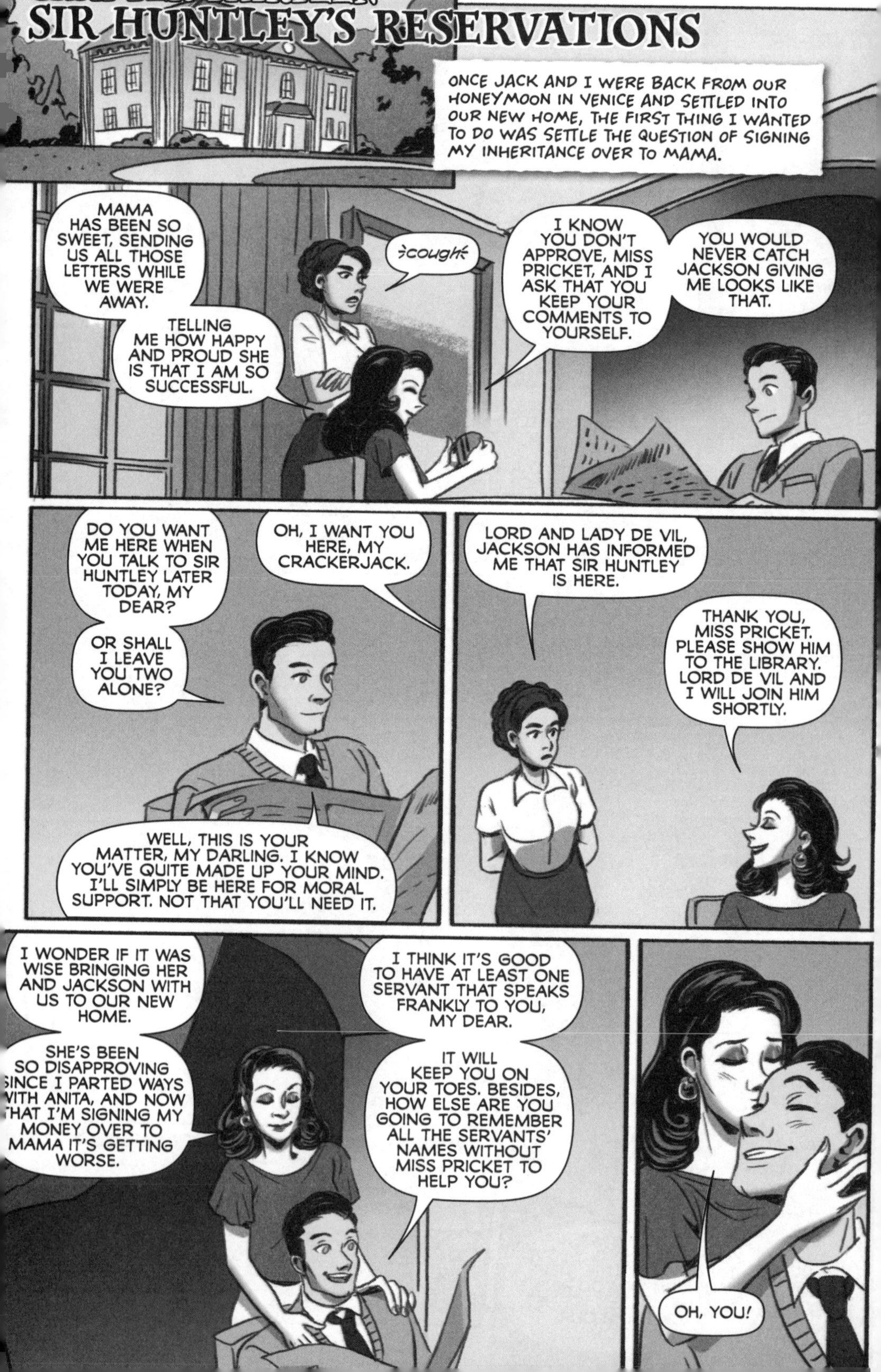
ONCE JACK AND I WERE BACK FROM OUR HONEYMOON IN VENICE AND SETTLED INTO OUR NEW HOME, THE FIRST THING I WANTED TO DO WAS SETTLE THE QUESTION OF SIGNING MY INHERITANCE OVER TO MAMA.
MAMA HAS BEEN SO SWEET, SENDING US ALL THOSE LETTERS WHILE WE WERE AWAY.
TELLING ME HOW HAPPY AND PROUD SHE IS THAT I AM SO SUCCESSFUL.
cough
I KNOW YOU DON'T APPROVE, MISS PRICKET, AND I ASK THAT YOU KEEP YOUR COMMENTS TO YOURSELF.
YOU WOULD NEVER CATCH JACKSON GIVING ME LOOKS LIKE THAT.
DO YOU WANT ME HERE WHEN YOU TALK TO SIR HUNTLEY LATER TODAY, MY DEAR?
OR SHALL I LEAVE YOU TWO ALONE?
OH, I WANT YOU HERE, MY CRACKERJACK.
WELL, THIS IS YOUR MATTER, MY DARLING. I KNOW YOU'VE QUITE MADE UP YOUR MIND. I'LL SIMPLY BE HERE FOR MORAL SUPPORT. NOT THAT YOU'LL NEED IT.
LORD AND LADY DE VIL, JACKSON HAS INFORMED ME THAT SIR HUNTLEY IS HERE.
THANK YOU, MISS PRICKET. PLEASE SHOW HIM TO THE LIBRARY. LORD DE VIL AND I WILL JOIN HIM SHORTLY.
I WONDER IF IT WAS WISE BRINGING HER AND JACKSON WITH US TO OUR NEW HOME.
SHE'S BEEN SO DISAPPROVING SINCE I PARTED WAYS WITH ANITA, AND NOW THAT I'M SIGNING MY MONEY OVER TO MAMA IT'S GETTING WORSE.
I THINK IT'S GOOD TO HAVE AT LEAST ONE SERVANT THAT SPEAKS FRANKLY TO YOU, MY DEAR.
IT WILL KEEP YOU ON YOUR TOES. BESIDES, HOW ELSE ARE YOU GOING TO REMEMBER ALL THE SERVANTS' NAMES WITHOUT MISS PRICKET TO HELP YOU?
OH, YOU!

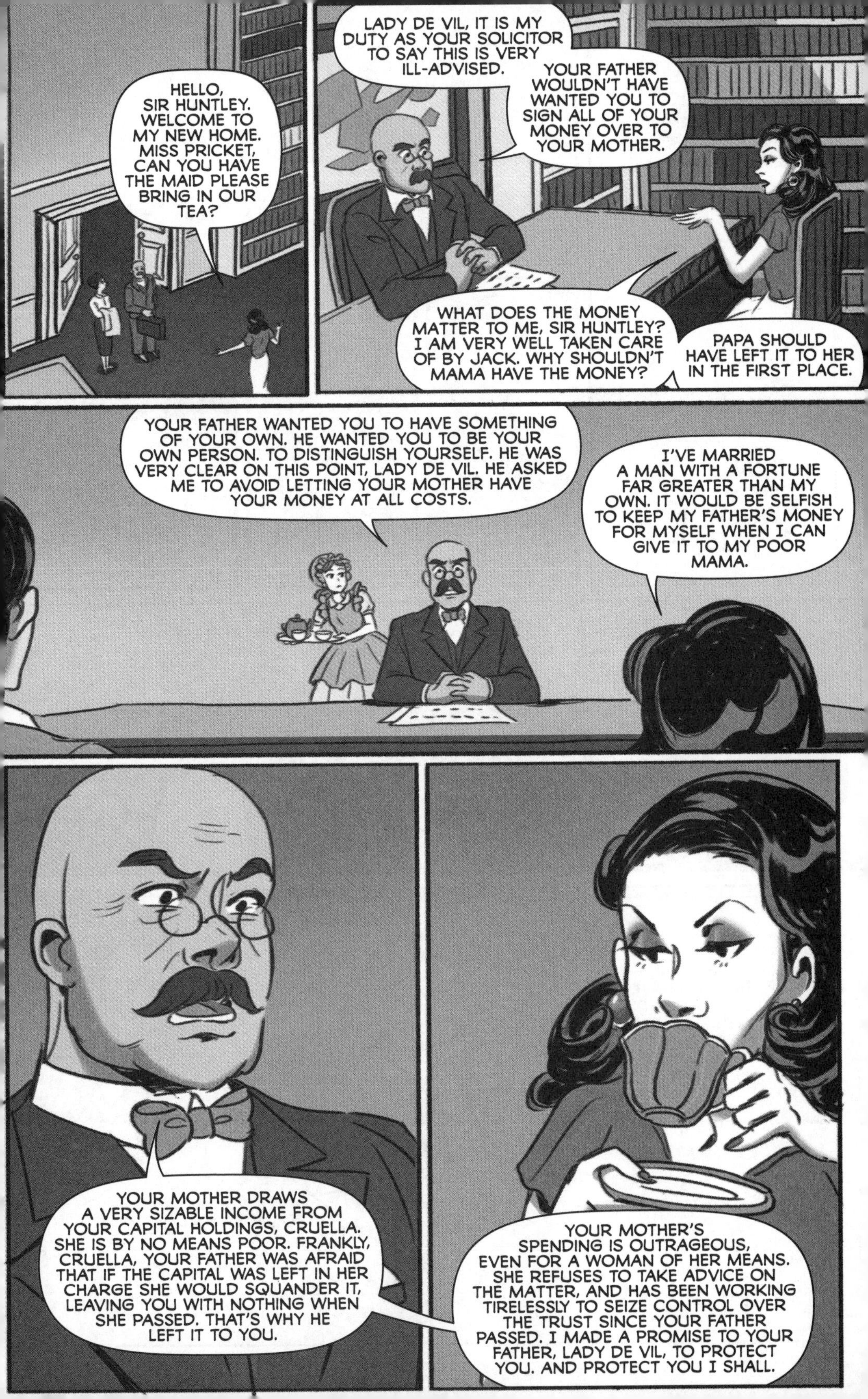
HELLO, SIR HUNTLEY. WELCOME TO MY NEW HOME. MISS PRICKET, CAN YOU HAVE THE MAID PLEASE BRING IN OUR TEA?
LADY DE VIL, IT IS MY DUTY AS YOUR SOLICITOR TO SAY THIS IS VERY ILL-ADVISED.
YOUR FATHER WOULDN'T HAVE WANTED YOU TO SIGN ALL OF YOUR MONEY OVER TO YOUR MOTHER.
WHAT DOES THE MONEY MATTER TO ME, SIR HUNTLEY? I AM VERY WELL TAKEN CARE OF BY JACK. WHY SHOULDN'T MAMA HAVE THE MONEY?
PAPA SHOULD HAVE LEFT IT TO HER IN THE FIRST PLACE.
YOUR FATHER WANTED YOU TO HAVE SOMETHING OF YOUR OWN. HE WANTED YOU TO BE YOUR OWN PERSON. TO DISTINGUISH YOURSELF. HE WAS VERY CLEAR ON THIS POINT, LADY DE VIL. HE ASKED ME TO AVOID LETTING YOUR MOTHER HAVE YOUR MONEY AT ALL COSTS.
I'VE MARRIED A MAN WITH A FORTUNE FAR GREATER THAN MY OWN. IT WOULD BE SELFISH TO KEEP MY FATHER'S MONEY FOR MYSELF WHEN I CAN GIVE IT TO MY POOR MAMA.
YOUR MOTHER DRAWS A VERY SIZABLE INCOME FROM YOUR CAPITAL HOLDINGS, CRUELLA. SHE IS BY NO MEANS POOR. FRANKLY, CRUELLA, YOUR FATHER WAS AFRAID THAT IF THE CAPITAL WAS LEFT IN HER CHARGE SHE WOULD SQUANDER IT, LEAVING YOU WITH NOTHING WHEN SHE PASSED. THAT'S WHY HE LEFT IT TO YOU.
YOUR MOTHER'S SPENDING IS OUTRAGEOUS, EVEN FOR A WOMAN OF HER MEANS. SHE REFUSES TO TAKE ADVICE ON THE MATTER, AND HAS BEEN WORKING TIRELESSLY TO SEIZE CONTROL OVER THE TRUST SINCE YOUR FATHER PASSED. I MADE A PROMISE TO YOUR FATHER, LADY DE VIL, TO PROTECT YOU. AND PROTECT YOU I SHALL.

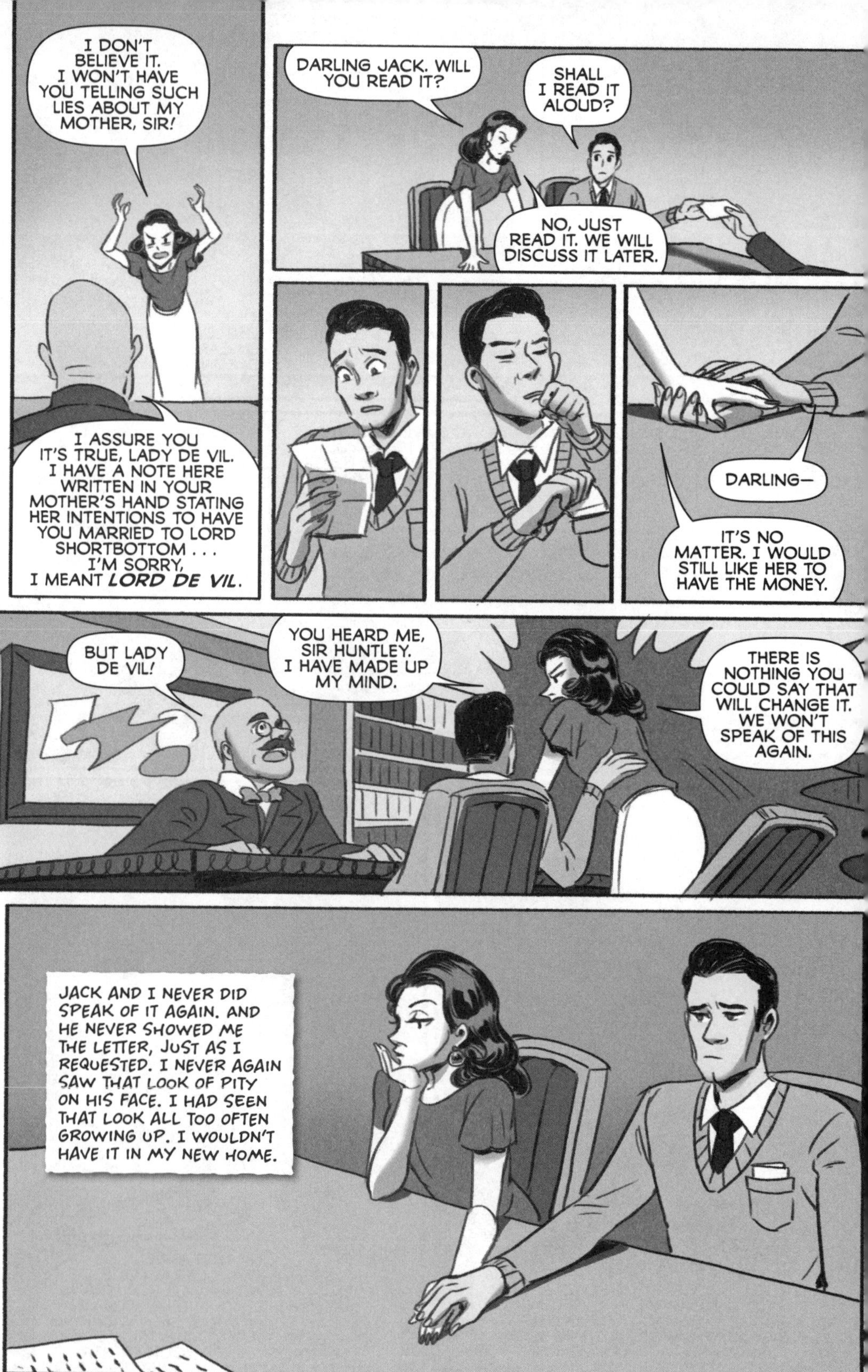
I DON'T BELIEVE IT. I WON'T HAVE YOU TELLING SUCH LIES ABOUT MY MOTHER, SIR!
I ASSURE YOU IT'S TRUE, LADY DE VIL. I HAVE A NOTE HERE WRITTEN IN YOUR MOTHER'S HAND STATING HER INTENTIONS TO HAVE YOU MARRIED TO LORD SHORTBOTTOM . . . I'M SORRY, I MEANT **LORD DE VIL**.
DARLING JACK. WILL YOU READ IT?
SHALL I READ IT ALOUD?
NO, JUST READ IT. WE WILL DISCUSS IT LATER.
DARLING—
IT'S NO MATTER. I WOULD STILL LIKE HER TO HAVE THE MONEY.
BUT LADY DE VIL!
YOU HEARD ME, SIR HUNTLEY. I HAVE MADE UP MY MIND.
THERE IS NOTHING YOU COULD SAY THAT WILL CHANGE IT. WE WON'T SPEAK OF THIS AGAIN.
JACK AND I NEVER DID SPEAK OF IT AGAIN. AND HE NEVER SHOWED ME THE LETTER, JUST AS I REQUESTED. I NEVER AGAIN SAW THAT LOOK OF PITY ON HIS FACE. I HAD SEEN THAT LOOK ALL TOO OFTEN GROWING UP. I WOULDN'T HAVE IT IN MY NEW HOME.

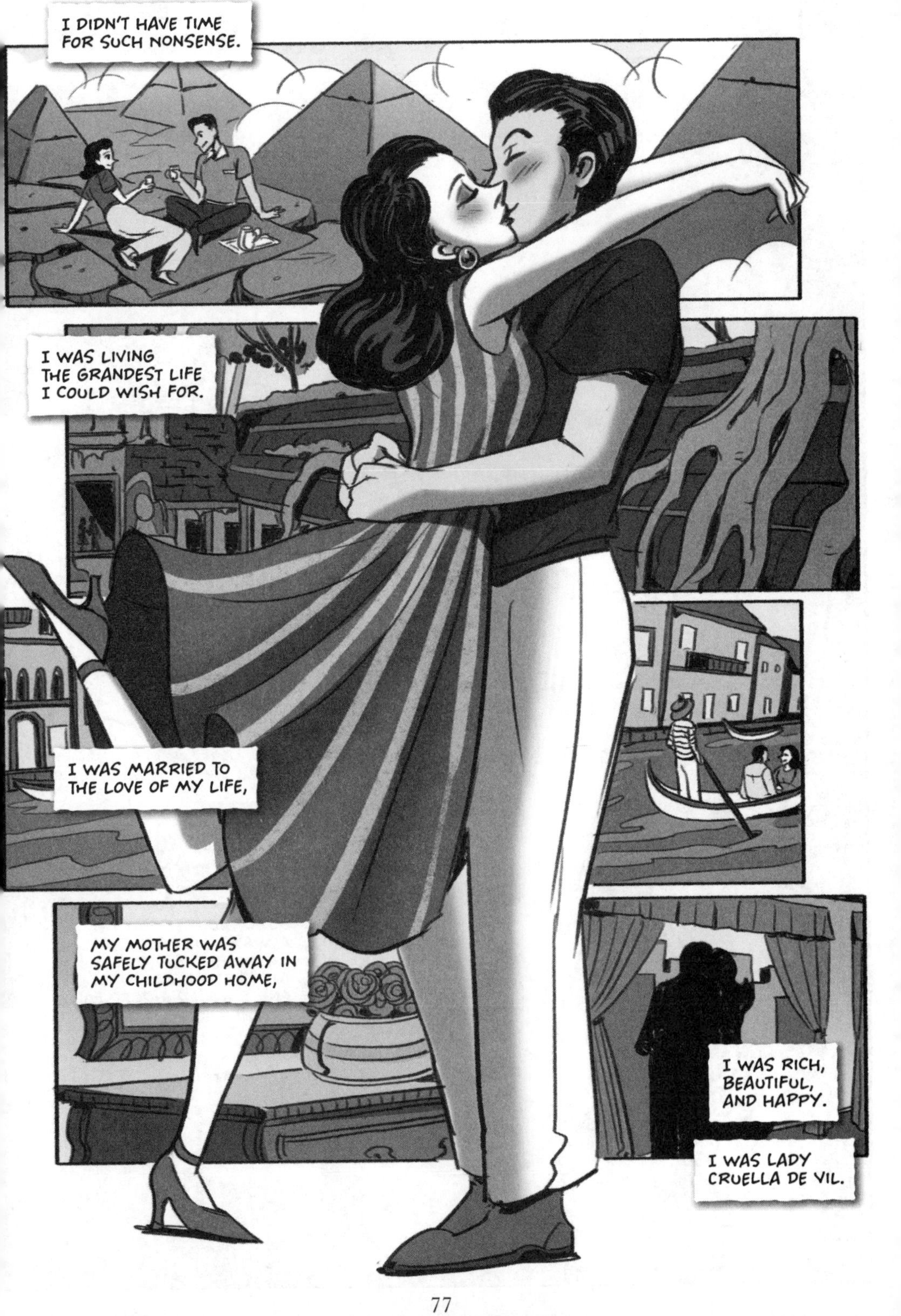
I DIDN'T HAVE TIME FOR SUCH NONSENSE.
I WAS LIVING THE GRANDEST LIFE I COULD WISH FOR.
I WAS MARRIED TO THE LOVE OF MY LIFE,
MY MOTHER WAS SAFELY TUCKED AWAY IN MY CHILDHOOD HOME,
I WAS RICH, BEAUTIFUL, AND HAPPY.
I WAS LADY CRUELLA DE VIL.

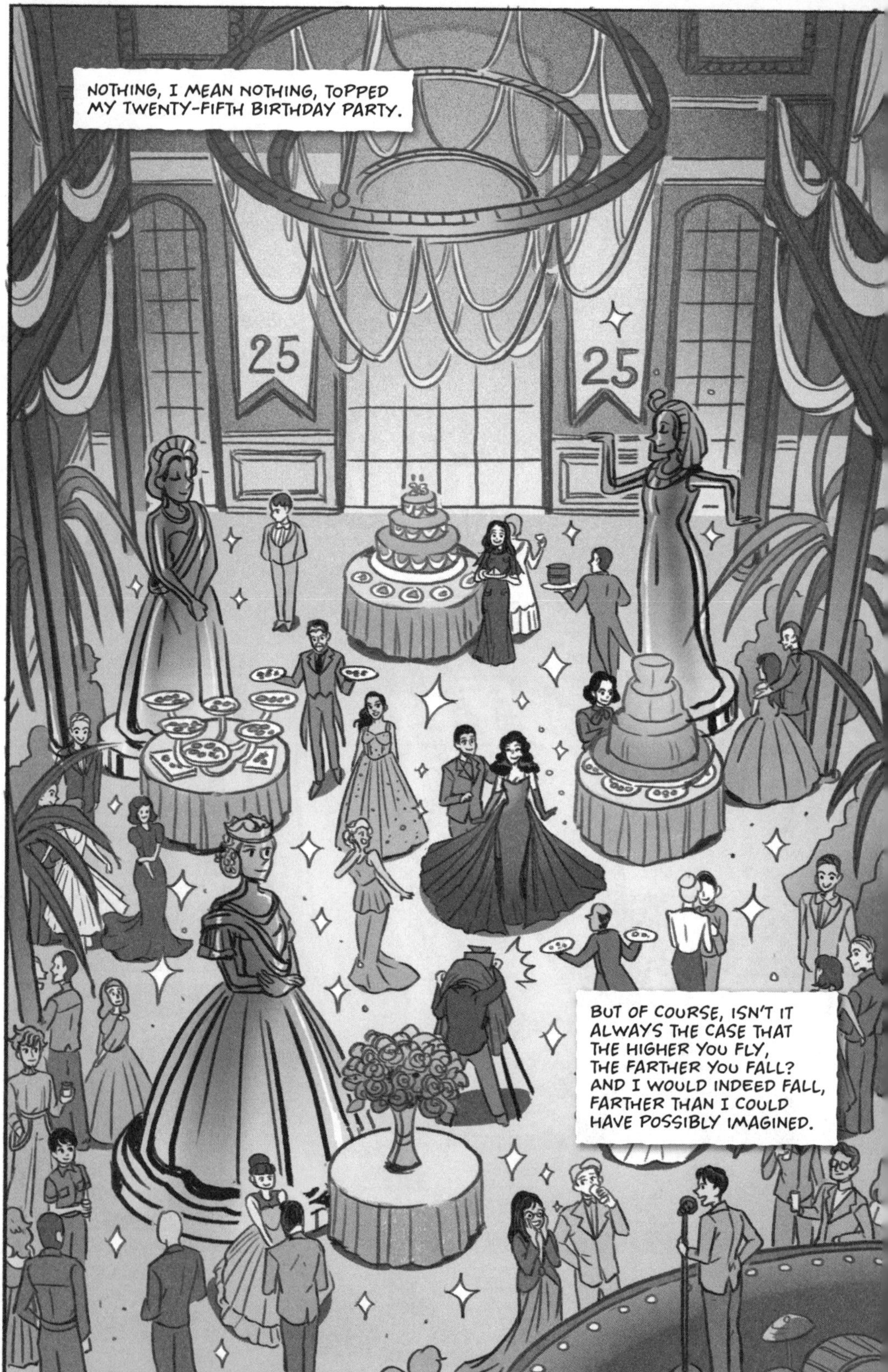
NOTHING, I MEAN NOTHING, TOPPED MY TWENTY-FIFTH BIRTHDAY PARTY.
25
25
BUT OF COURSE, ISN'T IT ALWAYS THE CASE THAT THE HIGHER YOU FLY, THE FARTHER YOU FALL? AND I WOULD INDEED FALL, FARTHER THAN I COULD HAVE POSSIBLY IMAGINED.

CHAPTER FOURTEEN
THE LITTLE BLACK DRESS

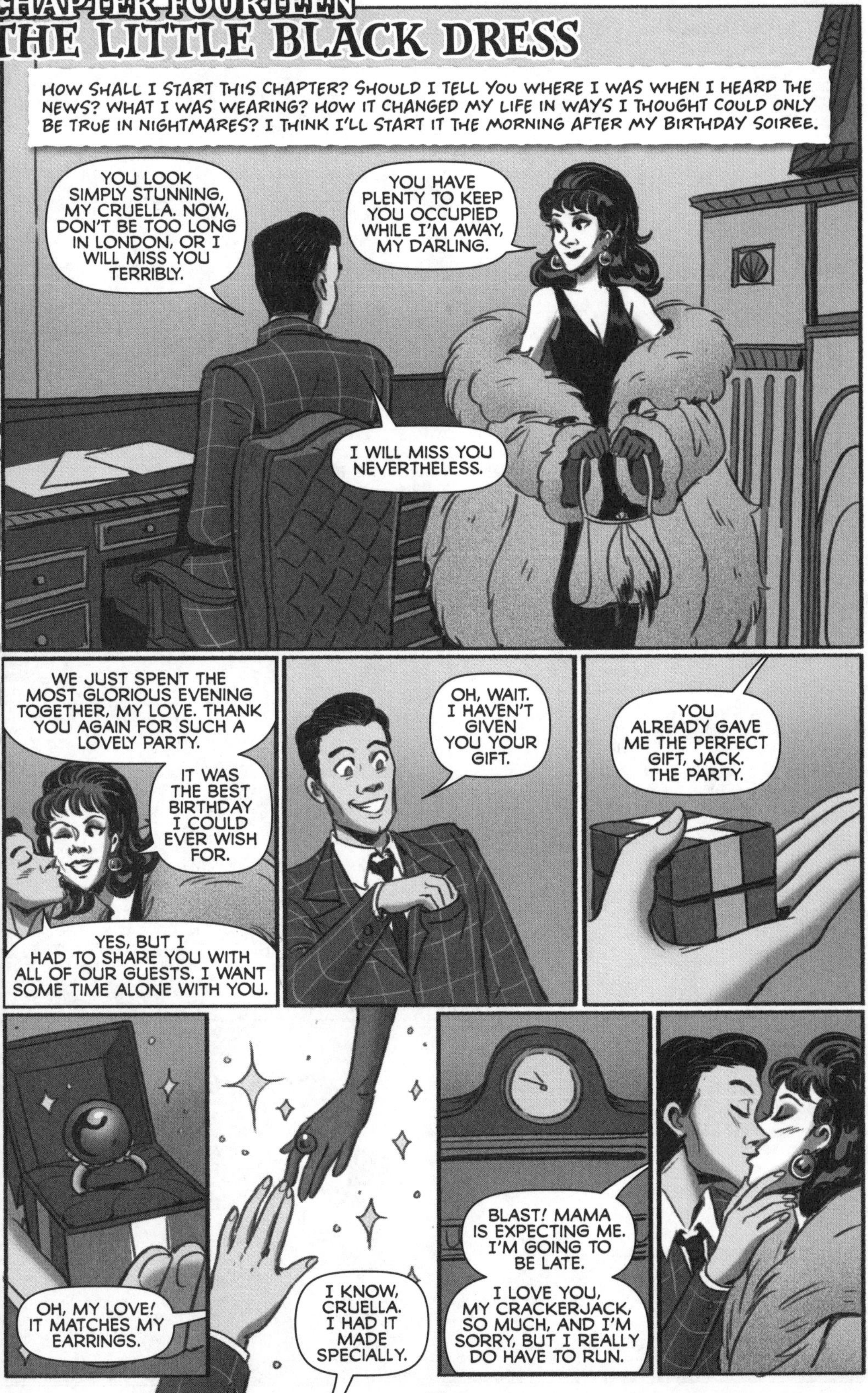

HOW SHALL I START THIS CHAPTER? SHOULD I TELL YOU WHERE I WAS WHEN I HEARD THE NEWS? WHAT I WAS WEARING? HOW IT CHANGED MY LIFE IN WAYS I THOUGHT COULD ONLY BE TRUE IN NIGHTMARES? I THINK I'LL START IT THE MORNING AFTER MY BIRTHDAY SOIREE.
YOU LOOK SIMPLY STUNNING, MY CRUELLA. NOW, DON'T BE TOO LONG IN LONDON, OR I WILL MISS YOU TERRIBLY.
YOU HAVE PLENTY TO KEEP YOU OCCUPIED WHILE I'M AWAY, MY DARLING.
I WILL MISS YOU NEVERTHELESS.
WE JUST SPENT THE MOST GLORIOUS EVENING TOGETHER, MY LOVE. THANK YOU AGAIN FOR SUCH A LOVELY PARTY.
IT WAS THE BEST BIRTHDAY I COULD EVER WISH FOR.
YES, BUT I HAD TO SHARE YOU WITH ALL OF OUR GUESTS. I WANT SOME TIME ALONE WITH YOU.
OH, WAIT. I HAVEN'T GIVEN YOU YOUR GIFT.
YOU ALREADY GAVE ME THE PERFECT GIFT, JACK. THE PARTY.
OH, MY LOVE! IT MATCHES MY EARRINGS.
I KNOW, CRUELLA. I HAD IT MADE SPECIALLY.
BLAST! MAMA IS EXPECTING ME. I'M GOING TO BE LATE.
I LOVE YOU, MY CRACKERJACK, SO MUCH, AND I'M SORRY, BUT I REALLY DO HAVE TO RUN.

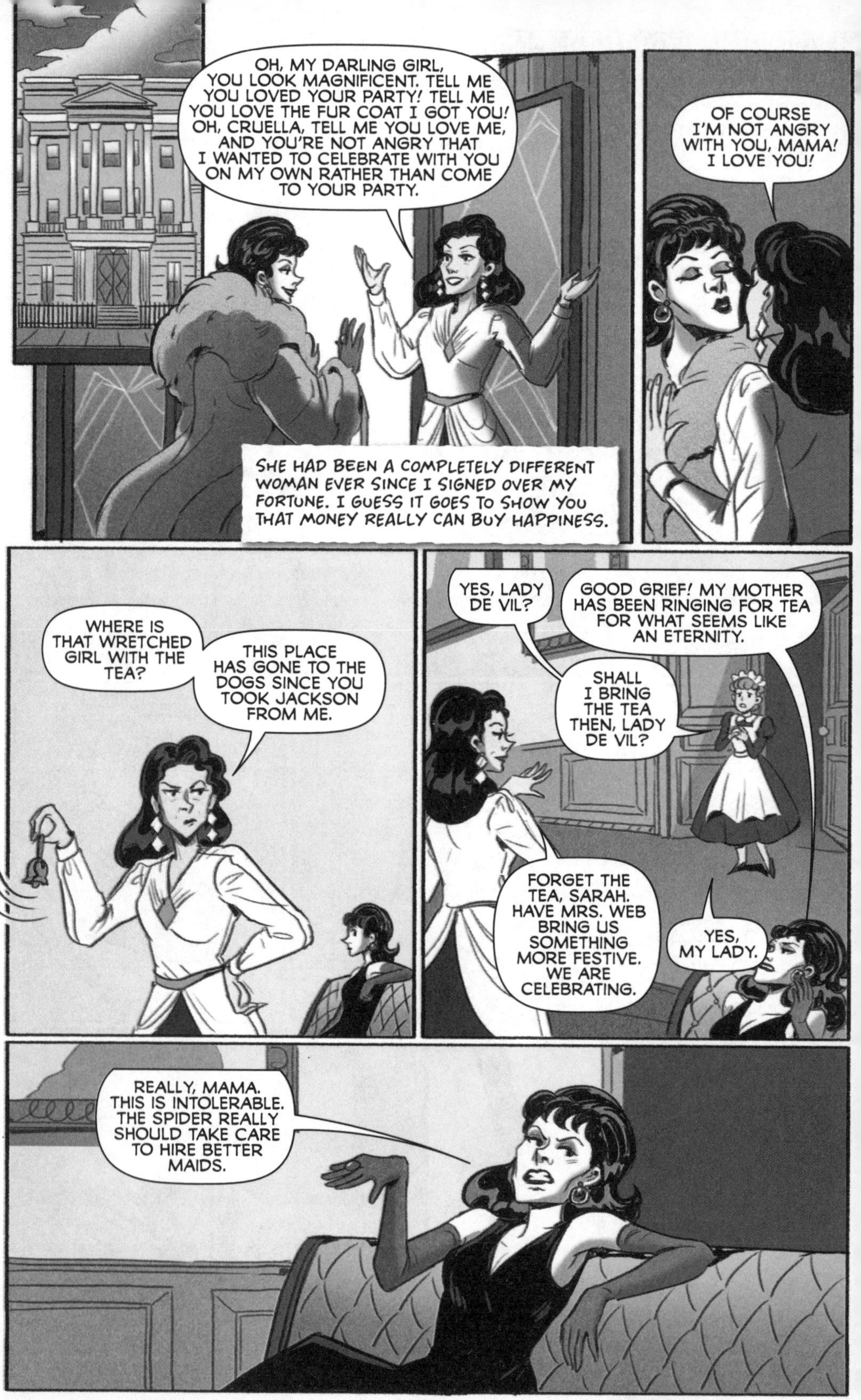
OH, MY DARLING GIRL, YOU LOOK MAGNIFICENT. TELL ME YOU LOVED YOUR PARTY! TELL ME YOU LOVE THE FUR COAT I GOT YOU! OH, CRUELLA, TELL ME YOU LOVE ME, AND YOU'RE NOT ANGRY THAT I WANTED TO CELEBRATE WITH YOU ON MY OWN RATHER THAN COME TO YOUR PARTY.
SHE HAD BEEN A COMPLETELY DIFFERENT WOMAN EVER SINCE I SIGNED OVER MY FORTUNE. I GUESS IT GOES TO SHOW YOU THAT MONEY REALLY CAN BUY HAPPINESS.
OF COURSE I'M NOT ANGRY WITH YOU, MAMA! I LOVE YOU!
WHERE IS THAT WRETCHED GIRL WITH THE TEA?
THIS PLACE HAS GONE TO THE DOGS SINCE YOU TOOK JACKSON FROM ME.
YES, LADY DE VIL?
GOOD GRIEF! MY MOTHER HAS BEEN RINGING FOR TEA FOR WHAT SEEMS LIKE AN ETERNITY.
SHALL I BRING THE TEA THEN, LADY DE VIL?
FORGET THE TEA, SARAH. HAVE MRS. WEB BRING US SOMETHING MORE FESTIVE. WE ARE CELEBRATING.
YES, MY LADY.
REALLY, MAMA. THIS IS INTOLERABLE. THE SPIDER REALLY SHOULD TAKE CARE TO HIRE BETTER MAIDS.

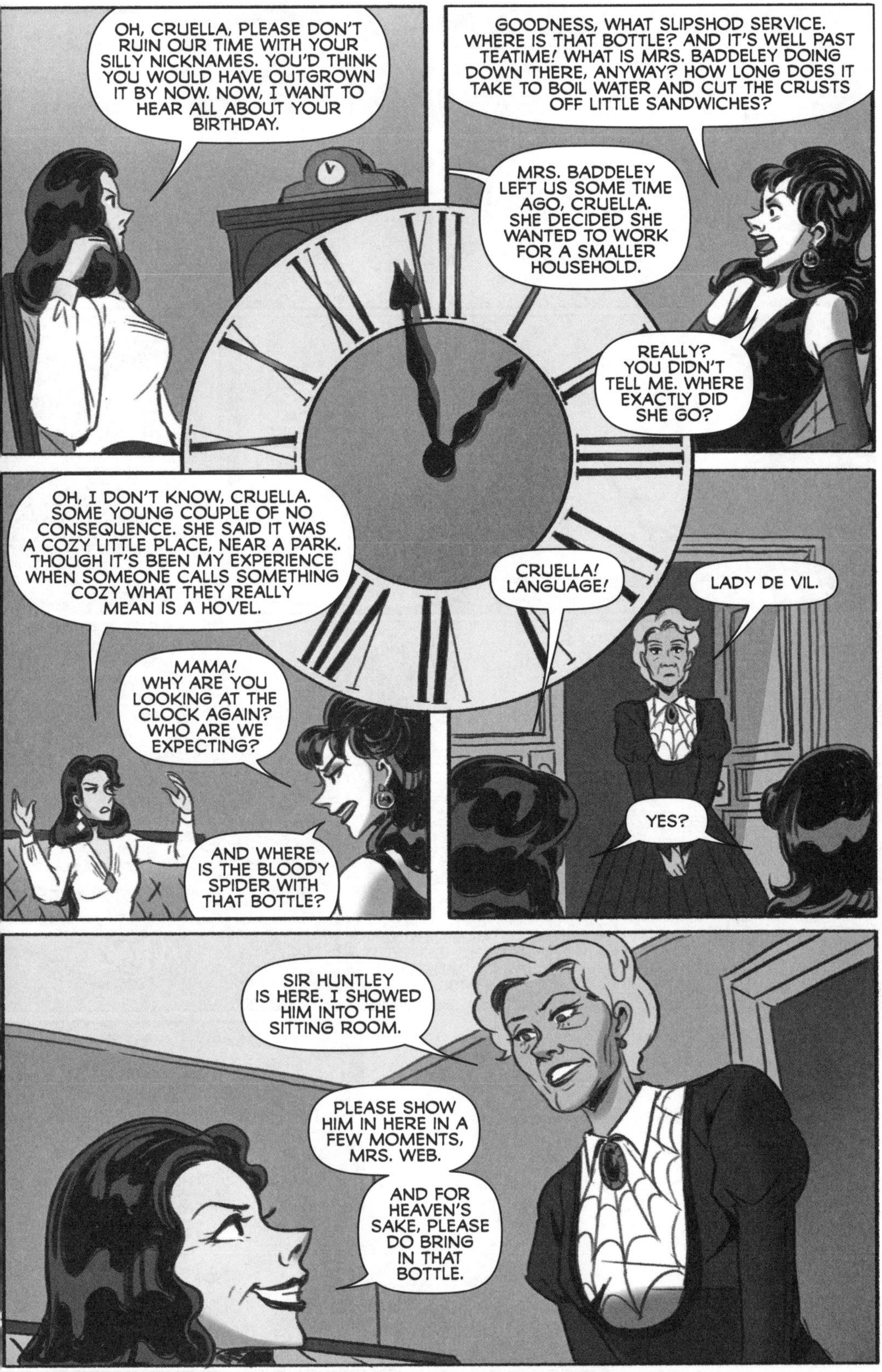
OH, CRUELLA, PLEASE DON'T RUIN OUR TIME WITH YOUR SILLY NICKNAMES. YOU'D THINK YOU WOULD HAVE OUTGROWN IT BY NOW. NOW, I WANT TO HEAR ALL ABOUT YOUR BIRTHDAY.
GOODNESS, WHAT SLIPSHOD SERVICE. WHERE IS THAT BOTTLE? AND IT'S WELL PAST TEATIME! WHAT IS MRS. BADDELEY DOING DOWN THERE, ANYWAY? HOW LONG DOES IT TAKE TO BOIL WATER AND CUT THE CRUSTS OFF LITTLE SANDWICHES?
MRS. BADDELEY LEFT US SOME TIME AGO, CRUELLA. SHE DECIDED SHE WANTED TO WORK FOR A SMALLER HOUSEHOLD.
REALLY? YOU DIDN'T TELL ME. WHERE EXACTLY DID SHE GO?
OH, I DON'T KNOW, CRUELLA. SOME YOUNG COUPLE OF NO CONSEQUENCE. SHE SAID IT WAS A COZY LITTLE PLACE, NEAR A PARK. THOUGH IT'S BEEN MY EXPERIENCE WHEN SOMEONE CALLS SOMETHING COZY WHAT THEY REALLY MEAN IS A HOVEL.
MAMA! WHY ARE YOU LOOKING AT THE CLOCK AGAIN? WHO ARE WE EXPECTING?
AND WHERE IS THE BLOODY SPIDER WITH THAT BOTTLE?
CRUELLA! LANGUAGE!
LADY DE VIL.
YES?
SIR HUNTLEY IS HERE. I SHOWED HIM INTO THE SITTING ROOM.
PLEASE SHOW HIM IN HERE IN A FEW MOMENTS, MRS. WEB.
AND FOR HEAVEN'S SAKE, PLEASE DO BRING IN THAT BOTTLE.

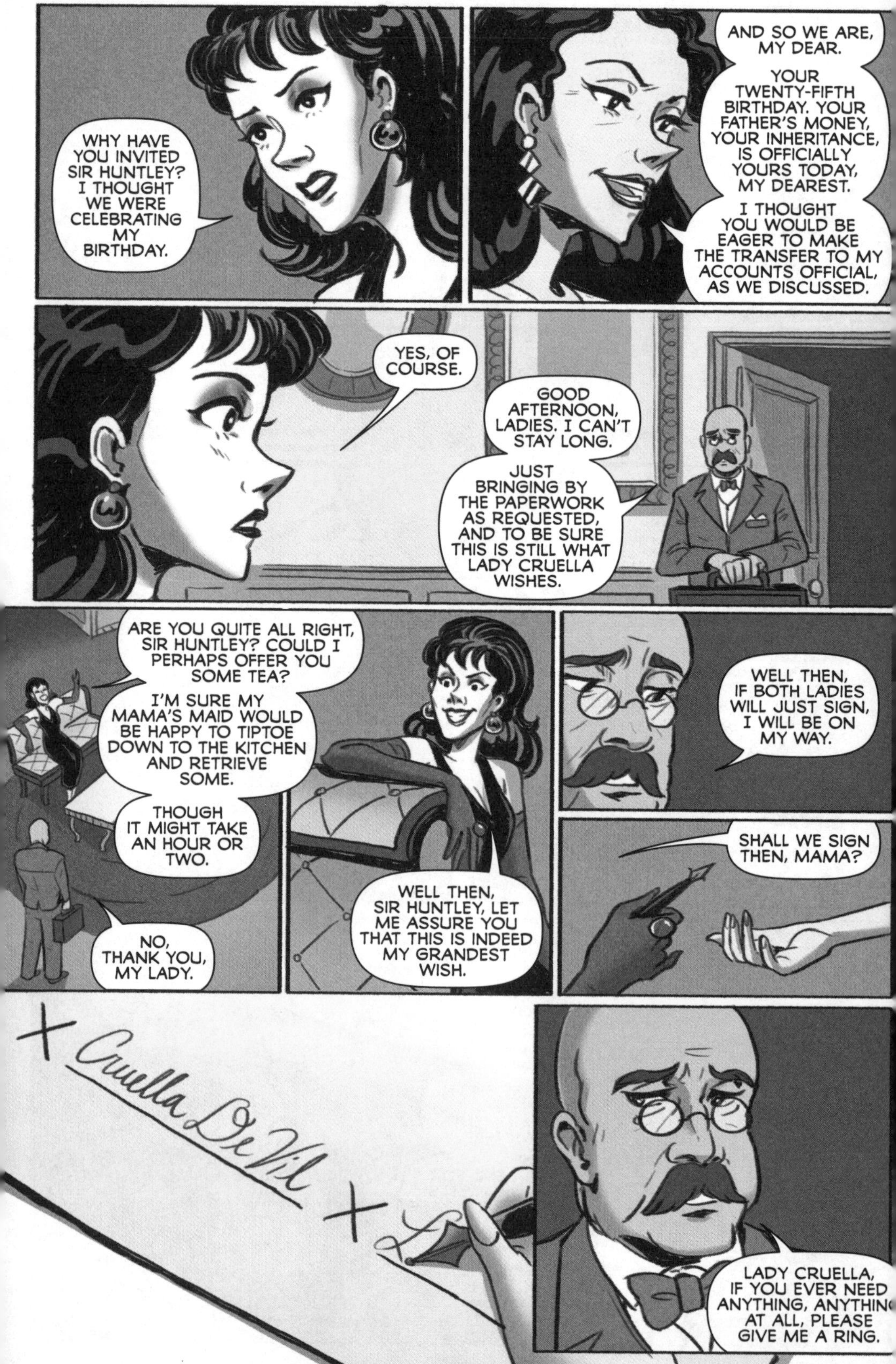
WHY HAVE YOU INVITED SIR HUNTLEY? I THOUGHT WE WERE CELEBRATING MY BIRTHDAY.
AND SO WE ARE, MY DEAR.
YOUR TWENTY-FIFTH BIRTHDAY. YOUR FATHER'S MONEY, YOUR INHERITANCE, IS OFFICIALLY YOURS TODAY, MY DEAREST.
I THOUGHT YOU WOULD BE EAGER TO MAKE THE TRANSFER TO MY ACCOUNTS OFFICIAL, AS WE DISCUSSED.
YES, OF COURSE.
GOOD AFTERNOON, LADIES. I CAN'T STAY LONG.
JUST BRINGING BY THE PAPERWORK AS REQUESTED, AND TO BE SURE THIS IS STILL WHAT LADY CRUELLA WISHES.
ARE YOU QUITE ALL RIGHT, SIR HUNTLEY? COULD I PERHAPS OFFER YOU SOME TEA?
I'M SURE MY MAMA'S MAID WOULD BE HAPPY TO TIPTOE DOWN TO THE KITCHEN AND RETRIEVE SOME.
THOUGH IT MIGHT TAKE AN HOUR OR TWO.
NO, THANK YOU, MY LADY.
WELL THEN, SIR HUNTLEY, LET ME ASSURE YOU THAT THIS IS INDEED MY GRANDEST WISH.
WELL THEN, IF BOTH LADIES WILL JUST SIGN, I WILL BE ON MY WAY.
SHALL WE SIGN THEN, MAMA?
X Cruella De Vil
X
LADY CRUELLA, IF YOU EVER NEED ANYTHING, ANYTHING AT ALL, PLEASE GIVE ME A RING.

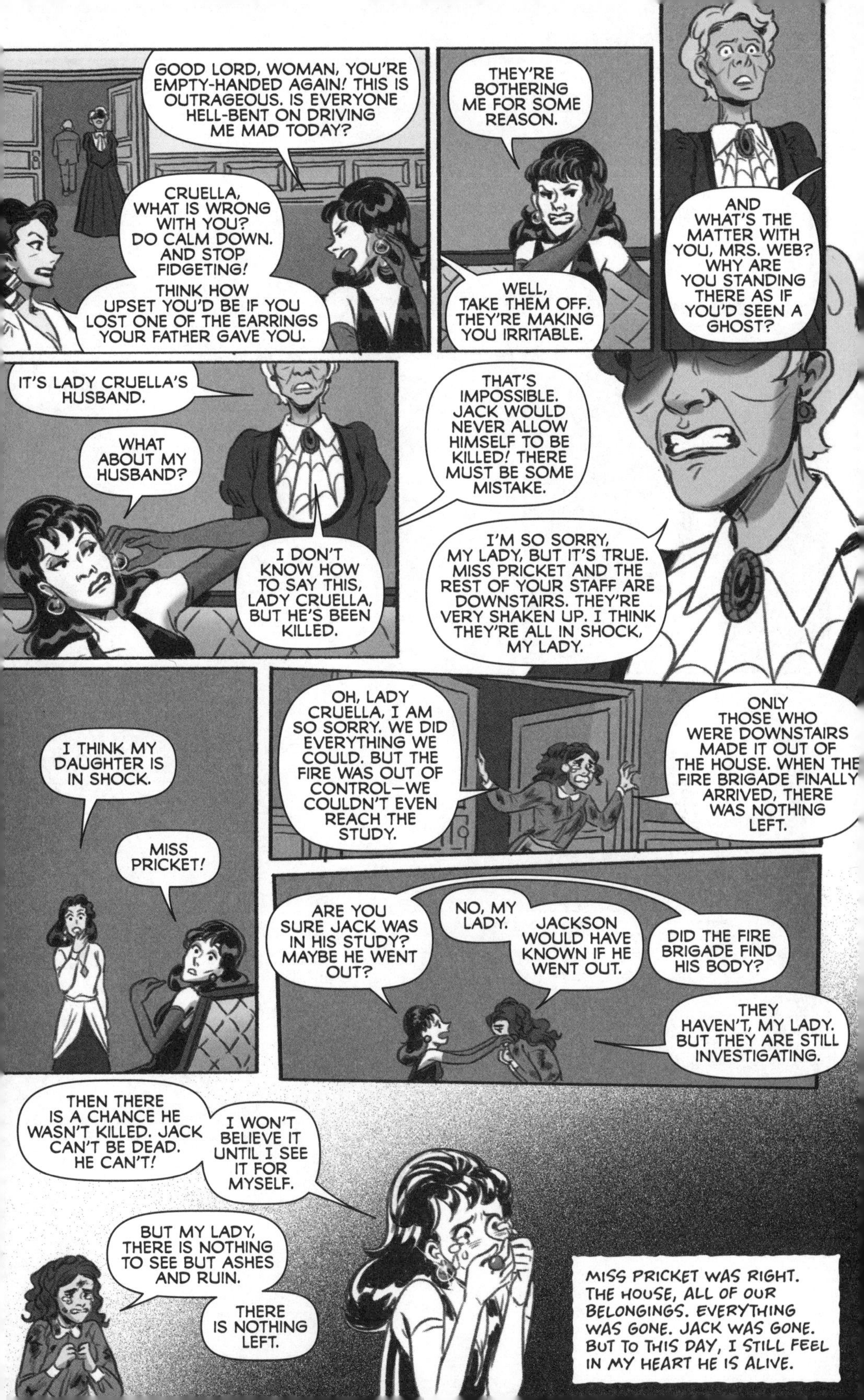
GOOD LORD, WOMAN, YOU'RE EMPTY-HANDED AGAIN! THIS IS OUTRAGEOUS. IS EVERYONE HELL-BENT ON DRIVING ME MAD TODAY?
CRUELLA, WHAT IS WRONG WITH YOU? DO CALM DOWN. AND STOP FIDGETING!
THINK HOW UPSET YOU'D BE IF YOU LOST ONE OF THE EARRINGS YOUR FATHER GAVE YOU.
THEY'RE BOTHERING ME FOR SOME REASON.
WELL, TAKE THEM OFF. THEY'RE MAKING YOU IRRITABLE.
AND WHAT'S THE MATTER WITH YOU, MRS. WEB? WHY ARE YOU STANDING THERE AS IF YOU'D SEEN A GHOST?
IT'S LADY CRUELLA'S HUSBAND.
WHAT ABOUT MY HUSBAND?
I DON'T KNOW HOW TO SAY THIS, LADY CRUELLA, BUT HE'S BEEN KILLED.
THAT'S IMPOSSIBLE. JACK WOULD NEVER ALLOW HIMSELF TO BE KILLED! THERE MUST BE SOME MISTAKE.
I'M SO SORRY, MY LADY, BUT IT'S TRUE. MISS PRICKET AND THE REST OF YOUR STAFF ARE DOWNSTAIRS. THEY'RE VERY SHAKEN UP. I THINK THEY'RE ALL IN SHOCK, MY LADY.
I THINK MY DAUGHTER IS IN SHOCK.
MISS PRICKET!
OH, LADY CRUELLA, I AM SO SORRY. WE DID EVERYTHING WE COULD. BUT THE FIRE WAS OUT OF CONTROL—WE COULDN'T EVEN REACH THE STUDY.
ONLY THOSE WHO WERE DOWNSTAIRS MADE IT OUT OF THE HOUSE. WHEN THE FIRE BRIGADE FINALLY ARRIVED, THERE WAS NOTHING LEFT.
ARE YOU SURE JACK WAS IN HIS STUDY? MAYBE HE WENT OUT?
NO, MY LADY.
JACKSON WOULD HAVE KNOWN IF HE WENT OUT.
DID THE FIRE BRIGADE FIND HIS BODY?
THEY HAVEN'T, MY LADY. BUT THEY ARE STILL INVESTIGATING.
THEN THERE IS A CHANCE HE WASN'T KILLED. JACK CAN'T BE DEAD. HE CAN'T!
I WON'T BELIEVE IT UNTIL I SEE IT FOR MYSELF.
BUT MY LADY, THERE IS NOTHING TO SEE BUT ASHES AND RUIN.
THERE IS NOTHING LEFT.
MISS PRICKET WAS RIGHT. THE HOUSE, ALL OF OUR BELONGINGS. EVERYTHING WAS GONE. JACK WAS GONE. BUT TO THIS DAY, I STILL FEEL IN MY HEART HE IS ALIVE.

CHAPTER FIFTEEN
THAT DE VIL WOMAN

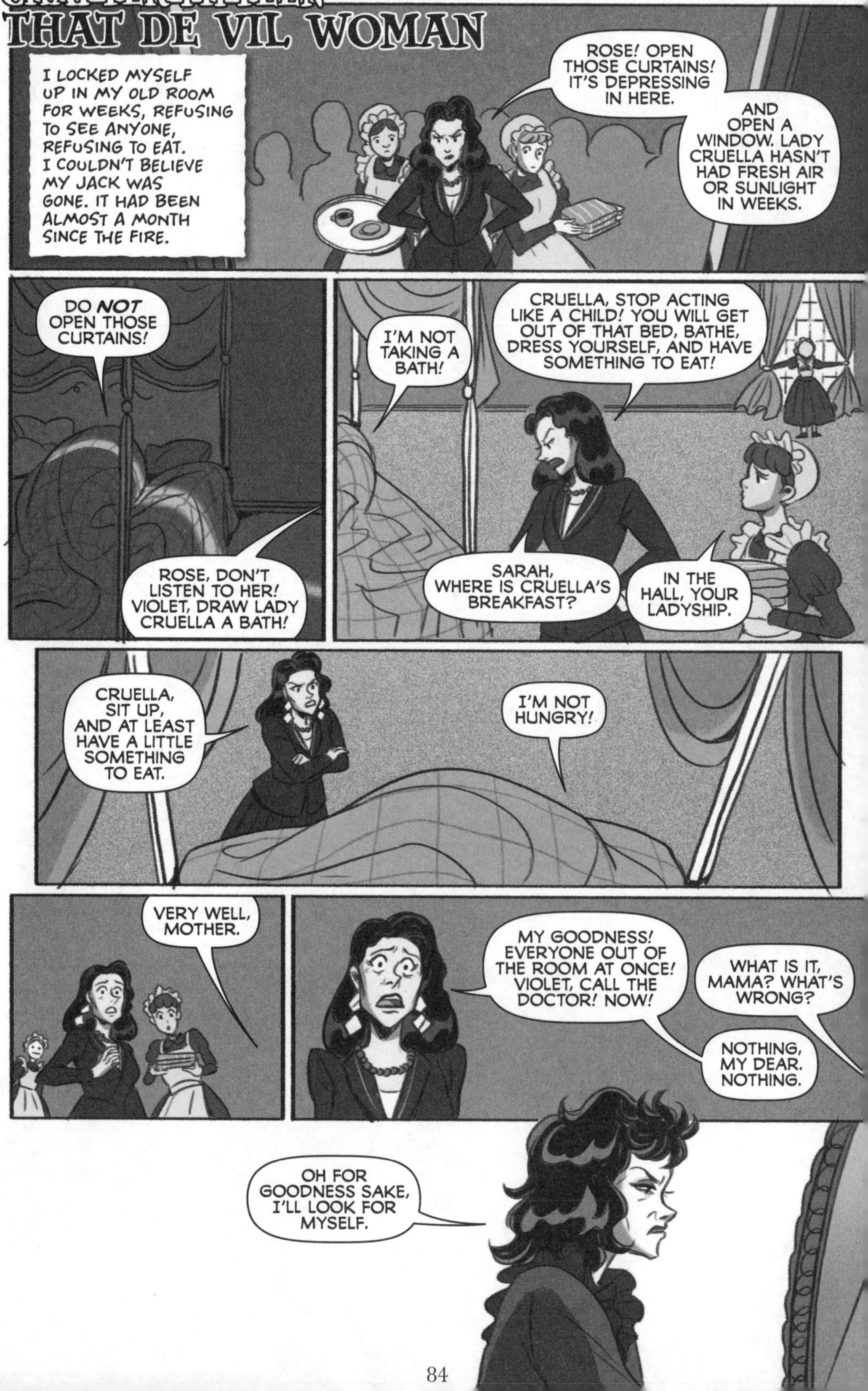

I LOCKED MYSELF UP IN MY OLD ROOM FOR WEEKS, REFUSING TO SEE ANYONE, REFUSING TO EAT. I COULDN'T BELIEVE MY JACK WAS GONE. IT HAD BEEN ALMOST A MONTH SINCE THE FIRE.
ROSE! OPEN THOSE CURTAINS! IT'S DEPRESSING IN HERE.
AND OPEN A WINDOW. LADY CRUELLA HASN'T HAD FRESH AIR OR SUNLIGHT IN WEEKS.
DO NOT OPEN THOSE CURTAINS!
ROSE, DON'T LISTEN TO HER! VIOLET, DRAW LADY CRUELLA A BATH!
I'M NOT TAKING A BATH!
CRUELLA, STOP ACTING LIKE A CHILD! YOU WILL GET OUT OF THAT BED, BATHE, DRESS YOURSELF, AND HAVE SOMETHING TO EAT!
SARAH, WHERE IS CRUELLA'S BREAKFAST?
IN THE HALL, YOUR LADYSHIP.
CRUELLA, SIT UP, AND AT LEAST HAVE A LITTLE SOMETHING TO EAT.
I'M NOT HUNGRY!
VERY WELL, MOTHER.
MY GOODNESS! EVERYONE OUT OF THE ROOM AT ONCE! VIOLET, CALL THE DOCTOR! NOW!
WHAT IS IT, MAMA? WHAT'S WRONG?
NOTHING, MY DEAR. NOTHING.
OH FOR GOODNESS SAKE, I'LL LOOK FOR MYSELF.

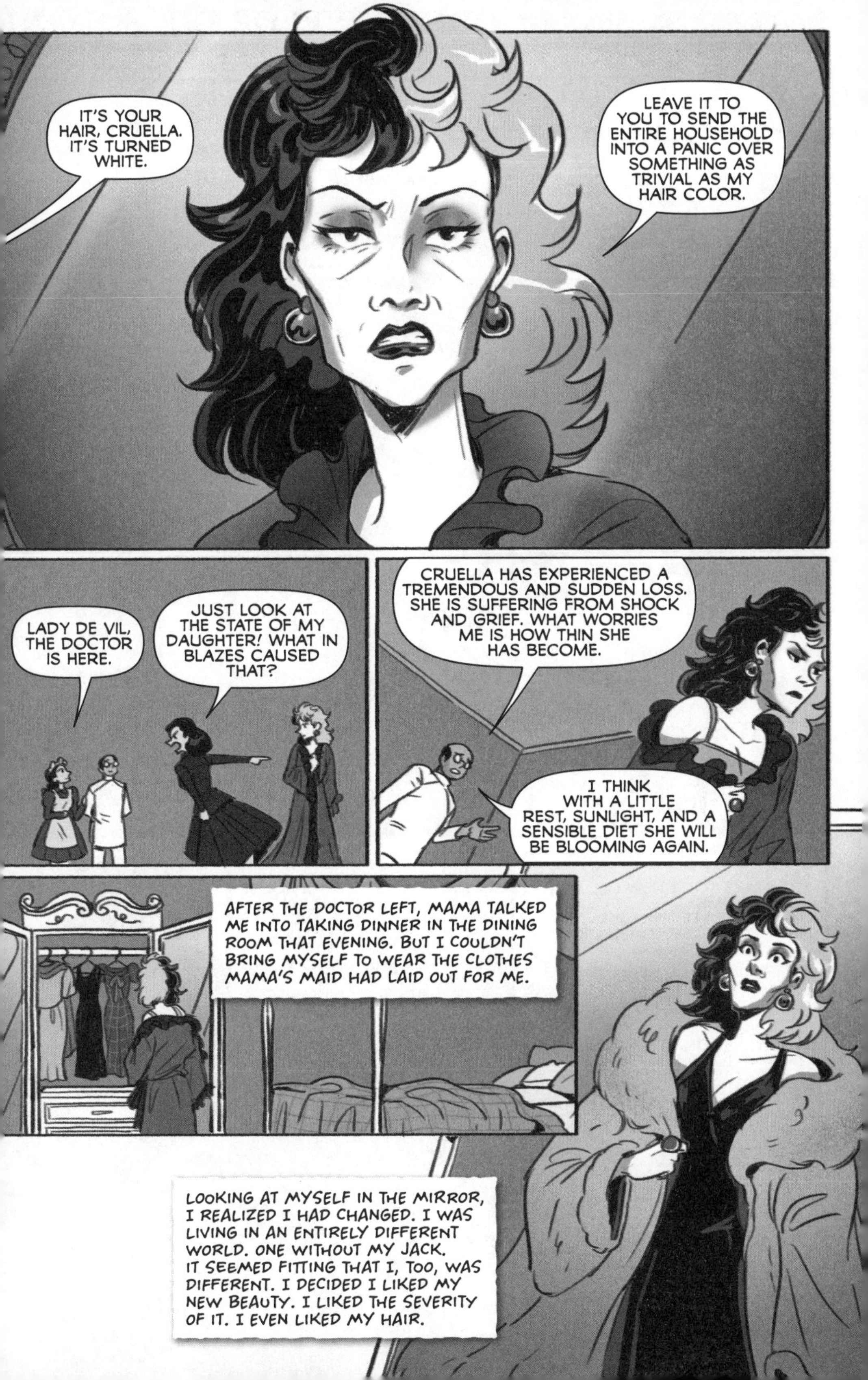
IT'S YOUR HAIR, CRUELLA. IT'S TURNED WHITE.
LEAVE IT TO YOU TO SEND THE ENTIRE HOUSEHOLD INTO A PANIC OVER SOMETHING AS TRIVIAL AS MY HAIR COLOR.
LADY DE VIL, THE DOCTOR IS HERE.
JUST LOOK AT THE STATE OF MY DAUGHTER! WHAT IN BLAZES CAUSED THAT?
CRUELLA HAS EXPERIENCED A TREMENDOUS AND SUDDEN LOSS. SHE IS SUFFERING FROM SHOCK AND GRIEF. WHAT WORRIES ME IS HOW THIN SHE HAS BECOME.
I THINK WITH A LITTLE REST, SUNLIGHT, AND A SENSIBLE DIET SHE WILL BE BLOOMING AGAIN.
AFTER THE DOCTOR LEFT, MAMA TALKED ME INTO TAKING DINNER IN THE DINING ROOM THAT EVENING. BUT I COULDN'T BRING MYSELF TO WEAR THE CLOTHES MAMA'S MAID HAD LAID OUT FOR ME.
LOOKING AT MYSELF IN THE MIRROR, I REALIZED I HAD CHANGED. I WAS LIVING IN AN ENTIRELY DIFFERENT WORLD. ONE WITHOUT MY JACK. IT SEEMED FITTING THAT I, TOO, WAS DIFFERENT. I DECIDED I LIKED MY NEW BEAUTY. I LIKED THE SEVERITY OF IT. I EVEN LIKED MY HAIR.

CHAPTER SIXTEEN GOODBYE, BELGRAVE SQUARE

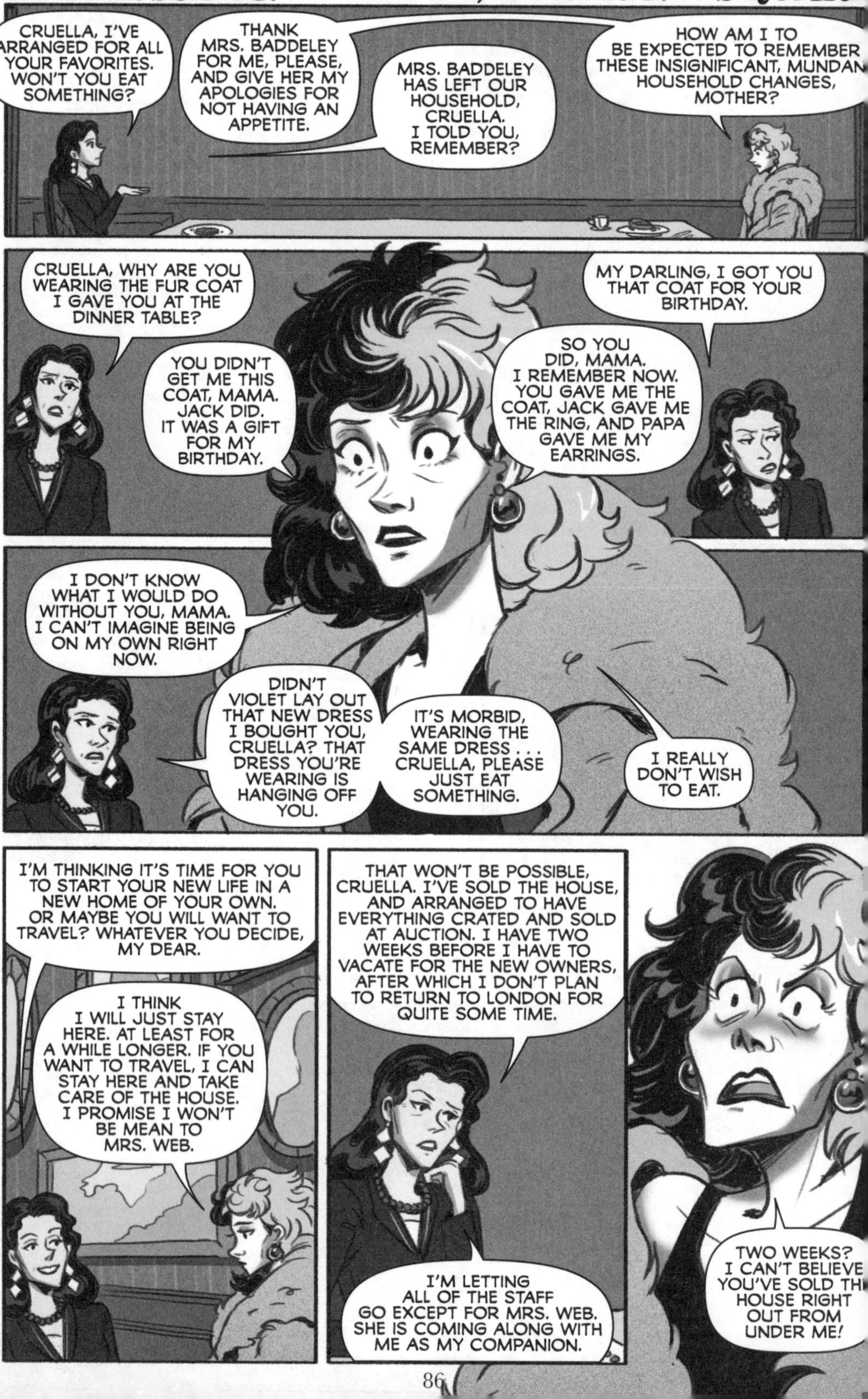
CRUELLA, I'VE ARRANGED FOR ALL YOUR FAVORITES. WON'T YOU EAT SOMETHING?
THANK MRS. BADDELEY FOR ME, PLEASE, AND GIVE HER MY APOLOGIES FOR NOT HAVING AN APPETITE.
MRS. BADDELEY HAS LEFT OUR HOUSEHOLD, CRUELLA. I TOLD YOU, REMEMBER?
HOW AM I TO BE EXPECTED TO REMEMBER THESE INSIGNIFICANT, MUNDAN HOUSEHOLD CHANGES, MOTHER?
CRUELLA, WHY ARE YOU WEARING THE FUR COAT I GAVE YOU AT THE DINNER TABLE?
YOU DIDN'T GET ME THIS COAT, MAMA. JACK DID. IT WAS A GIFT FOR MY BIRTHDAY.
MY DARLING, I GOT YOU THAT COAT FOR YOUR BIRTHDAY.
SO YOU DID, MAMA. I REMEMBER NOW. YOU GAVE ME THE COAT, JACK GAVE ME THE RING, AND PAPA GAVE ME MY EARRINGS.
I DON'T KNOW WHAT I WOULD DO WITHOUT YOU, MAMA. I CAN'T IMAGINE BEING ON MY OWN RIGHT NOW.
DIDN'T VIOLET LAY OUT THAT NEW DRESS I BOUGHT YOU, CRUELLA? THAT DRESS YOU'RE WEARING IS HANGING OFF YOU.
IT'S MORBID, WEARING THE SAME DRESS . . . CRUELLA, PLEASE JUST EAT SOMETHING.
I REALLY DON'T WISH TO EAT.
I'M THINKING IT'S TIME FOR YOU TO START YOUR NEW LIFE IN A NEW HOME OF YOUR OWN. OR MAYBE YOU WILL WANT TO TRAVEL? WHATEVER YOU DECIDE, MY DEAR.
I THINK I WILL JUST STAY HERE. AT LEAST FOR A WHILE LONGER. IF YOU WANT TO TRAVEL, I CAN STAY HERE AND TAKE CARE OF THE HOUSE. I PROMISE I WON'T BE MEAN TO MRS. WEB.
THAT WON'T BE POSSIBLE, CRUELLA. I'VE SOLD THE HOUSE, AND ARRANGED TO HAVE EVERYTHING CRATED AND SOLD AT AUCTION. I HAVE TWO WEEKS BEFORE I HAVE TO VACATE FOR THE NEW OWNERS, AFTER WHICH I DON'T PLAN TO RETURN TO LONDON FOR QUITE SOME TIME.
I'M LETTING ALL OF THE STAFF GO EXCEPT FOR MRS. WEB. SHE IS COMING ALONG WITH ME AS MY COMPANION.
TWO WEEKS? I CAN'T BELIEVE YOU'VE SOLD TH HOUSE RIGHT OUT FROM UNDER ME!

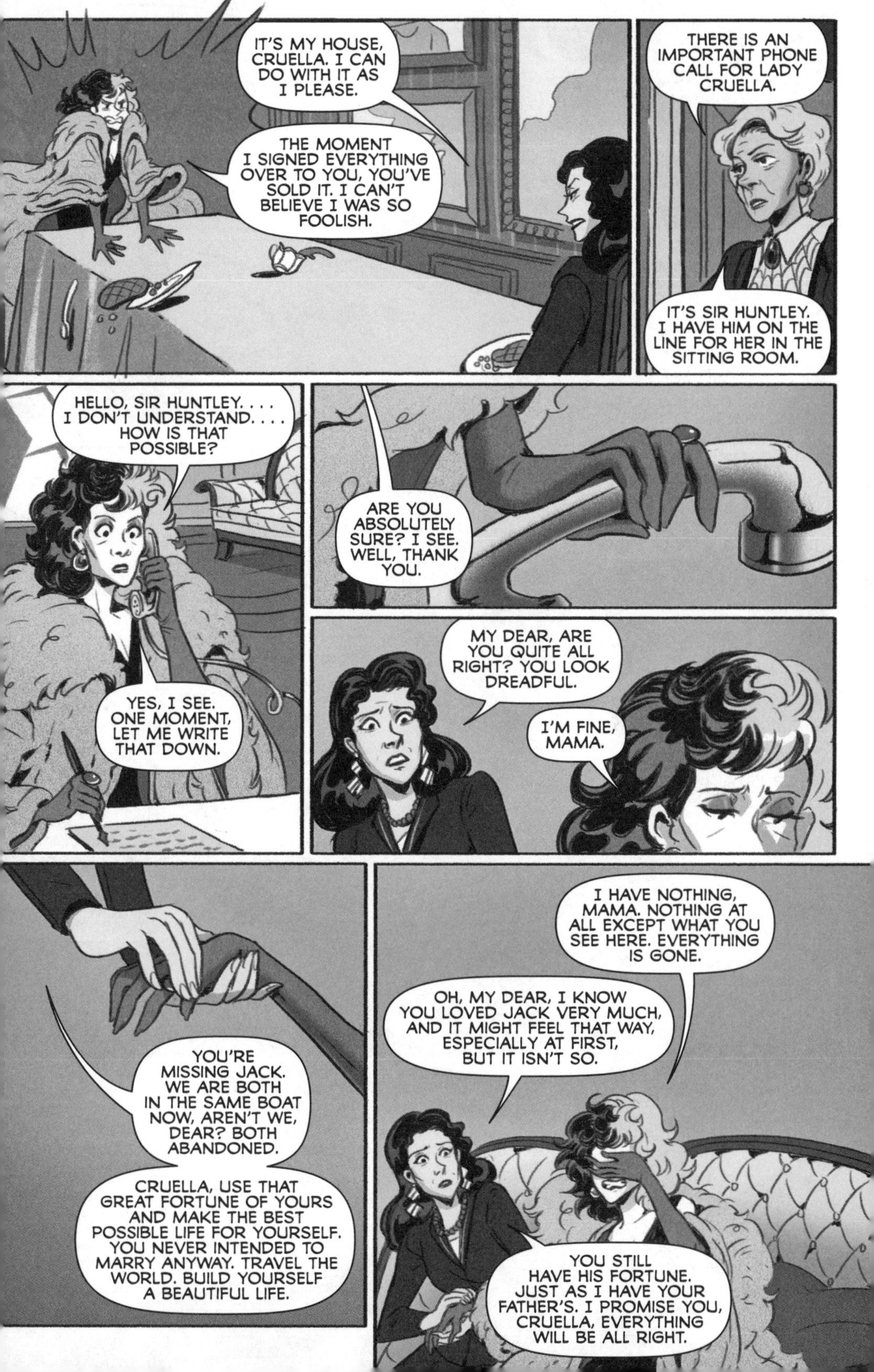
IT'S MY HOUSE, CRUELLA. I CAN DO WITH IT AS I PLEASE.
THE MOMENT I SIGNED EVERYTHING OVER TO YOU, YOU'VE SOLD IT. I CAN'T BELIEVE I WAS SO FOOLISH.
THERE IS AN IMPORTANT PHONE CALL FOR LADY CRUELLA.
IT'S SIR HUNTLEY. I HAVE HIM ON THE LINE FOR HER IN THE SITTING ROOM.
HELLO, SIR HUNTLEY. . . . I DON'T UNDERSTAND. . . . HOW IS THAT POSSIBLE?
YES, I SEE. ONE MOMENT, LET ME WRITE THAT DOWN.
ARE YOU ABSOLUTELY SURE? I SEE. WELL, THANK YOU.
MY DEAR, ARE YOU QUITE ALL RIGHT? YOU LOOK DREADFUL.
I'M FINE, MAMA.
YOU'RE MISSING JACK. WE ARE BOTH IN THE SAME BOAT NOW, AREN'T WE, DEAR? BOTH ABANDONED.
CRUELLA, USE THAT GREAT FORTUNE OF YOURS AND MAKE THE BEST POSSIBLE LIFE FOR YOURSELF. YOU NEVER INTENDED TO MARRY ANYWAY. TRAVEL THE WORLD. BUILD YOURSELF A BEAUTIFUL LIFE.
I HAVE NOTHING, MAMA. NOTHING AT ALL EXCEPT WHAT YOU SEE HERE. EVERYTHING IS GONE.
OH, MY DEAR, I KNOW YOU LOVED JACK VERY MUCH, AND IT MIGHT FEEL THAT WAY, ESPECIALLY AT FIRST, BUT IT ISN'T SO.
YOU STILL HAVE HIS FORTUNE. JUST AS I HAVE YOUR FATHER'S. I PROMISE YOU, CRUELLA, EVERYTHING WILL BE ALL RIGHT.

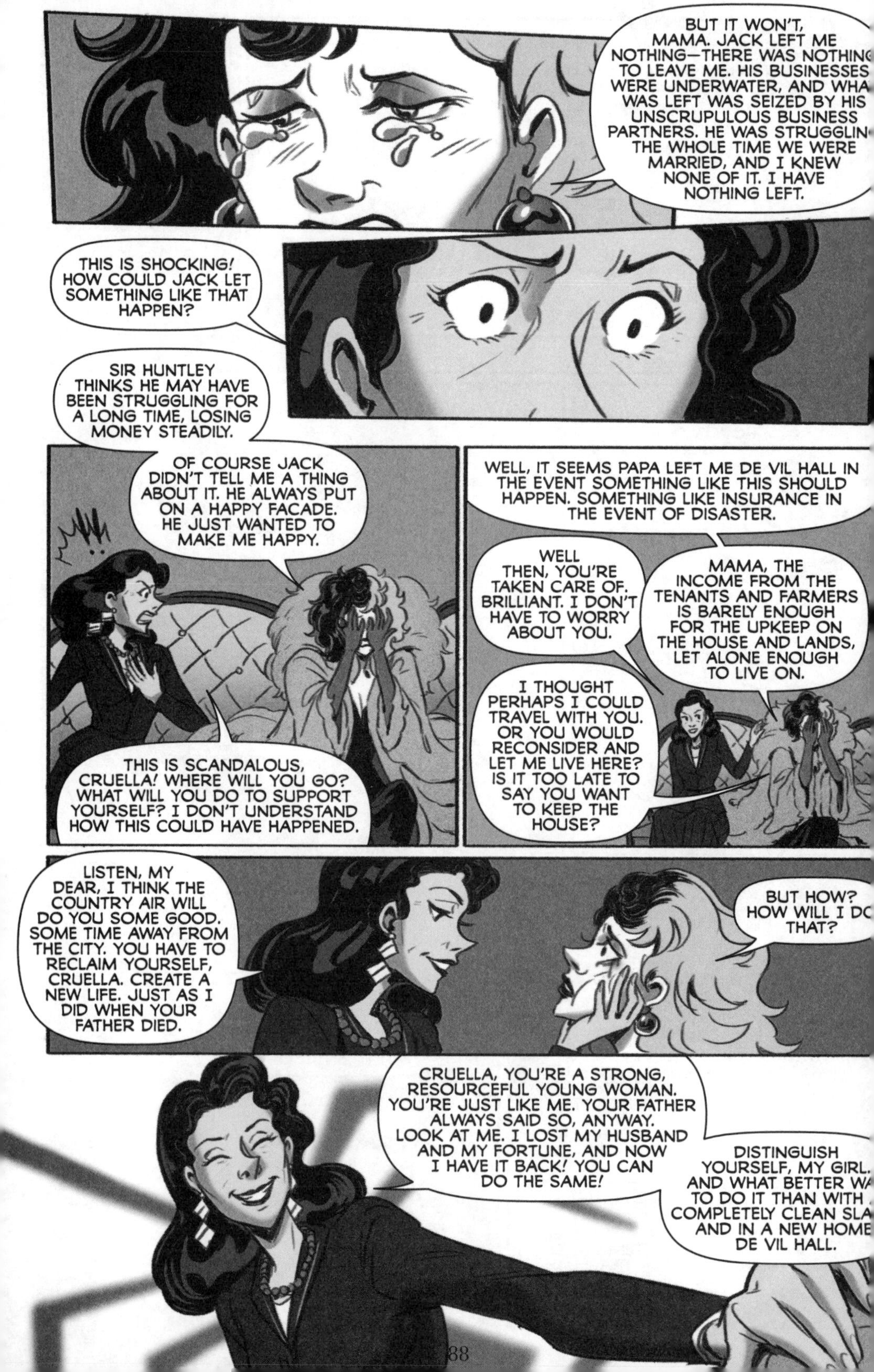

BUT IT WON'T, MAMA. JACK LEFT ME NOTHING—THERE WAS NOTHIN TO LEAVE ME. HIS BUSINESSES WERE UNDERWATER, AND WHA WAS LEFT WAS SEIZED BY HIS UNSCRUPULOUS BUSINESS PARTNERS. HE WAS STRUGGLIN THE WHOLE TIME WE WERE MARRIED, AND I KNEW NONE OF IT. I HAVE NOTHING LEFT.
THIS IS SHOCKING! HOW COULD JACK LET SOMETHING LIKE THAT HAPPEN?
SIR HUNTLEY THINKS HE MAY HAVE BEEN STRUGGLING FOR A LONG TIME, LOSING MONEY STEADILY.
OF COURSE JACK DIDN'T TELL ME A THING ABOUT IT. HE ALWAYS PUT ON A HAPPY FACADE. HE JUST WANTED TO MAKE ME HAPPY.
THIS IS SCANDALOUS, CRUELLA! WHERE WILL YOU GO? WHAT WILL YOU DO TO SUPPORT YOURSELF? I DON'T UNDERSTAND HOW THIS COULD HAVE HAPPENED.
WELL, IT SEEMS PAPA LEFT ME DE VIL HALL IN THE EVENT SOMETHING LIKE THIS SHOULD HAPPEN. SOMETHING LIKE INSURANCE IN THE EVENT OF DISASTER.
WELL THEN, YOU'RE TAKEN CARE OF. BRILLIANT. I DON'T HAVE TO WORRY ABOUT YOU.
MAMA, THE INCOME FROM THE TENANTS AND FARMERS IS BARELY ENOUGH FOR THE UPKEEP ON THE HOUSE AND LANDS, LET ALONE ENOUGH TO LIVE ON.
I THOUGHT PERHAPS I COULD TRAVEL WITH YOU. OR YOU WOULD RECONSIDER AND LET ME LIVE HERE? IS IT TOO LATE TO SAY YOU WANT TO KEEP THE HOUSE?
LISTEN, MY DEAR, I THINK THE COUNTRY AIR WILL DO YOU SOME GOOD. SOME TIME AWAY FROM THE CITY. YOU HAVE TO RECLAIM YOURSELF, CRUELLA. CREATE A NEW LIFE. JUST AS I DID WHEN YOUR FATHER DIED.
BUT HOW? HOW WILL I DC THAT?
CRUELLA, YOU'RE A STRONG, RESOURCEFUL YOUNG WOMAN. YOU'RE JUST LIKE ME. YOUR FATHER ALWAYS SAID SO, ANYWAY. LOOK AT ME. I LOST MY HUSBAND AND MY FORTUNE, AND NOW I HAVE IT BACK! YOU CAN DO THE SAME!
DISTINGUISH YOURSELF, MY GIRL. AND WHAT BETTER WA TO DO IT THAN WITH COMPLETELY CLEAN SLA AND IN A NEW HOME DE VIL HALL.

CHAPTER SEVENTEEN
HELL HALL

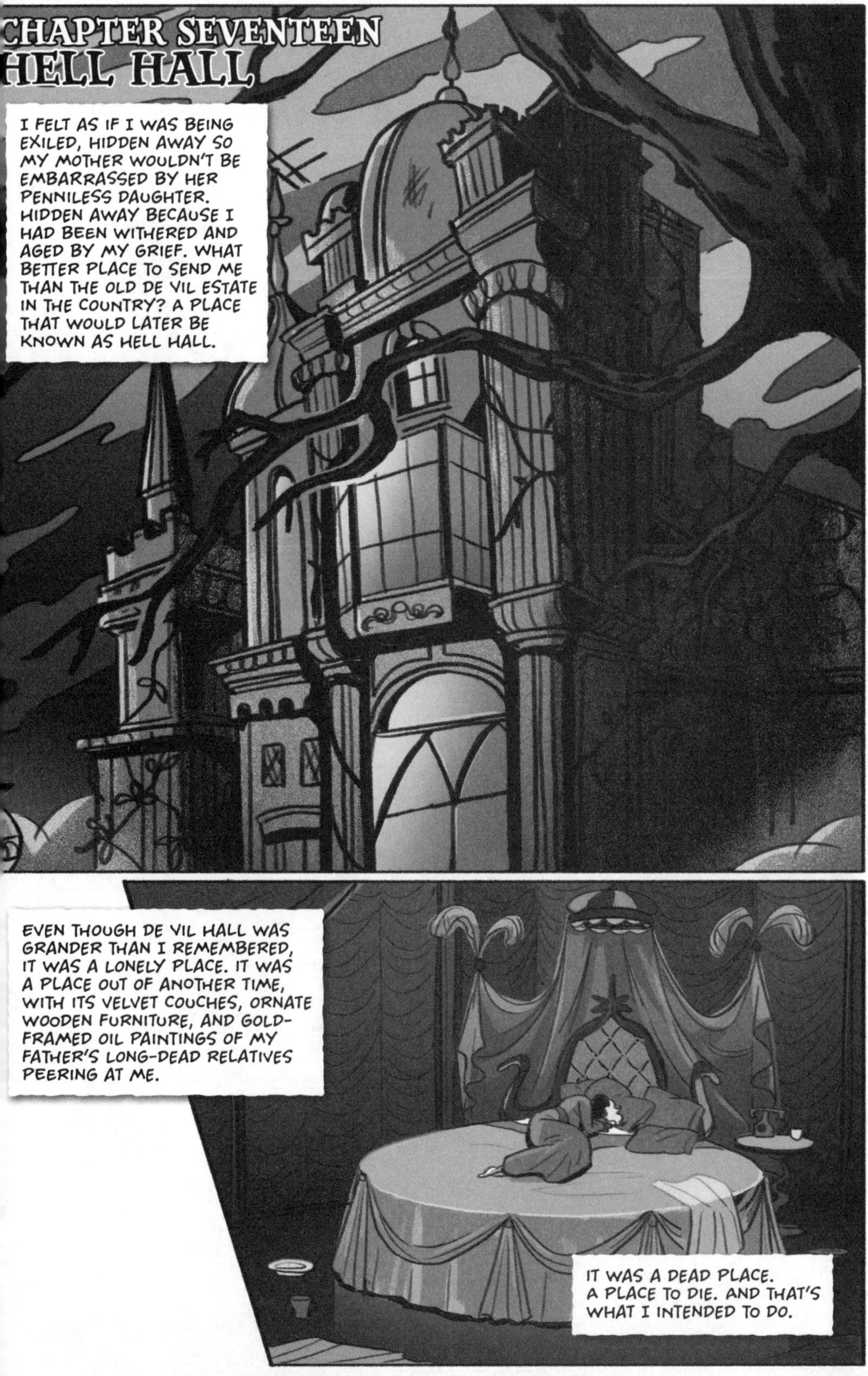
I FELT AS IF I WAS BEING EXILED, HIDDEN AWAY SO MY MOTHER WOULDN'T BE EMBARRASSED BY HER PENNILESS DAUGHTER. HIDDEN AWAY BECAUSE I HAD BEEN WITHERED AND AGED BY MY GRIEF. WHAT BETTER PLACE TO SEND ME THAN THE OLD DE VIL ESTATE IN THE COUNTRY? A PLACE THAT WOULD LATER BE KNOWN AS HELL HALL.
EVEN THOUGH DE VIL HALL WAS GRANDER THAN I REMEMBERED, IT WAS A LONELY PLACE. IT WAS A PLACE OUT OF ANOTHER TIME, WITH ITS VELVET COUCHES, ORNATE WOODEN FURNITURE, AND GOLD-FRAMED OIL PAINTINGS OF MY FATHER'S LONG-DEAD RELATIVES PEERING AT ME.
IT WAS A DEAD PLACE. A PLACE TO DIE. AND THAT'S WHAT I INTENDED TO DO.

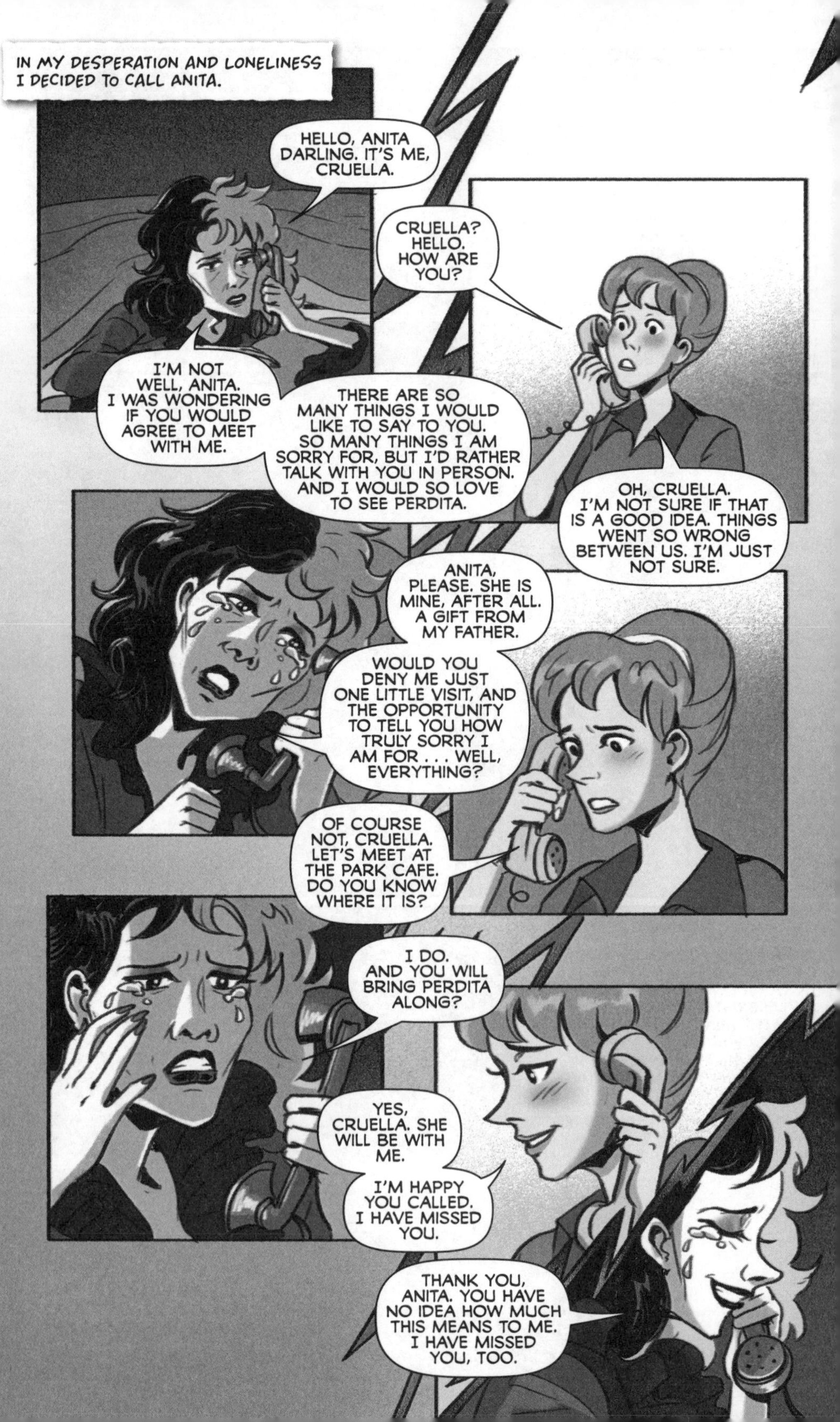
IN MY DESPERATION AND LONELINESS I DECIDED TO CALL ANITA.
HELLO, ANITA DARLING. IT'S ME, CRUELLA.
CRUELLA? HELLO. HOW ARE YOU?
I'M NOT WELL, ANITA. I WAS WONDERING IF YOU WOULD AGREE TO MEET WITH ME.
THERE ARE SO MANY THINGS I WOULD LIKE TO SAY TO YOU. SO MANY THINGS I AM SORRY FOR, BUT I'D RATHER TALK WITH YOU IN PERSON. AND I WOULD SO LOVE TO SEE PERDITA.
OH, CRUELLA. I'M NOT SURE IF THAT IS A GOOD IDEA. THINGS WENT SO WRONG BETWEEN US. I'M JUST NOT SURE.
ANITA, PLEASE. SHE IS MINE, AFTER ALL. A GIFT FROM MY FATHER.
WOULD YOU DENY ME JUST ONE LITTLE VISIT, AND THE OPPORTUNITY TO TELL YOU HOW TRULY SORRY I AM FOR . . . WELL, EVERYTHING?
OF COURSE NOT, CRUELLA. LET'S MEET AT THE PARK CAFE. DO YOU KNOW WHERE IT IS?
I DO. AND YOU WILL BRING PERDITA ALONG?
YES, CRUELLA. SHE WILL BE WITH ME.
I'M HAPPY YOU CALLED. I HAVE MISSED YOU.
THANK YOU, ANITA. YOU HAVE NO IDEA HOW MUCH THIS MEANS TO ME. I HAVE MISSED YOU, TOO.

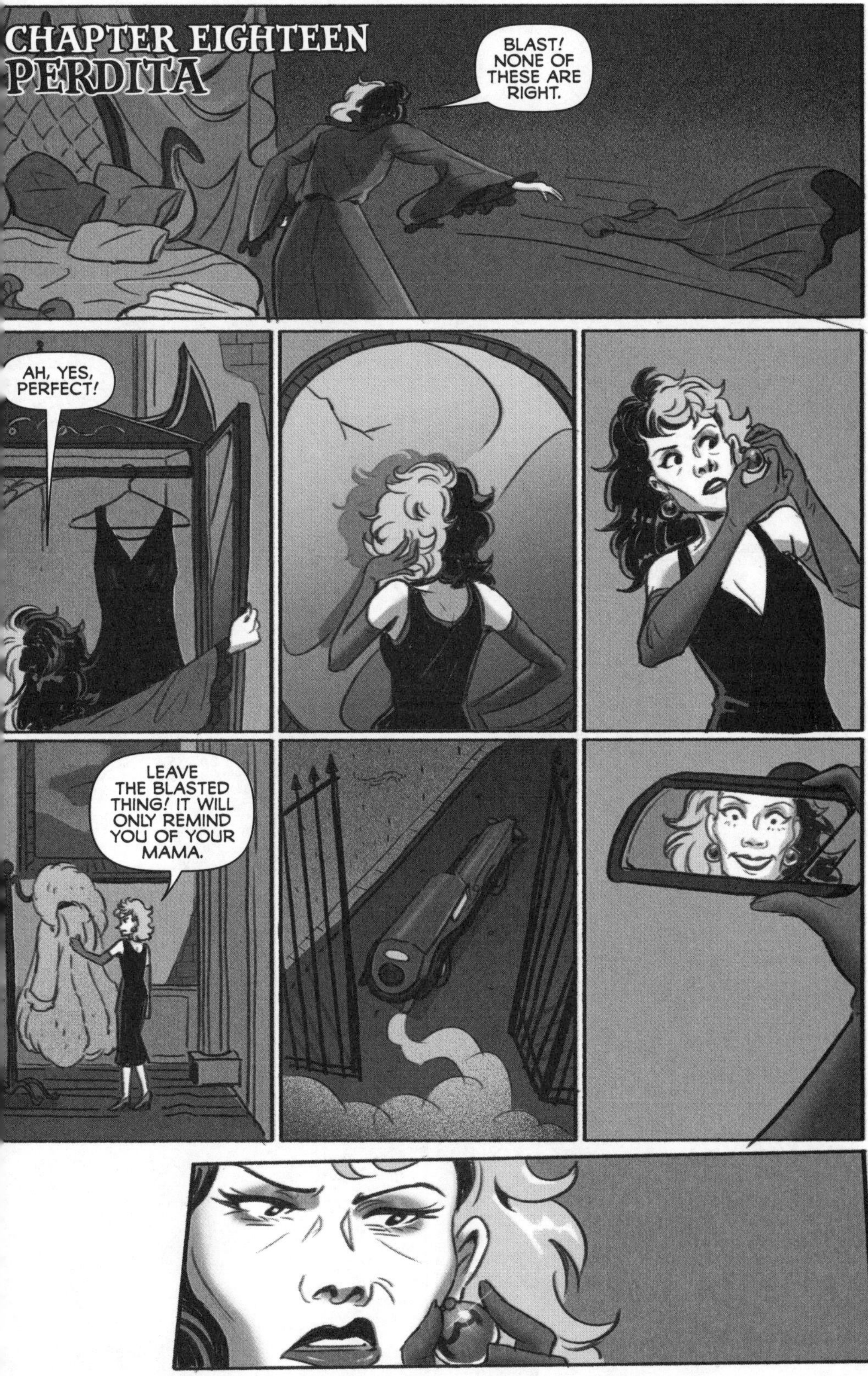
CHAPTER EIGHTEEN
PERDITA
BLAST! NONE OF THESE ARE RIGHT.
AH, YES, PERFECT!
LEAVE THE BLASTED THING! IT WILL ONLY REMIND YOU OF YOUR MAMA.

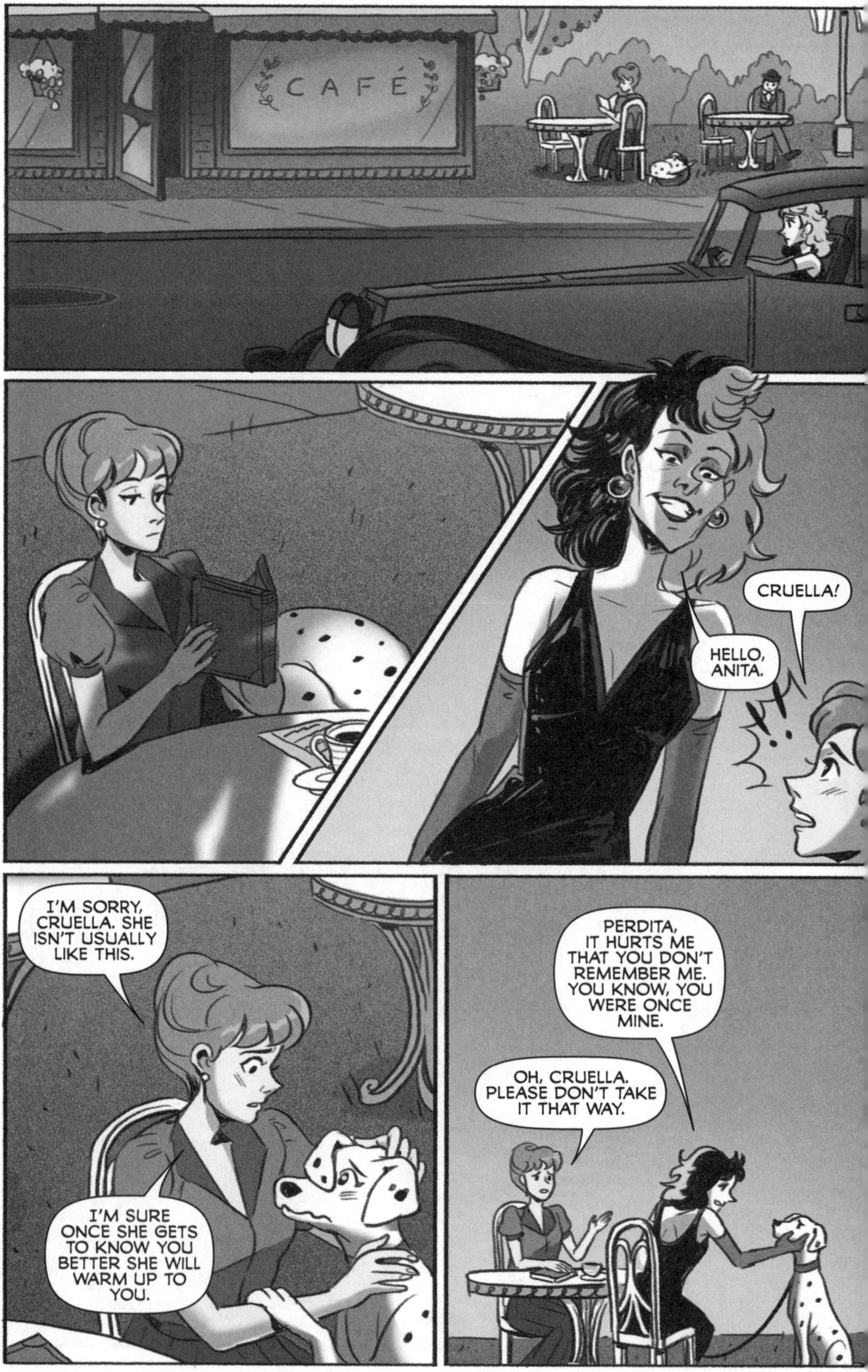
CAFÉ
HELLO, ANITA.
CRUELLA!
I'M SORRY, CRUELLA. SHE ISN'T USUALLY LIKE THIS.
I'M SURE ONCE SHE GETS TO KNOW YOU BETTER SHE WILL WARM UP TO YOU.
PERDITA, IT HURTS ME THAT YOU DON'T REMEMBER ME. YOU KNOW, YOU WERE ONCE MINE.
OH, CRUELLA. PLEASE DON'T TAKE IT THAT WAY.

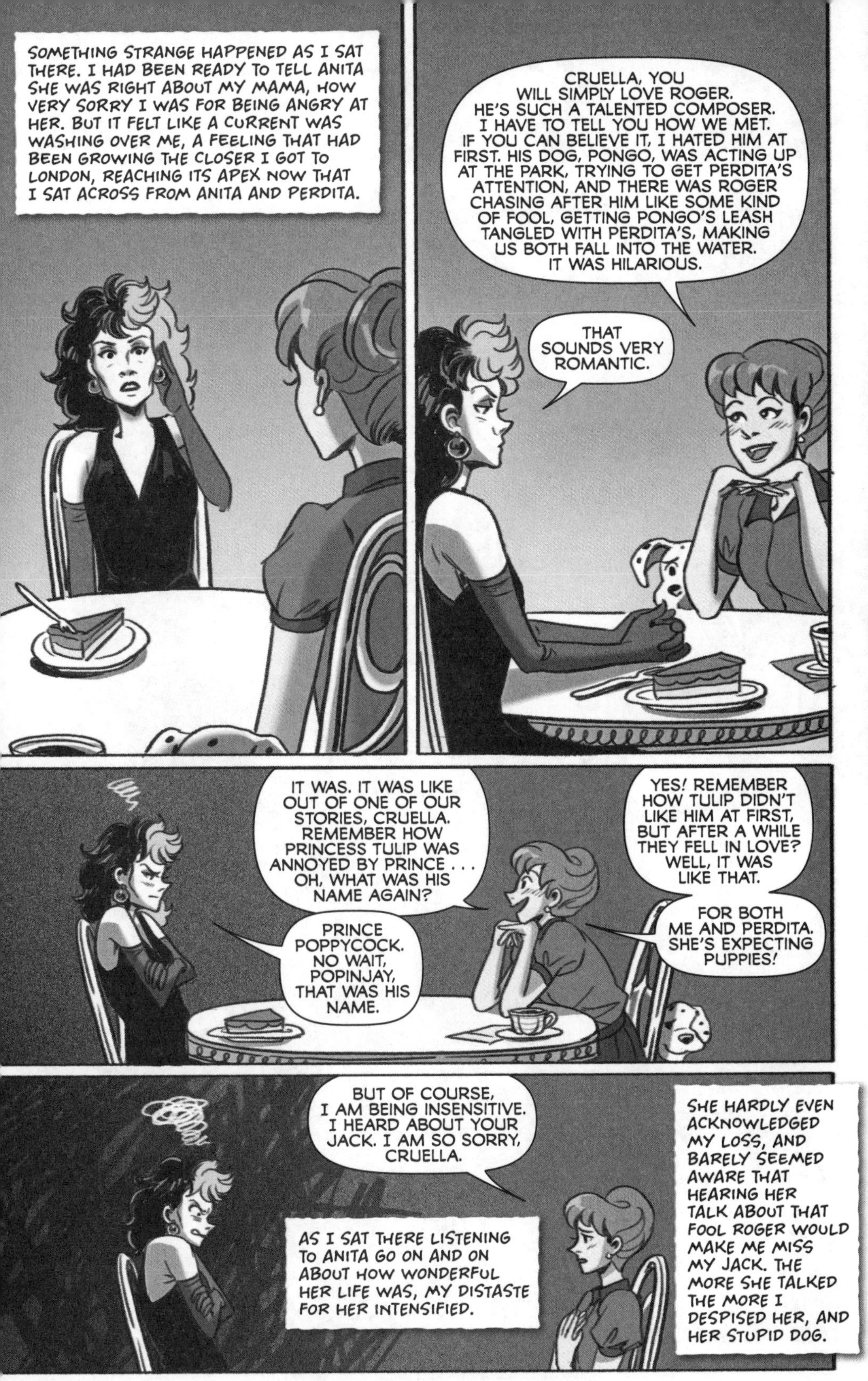
SOMETHING STRANGE HAPPENED AS I SAT THERE. I HAD BEEN READY TO TELL ANITA SHE WAS RIGHT ABOUT MY MAMA, HOW VERY SORRY I WAS FOR BEING ANGRY AT HER. BUT IT FELT LIKE A CURRENT WAS WASHING OVER ME, A FEELING THAT HAD BEEN GROWING THE CLOSER I GOT TO LONDON, REACHING ITS APEX NOW THAT I SAT ACROSS FROM ANITA AND PERDITA.
CRUELLA, YOU WILL SIMPLY LOVE ROGER. HE'S SUCH A TALENTED COMPOSER. I HAVE TO TELL YOU HOW WE MET. IF YOU CAN BELIEVE IT, I HATED HIM AT FIRST. HIS DOG, PONGO, WAS ACTING UP AT THE PARK, TRYING TO GET PERDITA'S ATTENTION, AND THERE WAS ROGER CHASING AFTER HIM LIKE SOME KIND OF FOOL, GETTING PONGO'S LEASH TANGLED WITH PERDITA'S, MAKING US BOTH FALL INTO THE WATER. IT WAS HILARIOUS.
THAT SOUNDS VERY ROMANTIC.
IT WAS. IT WAS LIKE OUT OF ONE OF OUR STORIES, CRUELLA. REMEMBER HOW PRINCESS TULIP WAS ANNOYED BY PRINCE . . . OH, WHAT WAS HIS NAME AGAIN?
PRINCE POPPYCOCK. NO WAIT, POPINJAY, THAT WAS HIS NAME.
YES! REMEMBER HOW TULIP DIDN'T LIKE HIM AT FIRST, BUT AFTER A WHILE THEY FELL IN LOVE? WELL, IT WAS LIKE THAT.
FOR BOTH ME AND PERDITA. SHE'S EXPECTING PUPPIES!
BUT OF COURSE, I AM BEING INSENSITIVE. I HEARD ABOUT YOUR JACK. I AM SO SORRY, CRUELLA.
AS I SAT THERE LISTENING TO ANITA GO ON AND ON ABOUT HOW WONDERFUL HER LIFE WAS, MY DISTASTE FOR HER INTENSIFIED.
SHE HARDLY EVEN ACKNOWLEDGED MY LOSS, AND BARELY SEEMED AWARE THAT HEARING HER TALK ABOUT THAT FOOL ROGER WOULD MAKE ME MISS MY JACK. THE MORE SHE TALKED THE MORE I DESPISED HER, AND HER STUPID DOG.

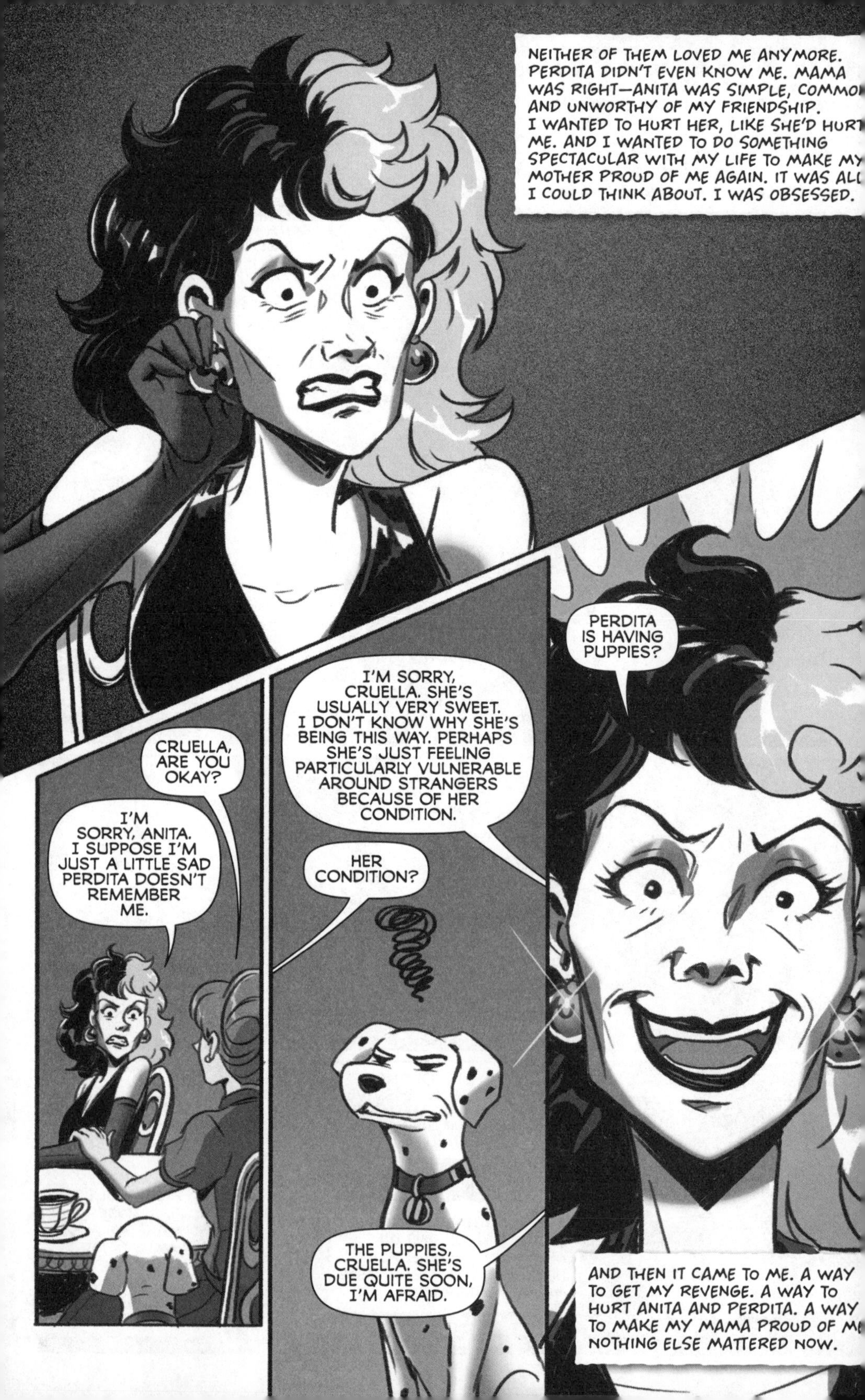
NEITHER OF THEM LOVED ME ANYMORE. PERDITA DIDN'T EVEN KNOW ME. MAMA WAS RIGHT—ANITA WAS SIMPLE, COMMO AND UNWORTHY OF MY FRIENDSHIP. I WANTED TO HURT HER, LIKE SHE'D HURT ME. AND I WANTED TO DO SOMETHING SPECTACULAR WITH MY LIFE TO MAKE MY MOTHER PROUD OF ME AGAIN. IT WAS ALL I COULD THINK ABOUT. I WAS OBSESSED.
CRUELLA, ARE YOU OKAY?
I'M SORRY, ANITA. I SUPPOSE I'M JUST A LITTLE SAD PERDITA DOESN'T REMEMBER ME.
I'M SORRY, CRUELLA. SHE'S USUALLY VERY SWEET. I DON'T KNOW WHY SHE'S BEING THIS WAY. PERHAPS SHE'S JUST FEELING PARTICULARLY VULNERABLE AROUND STRANGERS BECAUSE OF HER CONDITION.
HER CONDITION?
THE PUPPIES, CRUELLA. SHE'S DUE QUITE SOON, I'M AFRAID.
PERDITA IS HAVING PUPPIES?
AND THEN IT CAME TO ME. A WAY TO GET MY REVENGE. A WAY TO HURT ANITA AND PERDITA. A WAY TO MAKE MY MAMA PROUD OF M NOTHING ELSE MATTERED NOW.

HAPTER NINETEEN
BLAME THE HENCHMEN

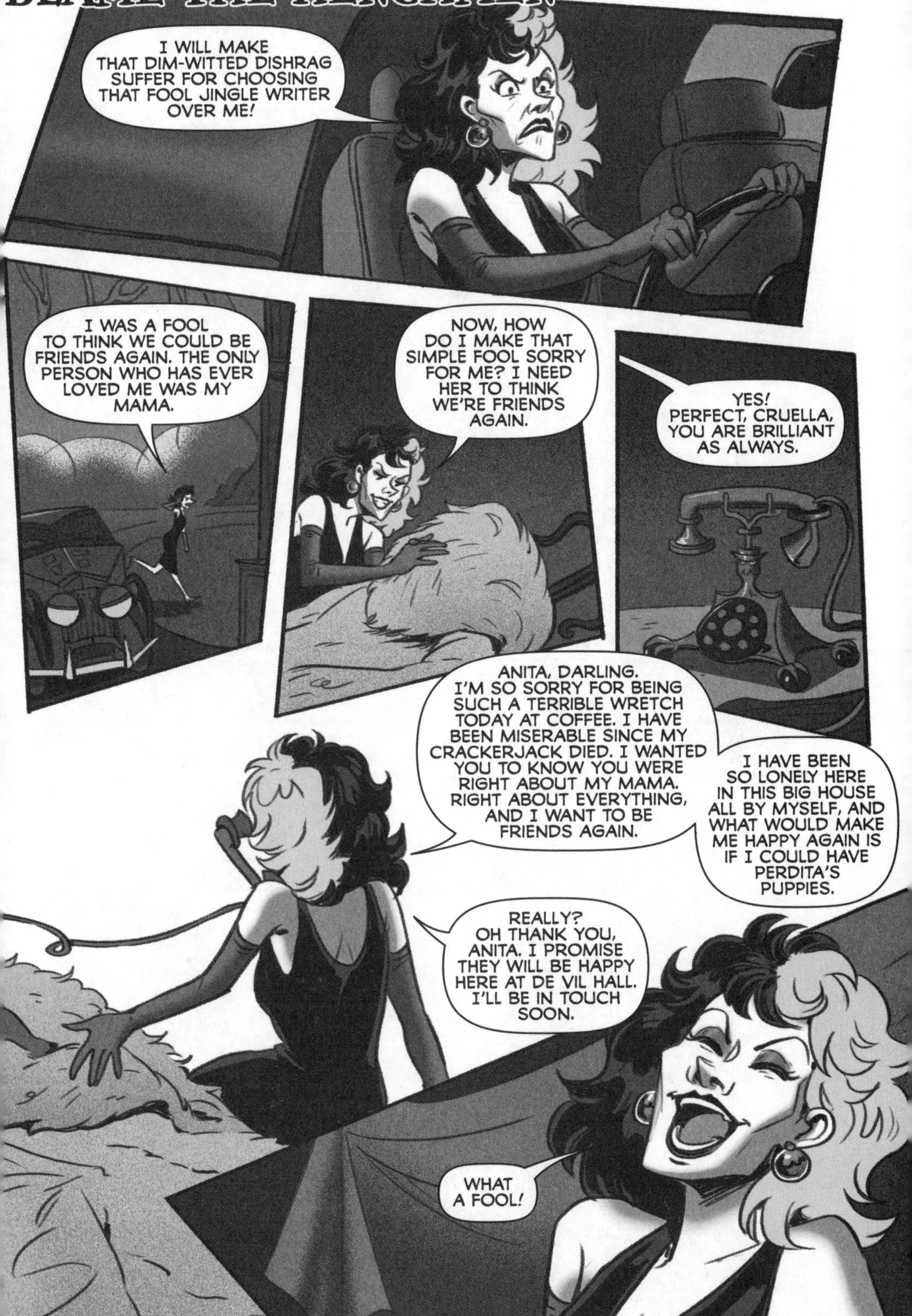

I WILL MAKE THAT DIM-WITTED DISHRAG SUFFER FOR CHOOSING THAT FOOL JINGLE WRITER OVER ME!
I WAS A FOOL TO THINK WE COULD BE FRIENDS AGAIN. THE ONLY PERSON WHO HAS EVER LOVED ME WAS MY MAMA.
NOW, HOW DO I MAKE THAT SIMPLE FOOL SORRY FOR ME? I NEED HER TO THINK WE'RE FRIENDS AGAIN.
YES! PERFECT, CRUELLA, YOU ARE BRILLIANT AS ALWAYS.
ANITA, DARLING. I'M SO SORRY FOR BEING SUCH A TERRIBLE WRETCH TODAY AT COFFEE. I HAVE BEEN MISERABLE SINCE MY CRACKERJACK DIED. I WANTED YOU TO KNOW YOU WERE RIGHT ABOUT MY MAMA. RIGHT ABOUT EVERYTHING, AND I WANT TO BE FRIENDS AGAIN.
I HAVE BEEN SO LONELY HERE IN THIS BIG HOUSE ALL BY MYSELF, AND WHAT WOULD MAKE ME HAPPY AGAIN IS IF I COULD HAVE PERDITA'S PUPPIES.
REALLY? OH THANK YOU, ANITA. I PROMISE THEY WILL BE HAPPY HERE AT DE VIL HALL. I'LL BE IN TOUCH SOON.
WHAT A FOOL!

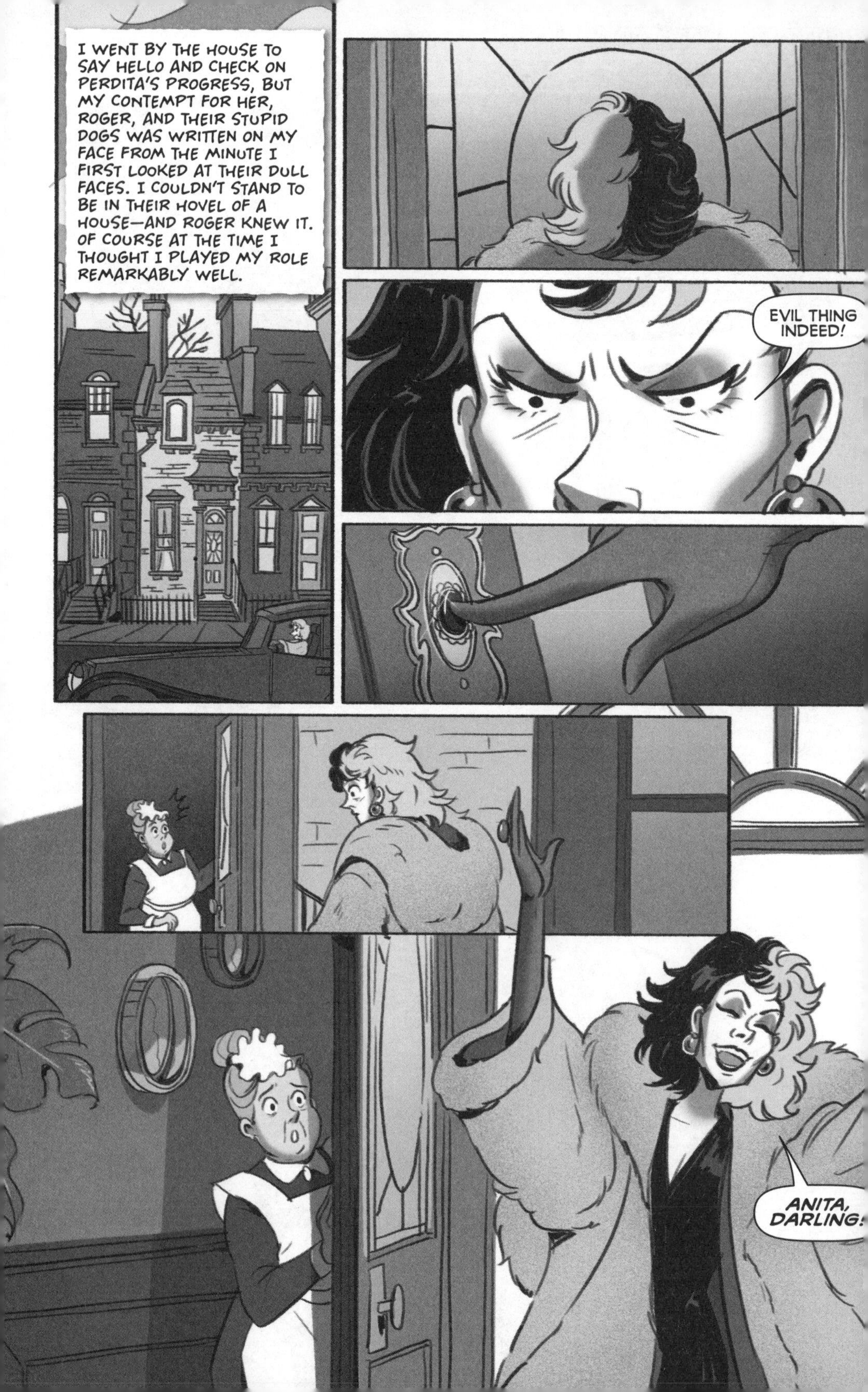
I WENT BY THE HOUSE TO SAY HELLO AND CHECK ON PERDITA'S PROGRESS, BUT MY CONTEMPT FOR HER, ROGER, AND THEIR STUPID DOGS WAS WRITTEN ON MY FACE FROM THE MINUTE I FIRST LOOKED AT THEIR DULL FACES. I COULDN'T STAND TO BE IN THEIR HOVEL OF A HOUSE—AND ROGER KNEW IT. OF COURSE AT THE TIME I THOUGHT I PLAYED MY ROLE REMARKABLY WELL.
EVIL THING INDEED!
ANITA, DARLING!

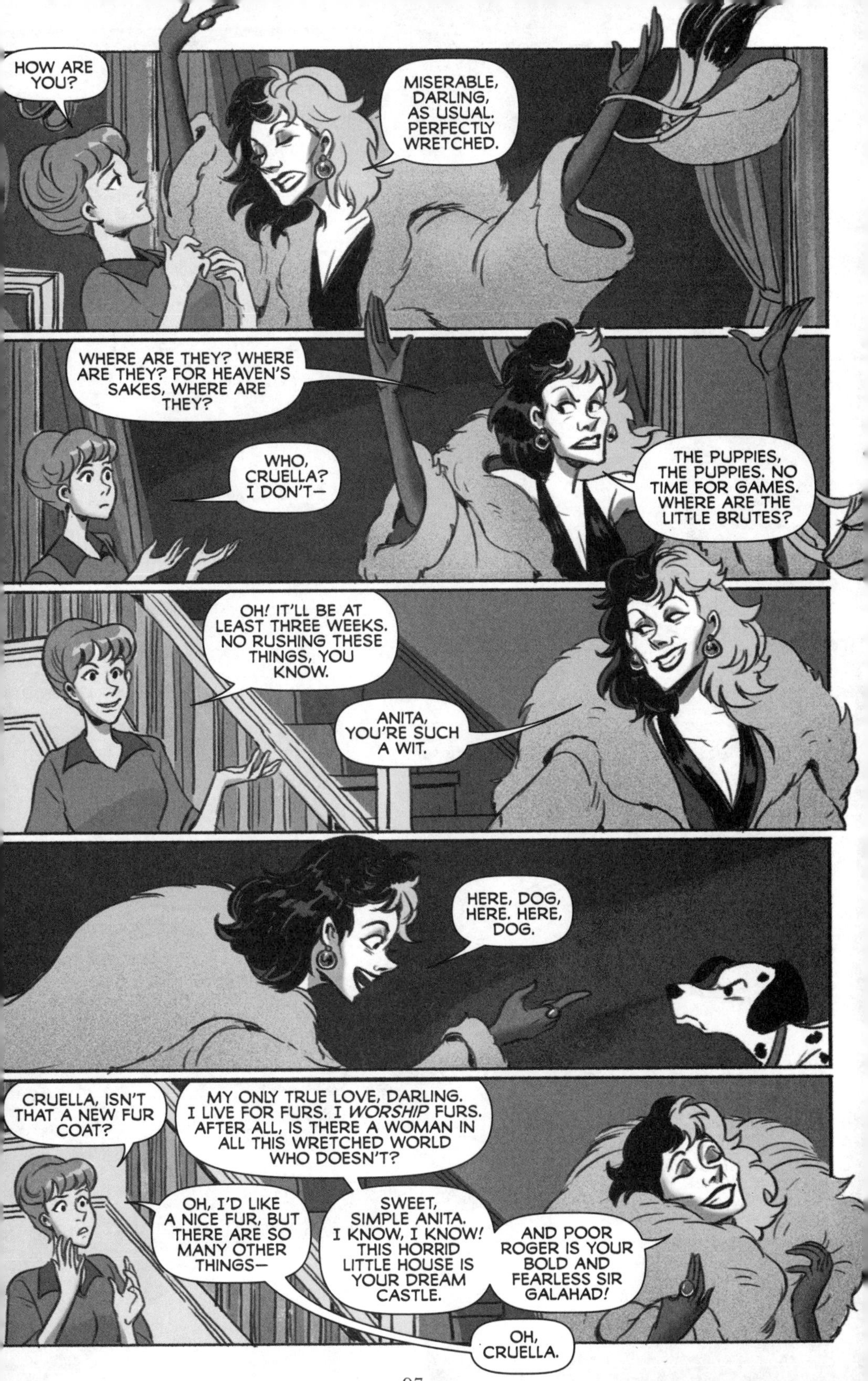
HOW ARE YOU?
MISERABLE, DARLING, AS USUAL. PERFECTLY WRETCHED.
WHERE ARE THEY? WHERE ARE THEY? FOR HEAVEN'S SAKES, WHERE ARE THEY?
WHO, CRUELLA? I DON'T—
THE PUPPIES, THE PUPPIES. NO TIME FOR GAMES. WHERE ARE THE LITTLE BRUTES?
OH! IT'LL BE AT LEAST THREE WEEKS. NO RUSHING THESE THINGS, YOU KNOW.
ANITA, YOU'RE SUCH A WIT.
HERE, DOG, HERE. HERE, DOG.
CRUELLA, ISN'T THAT A NEW FUR COAT?
MY ONLY TRUE LOVE, DARLING. I LIVE FOR FURS. I *WORSHIP* FURS. AFTER ALL, IS THERE A WOMAN IN ALL THIS WRETCHED WORLD WHO DOESN'T?
OH, I'D LIKE A NICE FUR, BUT THERE ARE SO MANY OTHER THINGS—
SWEET, SIMPLE ANITA. I KNOW, I KNOW! THIS HORRID LITTLE HOUSE IS YOUR DREAM CASTLE.
AND POOR ROGER IS YOUR BOLD AND FEARLESS SIR GALAHAD!
OH, CRUELLA.

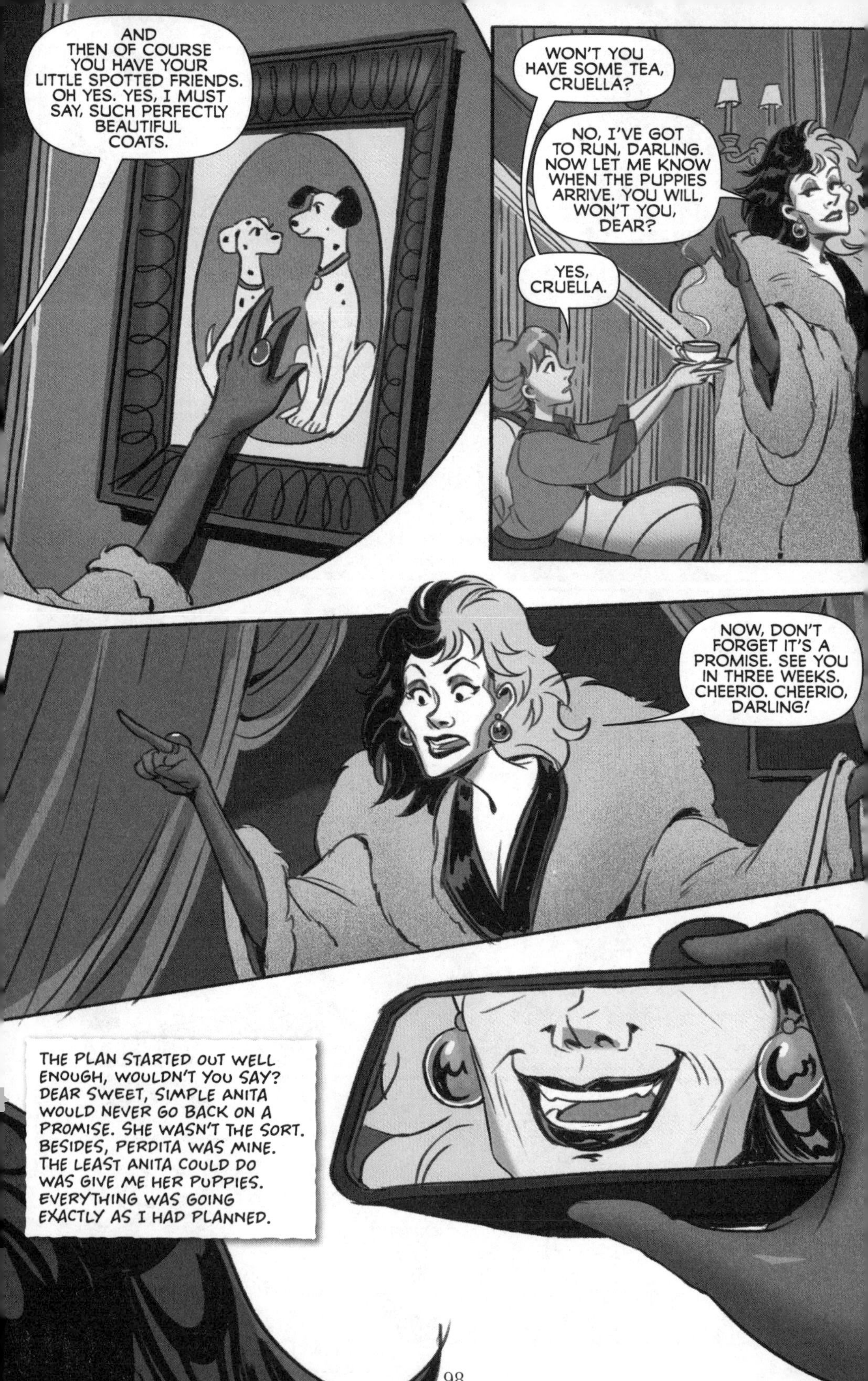
AND THEN OF COURSE YOU HAVE YOUR LITTLE SPOTTED FRIENDS. OH YES. YES, I MUST SAY, SUCH PERFECTLY BEAUTIFUL COATS.
WON'T YOU HAVE SOME TEA, CRUELLA?
NO, I'VE GOT TO RUN, DARLING. NOW LET ME KNOW WHEN THE PUPPIES ARRIVE. YOU WILL, WON'T YOU, DEAR?
YES, CRUELLA.
NOW, DON'T FORGET IT'S A PROMISE. SEE YOU IN THREE WEEKS. CHEERIO. CHEERIO, DARLING!
THE PLAN STARTED OUT WELL ENOUGH, WOULDN'T YOU SAY? DEAR SWEET, SIMPLE ANITA WOULD NEVER GO BACK ON A PROMISE. SHE WASN'T THE SORT. BESIDES, PERDITA WAS MINE. THE LEAST ANITA COULD DO WAS GIVE ME HER PUPPIES. EVERYTHING WAS GOING EXACTLY AS I HAD PLANNED.

APTER TWENTY
WILD AND STORMY NIGHT IN OCTOBER

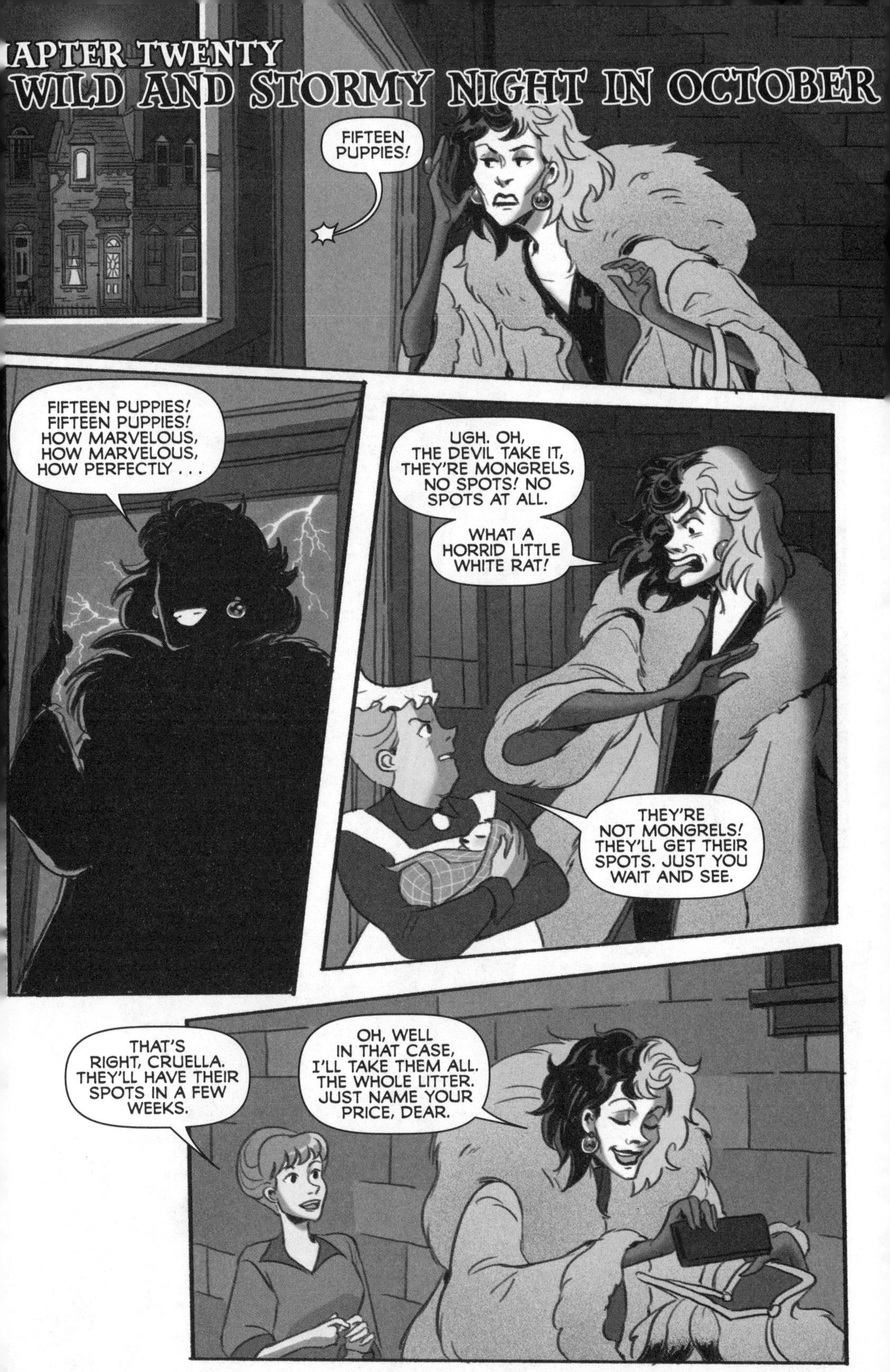

FIFTEEN PUPPIES!
FIFTEEN PUPPIES! FIFTEEN PUPPIES! HOW MARVELOUS, HOW MARVELOUS, HOW PERFECTLY . . .
UGH. OH, THE DEVIL TAKE IT, THEY'RE MONGRELS, NO SPOTS! NO SPOTS AT ALL.
WHAT A HORRID LITTLE WHITE RAT!
THEY'RE NOT MONGRELS! THEY'LL GET THEIR SPOTS. JUST YOU WAIT AND SEE.
THAT'S RIGHT, CRUELLA. THEY'LL HAVE THEIR SPOTS IN A FEW WEEKS.
OH, WELL IN THAT CASE, I'LL TAKE THEM ALL. THE WHOLE LITTER. JUST NAME YOUR PRICE, DEAR.

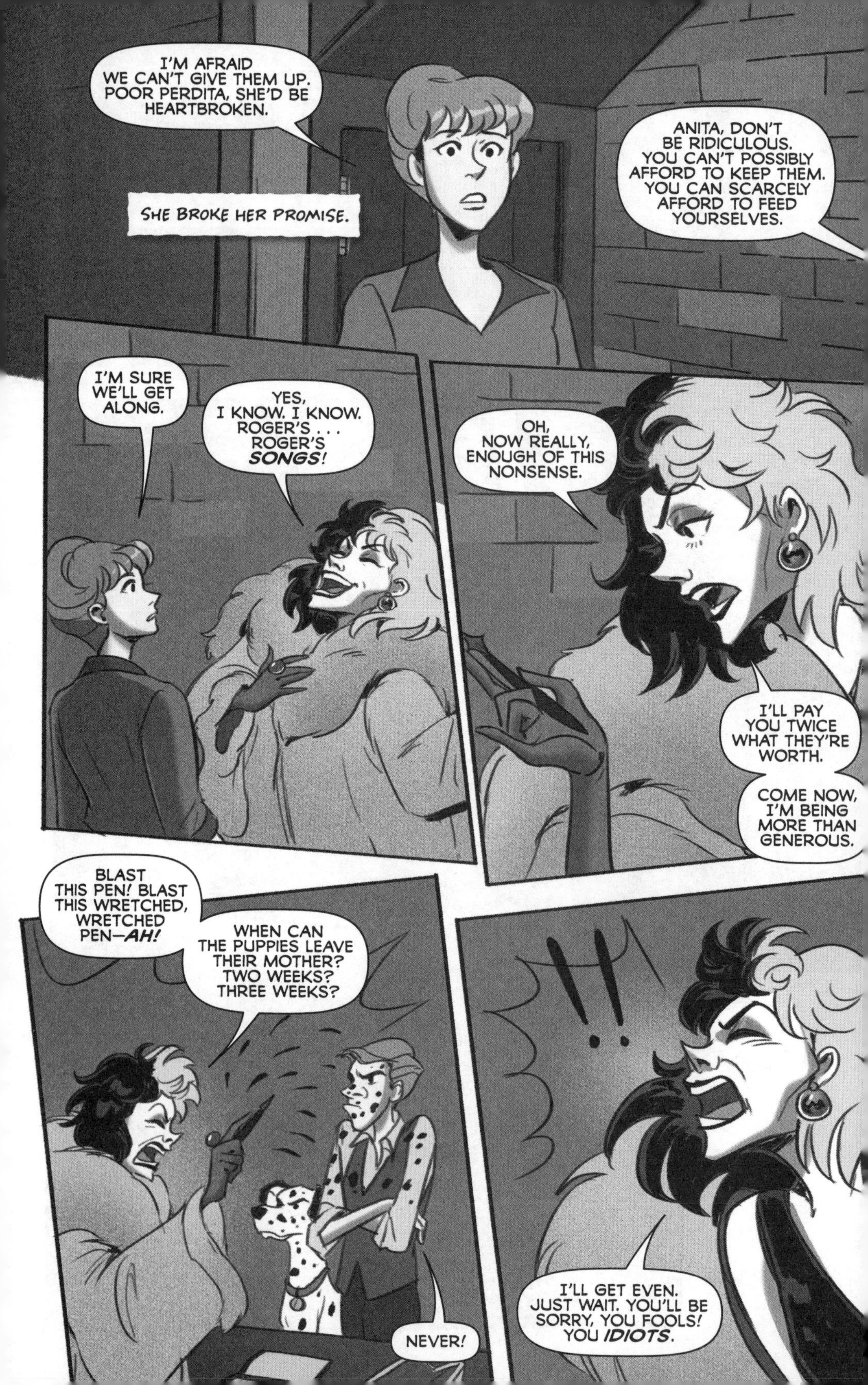

I'M AFRAID WE CAN'T GIVE THEM UP. POOR PERDITA, SHE'D BE HEARTBROKEN.
SHE BROKE HER PROMISE.
ANITA, DON'T BE RIDICULOUS. YOU CAN'T POSSIBLY AFFORD TO KEEP THEM. YOU CAN SCARCELY AFFORD TO FEED YOURSELVES.
I'M SURE WE'LL GET ALONG.
YES, I KNOW. I KNOW. ROGER'S . . . ROGER'S *SONGS*!
OH, NOW REALLY, ENOUGH OF THIS NONSENSE.
I'LL PAY YOU TWICE WHAT THEY'RE WORTH.
COME NOW, I'M BEING MORE THAN GENEROUS.
BLAST THIS PEN! BLAST THIS WRETCHED, WRETCHED PEN—***AH!***
WHEN CAN THE PUPPIES LEAVE THEIR MOTHER? TWO WEEKS? THREE WEEKS?
NEVER!
!!
I'LL GET EVEN. JUST WAIT. YOU'LL BE SORRY, YOU FOOLS! YOU *IDIOTS*.

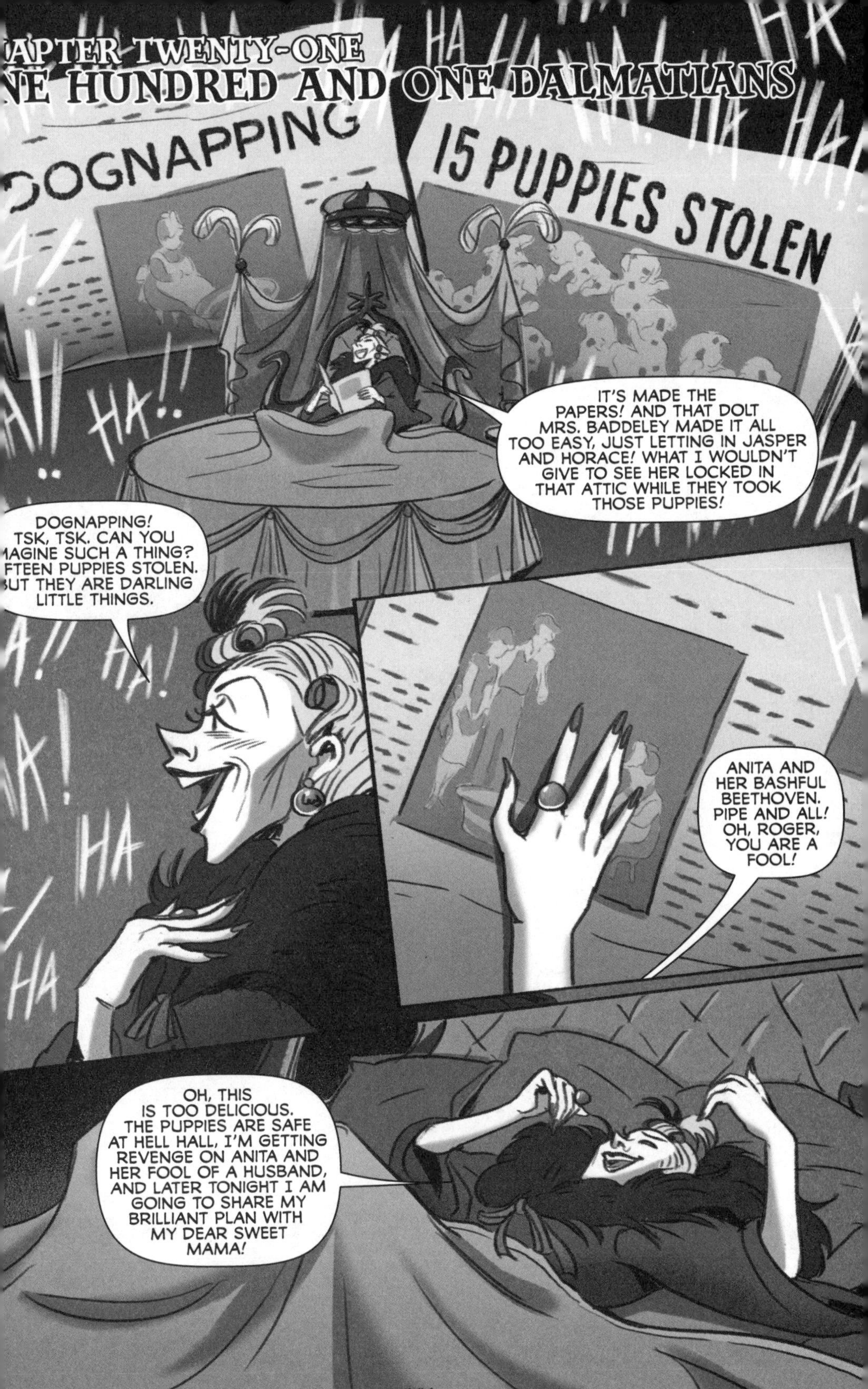

APTER TWENTY-ONE
NE HUNDRED AND ONE DALMATIANS
DOGNAPPING
15 PUPPIES STOLEN
HA HA HA HA!
IT'S MADE THE PAPERS! AND THAT DOLT MRS. BADDELEY MADE IT ALL TOO EASY, JUST LETTING IN JASPER AND HORACE! WHAT I WOULDN'T GIVE TO SEE HER LOCKED IN THAT ATTIC WHILE THEY TOOK THOSE PUPPIES!
DOGNAPPING! TSK, TSK. CAN YOU AGINE SUCH A THING? FTEEN PUPPIES STOLEN. UT THEY ARE DARLING LITTLE THINGS.
ANITA AND HER BASHFUL BEETHOVEN. PIPE AND ALL! OH, ROGER, YOU ARE A FOOL!
OH, THIS IS TOO DELICIOUS. THE PUPPIES ARE SAFE AT HELL HALL, I'M GETTING REVENGE ON ANITA AND HER FOOL OF A HUSBAND, AND LATER TONIGHT I AM GOING TO SHARE MY BRILLIANT PLAN WITH MY DEAR SWEET MAMA!

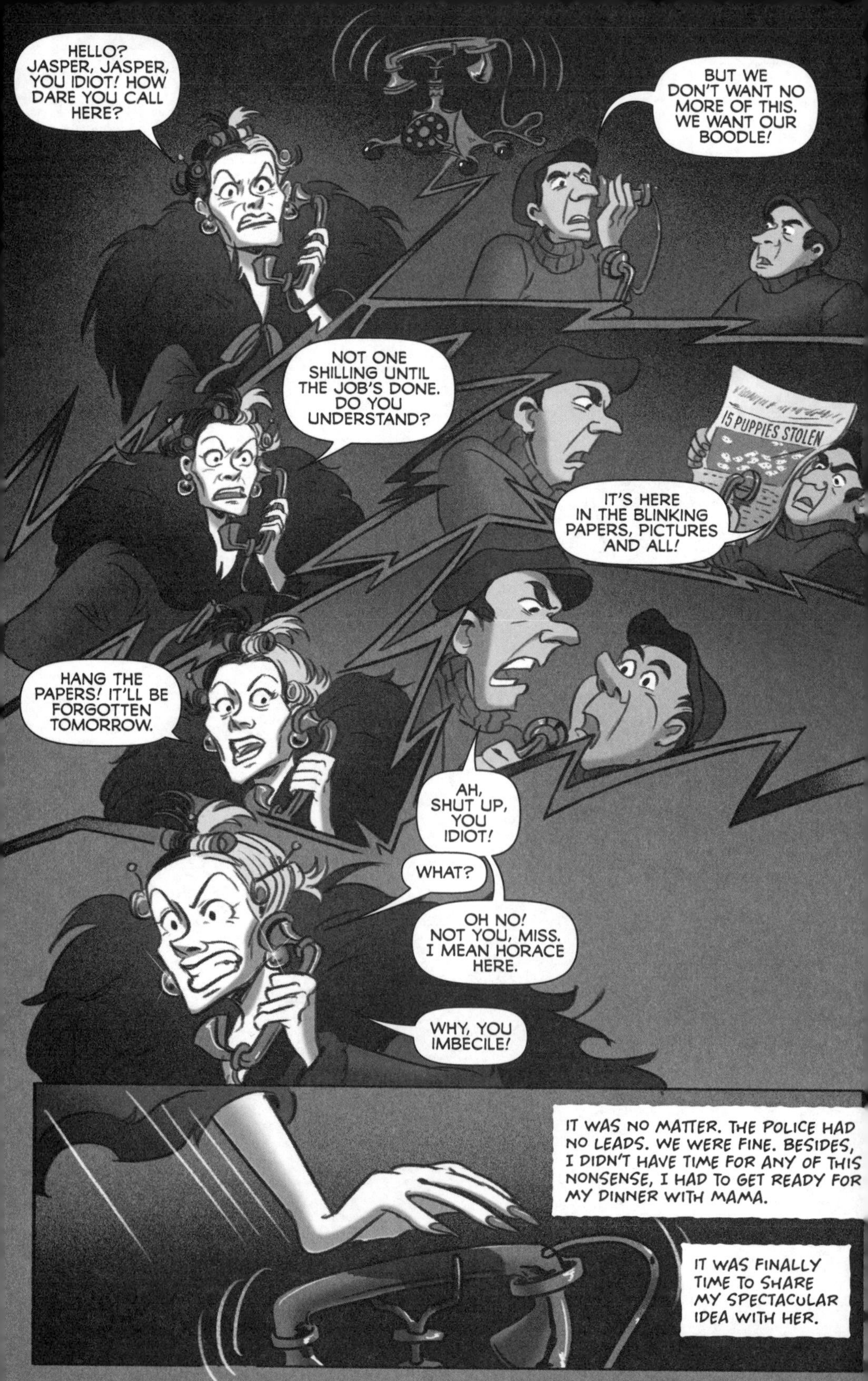
HELLO? JASPER, JASPER, YOU IDIOT! HOW DARE YOU CALL HERE?
BUT WE DON'T WANT NO MORE OF THIS. WE WANT OUR BOODLE!
NOT ONE SHILLING UNTIL THE JOB'S DONE. DO YOU UNDERSTAND?
15 PUPPIES STOLEN
IT'S HERE IN THE BLINKING PAPERS, PICTURES AND ALL!
HANG THE PAPERS! IT'LL BE FORGOTTEN TOMORROW.
AH, SHUT UP, YOU IDIOT!
WHAT?
OH NO! NOT YOU, MISS. I MEAN HORACE HERE.
WHY, YOU IMBECILE!
IT WAS NO MATTER. THE POLICE HAD NO LEADS. WE WERE FINE. BESIDES, I DIDN'T HAVE TIME FOR ANY OF THIS NONSENSE, I HAD TO GET READY FOR MY DINNER WITH MAMA.
IT WAS FINALLY TIME TO SHARE MY SPECTACULAR IDEA WITH HER.

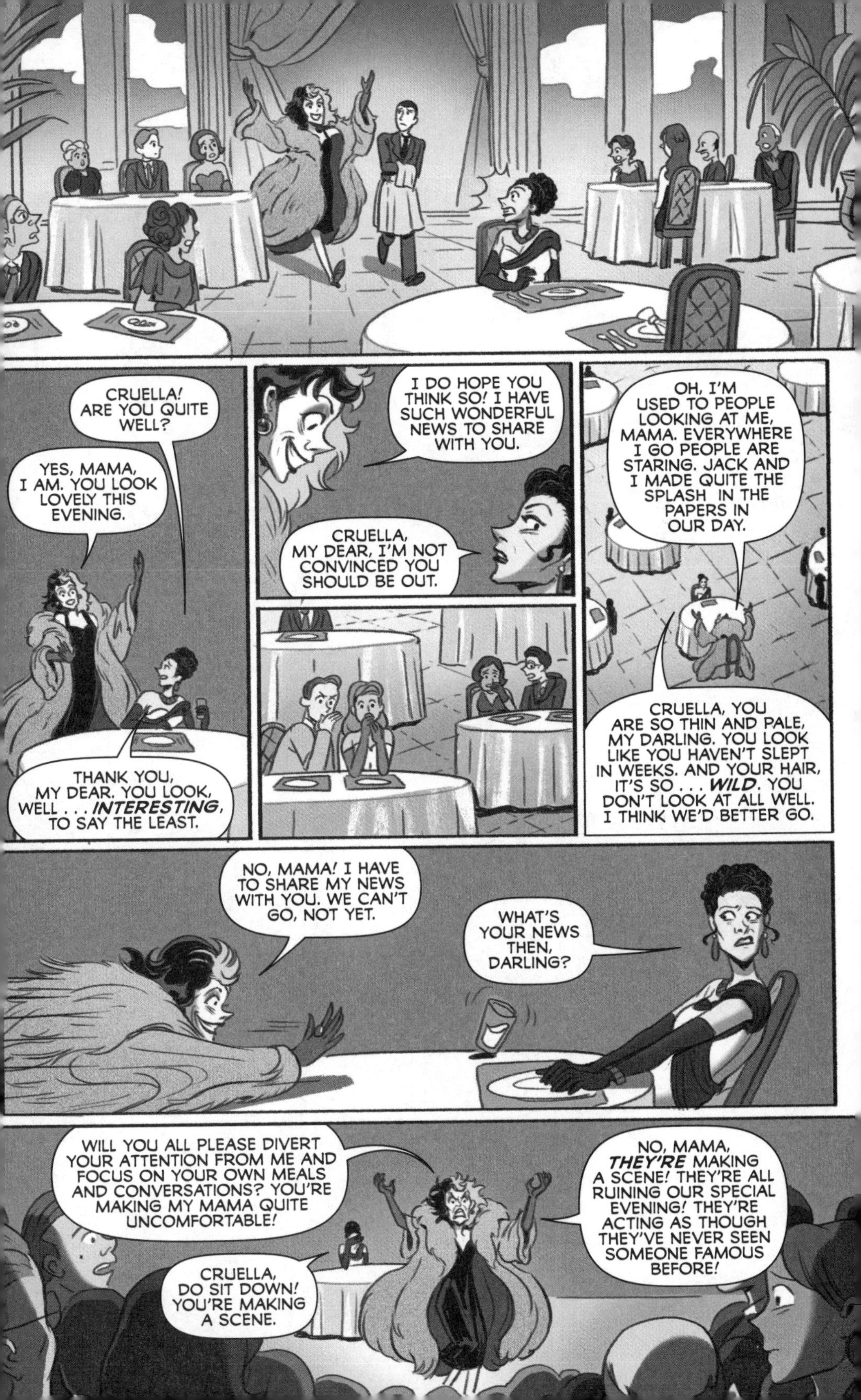
CRUELLA! ARE YOU QUITE WELL?
YES, MAMA, I AM. YOU LOOK LOVELY THIS EVENING.
THANK YOU, MY DEAR. YOU LOOK, WELL . . . *INTERESTING*, TO SAY THE LEAST.
I DO HOPE YOU THINK SO! I HAVE SUCH WONDERFUL NEWS TO SHARE WITH YOU.
CRUELLA, MY DEAR, I'M NOT CONVINCED YOU SHOULD BE OUT.
OH, I'M USED TO PEOPLE LOOKING AT ME, MAMA. EVERYWHERE I GO PEOPLE ARE STARING. JACK AND I MADE QUITE THE SPLASH IN THE PAPERS IN OUR DAY.
CRUELLA, YOU ARE SO THIN AND PALE, MY DARLING. YOU LOOK LIKE YOU HAVEN'T SLEPT IN WEEKS. AND YOUR HAIR, IT'S SO . . . *WILD*. YOU DON'T LOOK AT ALL WELL. I THINK WE'D BETTER GO.
NO, MAMA! I HAVE TO SHARE MY NEWS WITH YOU. WE CAN'T GO, NOT YET.
WHAT'S YOUR NEWS THEN, DARLING?
WILL YOU ALL PLEASE DIVERT YOUR ATTENTION FROM ME AND FOCUS ON YOUR OWN MEALS AND CONVERSATIONS? YOU'RE MAKING MY MAMA QUITE UNCOMFORTABLE!
CRUELLA, DO SIT DOWN! YOU'RE MAKING A SCENE.
NO, MAMA, *THEY'RE* MAKING A SCENE! THEY'RE ALL RUINING OUR SPECIAL EVENING! THEY'RE ACTING AS THOUGH THEY'VE NEVER SEEN SOMEONE FAMOUS BEFORE!

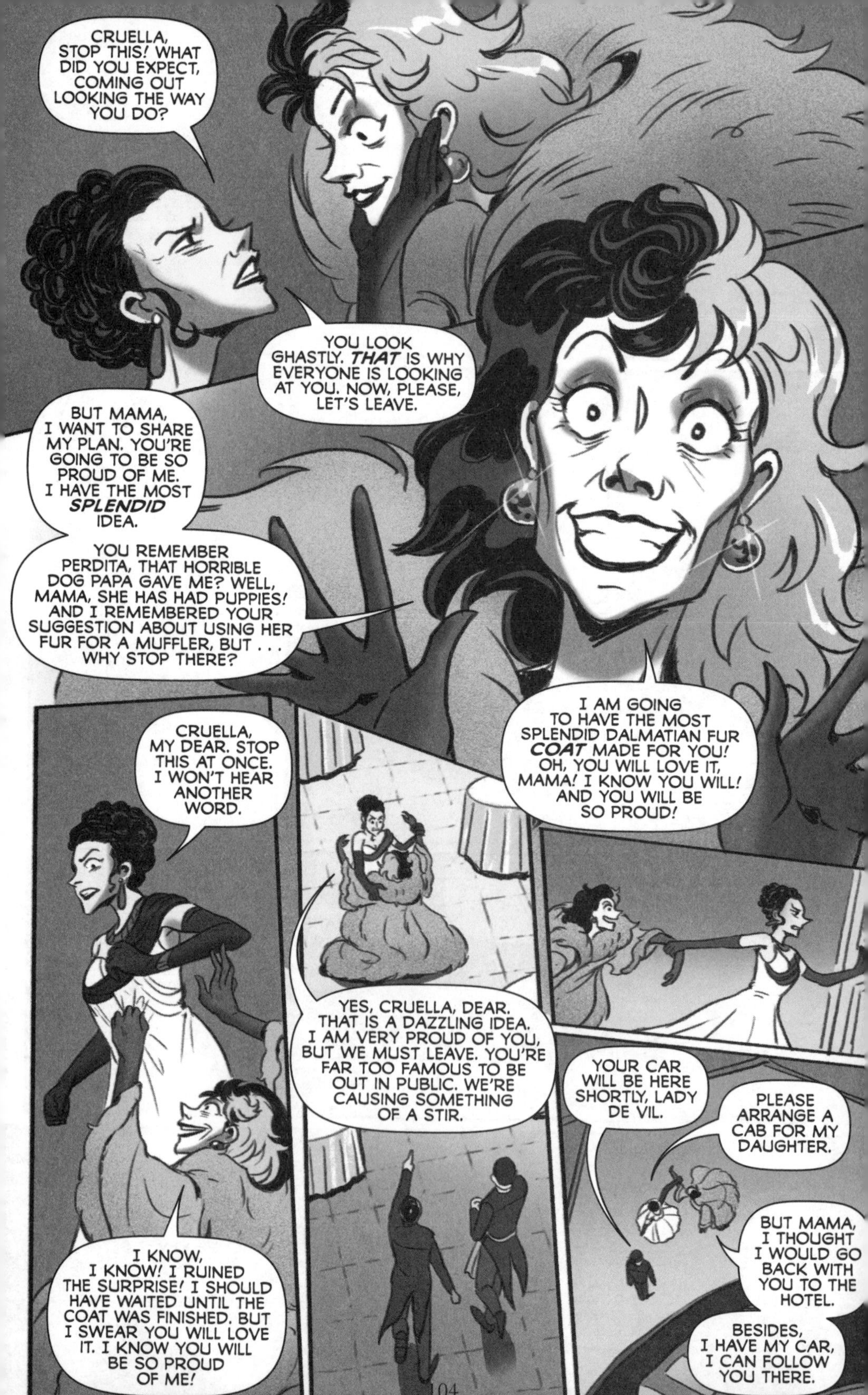

CRUELLA, STOP THIS! WHAT DID YOU EXPECT, COMING OUT LOOKING THE WAY YOU DO?
YOU LOOK GHASTLY. THAT IS WHY EVERYONE IS LOOKING AT YOU. NOW, PLEASE, LET'S LEAVE.
BUT MAMA, I WANT TO SHARE MY PLAN. YOU'RE GOING TO BE SO PROUD OF ME. I HAVE THE MOST SPLENDID IDEA.
YOU REMEMBER PERDITA, THAT HORRIBLE DOG PAPA GAVE ME? WELL, MAMA, SHE HAS HAD PUPPIES! AND I REMEMBERED YOUR SUGGESTION ABOUT USING HER FUR FOR A MUFFLER, BUT . . . WHY STOP THERE?
I AM GOING TO HAVE THE MOST SPLENDID DALMATIAN FUR COAT MADE FOR YOU! OH, YOU WILL LOVE IT, MAMA! I KNOW YOU WILL! AND YOU WILL BE SO PROUD!
CRUELLA, MY DEAR. STOP THIS AT ONCE. I WON'T HEAR ANOTHER WORD.
I KNOW, I KNOW! I RUINED THE SURPRISE! I SHOULD HAVE WAITED UNTIL THE COAT WAS FINISHED. BUT I SWEAR YOU WILL LOVE IT. I KNOW YOU WILL BE SO PROUD OF ME!
YES, CRUELLA, DEAR. THAT IS A DAZZLING IDEA. I AM VERY PROUD OF YOU, BUT WE MUST LEAVE. YOU'RE FAR TOO FAMOUS TO BE OUT IN PUBLIC. WE'RE CAUSING SOMETHING OF A STIR.
YOUR CAR WILL BE HERE SHORTLY, LADY DE VIL.
PLEASE ARRANGE A CAB FOR MY DAUGHTER.
BUT MAMA, I THOUGHT I WOULD GO BACK WITH YOU TO THE HOTEL.
BESIDES, I HAVE MY CAR, I CAN FOLLOW YOU THERE.

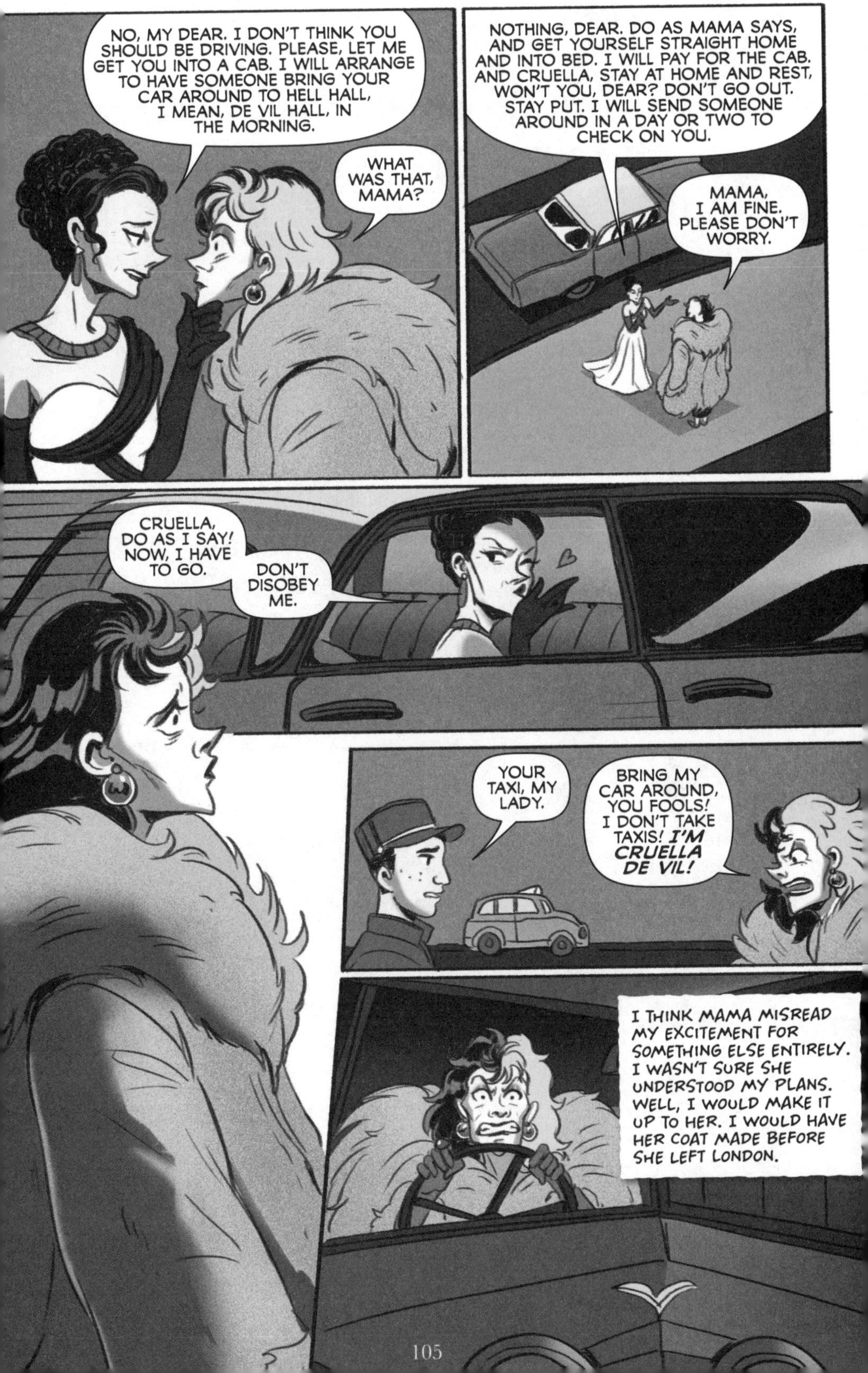
NO, MY DEAR. I DON'T THINK YOU SHOULD BE DRIVING. PLEASE, LET ME GET YOU INTO A CAB. I WILL ARRANGE TO HAVE SOMEONE BRING YOUR CAR AROUND TO HELL HALL, I MEAN, DE VIL HALL, IN THE MORNING.
WHAT WAS THAT, MAMA?
NOTHING, DEAR. DO AS MAMA SAYS, AND GET YOURSELF STRAIGHT HOME AND INTO BED. I WILL PAY FOR THE CAB. AND CRUELLA, STAY AT HOME AND REST, WON'T YOU, DEAR? DON'T GO OUT. STAY PUT. I WILL SEND SOMEONE AROUND IN A DAY OR TWO TO CHECK ON YOU.
MAMA, I AM FINE. PLEASE DON'T WORRY.
CRUELLA, DO AS I SAY! NOW, I HAVE TO GO.
DON'T DISOBEY ME.
YOUR TAXI, MY LADY.
BRING MY CAR AROUND, YOU FOOLS! I DON'T TAKE TAXIS! I'M CRUELLA DE VIL!
I THINK MAMA MISREAD MY EXCITEMENT FOR SOMETHING ELSE ENTIRELY. I WASN'T SURE SHE UNDERSTOOD MY PLANS. WELL, I WOULD MAKE IT UP TO HER. I WOULD HAVE HER COAT MADE BEFORE SHE LEFT LONDON.

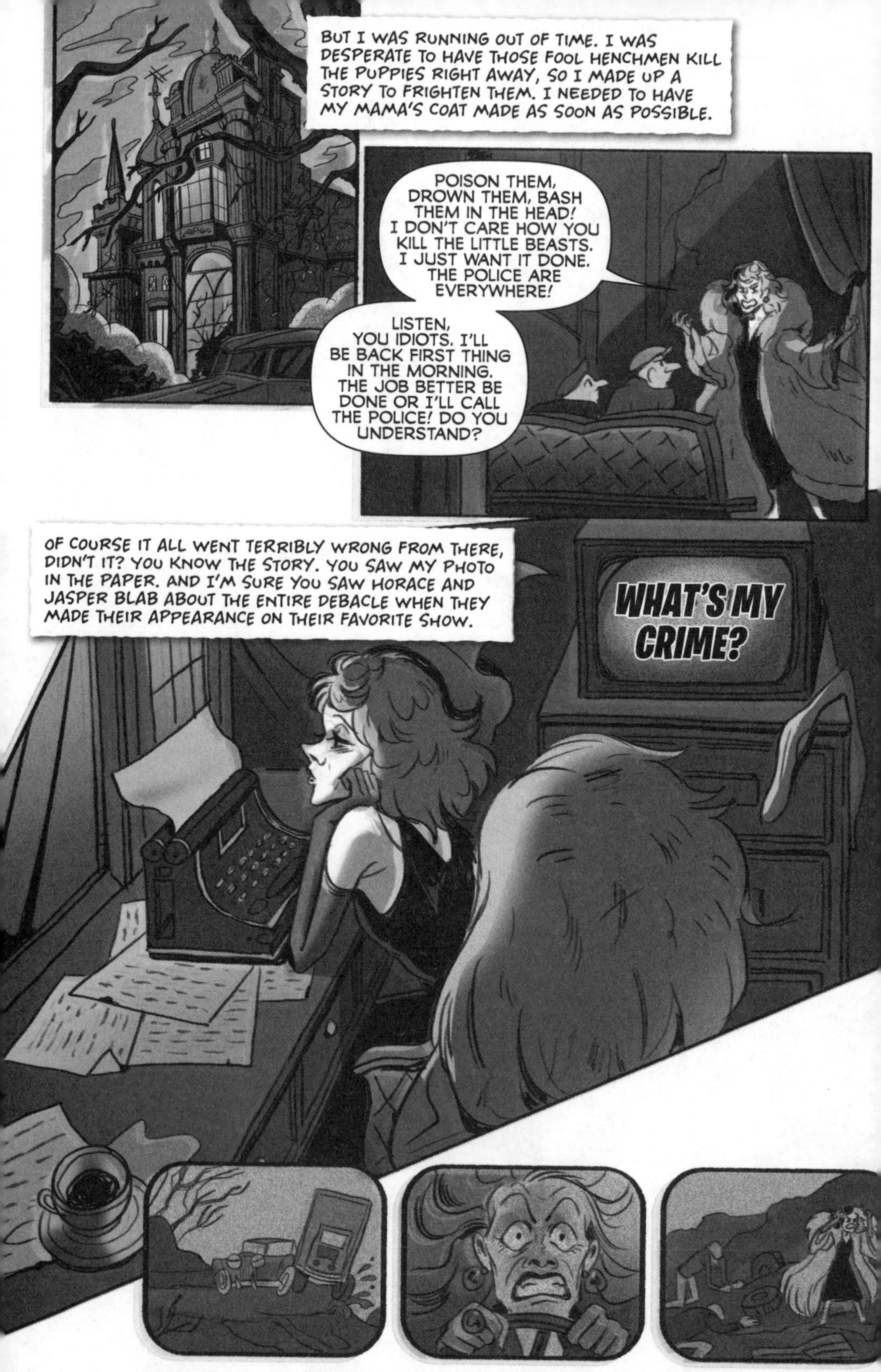
BUT I WAS RUNNING OUT OF TIME. I WAS DESPERATE TO HAVE THOSE FOOL HENCHMEN KILL THE PUPPIES RIGHT AWAY, SO I MADE UP A STORY TO FRIGHTEN THEM. I NEEDED TO HAVE MY MAMA'S COAT MADE AS SOON AS POSSIBLE.
POISON THEM, DROWN THEM, BASH THEM IN THE HEAD! I DON'T CARE HOW YOU KILL THE LITTLE BEASTS. I JUST WANT IT DONE. THE POLICE ARE EVERYWHERE!
LISTEN, YOU IDIOTS. I'LL BE BACK FIRST THING IN THE MORNING. THE JOB BETTER BE DONE OR I'LL CALL THE POLICE! DO YOU UNDERSTAND?
OF COURSE IT ALL WENT TERRIBLY WRONG FROM THERE, DIDN'T IT? YOU KNOW THE STORY. YOU SAW MY PHOTO IN THE PAPER. AND I'M SURE YOU SAW HORACE AND JASPER BLAB ABOUT THE ENTIRE DEBACLE WHEN THEY MADE THEIR APPEARANCE ON THEIR FAVORITE SHOW.
WHAT'S MY CRIME?

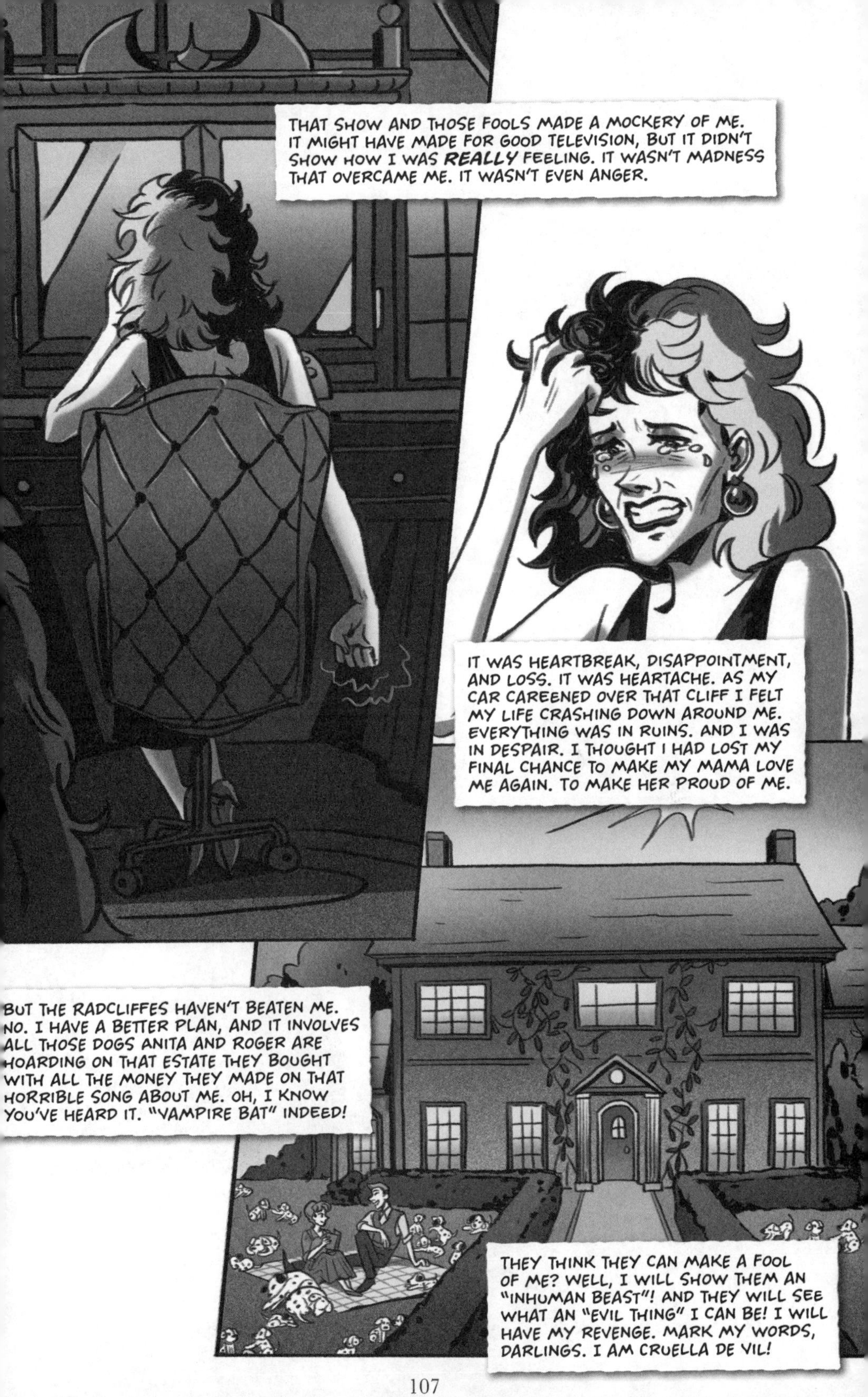
THAT SHOW AND THOSE FOOLS MADE A MOCKERY OF ME. IT MIGHT HAVE MADE FOR GOOD TELEVISION, BUT IT DIDN'T SHOW HOW I WAS **REALLY** FEELING. IT WASN'T MADNESS THAT OVERCAME ME. IT WASN'T EVEN ANGER.
IT WAS HEARTBREAK, DISAPPOINTMENT, AND LOSS. IT WAS HEARTACHE. AS MY CAR CAREENED OVER THAT CLIFF I FELT MY LIFE CRASHING DOWN AROUND ME. EVERYTHING WAS IN RUINS. AND I WAS IN DESPAIR. I THOUGHT I HAD LOST MY FINAL CHANCE TO MAKE MY MAMA LOVE ME AGAIN. TO MAKE HER PROUD OF ME.
BUT THE RADCLIFFES HAVEN'T BEATEN ME. NO. I HAVE A BETTER PLAN, AND IT INVOLVES ALL THOSE DOGS ANITA AND ROGER ARE HOARDING ON THAT ESTATE THEY BOUGHT WITH ALL THE MONEY THEY MADE ON THAT HORRIBLE SONG ABOUT ME. OH, I KNOW YOU'VE HEARD IT. "VAMPIRE BAT" INDEED!
THEY THINK THEY CAN MAKE A FOOL OF ME? WELL, I WILL SHOW THEM AN "INHUMAN BEAST"! AND THEY WILL SEE WHAT AN "EVIL THING" I CAN BE! I WILL HAVE MY REVENGE. MARK MY WORDS, DARLINGS. I AM CRUELLA DE VIL!

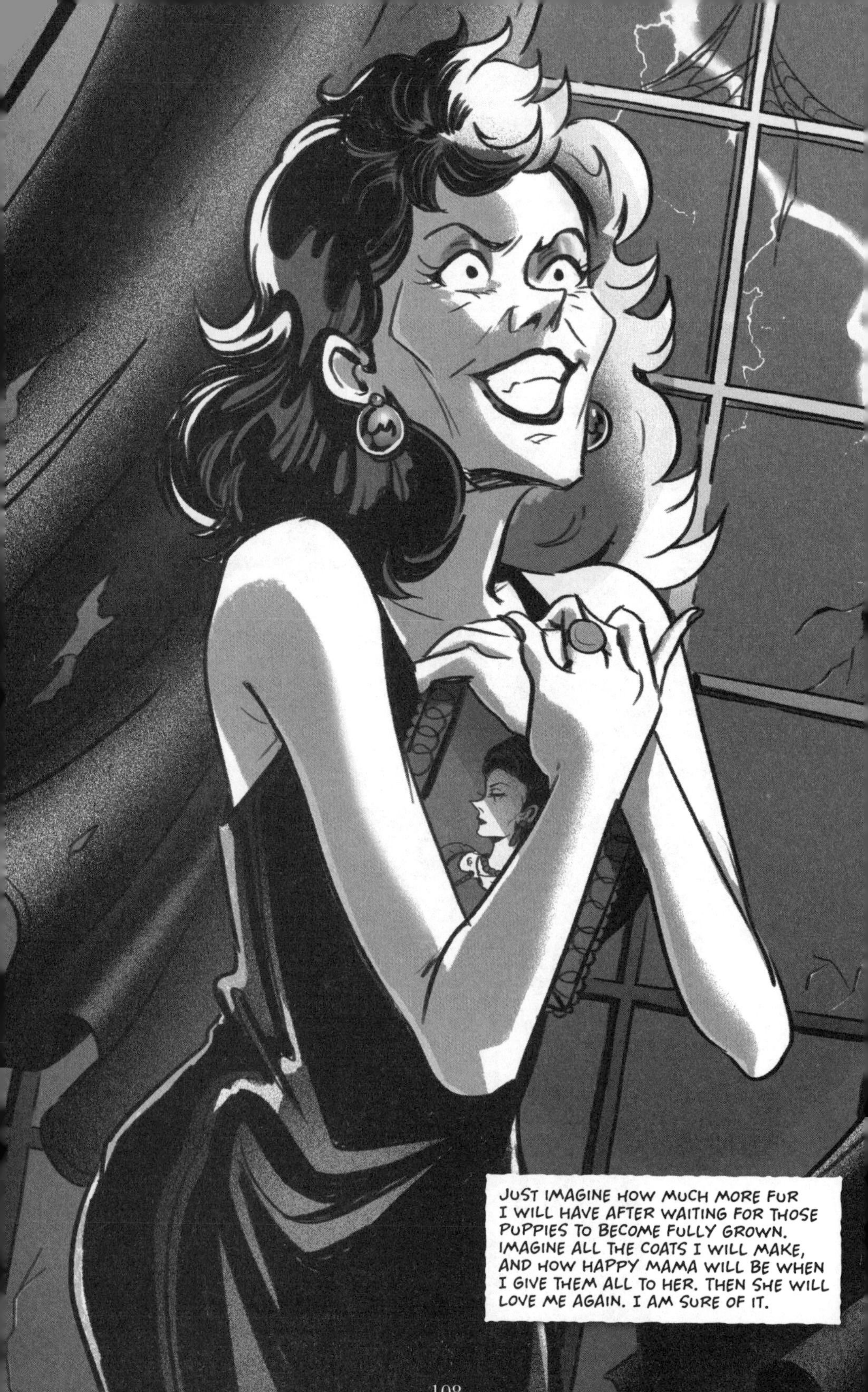
JUST IMAGINE HOW MUCH MORE FUR I WILL HAVE AFTER WAITING FOR THOSE PUPPIES TO BECOME FULLY GROWN. IMAGINE ALL THE COATS I WILL MAKE, AND HOW HAPPY MAMA WILL BE WHEN I GIVE THEM ALL TO HER. THEN SHE WILL LOVE ME AGAIN. I AM SURE OF IT.

AFTERWORD

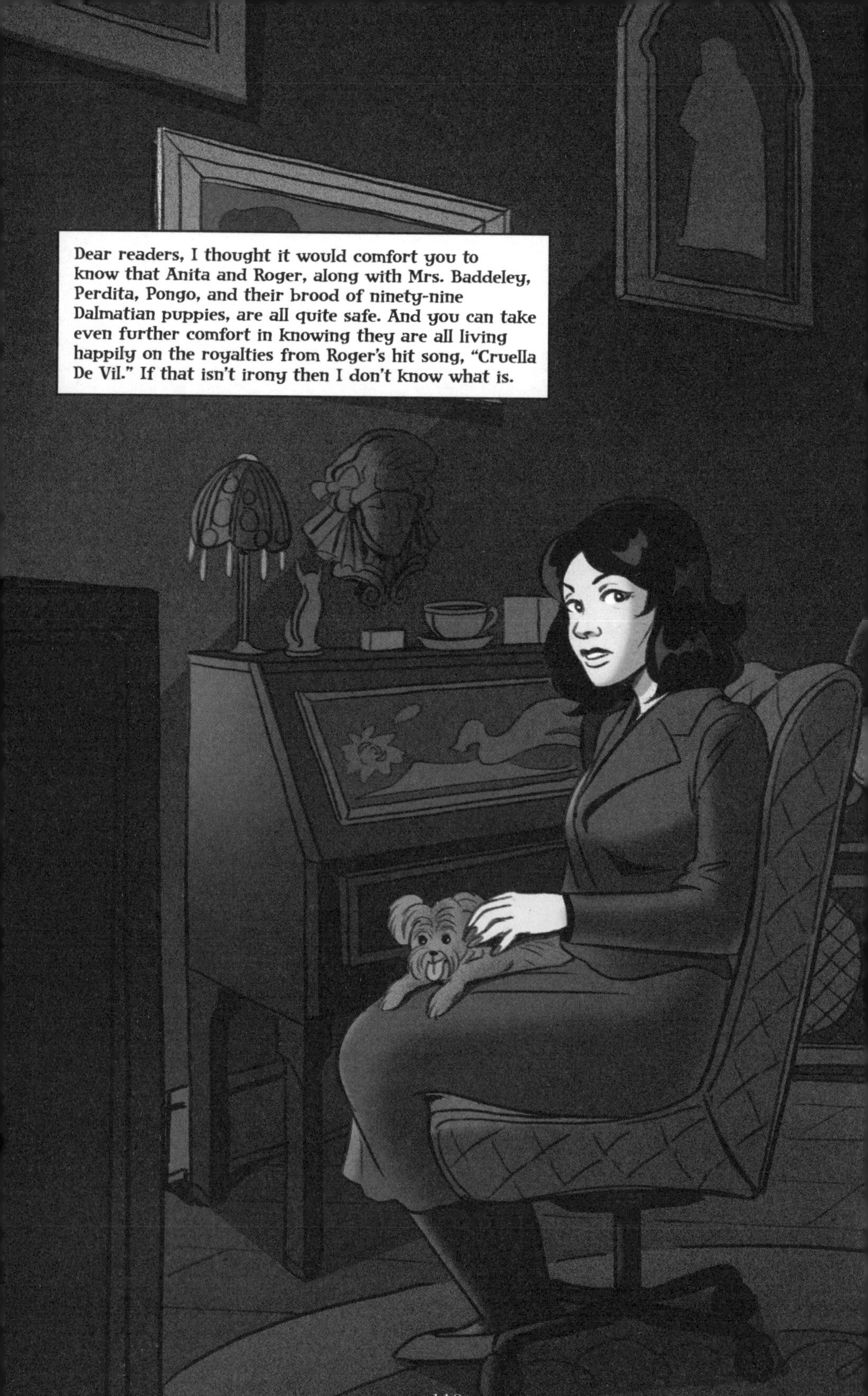
Dear readers, I thought it would comfort you to know that Anita and Roger, along with Mrs. Baddeley, Perdita, Pongo, and their brood of ninety-nine Dalmatian puppies, are all quite safe. And you can take even further comfort in knowing they are all living happily on the royalties from Roger's hit song, "Cruella De Vil." If that isn't irony then I don't know what is.

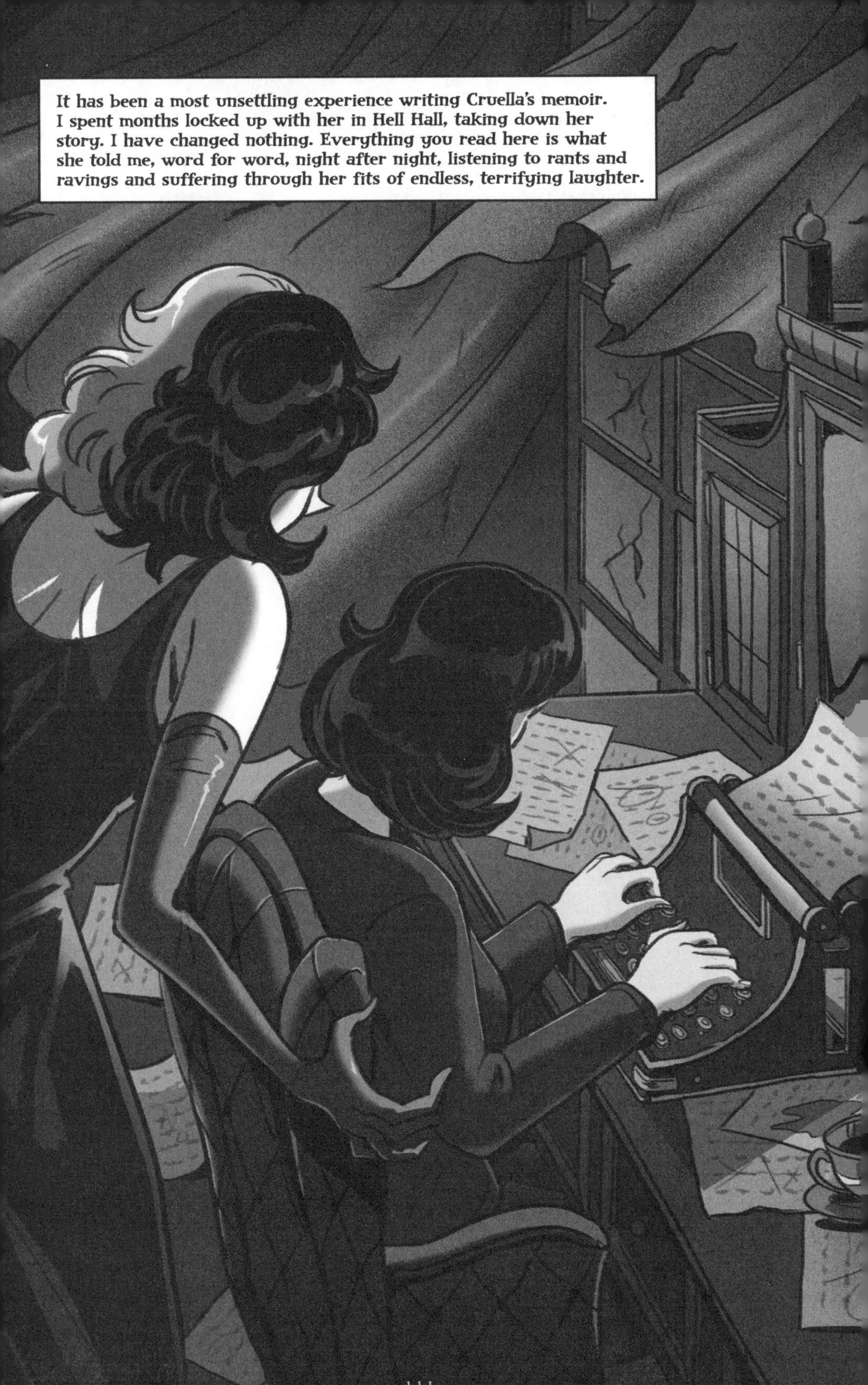
It has been a most unsettling experience writing Cruella's memoir. I spent months locked up with her in Hell Hall, taking down her story. I have changed nothing. Everything you read here is what she told me, word for word, night after night, listening to rants and ravings and suffering through her fits of endless, terrifying laughter.

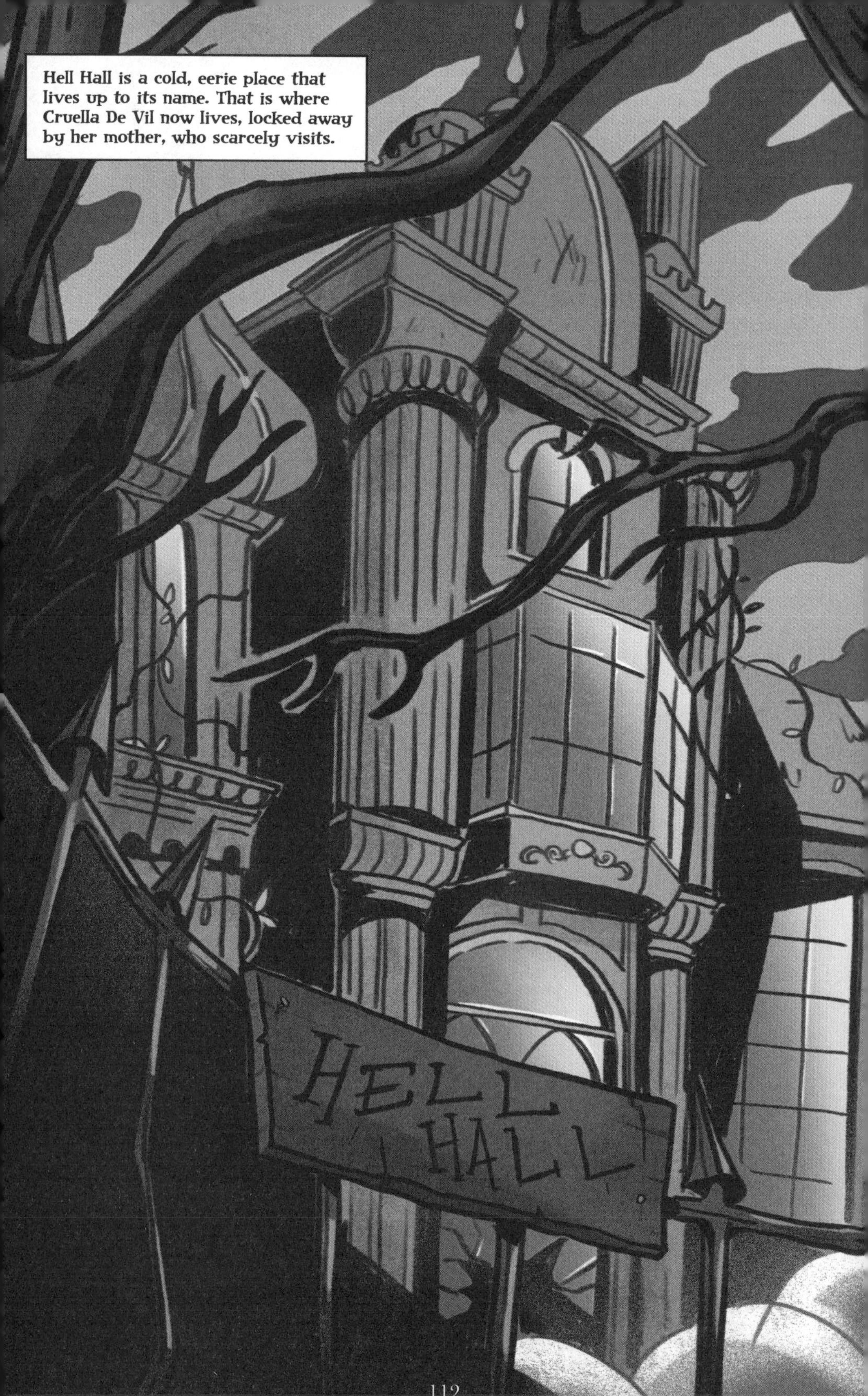
Hell Hall is a cold, eerie place that lives up to its name. That is where Cruella De Vil now lives, locked away by her mother, who scarcely visits.
HELL HALL

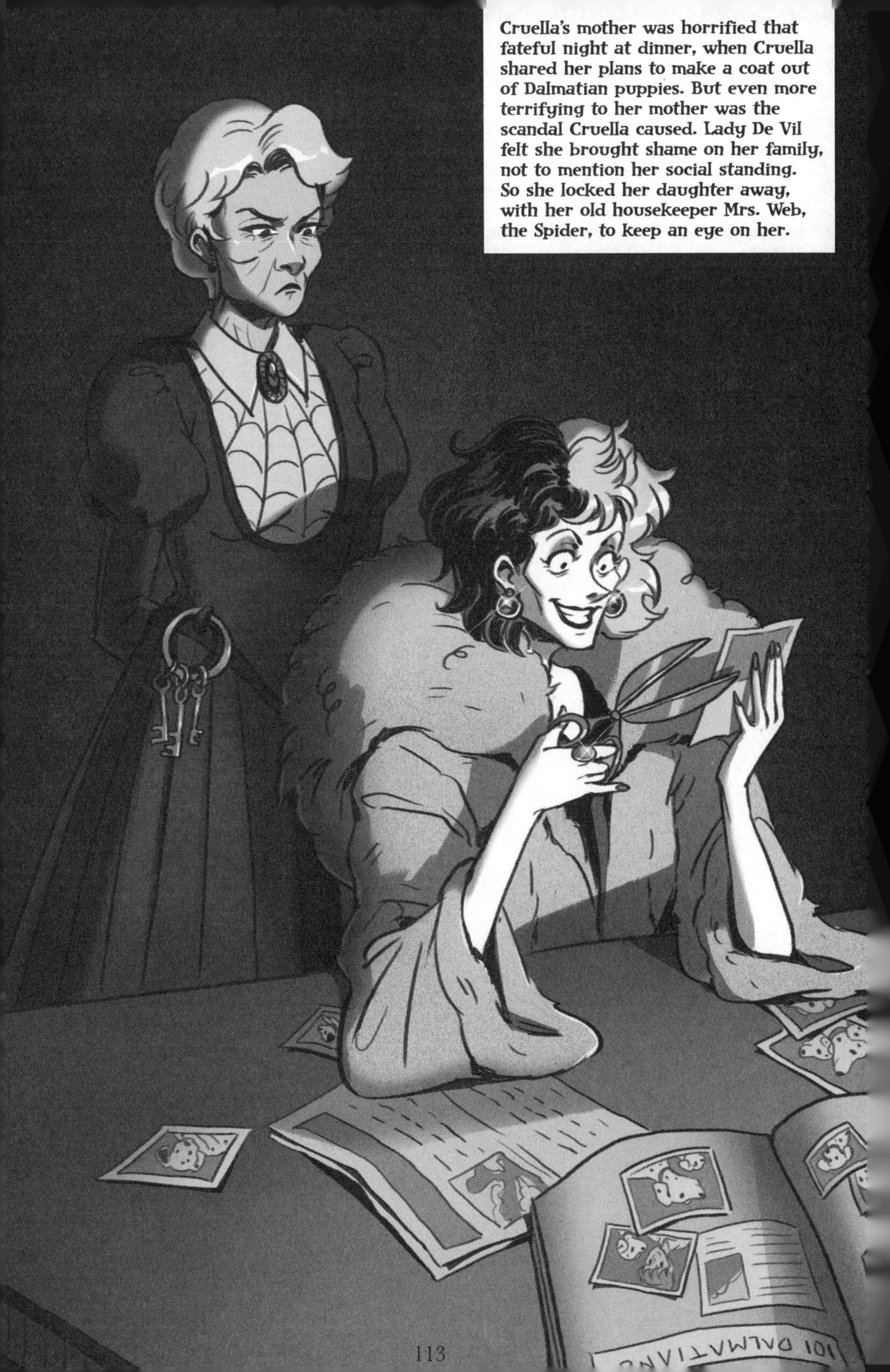
Cruella's mother was horrified that fateful night at dinner, when Cruella shared her plans to make a coat out of Dalmatian puppies. But even more terrifying to her mother was the scandal Cruella caused. Lady De Vil felt she brought shame on her family, not to mention her social standing. So she locked her daughter away, with her old housekeeper Mrs. Web, the Spider, to keep an eye on her.

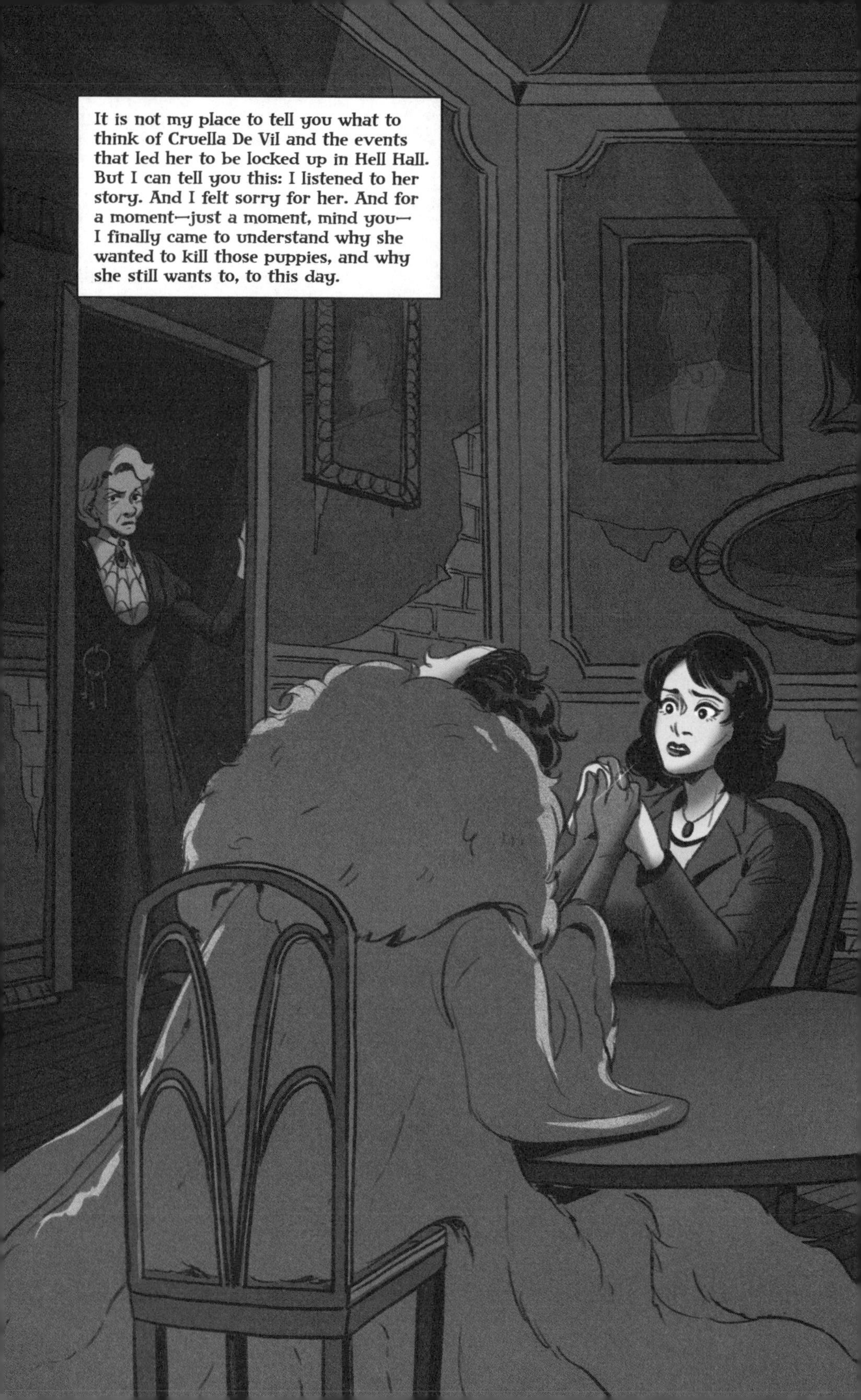
It is not my place to tell you what to think of Cruella De Vil and the events that led her to be locked up in Hell Hall. But I can tell you this: I listened to her story. And I felt sorry for her. And for a moment—just a moment, mind you—I finally came to understand why she wanted to kill those puppies, and why she still wants to, to this day.

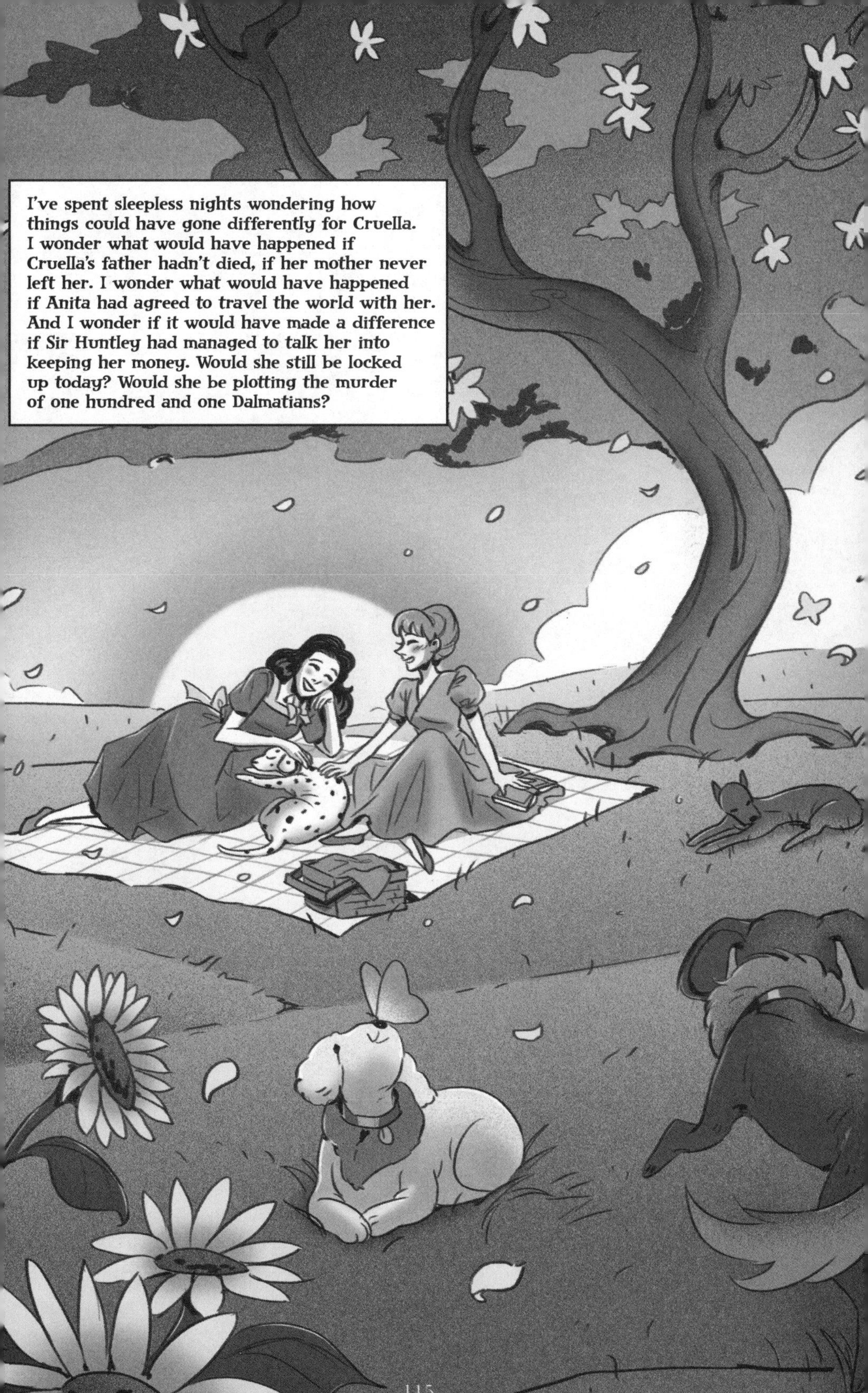
I've spent sleepless nights wondering how things could have gone differently for Cruella. I wonder what would have happened if Cruella's father hadn't died, if her mother never left her. I wonder what would have happened if Anita had agreed to travel the world with her. And I wonder if it would have made a difference if Sir Huntley had managed to talk her into keeping her money. Would she still be locked up today? Would she be plotting the murder of one hundred and one Dalmatians?

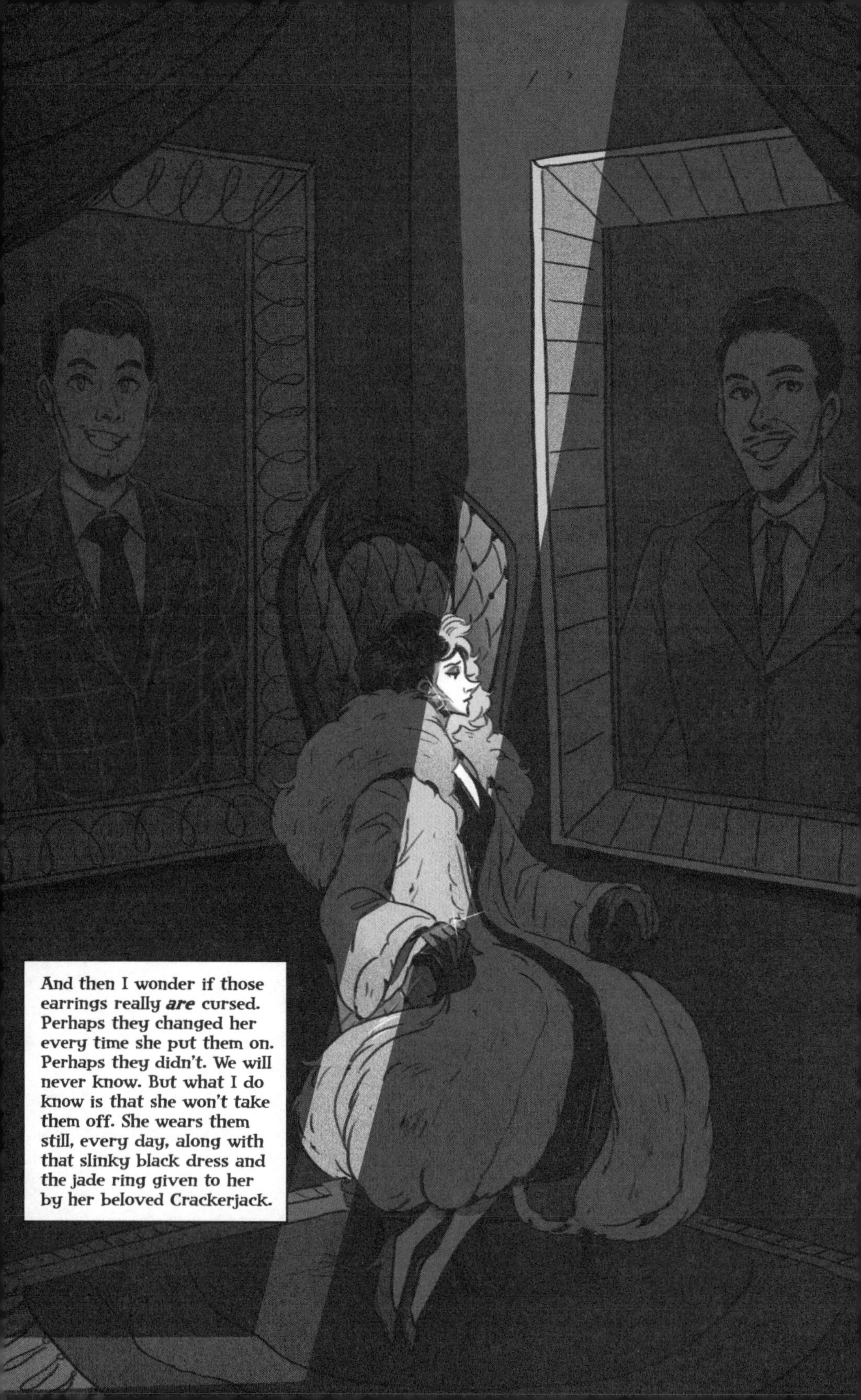
And then I wonder if those earrings really *are* cursed. Perhaps they changed her every time she put them on. Perhaps they didn't. We will never know. But what I do know is that she won't take them off. She wears them still, every day, along with that slinky black dress and the jade ring given to her by her beloved Crackerjack.

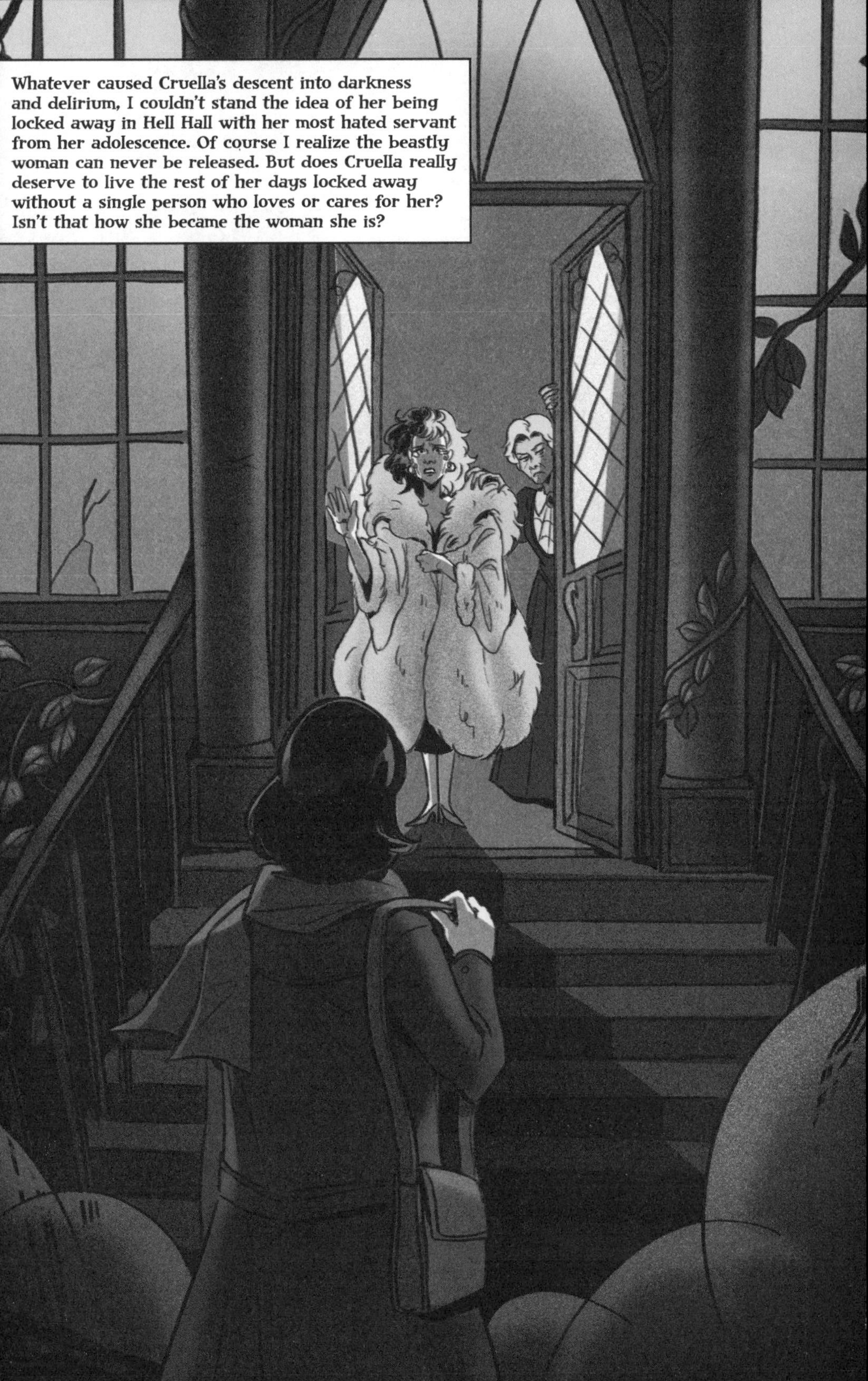
Whatever caused Cruella's descent into darkness and delirium, I couldn't stand the idea of her being locked away in Hell Hall with her most hated servant from her adolescence. Of course I realize the beastly woman can never be released. But does Cruella really deserve to live the rest of her days locked away without a single person who loves or cares for her? Isn't that how she became the woman she is?

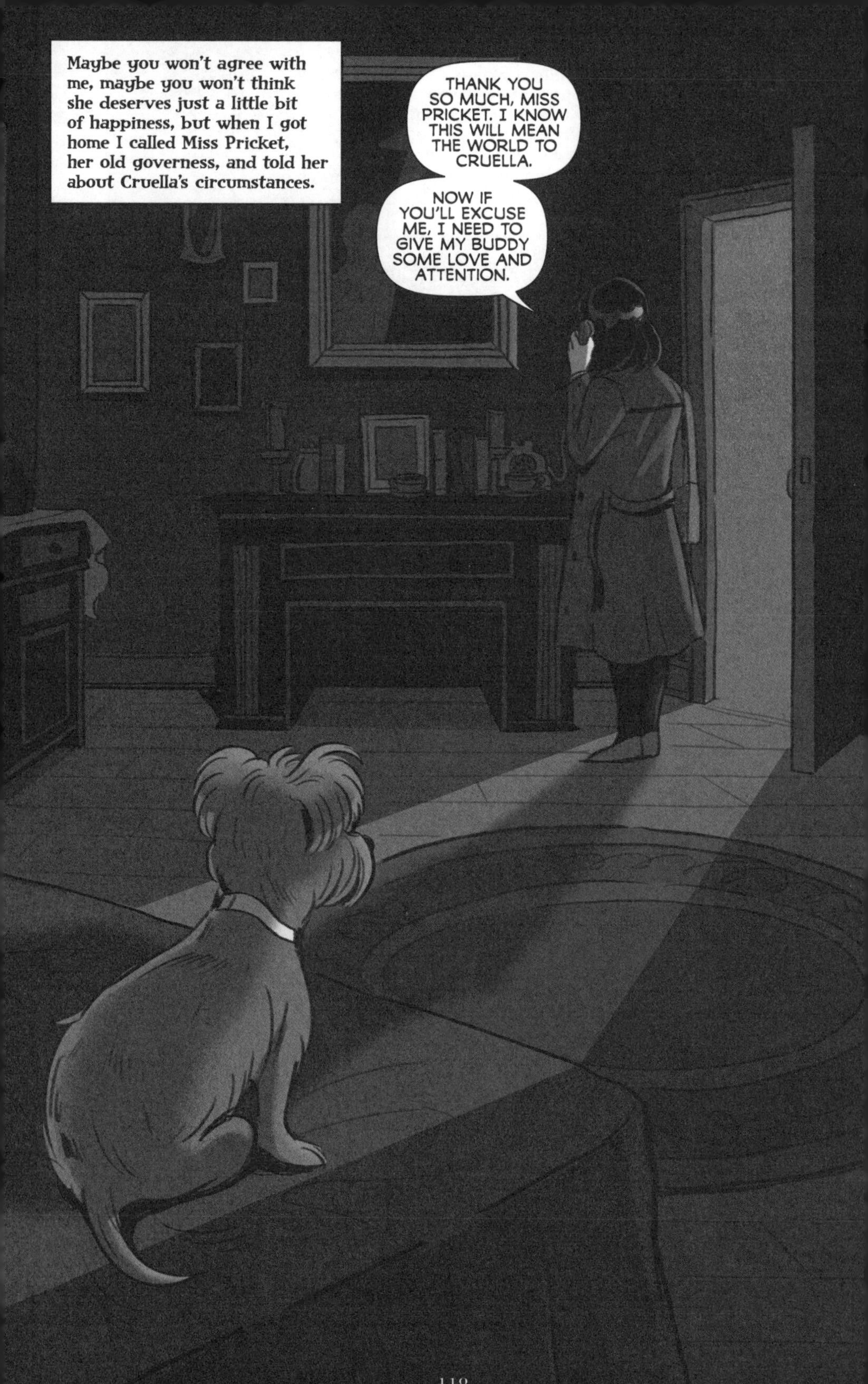
Maybe you won't agree with me, maybe you won't think she deserves just a little bit of happiness, but when I got home I called Miss Pricket, her old governess, and told her about Cruella's circumstances.
THANK YOU SO MUCH, MISS PRICKET. I KNOW THIS WILL MEAN THE WORLD TO CRUELLA.
NOW IF YOU'LL EXCUSE ME, I NEED TO GIVE MY BUDDY SOME LOVE AND ATTENTION.

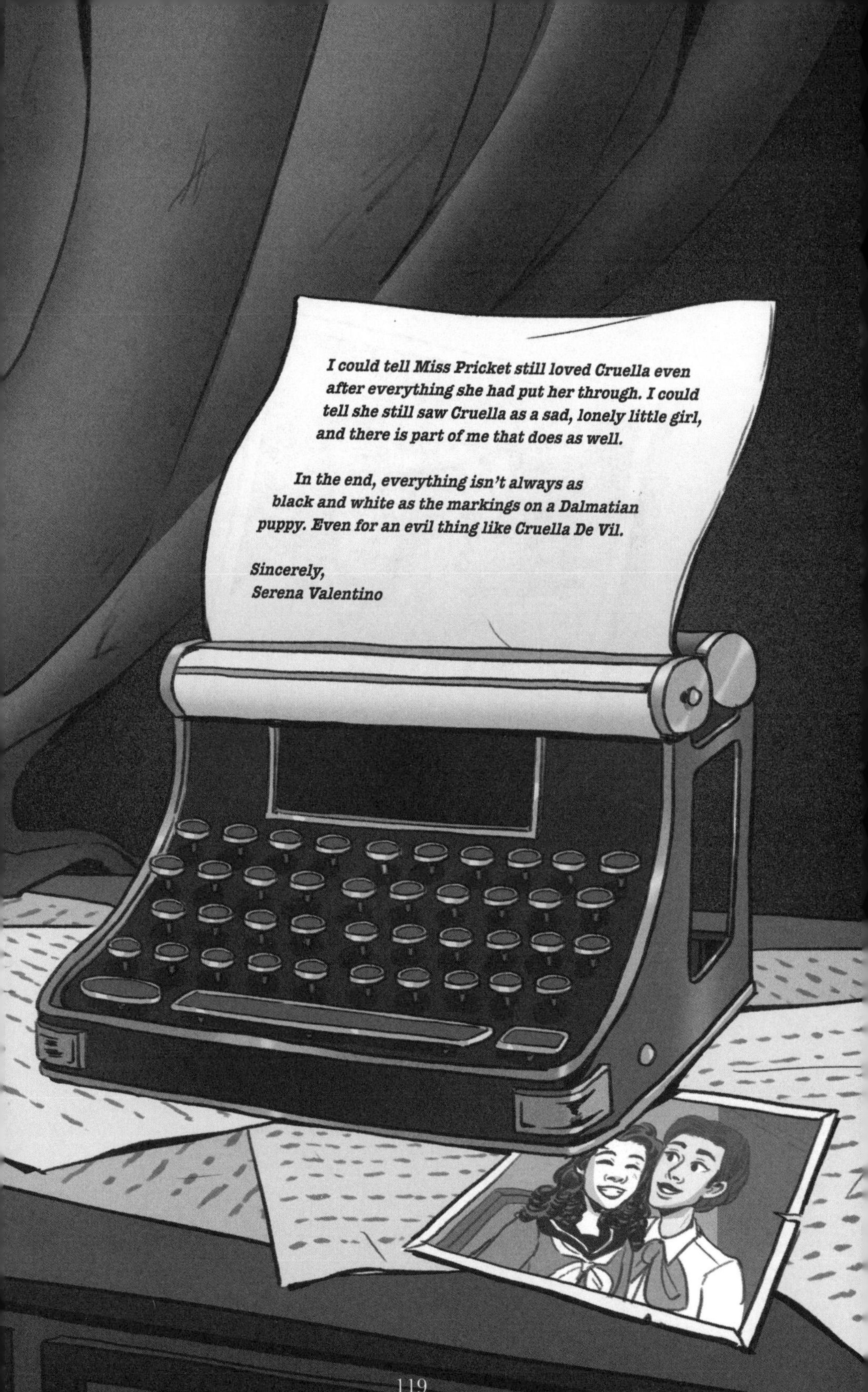
I could tell Miss Pricket still loved Cruella even after everything she had put her through. I could tell she still saw Cruella as a sad, lonely little girl, and there is part of me that does as well.
In the end, everything isn't always as black and white as the markings on a Dalmatian puppy. Even for an evil thing like Cruella De Vil.
Sincerely,
Serena Valentino

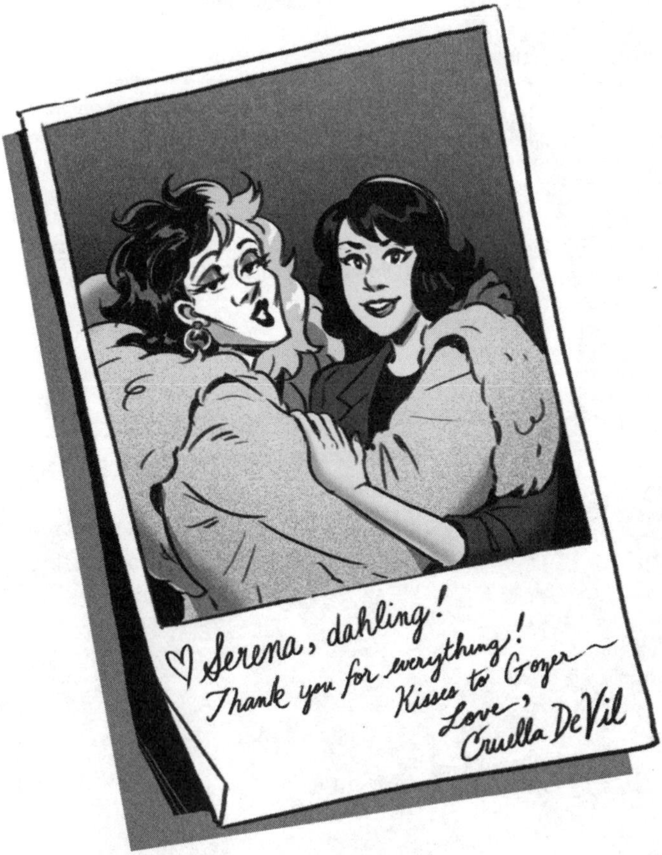
♡ Serena, dahling!
Thank you for everything!
Kisses to Gozer~
Love,
Cruella De Vil

ACKNOWLEDGMENTS

First, thank you to the whole team at Disney Hyperion and Lauren Ashleigh at Illustration Ltd., without whom this project would not be possible. Shout-out to Rachel Stark for being our cheerleader in the editing notes. We're honored and gratified to bring Serena Valentino's wonderful story to life.

Huge thanks to our color assistants Beau Pirrone and Shawna Saycocie for their tireless effort in helping us get this book done.

Special appreciation goes to Jordan Gibson, Nick Iluzada, Alyssa Jovellanos, and Jaemari Garcia. You are all treasures.

Shout-outs to Lorraine, Ally, Gail, Melva, Nicole, Marienella, and Rosa for their extra support on long work nights. And also the Bangtan Boys, for keeping us entertained and energized.

We would be remiss not to acknowledge Mr. Richard Gorey, who once gave a very passionate lecture at Parsons School of Design in which he thoroughly analyzed the visual language and storytelling of Cruella De Vil's introduction in *One Hundred and One Dalmatians*. Arielle has regularly thought about that class ever since, and hopes that knowledge has seeped into the pages of this book.

Lastly, it has been an honor to follow legendary animator Marc Davis's footsteps. His amazing work on the original Cruella is iconic and timeless.

Just like Cruella and Anita, Arielle and Janet were schoolmates. Who would have known we would eventually draw and color a book together? :)

Distinguishing ourselves,

Arielle Jovellanos & Janet Sung